A flicker of fear raced through her.

Beside her, Garrett reached for his gun. "Stay here," he commanded. "Someone tried to kill you today. He could be back to finish the job." He pushed open her front door and entered the house.

But she wasn't going to obey his command. Her son was inside that house!

"Jacob!" She ran past Garrett and inside.

"Ashlynn, wait."

Sounds from the TV greeted her, but she heard nothing else. The house was too quiet. Panic ripped through her and she searched in a haze of anxiety and fear…but he wasn't anywhere to be seen.

"Jacob!"

She rushed into the next room and tripped over something. A leg jutting out from behind the couch. The nanny. Ashlynn didn't need to check for a pulse to know she was dead.

Garrett grabbed her shoulders and she sank into his arms. The nanny was dead, murdered, and Jacob… If something had happened to him…

Anguish rushed through her.

Where was her child?

Virginia Vaughan is a born-and-raised Mississippi girl. She is blessed to come from a large Southern family, and her fondest memories include listening to stories recounted around the dinner table. She was a lover of books from a young age, devouring tales of romance, danger and love. She soon started writing them herself. You can connect with Virginia through her website, virginiavaughanonline.com, or through the publisher.

By day **Liz Johnson** works as a marketing director. She makes time to write late at night and is a two-time ACFW Carol Award finalist. She lives in Tucson, Arizona, and enjoys exploring local theater and doting on her nieces and nephews. She writes stories filled with heart, humor and happily-ever-afters and can be found online at lizjohnsonbooks.com.

Peril at Christmas

Virginia Vaughan

&

Liz Johnson

2 Thrilling Stories
Mistletoe Reunion Threat and *Christmas Captive*

LOVE INSPIRED
INSPIRATIONAL ROMANCE

LOVE INSPIRED®

INSPIRATIONAL ROMANCE

Recycling programs for this product may not exist in your area.

ISBN-13: 978-1-335-42989-6

Peril at Christmas

Copyright © 2022 by Harlequin Enterprises ULC

Mistletoe Reunion Threat
First published in 2016. This edition published in 2022.
Copyright © 2016 by Virginia Vaughan

Christmas Captive
First published in 2017. This edition published in 2022.
Copyright © 2017 by Elizabeth Johnson

For questions and comments about the quality of this book, please contact us at CustomerService@Harlequin.com.

Love Inspired
22 Adelaide St. West, 41st Floor
Toronto, Ontario M5H 4E3, Canada
www.LoveInspired.com

Printed in U.S.A.

CONTENTS

MISTLETOE REUNION THREAT

Virginia Vaughan

This book is lovingly dedicated to my family.
Thank you all for putting up with me
during this incredible journey.
You know me at my best and at my worst
and still love me.

He has watched over your journey through this vast desert. These forty years the Lord your God has been with you, and you have not lacked anything.

—*Deuteronomy 2:7*

Chapter One

Assistant District Attorney Ashlynn Morris's hands were shaking as she hurried down the steps of the courthouse toward her car. It couldn't be him. It just couldn't. But it had been Garrett Lewis in the foyer of the courthouse. The one man she'd never expected to see again.

She hadn't seen him in years—five to be exact—and she hadn't allowed herself to think about him in all that time except when she looked into her son Jacob's face and saw Garrett's eyes staring back at her. But she wouldn't give him the satisfaction of knowing how he'd devastated her when he abruptly ended their engagement, choosing his life as an army ranger over a life with her and Jacob.

The December wind nipped at her cheeks as she reached her car and opened the door, dumping belongings that had been in her briefcase onto the seat. She hadn't even bothered to slip on her coat in her haste to get out of the courthouse. She'd gone stone cold when she'd seen Garrett standing in the hall, his hands casually in his pockets and his easygoing manner apparent. His sandy hair was long on his neck and ears, and a goatee decorated his face, but his eyes were unmistakably kind when he turned to look at her, his expression just as surprised as she knew her own must be. She'd frozen in place, engulfed in a trance until someone had bumped into her, knocking her briefcase from her hands and spilling its contents on the floor. After quickly recovering her items with the stranger's help, she'd turned and rushed from the courthouse.

"Ashlynn," Garrett called, his baritone voice another shock to her system. "Ashlynn, wait."

How could she face him now when she'd loved him so amazingly deeply? He'd shattered her world by rejecting her, leaving her a twenty-two-year-old law school student suddenly on her own with a baby on the way.

It had been a struggle to raise a child alone and finish law school, but she hadn't given up. She'd fought for a better life for herself and Jacob just as she'd battled for everything good in her life. Her mentor, Judge Warren, often called her a survivor, and she was. She handled more pressure on a daily basis in her job as a prosecutor than most people ever faced, and she never blinked. She wouldn't—she couldn't—let Garrett see her blink, either.

Steeling herself against the emotions that threatened to overwhelm her, she shut her car door quickly before she acted on her need to jump inside and roar away. She would face him. It was time to finally put this behind her once and for all. Tucking her hair behind her ear, she took a deep, fortifying breath then turned and closed the distance between them. "Garrett, what are you doing here?"

His green eyes bored into hers so intensely that it made her breath catch, and when he spoke, his low, husky voice was just as she remembered; his deep southern drawl unmistakable. "I've started mentoring foster kids through my local church, and one of the boys is here to see his mother, who was picked up for drugs. I'm here to support him."

Her mind spun at the idea that he was mentoring foster kids. Yes, he'd been one, and yes, he'd found a successful career as an army ranger, but what kind of role model ran out on the people who needed him most? He might fool some with his good-guy act, but not her, not after how he'd abandoned her. But he'd misunderstood her question. "No, what are you doing here in Jackson?"

"Oh, that. I've been back in town for a while now. I'm living over on Sutton Lane out by the Reservoir." He gave her an uncertain shrug. "I didn't know whether or not to call. I heard you'd gotten married and started a family."

Yes, she'd gone on with her life after he'd left her. No need for him to know how it was currently falling apart. Her marriage was over, and her ex-husband wanted Jacob to live with him full-time. But those were her problems, and he didn't need to know about them.

"It's better you didn't," she said, determined not to let her vulnerability show. "We've both moved on."

"I'm working with the police now. I took a job training local law enforcement in anti-terror response tactics."

She gasped at this revelation. "You left the army?" Being a ranger had been everything to him. He'd chosen that life over a life with her, having promised to marry her during an extended leave from the rangers only to change his mind once he rejoined his unit.

He nodded, but his voice caught and she thought she spotted something lurking in his eyes—pain? "I did."

For Ashlynn, that was a final blow to her ego. He'd told her he couldn't be a ranger and be with her, then he'd abandoned them both. Now he would be around town and working with the police. She might see him through the course of her work. Jackson, Mississippi, was a big town, but law enforcement was a small community, and in her job as a prosecutor she often worked closely with the police. It was just one more insulting kick in the teeth to her already encumbered life. "I have to go. I'm expected at home."

She hurried away from him and back toward her car. It unnerved her to think he was so close now and she might see him regularly. She made a mental note to conduct as much of her business as possible at the secondary jailhouse, where she would be less likely to run into him again instead of the primary jailhouse where he was now working. But, for now, she needed to concentrate on Jacob and looked forward to winding down after an incredibly hectic day by snuggling with him on the couch tonight and watching *A Charlie Brown Christmas* on television.

She was nearly to her car when an explosion rocked the air. Ashlynn was thrown backward, landing hard on the asphalt. She tumbled back against a car, ram-

ming her head. Blinding pain ripped through her and her head felt heavy, but she managed to glance up to see her car in flames and debris falling all around. People were running toward her. Garrett was the only one she could make out clearly. He appeared to be screaming, but she couldn't hear him or anything over the ringing in her ears.

He reached her and pulled her to her feet then hurried her away from the debris and flames. Her body was numb, but when her knees buckled beneath her, he scooped her into his arms and carried her. Noise began to seep back through to her—the huff of air through Garrett's lungs as he ran, the distant wail of sirens and the roar of the fire raging a few feet away. The overwhelming smell of burning rubber permeated the air. She caught the worried expression on Garrett's face as her vision faded, and she laid her head against his chest and slipped into unconsciousness.

The sky was on fire from the force of the blast and the heat radiating from what was left of the car. As she passed out in his arms, a horrible realization rushed through Garrett. He'd seen her put her things into the vehicle that was now ablaze. That was definitely her car. A sickening feeling pulsed through him. If he hadn't stopped her, she would have been inside the car when it had blown up.

The explosion immediately made him think of his time in the army and the night his ranger team was ambushed. Five years later and he was still reliving it. Anything could bring those memories front and center again, whisking him back to that dark place. To the echoing blasts of mortars and gunfire, the cries of agony and the anguish of hauling his best friend from the battle only to have him die in Garrett's arms. This was his Ashlynn in the line of fire. And here he was, carrying someone he cared for out of danger once again. The way she slumped in his arms filled him with terror.

Please, God, don't let her be seriously injured.

People rushed from the courthouse and surrounding downtown buildings. The fire still raged and the air smelled putrid. He carefully set Ashlynn down in a patch of grass beside the courthouse steps. She was light as a feather in his arms, and her skin was soft as he touched her face. Her brown hair spilled from a clip at the back of her neck. And he'd noticed while they were talking that her eyes still blazed with fire and her chin jutted when she spoke. She was a petite powerhouse of dedication and energy when she fixated on something important to her. He'd always loved that about her.

He turned back to look at the car. Black smoke was pouring from it. He'd broken their engagement five years ago in order to keep her safe. His job as an army ranger had been a dangerous one, something he hadn't fully considered in the midst of their whirlwind courtship. But on returning to the army after proposing, he had, in fact, been scarred by war and the ambush that wiped out his ranger squad.

It was that ambush, and watching his friends die and turn their wives into widows and their kids into orphans, that had convinced him he didn't want that life for Ashlynn. He hadn't wanted to saddle her with wondering if he would come home from a mission. He was glad she'd gotten on with her life, glad she'd found someone else to love and start a family with. Yet he'd always assumed her life without him would be quiet and uneventful. He'd never once dreamed she might become the victim of a car bomb.

The police arrived from the downtown precinct behind the courthouse. He could see the confusion on their faces as they wondered what had happened. Their first priority would be to keep the public safely away from the blaze and then scope out the area for other threats of danger.

He spotted his friend Vince Mason, his liaison with the Jackson police department, and called to him.

"What happened?" Vince asked, running up to him. "Did you see?"

Garrett swallowed the lump forming in his throat. "It was a car bomb."

"Do we know whose car it was?"

Again Garrett held the answer. He glanced at Ashlynn lying unconscious on the grass. "It was hers."

Vince stepped around him and saw her on the grass. "An attack on an ADA? That's not good. How is she?"

"She needs medical attention."

"Paramedics are on the way. Stay with her. We're going to have to question you about what you saw," he said, hurrying away. "Don't go anywhere."

He needn't have worried. Garrett wasn't leaving, not until he knew Ashlynn was all right. It had been her dream to become a lawyer and then a prosecutor ever since Judge Warren had encouraged her pursuit of law after her testimony against her abusive foster mother helped send the woman to jail. He was proud of her for accomplishing her dreams, but he'd never considered the danger such a job might place her in.

What else had changed in her world, he wondered. Had she found God since their time together? He hoped she had. His newfound faith was the only thing that had sustained him through the past years since the ambush. And while he still struggled, he was thankful to have God on his side. He hoped Ashlynn had found the same comfort in Jesus that he had, especially when he realized how close she'd just come to meeting Him.

Ashlynn began to squirm. Her hand went to her head and she groaned. "What happened?"

He knelt beside her, in his heart a mix of relief that she seemed okay and horror over what had happened. "There was an explosion. How do you feel?"

She sat up and looked at him, her expression confused as if she didn't remember why he was there. She glanced past him toward the flames. The fire department had arrived on scene and was working to contain the blaze while the police were keeping people back, questioning witnesses and searching for other explosives. "My car."

"It could have been worse," he stated. "You could have been in it."

Again that thought sent shivers through him. He took a deep breath and thanked God for His intervention today in keeping Ashlynn safe. Garrett had let her go five years ago in order to keep her safe.

Yet it seemed she'd managed to find danger all on her own.

* * *

Ashlynn allowed the paramedics to check her out and bandage a few scrapes she'd sustained in the explosion, but she waved off any talk of going to the hospital. She wasn't seriously injured and she needed to get home to be with her son and relieve her nanny, Mira. Her mind was scrambled by the thought that someone had tried to kill her. Who had placed that bomb in her car? And why? She didn't know, but the idea that someone might want her dead shook her.

Garrett approached with the precinct commander and Ashlynn realized that seeing Garrett again after all this time had shaken her nearly as much as the threat against her life. At first, she'd thought he was a dream or a flashback when she'd opened her eyes and seen him hovering over her, but then the events of the afternoon had come rushing in. Garrett Lewis was back in her life.

"Ashlynn, this is Vince Mason, he's—"

"I know who he is," she insisted, suddenly irritated that he thought he could waltz into town and act like she was the outsider. "I work with this police force every day." She'd struggled to put herself through law school after Garrett left her, and she had been working in the DA's office for nearly two years now.

Vince nodded. "Yes, we've worked together on cases many times. How are you feeling, counselor?"

Her ears were still ringing and she was sore, but mostly she was ready to wrap her son in a big hug. "I'm fine. I'm anxious to get home."

"I know you are. I need to ask you some questions

first, though. Do you have any idea who would place a bomb on your car?"

"Not at all." It was the truth. She hadn't worked any high-profile cases during her time in the DA's office. In fact, she hadn't worked any cases she could remember involving explosives of any kind.

"Have you received any threats recently?"

"No."

"Can you think of anyone, perhaps someone you prosecuted, who would want to do you harm? We can check on people you've convicted that might have recently been released from prison or escaped."

"I don't make a lot of friends in my job as a prosecutor, but no one has made overt threats. I can have my investigator send you some names to check out. He's familiar with all the threats the office receives."

He nodded. "Tell him to call me. Meanwhile, I'm going to follow up with forensics to see if there's any identifying information about that bomb. Fortunately, we haven't discovered any further devices. Until we determine otherwise, it appears you were the primary target. Would you like me to have an officer drive you home?"

"Yes, that would be good," Ashlynn said. She couldn't wait to go home and wash this day from her memory.

"No need. I'll take her," Garrett said.

Vince looked at her questioningly, allowing her to make the decision.

"It's fine," she said, and Vince nodded.

"I'll be in touch, then." He walked off, leaving Ashlynn alone with Garrett as he hurried back to the scene.

"You didn't have to offer," she said. She didn't want him thinking she couldn't take care of herself. She was a successful career woman. She'd built a life without him.

But the glint of his smile melted her resolve. "I would feel better knowing you made it home safely. Besides, I don't mind."

She hated that he could still have such an effect on her, but she'd been captivated by Garrett ever since he first smiled at her at a friend's party. She'd been fresh out of college and he was already a decorated soldier home on an extended leave. She'd fallen hard and fast, and his protective manner had made her feel safe and loved for the first time in her life. But she wasn't that young girl anymore and she didn't need rescuing…yet she did like the way his hand rested protectively on the small of her back, guiding her and keeping her steady as they walked toward his truck.

He opened the door for her to sit in the passenger's seat then walked around and slid behind the wheel. He grinned at her in a familiar manner she remembered so well, and she felt her heart flutter. Maybe this wasn't such a good idea. She'd just wanted to get home. But now, the twenty-minute drive to her neighborhood seemed like an eternity. What did one say to the man who'd promised to spend his life with her then left her and her unborn child to pursue his career as a ranger?

After giving him directions to her home, she decided avoiding anything personal was the best solution. She should call Ken Barrett, her investigator at the DA's office, and get him started on gathering those names for Vince. But her phone was a charred mess in what was left of her car. "May I borrow your cell phone to call my investigator?" Her first task tomorrow would be obtaining a new phone.

He handed it over and she dialed Ken's number, thankful she knew it by heart. He answered, his deep bass voice familiar and reassuring. She had only known him six months, but they had become fast friends in that time, and she often looked to him as a brotherly figure, though they were only ten years apart in age.

"Ashlynn? Are you okay? I heard about what happened downtown. Is it true someone placed a bomb in your car?"

"It does look that way," she admitted. "Vince Mason wants a list of all the threats our office has received, especially any directed at me specifically or any involving explosive devices."

"I'll take care of it," he said, then in a tone of concern added, "I'm glad you're safe. I wish you'd be more careful, Ashlynn. I've tried to warn you that there are a bunch of crazies out there."

"I know, Ken, but I'm fine. I just want to get home. I'll see you tomorrow at the office."

She ended the call, then handed the phone back to Garrett. He slid it into a holder on the dashboard. Suddenly, the silence grew awkward between them, and she realized she should have kept Ken on the phone longer. She could have asked him for an update on any number of cases they were working on together.

The uncomfortable silence lengthened. At least they were nearly to her house.

"So, you have a son," he said. "What's his name?"

Her heart hammered in her chest at his question. She didn't like where this conversation was going. Didn't want him asking about Jacob. He'd given up that right when he'd abandoned them, and she already had one man trying to pull her child from her. She didn't need another. She had to keep him at arm's length when it came to her little boy. How could he ever make up for the fact that he hadn't wanted her and his child?

"Jacob," she said, then thankfully noticed they were nearing her home. "That's my house," she said, pointing out the driveway. He pulled in and parked beside Mira's small sedan.

"Thank you for the ride," she said, hoping that would be the end of it and they could each go their separate ways.

But Garrett was already getting out. "I'd feel better if you let me check inside."

"That's really not necessary."

"Someone tried to kill you today, Ashlynn. Who's to say they haven't come here to finish the job?"

"I would know if someone had been here, Garrett. I have a security system."

He spotted the car in the driveway. "I guess your husband would have phoned you, huh?"

It was none of his business about her marriage, and she didn't want him to think she'd failed without him. "My nanny and son are in the house. Mira would have called me if something was wrong."

"Still, I would feel better if you'd let me check it out. It won't take long."

She finally relented and walked to the front door.

Anything to satisfy him and get him away from her home and away from her son. However, she stopped walking when she noticed the front door ajar, a flicker of fear racing through her.

Garrett saw it too and stiffened as he reached for his gun, pushing past her. "Stay here," he commanded. He shoved open the door and entered the house.

But she wasn't going to obey that command. Her son was inside that house. If someone else was there, someone who meant to get back at her by harming her son, she wasn't going to be still.

"Jacob!" she screamed, hurrying past him and running up the stairs.

"Ashlynn, wait."

She heard his footsteps behind her but she wouldn't stop until she knew Jacob was safe.

Sounds from the TV in the playroom greeted her at the top of the stairs, but she heard nothing else. Jacob was a rambunctious four-year-old and the house was too quiet. Panic ripped through her and she took the last few stairs in a haze of anxiety and fear. She pushed open the playroom door. Jacob's toys littered the floor and the television was still playing his favorite evening show…but he wasn't anywhere to be seen.

"Jacob!"

She rushed into the room, intent on looking in his favorite hiding spots. She tripped over something beside the couch and hit the floor, landing hard on her hands. Ashlynn turned to see what she'd tripped over and saw a leg jutting out from behind the couch. Panic hit her at the sight. It was too big to be Jacob's leg, but…

She looked up at Garrett, who now stood in the doorway, his gun drawn. His eyes focused on the leg. She moved to look behind the couch and saw Mira on the floor. The young girl wasn't moving, her eyes were vacant, and the carpet was stained red with blood around her.

Ashlynn didn't need to check for a pulse to know Mira was dead.

She screamed Jacob's name and leaped to her feet. If someone had broken in and killed Mira, Jacob might have gotten scared and hidden.

"Jacob!" She ran down the hall to his bedroom and burst in, searching under the bed and in the closet. He wasn't there. She checked her bedroom then rushed downstairs. She called for him, frantic with worry as she checked every nook and cubby, searching for any place he might have hidden.

He was nowhere to be found.

Panic filled her. Mira was dead, murdered, and Jacob was missing. If something had happened to him...

Ashlynn dropped to her knees as anguish rushed through her.

Where was her child? *Oh, God, where is Jacob?*

Seeing her this way was like a sucker punch to his gut, and all Garrett wanted to do was sweep her up into his arms and make everything better. He checked that response, realizing not only might she object, but her husband wouldn't be too thrilled with him, either. He'd noticed the family portrait of them when he entered the house. And he no longer had that right. Even if she hadn't been married with a child, there could never be a future for them, not after all he'd seen and all he'd done. He'd walked out of a firefight unscathed when other men, better men with families, had died, and his grief had pushed him to kill and maim all in the name of war.

But his heart hurt for her. He couldn't imagine the devastation of having her child ripped from her. She'd already had such a difficult life, having lost her parents in a car accident when she was eight then being placed in an abusive foster home and nearly beaten to death by her foster mother. But it seemed she'd turned that all around now. She had a nice home in a fancy neighborhood, a good job in the DA's office and a beautiful family.

He holstered his gun and pulled out his cell phone to alert the police about the dead girl in the playroom and the missing child. This couldn't be a coincidence. It had to somehow be connected to the bomb in her car earlier today.

Garrett stopped dialing when he heard a noise from outside the house. His ears perked up and all his senses went on alert. He put away his phone and retrieved his gun. Someone was here. He grabbed Ashlynn's hand, pulled her to her feet and pressed his hand against her mouth to keep her from speaking. Her eyes widened in fear and her lashes were wet with tears, but she didn't ask questions.

"Follow me," he whispered, his instincts warning him to tread cautiously. He led her away from the front windows but peered out of them from the side, peeking through the heavy curtains. He saw nothing but the setting sun.

Something was wrong. He felt it in his gut. He sensed someone watching them. His truck was parked in the driveway but the direct route to it would be dangerous if he was right and someone was out there.

He grabbed a lamp from the end table and waggled it in front of the window. A shot rang out, bursting through the glass and shattering the lamp in his hand. Ashlynn screamed, but Garrett grabbed her arm and pulled her back up the stairs, his heart heavy at the continuing threat against her. Now that the shooter had made himself known, but failed to kill them, he would watch the exits closely or possibly come inside to finish them off. They had to find a way out of the house.

He led her into the master bedroom and locked the door. It wouldn't hold off an intruder with a gun for long, but possibly long enough for them to escape. He had his weapon, but it would be no match for the shooter's gun which, by the sound of it, Garrett recognized as a semi-automatic rifle, a serious weapon with serious intent. He hurried to the balcony and swung open the doors. Their only chance was to get out of this house, and now that they were upstairs this was their only way out. They would have to jump. He glanced down and saw a concrete patio below. It wasn't a high drop, but it would hurt. He holstered his gun.

"I'll go first. Then you follow behind me."

She shook her head, fear pooling in her wide brown eyes. "I can't."

"You have to, Ashlynn. You have to stay alive for

Jacob." His words were meant to provoke her to action, knowing she would do whatever she had to in order to find her son. It worked. She considered his words for only a moment before fortifying herself and nodding.

He crawled over the railing and climbed down, letting himself drop and hitting the ground. Pain ripped through his leg, but he ignored it. He'd sustained worse injuries and kept moving. He looked up and motioned for Ashlynn to jump.

She nodded and swung one leg over the railing. Just then, he heard the sound of the door cracking open and the shout of the gunman as he burst into the room. Ashlynn's head jerked up and the *dat-dat-dat* of gunfire filled the air. His gut clenched as her fingers slipped from the railing and she fell, tumbling backward toward the ground.

Chapter Two

She felt herself falling, and her only thoughts were of Jacob and to wonder if he was crying for her. She was going to die without ever knowing what had happened to him.

She slammed into something hard and felt Garrett's arms surround her as they both fell to the ground. He scrambled up before she could even process what was happening and pulled them both toward the safety of the house as the shooter fired over the balcony. Garrett's arm tightened protectively around her and Ashlynn was surprised by the way her heart picked up speed at being this close to him. She chided herself. Her son was missing and someone was shooting at her, but she felt safe swept up in his arms.

Garrett pulled his gun and fired upward into the balcony. Tension was rolling off him in waves. The shooter scrambled back into the room to avoid the shots.

"Run to my truck now," Garrett commanded, and Ashlynn did as she was told without question. She heard shots and screamed at the fear that ripped through her, but she didn't stop running. She was also keenly aware that Garrett was beside her, matching her steps and stopping every now and then to return fire into her house before easily catching up with her. The Christmas lights she'd placed on a timer flickered on, illuminating her bullet-riddled home and making this entire situation seem less real and more like a terrible action movie gone wrong.

She reached the pickup and slid into the passenger's seat. He jumped behind the wheel and started the engine, roaring away a moment later. The shooter started firing again and shots hit the vehicle. One pinged the rear windshield, causing it to shatter. Ashlynn winced as glass spilled over her but she knew it could have been so much worse.

She glanced in the side mirror and saw a masked man with a long gun run toward a waiting car.

"Hang on," Garrett said, then punched down on the accelerator, putting distance between them and the man, their attacker.

Ashlynn was shivering by the time they reached the downtown police precinct and it wasn't from the chill in the December air. Whoever had been shooting at them either hadn't been able to keep up with Garrett's driving or had given up. It didn't matter if they didn't kill her right then. They had her son, which meant they could have whatever they wanted from her. She would do anything to get him back.

Garrett led her inside, telling the on-duty officer about the incident. Within minutes, the precinct was on alert.

Garrett slipped his jacket around her shoulders and tried to offer her comfort as he led her to a quiet office. "They've got officers headed to your house right now to process the scene. They're also trying to contact your husband. Is it possible Jacob is with him?"

She saw a hopeful look in his expression, but she knew that wasn't the case and shook her head. "Mira doesn't live with us. If Stephen had picked up Jacob, she would have gone home."

"You don't live together?" Garrett asked, surprise coloring his face.

She shook her head. "He lives on Barrister Avenue in the Wood Hills subdivision. We divorced a few months ago." She didn't want to discuss such personal matters with Garrett, and thankfully, he didn't ask any further questions about her and Stephen. It was embarrassing to admit to him that her marriage had broken down.

Ashlynn felt numb. Her thoughts were all about Jacob. Her arms ached at the thought of not being able to hold him and her heart broke at the idea that he was probably crying for her. It wasn't fair! Ripping a child from his mother's arms was the cruelest thing anyone could do.

She'd never been much of a praying woman. Her anger at God was too strong. He had allowed too many bad things to come into her life. She'd foolishly thought things were turning around when she'd met Garrett, but then he'd turned against her, too, choosing the rangers over her and Jacob. And now it seemed God was still not on her side.

Vince arrived at the station, his hair tousled and his clothes dirty. Since she'd known him, he'd always been cool under pressure and presented a well-kept appearance. It was the first time she could remember seeing him look so disheveled. He apologized for not being there when they'd arrived and explained he'd had to leave to fix his wife's car that had stalled on the interstate. Garrett filled him in on what had happened, how they'd entered the house and found Mira dead, then been attacked by an armed gunman.

"Did you see the man?" Vince asked her once Garrett told him about the incident on the balcony. "Can you describe him?"

She thought back, reliving the terror of the man bursting into the room and raising his gun at her. But she wasn't able to offer much in the way of description. "He was wearing a dark mask over his face, like a ski mask, and he was dressed all in black. I couldn't see any of his features, but he was a large man, tall with big shoulders."

"He had an automatic weapon," Garrett added. "I would say by his tactics he's probably had some military experience. He came prepared."

Vince nodded. "The question is, did he come prepared to take the child or was it an impromptu decision? And why kill the nanny if Ashlynn is the one he wants?"

"We didn't see Jacob, but he could have had him tied up in the car."

Vince's face grew grim. "Whoever this guy is, he has access to both automatic weapons and explosives."

Ashlynn shuddered and folded her arms around her. They were talking so clinically, as if it wasn't her child missing or her world falling apart.

"Did Mira have any family that needs to be notified?" Vince asked her.

Ashlynn nodded. "Her parents live in Memphis."

"Is it possible this is about her?" Garrett asked.

"It's possible, but unlikely given the bomb was in Ashlynn's car." Vince looked at her. "What about your husband? I understand you divorced recently. Was it an amicable split?"

Ashlynn swallowed hard and wished Garrett wasn't listening to every word she said. She didn't like sharing information about her personal life, especially unpleasant details. She nodded. She doubted Stephen was involved in this. He was a good man and loved Jacob like his own son. "Stephen isn't a violent person. I can't believe he would try to kill me."

"But he could have hired someone to do it. It wouldn't be the first time a man has tried to off his ex-wife over a custody dispute. I'll send someone to his house to update him on what's happened and try to ascertain his involvement, if any." Vince's phone rang and he pulled it out. "It's the commander on scene at your house." He answered the call and listened intently.

Garrett walked over to her and rubbed her arms. "How are you holding up?"

She wanted to scream and rant, but her arms and legs were numb with shock and fear. Her chin trembled as she spoke. "I just want him back," she whispered, fighting with everything she had to keep her emotions under control. Falling apart now wouldn't do any good. She had to keep her wits about her in order to figure out who was targeting her and who had Jacob.

Vince ended his call and turned back to them.

"My men have been through the house and there's no sign of your son. We did gather photos of him." He pulled up one that had been sent to him. "Is this a recent snapshot?"

She looked at the photo and bit back tears. It was his preschool Christmas photo, taken only two weeks earlier. She traced the outline of his face, her heart breaking at the sight of his beautiful green eyes and his wide, mischievous smile. "Yes, it's very recent."

He nodded. "We'll add this photo to our Amber Alert. Don't worry, Ashlynn. We'll find him. Ken sent me those names and my officers are checking them all."

"How sure are you that this has to be someone she's prosecuted?" Garrett asked.

"Without any other identifiable enemies, it's a logical place to start. We're still on the scene processing the house and interviewing neighbors so we may find some more evidence that might lead us in the right direction there." He looked at her and his face softened. "You can't go home. Do you have somewhere to go, Ashlynn? Somewhere safe?"

"I'm not going anywhere until Jacob is found."

"You won't do anybody any good here. You need to get some rest."

"I can't rest until I know he's safe. Besides, with someone trying to kill me, I couldn't possibly put any of my friends in danger that way."

Garrett placed an arm on her back, but he addressed Vince when he spoke. "She can come home with me. I'll keep her safe."

"No!" Ashlynn insisted. "I said I'm not leaving."

"I need you to rest, Ashlynn," Vince told her and Garrett agreed.

"You can't do Jacob any good if you're so tired you can't function. There's nothing you can do here."

She wanted to lash out at him for using Jacob against her. He had no right to act so concerned. He'd lost that right when he'd abandoned them five years ago. Yet she knew he was right. She needed to be at her best for Jacob's sake.

She stared up into Garrett's face and saw the worry in his expression. He wanted her to trust him and she instinctively desired to. She'd trusted him with everything she'd had once upon a time He'd been her rock and her protector, and she had to admit she was glad he was by her side now. Her initial displeasure at seeing him was beginning to fade. What would she have done if he hadn't been there? She would have been dead in her car this afternoon or at the very least in her house tonight.

But how could she rest when her child's life was at stake? She shuddered thinking of the possibility that Jacob might need her and she wasn't close by. She shook her head stubbornly. "I'm not going anywhere."

Garrett glanced over at Vince then tried a different tactic. "Okay then, we won't go anywhere. We'll stick around and man the phones for the Amber Alert." He looked at Vince, who nodded his agreement.

"I'll keep you updated if we get any new leads," he promised then walked off.

She was glad that was settled. She wasn't just any crime victim. She was also a prosecutor and she didn't want to be handled. She had to stay strong and make certain every lead and angle was being investigated in finding her son.

Garrett reached out and placed a reassuring hand on her arm that sent tingles through her. "We'll find him. I promise." She stared into his green eyes and melted a little inside, remembering how much she'd once loved this man. "Do you trust me, Ash?" he asked, using his old nickname for her.

She stared at her hands to avoid looking into his eyes. Every instinct told her she could trust him, but her heart knew better. She'd once trusted him more than anyone in the world. She'd believed he was someone she could count on forever, but that trust had ended when he'd shut them out after discovering she was pregnant. The memory of how alone and broken she'd been brought back anger and bitterness so intense that she nearly couldn't breathe.

Instead of answering him, she asked a question. "When did you leave the rangers?"

He looked like he didn't want to answer, but he did. "Two years ago."

So he'd given up on them for something he hadn't even stayed with.

He sighed. "I owe you an apology, Ash."

"No, you don't."

"Yes, I do, and I want to explain. I never told you this, but after I left you to return to my unit, my ranger team was ambushed. I saw men with wives and families who were suffering because their husbands and fathers had decided to take on a dangerous task. I knew I couldn't let you have that kind of life. My life, my work, is dangerous. I was trying to protect you from that."

She cut him off, anger pulsing through her at the idea that he was going to try to justify abandoning his family. "What you did was to make the choice for me. You made a decision that affected us without even consulting me. You cut me out of your life."

His expression held regret and pain, but he nodded reluctantly. "I know."

"I can't even begin to fathom how I can trust you to help me look for Jacob."

"I know I've let you down in the past, Ash, but I'm here now and I won't leave you again. I'm right here by your side and I promise you I'll find your son."

His eyes steeled with determination, but she noticed he still referred to Jacob as *her* son, not *their* son. Well, he was right. Jacob was her son. He'd abandoned them when they'd needed him most. But he had skills that could help her. He had been an army ranger. She needed him in order to find Jacob. And even though she didn't want to, she instinctively trusted him in that regard.

Garrett hung around the precinct and kept an eye on Ashlynn. For the next few hours, she answered calls from the Amber Alert and he could see the devastation on her face when each lead proved unworthy. He agreed with Vince that she didn't need to be here in the center of all this. She needed to distance herself and allow others to field through the evidence. Yet he also knew she wasn't the type of person to sit around and wait for answers. Like him, she was action oriented. It was one of those things he'd once loved most about her.

She'd never played the part of a victim no matter how many obstacles life threw at her. He knew she wouldn't now, either.

He had to admit he was feeling antsy himself. He needed to do something and his mind was focused on speaking with Ashlynn's ex-husband, Stephen Morris. He'd been surprised to learn of their divorce. It wasn't really his business, but this was Ashlynn they were talking about, and as far as he was concerned she was still his business.

Despite what she'd told Vince earlier, his stomach constricted as he realized the attempt on her life along with her son's abduction made much more sense when you added an angry ex-husband to the mix, especially since they had yet to receive a ransom call. Had Stephen hired someone to plant that bomb in Ashlynn's car? And was he behind the murder of their nanny? He wanted to believe such a thing would shock him, but unfortunately he'd seen too much and was no longer surprised by the depravity of the world. Both his time in the rangers and his private search-and-rescue missions had cemented his belief that evil knew no bounds and betrayal was a bitter pill. It pained him to think that Ashlynn might have been betrayed by someone she'd once cared for.

He tracked down the detective Vince had sent to interview Ashlynn's ex and asked him what his take was on Stephen Morris.

"The husband would automatically become a person of interest in an attack on his wife, but this guy seemed genuinely shocked at the nanny's death and understandably worried about his kid. We'll keep looking into his business dealings and financials, but my personal opinion is that he's not involved."

Garrett hoped the detective was correct, but it was hard to take the man's opinion at face value. He didn't know him that well and didn't yet trust his judgment. In fact, there wasn't anyone on the force he trusted that much yet. Garrett wanted to look into Stephen's eyes himself in order to know for sure he wasn't involved in this.

But he wasn't leaving Ashlynn alone. He found her refilling a cup of coffee in the break room and pulled her aside. Her face showed signs of weariness and her eyes were red and sad. He hated seeing her this way and had the sudden urge to take her in his arms. Instead, he dug his hands into his pockets before he acted on it.

"How are you holding up?"

She shook her head. "It's frustrating. The Amber Alert isn't generating much usable information. I feel like I should be out doing something, even if it's just driving around with my head out the window screaming Jacob's name."

He smiled at that image, but he agreed with her sentiment. They'd been at the precinct for hours. They both needed to be out doing something.

"I was thinking we should go talk with your ex-husband. I know the police have already questioned him, but he may say something to you that he wouldn't say to the police."

"I know Stephen is the most logical suspect given that the bomb was in my car, but I still have a hard time believing he would kill Mira."

"This may have nothing to do with him or he could be involved indirectly. What if someone is targeting his family to get back at him? We should check out every possibility."

He could see she was still hesitant to believe Stephen could be involved, but her urge to do something obviously won out because she agreed to go with him. She followed him outside and slid into the passenger seat of his truck. The back window was still out so he cranked up the heater to knock off the chill of the December night air.

He headed for the neighborhood where Stephen Morris now lived. Garrett knew it by reputation. It was an upscale area in a well-to-do part of town. Stephen obviously made a good living. Garrett didn't like the twinge of jealousy that nicked at him. He wasn't some poor kid from the wrong side of town anymore. He, too, made a good living and while his house might not be as large or grand as this one, it offered him all he needed.

He slowed as they approached the house and he memorized the layout as he passed it. The garage door was closed. All the window blinds were down. The house seemed dark, but Garrett noticed a faint light in the kitchen window. It wasn't unusual even this close to midnight, but it caught his attention. He scanned the area looking for suspicious cars or activity that might indicate that whoever was after Ashlynn had either followed them there or was waiting for them.

"That's his house," Ashlynn stated, pointing. "You just passed Stephen's house."

He sped up and turned, circling the block. "I know. I'm checking out the area first."

"Oh." She glanced out the windshield and tried to see something. "Do you see anything?"

"No. Everything looks clear." He wished they had stopped by his house first so he could grab his gun bag. The only weapon he had on him was the pistol he always carried. He didn't like to walk into any situation unprepared. Ashlynn didn't believe her ex could be involved, but Garrett had seen too many relationships go bad to take anything for granted. "I see a light coming from the side window. Looks like he might be up." But was he awake because he was hiding his son in the house or because he was concerned about the shooting gone wrong at his former home?

Garrett parked several houses down and got out. He placed his arm on her elbow as they approached the house. She headed for the front door, but he stopped her.

"We're not going in that way."

"Why not?"

"Ashlynn, we have to make sure he isn't in on this. I want to know what's going on inside that house before we enter. If he's involved, he might have Jacob inside."

He moved quietly around the side until they reached the back. He glanced in through a window. The kitchen was dark except for a light above the sink, but Stephen Morris sat at the table poring over his laptop. Garrett pushed Ashlynn behind him then found a stick and used it to scratch against the back door. He watched Stephen react to the sound. Stephen stood and glanced out the window but Garrett pushed Ashlynn down so they wouldn't be seen. He heard the locks on the door unlatch and knew Stephen was coming out to investigate.

Garrett readied his weapon and when the door opened, he leaped forward and pushed Stephen back into the house, his gun raised and aimed at the man's head. Stephen stumbled backward, his hands up in a surrendering manner until he saw Ashlynn enter behind Garrett.

She rushed past him and ran toward the bedrooms, calling her son's name. She reappeared several moments later, disappointment coloring her face. "He's not here."

Stephen's eyes rounded in surprise as he stared at her, then anger set in. "Of course he's not here. I wish he was. The police have already been here and filled me in on what's happened." His eyes bored into hers. "I knew working that job in the DA's office would bring nothing but trouble. It's already destroyed our marriage. Now it's taken our son."

"Did you have anything to do with that, Stephen?"

He sighed. "No, Ashlynn, of course not. How could you think I could be involved?"

Garrett motioned for Stephen to sit down at the table and he put away the gun. He pulled the laptop to him and examined the screen. Stephen Morris appeared to be looking up only investment statistics. It seemed an odd thing to focus on when your child was missing, but other than that it didn't strike him as a suspicious activity. Perhaps he was merely trying to keep his mind off his missing child.

It was looking more and more possible that he wasn't involved, and Garrett was glad. He would hate to believe Ashlynn had been betrayed again by someone she thought cared for her.

But then who had Jacob, and why?

Ashlynn sat down and her shoulders slumped, defeated. He knew she hadn't really thought her ex was involved, but it must be hitting her hard that Jacob wasn't here. At least if he'd been with his father, she would know he wasn't in any danger. She no longer had that assurance. The lack of a ransom request after all these hours didn't bode well for Jacob's safe homecoming. Kidnappers who didn't want a ransom generally had no intention of returning the child. That meant finding him soon became much more urgent for his safety.

Garrett faced Stephen Morris and got down to business. "Someone is targeting your ex-wife and son, Stephen. Family can be a powerful weapon to use against a person. What are you into?"

"I don't know what you are talking about. I'm not into anything." Stephen grew a little more confident and gave Garrett a harsh look. "Who are you, anyway?"

"I'm an old friend of your wife's and I'm the one who is going to find out what's going on here."

Stephen looked at Ashlynn. "You have to believe me. I have no idea why someone would be doing this to us. It must have something to do with one of your cases."

She closed her eyes against his accusation. Garrett knew she was already worrying that her job could have made her son a target. She didn't need Stephen reminding her. A tear slipped from her eye. She wiped it away before rushing to the bathroom.

Garrett gave him a long, hard stare, not liking the accusation he'd hurled at Ashlynn. "The police are sifting through her files and following up on that. We're looking into different angles."

"I'm telling you I had nothing to do with this. I want to find Jacob and bring him home."

"Ashlynn told me you're suing for custody. If you thought you might lose, that's a good motive to have her killed."

Stephen shook his head. "I've already decided to drop that suit. I called my attorney this afternoon. I hoped Ashlynn and I could work this out between ourselves."

"That's convenient. You drop the custody suit and suddenly Jacob goes missing."

"I've already told you I had nothing to do with that. I would never hurt Jacob. I've helped raise him these past three years. I love him like he's my own child." He fidgeted uncomfortably in his chair but his words had a feel of truth to them.

But one point struck Garrett as odd. "When you say you love him like he's your own child, are you implying that Jacob isn't your biological son?"

Stephen nodded. "Jacob was already born when Ashlynn and I got married, but that doesn't mean he's not my son. He is."

Garrett looked toward the closed door where she'd disappeared as a rush of thoughts flooded him. If it was true that Ashlynn's ex wasn't the father of her child… who was?

Ashlynn went to the bedroom Stephen had fixed up for Jacob. The boy loved being here and Stephen was a good father. She picked up one of the stuffed animals on the bed and hugged it to herself. Where was Jacob right now? She couldn't help wondering if he was safe.

Was he crying for her? Shame and guilt filled her. She should have been there for him.

That's why her marriage had broken down, too. Stephen had told her she spent too much time worrying about work and not about him. He'd called her obsessed and maybe he was right.

She'd always hated the injustice of the world, mostly because in her childhood she'd been a victim of life. She'd made a vow to herself that she would provide a better life for her child, and while she hadn't gotten off to a good start—his own father hadn't wanted him— she had mostly succeeded.

Jacob would never have to worry about the lights being turned off for lack of payment or going hungry because his father spent all their grocery money on booze. Yes, Stephen had been a good husband and father. He'd provided for them well, and still did. Yet she hadn't been able to keep it all together for him and he'd obviously sensed it and felt alienated. She'd never loved Stephen the way he'd wanted her to, and she knew the reason was standing in his kitchen right now.

The connection she'd shared with Garrett could never be topped. She'd done a disservice to Stephen by marrying him when she couldn't forget Garrett, but she'd done what she'd thought was best for her baby at the time. She'd given him the father who wanted him and could provide a good life for him. And she had loved Stephen and been hurt when he'd left her, although that pain had been nothing like she'd felt when Garrett walked away.

Indignation bristled through her at that reminder. She would never allow him to hurt Jacob. She may need him, even be grateful to him, for helping her find Jacob, but once her son was home safely, Garrett Lewis could not be a part of their lives.

Garrett scanned the living room, looking at photos that were all around. A large Christmas tree that looked flawlessly decorated stood in the corner. Not an ornament was out of place. It looked too picture-perfect for a house with a four-year-old and he doubted Stephen Morris had done the job himself. His gaze landed on the mantel and pictures depicting happier times with Stephen, Ashlynn and Jacob—a trip to Niagara Falls, a photo in front of the Eiffel Tower, Jacob's second birthday party, complete with cake and candles and Billie the Bear, a franchise he recognized as a local favorite for kids.

He turned away from the photos. They were painful to look at. That should have been him with Ashlynn and only his foolishness had prevented it. Letting her go had been one of his greatest mistakes, but at the same time he knew it had been for the best. He hadn't been seriously injured in the ambush that took the lives of many of his friends, but it had shattered his life in ways he was still discovering.

Only Colton had escaped physically unscathed, although Garrett knew he'd carried emotional wounds deep inside him until he'd met Laura Jackson recently and found a reason to believe in life again. Garrett missed the times he and Colton had spent working together after leaving the rangers, just the two of them on privately funded search-and-rescue missions. After Colton had hung up his gear and retired to ranch life, the solitude had quickly turned to loneliness for Garrett.

That was when his friend and former Ranger buddy Josh Adams had heard about the opening at the local police agency and all his ranger friends had encouraged him to take the job. Garrett was glad he'd finally relented. He enjoyed the camaraderie with others and enjoyed putting his skills in action in a way that didn't always have to put his life in danger. Only a few days ago, he'd convinced himself he was content with his life now, but seeing Ashlynn, hearing her voice and having her need him, had sent him once again into a tailspin. And having evidence of her perfect life before him in high-quality photos didn't make it any easier. Ashlynn might now be single, but he'd done too much to ever be worthy of a woman like her.

"Are you him?" Stephen asked from the doorway, causing Garrett to startle. "Are you the one who broke her heart?"

Heat rose in his face as he realized Stephen Morris had just managed to sneak up on him, all because he'd had Ashlynn on his mind.

"She never got over it," Stephen continued. "I tried to make it work between us. I thought she would learn to love me the way I loved her, but that never happened. I just wish she could have—"

Suddenly, a shot rang out. Garrett ducked, reaching for his gun as he watched the bullet burst through the glass in the window and slam into Stephen's chest. The force of it knocked Stephen from his feet, tossing him backward. He landed on the edge of the sofa then slid to the floor, the life draining from him in a matter of moments.

Chapter Three

Ashlynn ran into the room at the sound of the shot. She saw Stephen on the floor and called out his name, trying to reach him. Garrett grabbed her around the waist and threw her to the floor. Whoever had made that shot was still out there and Garrett was certain he or Ashlynn would be his next target.

Yet he also knew they couldn't stay here. The shooter would be coming inside soon to finish the job, just as he'd done at Ashlynn's house. Garrett considered their options. No way they would make it all the way to his truck without being seen. He slid across the floor to where Stephen lay motionless and searched through his pockets for his car keys. He hadn't seen Stephen's car in the driveway, so it had to be in the attached garage. If they could make it there, they might have a chance.

He reached for Ashlynn's hand. "We're going to the garage. Stay low and remain quiet."

She nodded her agreement then followed him, her hand pressing tightly into his. He had his gun in his other hand, but it wouldn't do much good against a long-range shooter. He'd have to get closer to do any real damage, but he could and would use it for cover fire if necessary. After all, whoever was shooting didn't know what kind of weapon he had on him.

He led Ashlynn through the kitchen to the garage entrance. There were no windows so they were able to stand normally in here. They rushed to the car and Garrett was glad to see it was a BMW. The higher quality German-made steel would be better able to withstand the gunshots that were sure to be fired at them and the engine was powerful enough to whisk them away quickly.

He slid behind the wheel while Ashlynn dived into the passenger seat, pulling on her seatbelt. He paused. Once he started the car, it was do or die for them. He glanced at Ashlynn to make sure she was ready. Her nod told him she was.

He lifted a silent prayer that they would make it through this, then hit the start button and pressed the automatic opener on the visor.

"Hang on," he told her as the garage door rumbled open.

He shifted into reverse and barreled out of the garage straight into the street, stopping only to shift back into Drive and take off down the road. The *dat-dat-dat* of gunfire rang in his ears and he heard several of the shots ping against the car. Ashlynn slid down in her seat to avoid the windows.

Garrett roared out of the neighborhood, employing all the skills he'd learned in driving during combat situations. Thankfully, traffic was light even when he hit the interstate, but he didn't let up until he'd determined for certain no one was following them. They'd escaped again, but it hadn't been clean. Stephen was dead and Jacob was still missing. But how had the killer tracked Ashlynn there? And why kill Stephen if they were after her? Was it possible this was all about something Stephen had been into? He needed to know more about Ashlynn's ex.

He turned to her to demand more information but stopped himself when he saw she was shaking. Her arms were folded over her chest and she appeared small and frightened in the lush leather seat.

Garrett came to a stop at the side of the road and pulled her close.

She wrapped her arms around him and pressed her face deep into his shoulder as sobs racked her body. She had every right to be upset. She'd been through a lot in the past several hours. Her son was missing, both her nanny and her ex-husband were dead, and someone was trying to kill her, too.

He might not be able to ever be a real part of her life, but Garrett knew he wouldn't rest until Jacob was back safely in her arms.

"What do we do now?" Ashlynn asked when her tears were spent.

She knew she should pull away from Garrett's embrace, but she couldn't. She felt safer here with him than she had since this mess started. If anyone could help her through this and get her son back alive, it was Garrett.

"I'll call Vince and let him know about Stephen, then we'll head to my house. You'll be safe there, I promise."

He drove while Ashlynn tried to keep her bubbling emotions in check. She hated that she'd lost control. He'd been understanding about it, but she didn't like being so vulnerable in front of Garrett. She had to keep her emotions in check around him or she would be of no help in finding her son. She needed to remain strong, at least until they found Jacob. After that, Garrett would be on his way, moving on with his life and she with hers.

He pulled into the driveway of a craftsman-style house in a neighborhood she recognized and led her inside. The house was neat and orderly but homey. Garrett motioned toward the living room. "I'll take the couch tonight. You can have the bedroom."

She nodded absently. Of all that had happened to her tonight, being here seemed the most surreal. She'd first met Garrett when she was placed in a group home after her foster mother had nearly killed her. He'd been young and rebellious, and into more trouble than she'd known at the time. She hadn't fallen for him then, but many years later, when they reconnected at a party given by one of her college friends, she'd fallen hard and fast.

He went to a cabinet and pulled something out of a box. It was a cell phone. "I know you lost yours this afternoon. This one is clean and no one can track you with it. I'm not planning on us splitting up, but in case it happens you'll be able to contact me." He quickly programmed his number into it then handed her the phone. "Do you have any other electronic devices on you that the killer could be using to locate you?"

She shook her head. "No, everything I had was in the car when it exploded. Why?"

"The killer found you at Stephen's house. Possibly he was there for Stephen, but we need to be sure he doesn't have some way of finding you." He reached out and took her hand, an act that put her nerve endings on alert. "Don't worry, Ashlynn. We'll figure out who is after you and why. And I promise you I won't rest until we've found your son and brought him home."

She thanked him again for his help, claimed she was tired and went upstairs. While it was true she was exhausted, she wouldn't be getting any sleep tonight. How could she with Jacob still missing?

She pulled out the phone Garrett had given her and dialed her friend and neighbor, Olivia Williams, thinking she should at least let someone know she was safe. But it was more than that. She longed for someone to talk to about what was happening.

Olivia sounded stunned to hear from her. "I thought you were dead," she whispered, her voice choked with grief. "Your house is surrounded by police and crowds. The news has been saying there was a shooting there and a woman was killed."

"It wasn't me," Ashlynn told her, then recounted the events of the night.

Once the shock of the situation wore off, Olivia turned to worrying about Ashlynn's safety. "So where are you now? Are you safe?"

"I'm safe. Remember I told you about my old friend Garrett Lewis?"

"The hunky army ranger?"

She smiled at Olivia's very accurate description of him. "That's the one. I ran into him at the courthouse this afternoon. I'm with him. If anyone can help me find Jacob, it's him."

"I hope you're right. Jacob is such a sweet little boy. He doesn't deserve this. I'm just happy you're alive," Olivia said. "I thought I'd lost my best friend. Is there anything else I can do?"

"I don't know," Ashlynn said honestly. "The police will probably question you if they haven't already. If there's anything you can tell them that might help find Jacob..."

"Of course. I just don't know how helpful I can be. I didn't see anything. In fact, the first I'd heard about this was from the news." She huffed. "That just goes to prove you can't believe everything you see on television. Be safe. I'll be praying for you," Olivia told her before hanging up.

Ashlynn clicked off with her friend. She was glad she'd phoned her and glad Olivia was the praying type. Maybe God would listen to her and intervene to bring Jacob home safely. Ashlynn suspected they would need all the prayers they could get.

Garrett stretched out fully clothed on the couch. His mind was alert, replaying every moment of the night. Someone with serious firepower was after Ashlynn, and there was no denying that. That man had come prepared to kill her. Garrett knew she was terrified. He'd been in combat, was trained and experienced to handle such incidents, but he'd certainly never expected to come across them in his hometown in Mississippi.

He liked Vince and the other guys he worked with, but he couldn't say he trusted any of them with his life. There were only five men who'd garnered that kind of confidence—Josh, Colton, Matt, Levi and Blake, all that remained of his ranger squad after the ambush. Since the night the rest of his friends, including his best friend, Marcus, were killed, trusting had come as hard for him as it had for the others. They'd been betrayed by someone they'd relied upon, their translator, who'd turned out to be an enemy spy.

He glanced at the ceiling, knowing that Ashlynn was only one floor away from him yet they remained so far apart. He'd chosen this life and he deserved it, but a pang of jealousy still nipped at him that she'd gotten on with her life. She'd married and started a family. Logic told him he had no right to be angry about that, but when had logic ever factored into his feelings?

He should have died on that mountain with his friends, but God had allowed him to live and there had to be a reason for that. He thought that reason might be sleeping upstairs in his bed right now. She needed him and, if he was honest, it felt good to have her need him again. He'd been crazy to let her go. It had taken him years to realize he'd made the biggest mistake of his life. He didn't deserve her and he knew she could never love her again after all that he'd done, but he couldn't deny he still cared for her.

A light shone through the living room window, grabbing his attention. It was a red light, like the kind on high-powered targeting rifles. He knew exactly what it was the moment he saw it. The killer had found them.

He slid from the couch to the floor and crawled toward the hall where he'd be able to safely stand without being exposed. He had to get to Ashlynn and warn her. They had only minutes to escape before the killer came bursting through the door, and Garrett had no way of knowing how many there were. He'd only seen one man at her house, but the more he considered it, the more he thought the shooter had made it inside a little too quickly. He might not have been acting alone.

But how had they been found, and so quickly? No one knew he and Ashlynn had a connection so no one should know to look for her here. Yet here they were, approaching with guns, ready to kill her as if stealing away her child wasn't punishment enough for whatever the reason was behind this attack.

Garrett burst through the bedroom door and Ashlynn jerked up from the bed. She was also fully clothed and lying on top of the covers. "We have to go," he said. "They found us." He stopped at his closet and pulled out his emergency gun bag. He kept it loaded with weapons and ammunition for situations just like this. His time with the rangers, as well as his freelance jobs, had taught him to always be ready to protect his back.

Leading her down the stairs and to the side door, he handed over the keys to the BMW while pulling a rifle from his go bag along with his night-vision goggles, which he slipped on. "You run to the car and start it up. I'm going to give us some cover fire." She nodded at his instructions.

He raised the weapon and stepped out, scanning the landscape for any trace of movement. He didn't want to just fire blindly. This was a family neighborhood, and he didn't want to take the risk of unintentional casualties. As Ashlynn reached the BMW, he saw movement behind a bush. He held his breath, waiting to make sure it wasn't a stray dog or a possum. Through his NVGs he saw the figure of a man rise and the outline of a weapon point at the vehicle. Garrett pulled the trigger, taking out the intruder as the engine on the BMW revved up. The man fell unmoving behind the bush where he'd been hiding. Garrett jumped into the car, aware that if the shooter was wearing a bulletproof vest, he would be back on his feet soon. Ashlynn quickly backed out of the driveway and took off down the street before more shooters became visible. But the sounds of gunfire from another direction as they roared away played in his ears confirming to him that whoever was after Ashlynn wasn't acting alone. He prayed none of his neighbors had been collateral damage.

Ashlynn attempted to concentrate on the road, but the thumping of her heart in her chest demanded all her attention. She tried to push through the trembling fear that raced into every nerve in her body, steadying her breath and gripping the steering wheel until her knuckles were pale. And she didn't let up on the accelerator, either. Thankfully, the roads were nearly deserted this time of night.

Over her pounding heart, she heard a noise and realized Garrett was speaking to her. She turned to look at him. His face was flushed with adrenaline, but that was the only sign that some madman had been shooting up his house mere minutes ago. "You can slow down now. We're not being followed."

She nodded, but her hands seemed glued to the steering wheel and her foot to the pedal. Finally, he touched her arm. "You want to pull over and let me drive?"

"No, I'm fine," she said. Her voice was clipped and edgy. She hadn't meant it to be. She was just trying to hold all her emotions together, but she wasn't stopping this car for anything, not now, not until her heart returned to a normal beat and she was certain no one was behind them.

"How did they find us?" she asked him.

"I don't know," he admitted. "I disabled the GPS on our phones and on the car. You said you didn't have anything on you that could be tracked. So they can't be tracking us electronically. It has to be someone who knows our whereabouts, but the only person I told was Vince. I suppose anyone who works around the police would know about our reconnection, but other than that, who is even aware we know one another?"

Her gut constricted at that suggestion. Had someone in the police department betrayed them to a killer?

He pulled out his phone. "I'm going to call my friend Josh Adams. He's a former ranger buddy who lives here in town. His wife works at the FBI office in Jackson. They're good people."

She glanced at him, nervousness ticking through her. "How do you know you can trust him?"

"There's no one I trust more than my fellow rangers. Josh is on our side. If I can't believe in anything else, I believe that."

"I can't trust him. I don't even know him."

He looked at her, eyes wide and surprised. He must have seen the fear on her—it had to be pouring off of her—because he gave her a reassuring nod and his voice quieted. "Then maybe you can trust me? I know I let you down before when I promised you'd be safe at my house. You weren't and that's on me. But believe me now, Ash. We absolutely can count on Josh." He held up his phone as if asking her permission to make the call.

She pondered the decision only for a moment. She had no choice, really. She needed to trust someone and it wasn't his fault she hadn't been safe at his house.

Finally, she nodded and he hit the button and placed the call.

She gripped the steering wheel again and took a deep breath, hoping against hope she could believe in Garrett's judgment about his friend.

He put the phone on speaker and when Josh answered, Garrett quickly updated him on the attacks against Ashlynn and the kidnapping.

"I heard about that on the news. How can I help?"

"We need a safe place to stay. Whoever is after Ashlynn is still managing to track us. I haven't figured out how yet. We need somewhere off the grid."

"I have just the place," Josh said. "Elise has a great-uncle who left her a cabin outside of town. No one should be able to trace it to you. I'm texting you the address of a convenience store. I'll meet you there in a half hour with the keys and a map to the cabin."

When he received the text, he called out the directions to Ashlynn and she headed north on the interstate. Rain turned to sleet as she drove and the quiet in the car grew deafening. The windshield wipers swished back and forth in a timed motion. That and the hum of the tires against the road were the only sounds. She felt tension pouring from Garrett as he rummaged through his bag and checked his weapons. Seeing him in combat mode was unnerving. When she'd known him before, he'd been rakish and charming, a dangerous combination in itself, but she'd not seen this side of him until today. He'd grown into a serious and brooding man with muscles for days and firsthand knowledge of guns and ammunition. Five years had changed him from a boy to a man…but was he now a man she could count on to bring Jacob home?

As she added Stephen's death to the killer's toll on her life, she realized the truth. If she wanted to live long enough to find her son and bring him home, she had no choice but to trust Garrett.

They pulled into the convenience store but didn't see Josh's car. It had been hours since this mess first started and neither of them had eaten anything. They both needed food in their stomachs and a few hours of sleep if they hoped to keep their wits about them. "Let's go inside and get some provisions," Garrett suggested.

Ashlynn agreed and shut off the engine then followed him inside, but he couldn't help but notice she looked like she was moving on autopilot. He lifted a silent plea skyward. They needed God's help to get through this and he could only hope that the Almighty would look past his shortcomings to see how deserving Ashlynn was of His help. He had no right to ask God for anything, not after the mess he'd made of his life, but Ashlynn didn't deserve the danger she'd found herself in.

As he carried two bags of groceries to the car, Josh pulled up. He jumped from his car and greeted them both.

"I'm sorry to hear about your son," Josh told Ashlynn. "But I have every confidence you're in good hands with Garrett. I also phoned Elise and updated her about the situation." He glanced at Ashlynn again. "Elise is FBI. She specializes in child abductions. Unfortunately, she's in Nashville at the moment working as part of a task force. But she did promise to contact the locals and examine the evidence they've collected."

"Thank you for your help," Ashlynn said. "And thank your wife, too."

Josh handed Garrett a hand-drawn map to the cabin and the keys. "I'm glad to see you bought some supplies. We haven't been up there in quite a while so the cupboards are pretty bare. What else can I do?"

Garrett didn't hesitate. "The men who attacked us had automatic weapons and a sniper's aim. I might need some backup before this is over."

Josh nodded. "I'll call around and see who else is close. How are you set for weapons?"

"I was able to grab my gun bag. It's enough to last as long as we don't get into a major firefight."

"I've also got a storage locker with weapons and ammunition. I'll get some things ready."

"Is all that really necessary?" Ashlynn asked.

"Let's hope not, but if it is, we'll be ready." Garrett wasn't going to find himself outgunned again.

Josh shook his hand firmly. "Be safe, and remember I'm only a phone call away if you need me. I'll be on alert."

"We will. Thanks, Josh."

He climbed back into the car, waving as he drove off.

Josh's handwritten map led him straight to the cabin. As he'd stated, it was isolated and set back on a lake in the woods. It was a perfect place to hide out and he couldn't imagine how anyone could find them here.

He led Ashlynn inside and she looked around, glancing through the window as the sun rose over the lake. The cabin, while isolated, had modern amenities. Garrett headed over to the kitchen and placed the grocery bags on the counter. It helped to keep his hands busy unpacking the groceries. They would have to stock up if they planned to stay there long, but for now, this would do. He heated up a can of soup, poured it into two mugs and handed one to Ashlynn, who had curled up on the couch, a blanket wrapped around her and her legs tucked beneath her.

She shook her head, not wanting the soup, but Garrett insisted. "You need it. You have to stay strong for Jacob, remember?"

She relented and took it from him, though she didn't drink any of it. "I don't understand why this is happening," she said instead, her voice small and frail. "I don't know why God is doing this to me. What have I ever done that I would deserve any of this?"

She hadn't had an easy life, but he knew better than most that life wasn't always fair. If he could go back in time and change things, he would. He longed to change the past and his actions. But all he could do was be here for her now, comfort her as best he could and do everything in his power to bring her son home safely to her.

He was a believer. Had asked Jesus into his heart during his first year with the rangers, and he felt certain God was watching out for Jacob. Yet he also knew bad things happened in this world and God didn't often intervene in man's sinful behavior. Evil existed on Earth. He knew it firsthand. He'd witnessed it in action and asked himself many times the same questions she was now asking him. Why did God allow bad things to happen?

"I don't have all the answers for you, Ash. I can't fix what has happened, but I can be here for you and Jacob. I want to be here for you."

Her eyes were cold and hard as she looked at him. "I wish I could believe you," she told him in a flat voice. "But I can't forget how you left us. You abandoned me when I needed you most, Garrett. How can I trust you now? How can I know for certain that you won't leave again?"

"I won't leave. I'm not that same person, Ash."

She shook her head. "Neither am I. I've been through too much to be that trusting young girl I once was. I always thought you were the one person in this world I could count on. Then you left me. You left me when I needed you more than I'd ever needed anyone."

He didn't understand exactly what she was talking about, but she didn't understand what he'd gone through, either. "I thought I was protecting you. I didn't mean to hurt you."

"It doesn't matter what your intention was. It still hurt." She wiped away a tear that slipped through. "And the way you cut me off after you'd made your decision was cruel. You wouldn't even speak to me. I sent you letters. I emailed you. But you never responded. I didn't even have any way to know for sure that you received them."

"I got your letters, Ashlynn, and your emails. But you have to understand, I thought I was protecting you. I looked at our future and all I saw was your pain and heartache if I married you."

"You made that future of pain and heartache come true for me when you abandoned us, Garrett."

Her words stopped him. "What do you mean *us*?" Stephen's words came back to him in a wave. *I'm not Jacob's biological father.* Did that mean...?

She placed the cup of soup on the table and turned to him, her eyes blazing with anger and indignation. "You claim you didn't want to leave me to raise a family alone, but that's exactly what you left me to do. You turned me into a single parent."

He felt his face flush at the realization of what she was saying. "Are you telling me Jacob...?" He stopped, his question hanging in the air.

Her expression changed to one of confusion. "You said you'd received my letters and emails."

"Yes, I received them, but I didn't read them. I couldn't.

I thought you were trying to change my mind. I never read them."

He set down his cup and stood, his turn to feel overwhelmed. She acted as if he'd known all along, as if her letters and emails had come with the words *you're going to be a father* written in big, bold letters across the front and in the subject line. Maybe if they had, he would have opened them.

She stood and touched his arm, the graze of her fingers whisper soft. He looked at her and saw tears pooled in her eyes and the sudden realization hit him that she'd believed all this time he'd known and he'd rejected her because of it.

Her manner softened but the truth hung out there for several moments that seemed to last an eternity. Finally, she spoke the words that would change his life forever.

"Garrett, Jacob is your son."

Chapter Four

Garrett lowered himself slowly back into the cushions of the couch. Hearing her words was a blow like no other he'd ever sustained. He was sick and excited at the same time. It was the strangest mixture of emotions he'd ever felt.

She sat beside him and placed her hand over his, her touch only serving to rev up the emotional turmoil he was currently experiencing. "I'm sorry. I thought you knew."

He raked a hand over his face as the weight of her words continued to sink in. "Are you telling me that I'm searching for my own son?"

"Yes."

He stood, his mind spinning with this new information. *His* son was the boy missing. His *son* was out there somewhere. Someone had kidnapped *his son*.

He spun around and glared at Ashlynn. "How could you let this happen?"

Hurt and anger flashed in her eyes, but she stood to

face him, her chin jutting out stubbornly. "I don't even know why this is happening."

"You should have done a better job of protecting him."

Now her face flushed with anger. "Don't you dare stand there and criticize my parenting, Garrett Lewis. You were the one who ran out on us."

"Not by choice."

"Do you think that matters? Do you believe for one second that your intentions make any difference in our lives? You promised you would help me find Jacob and bring him home. Once that's done, you can leave again and never have to worry about us."

She turned and rushed into the bedroom, slamming the door behind her. He heard the click of the lock and grimaced at his own reaction. What was he doing? He was taking out his frustrations on her and that wasn't fair. She already had too many people blaming her for her choices. He didn't want to be one of them.

He stood at the back door and stared out at the lake, his mind struggling to process this new information that changed everything he knew about his life. Every decision would now have to be made in the context of how it would affect his child. The idea terrified him. He'd never had a dad and he had no idea how to be one. His best friend, Marcus, who had died in the ambush, had always had his family in his thoughts, or so it seemed, because he always had a funny story to share about something that had happened when he was home or else he was showing off a drawing one of his kids had colored for him.

In Garrett's mind, that was what a father looked like. *His* first official act as a father had been to abandon the mother of his child. Now he'd accused her of allowing his abduction. Not a great start to fatherhood.

He pushed the door open and walked outside, needing the brisk morning air to clear his mind. He stared up at the sky and had to question why God would allow this to happen. Why had he been allowed to live while a terrific dad like Marcus had been taken? He tried to shake those feelings away. He couldn't let emotion and guilt jeopardize what he needed to do. He had to focus on the job of finding Jacob. Everything else could be worked out once he was home safe and sound.

Yet even as that thought crossed his mind, another countered it. If he'd been killed instead of Marcus, who would be here to look for his son now? Jacob's safety would be in the hands of strangers. He liked several of the men he'd met on the force, but did he trust any one of them to find his kid? The answer was a resounding *no*.

He picked up a stick and hurled it into the lake.

For the first time since the night of the ambush, he couldn't feel guilty for staying alive because it allowed him to be here now when his son needed him.

Ashlynn flung herself across the bed, angry at him for letting her down again and even more at herself for daring to believe in him. He couldn't have faked that reaction. He honestly hadn't known she was pregnant when he'd broken their engagement. But that gave him no right to blame her for Jacob being kidnapped.

But her anger extended even further. Life had once

again used her as a pawn in its game and Ashlynn wasn't amused. She didn't understand why God continued to allow such terrible events to happen to her. She'd never done anything to the Great Almighty.

Tears slipped from her eyes as she remembered her foster mother telling her she'd offended God just by being born. She'd had no control over that or over any of the terrible events that had made up her life. Her mother's death along with her father's alcoholism had led her into foster care and into the home of Kathryn Rollins, who had singled her out for a reason only she knew to suffer repeated abuse and neglect. The other children in the home—six in all, including Kathryn's own biological son—had not shared in her torment, and Ashlynn had grown up believing something was inherently wrong with her.

She often still pondered that thought. Did she truly not deserve a family of her own? Or a happy life for her son? Judge Warren would call that kind of thinking utter nonsense and assure her that she did, indeed, deserve such things. But the older she got and the more she struggled, the less she tended to believe it.

But that didn't mean she would quit fighting, if not for herself then for Jacob's sake. He deserved a happy life even if she didn't.

A few hours later, Garrett heated up two breakfast burritos he'd gotten at the convenience store. It wasn't much, but it was all he had to offer until they made a run for supplies. He tensed when he heard the bedroom door unlock. He watched Ashlynn walk out and shuffle across the floor to the kitchen. She looked better after a few hours of rest, but he doubted she'd slept well. He also couldn't miss the red, swollen eyes that indicated she'd spent at least part of the time crying. He kicked himself, feeling guilty for causing at least some of that.

"I made breakfast," he said, sliding a burrito to her. She hadn't eaten any of the soup he'd heated for her earlier, which meant she hadn't eaten since before he'd first seen her yesterday afternoon.

She shook her head at the offer of food. "Just coffee, please."

He poured her a cup from the pot he'd started and handed it to her. Then he sighed and got ready to eat crow. "Look, Ash, I owe you an apology. I think I was taking out my frustrations on you earlier. I was just so shocked by what you told me."

She sipped her coffee, but her expression was guarded as she glanced at him. "No apology is required."

He saw the lift of her chin and the determined look in her eye. He knew that stance. She was shutting herself down, hiding her hurt and pain away so she wouldn't seem weak. He'd seen her do it before. If she could protect herself, then she would never have to admit to being hurt.

"Don't do that. Don't shut me out like that."

"I don't know what you're talking about. I'm fine."

He walked around the island separating them. "I'm trying to say I'm sorry I hurt you, and before you say I didn't, I know good and well I did. I was wrong to blame you for Jacob's abduction. You had no control over what some psychotic did." He reached out and caressed her arm. He'd wanted to comfort her but instead he'd jabbed her. He longed now to pull her into his arms. She looked like a wounded bird, so sad and helpless, but he knew from experience that that look was deceiving. She was a mother lion who would pounce when her cub was in danger.

"You only said what everyone is probably thinking. This is my fault."

"Anyone who knows you understands how much that little boy means to you."

He did pull her into his arms now, drawing her closer and pressing her against him. After a moment, she burrowed her head into his chest and he was glad he could at least offer her a shoulder on which to cry. But he didn't expect the dizzying way the scent of her shampoo or the feel of her soft, smooth skin made him feel.

"I just want him back," she whispered and the torment in her voice made his heart constrict. She stared up into his eyes, but something about her expression told him she wasn't seeing him right at that moment. She reached up and touched his face. "Jacob has your eyes." Tears pooled in hers.

He caressed her cheek and found her leaning into his hand. His eyes fell on her lips and he remembered the sweet taste of them that had never strayed far from his memory. How many nights had he dreamed about holding her again? Now she was here, in his arms, needing his comfort. Her chin lifted again and this time it wasn't out of defiance. Her lips were close to his and he breathed in the heady scent of her. Even after a day of car bombs and running for her life, she smelled sweet, like cucumber. He wanted so much to kiss her, to re-kindle the spark that had once been between them.

But he didn't.

He pulled himself away emotionally and then phys-ically before he crossed a line and enveloped her lips with his. He shouldn't get to go on with his life when others didn't. Marcus would never kiss his wife again. Why shouldn't Garrett face similar consequences?

His phone rang and he gave a deep, relieved sigh. Seeing it was Vince, he put some distance between Ashlynn and himself as he pressed the answer key and placed the call on speaker.

"Hey, Vince. Any news?"

"Some. We've scheduled a press conference for eleven a.m. It's time we address the public. I'd like Ash-lynn to say a few words if she's up to it."

Ashlynn nodded. "Of course I will."

"Good. I'll see you both at the precinct."

Garrett pressed the button to end the call. Narrow-ing his eyes, he gave Ashlynn a quizzical look. "Are you sure you're up for a press conference?"

But she batted away tears and straightened her shoul-ders in steady determination. "It won't be easy, but I'll do whatever I need to do to bring home Jacob."

"Well, you won't have to do it alone." He placed a reassuring hand on her shoulder. It wasn't much after how close he'd come to kissing her, but it was the best he could offer. "I'll be right there beside you."

What had almost happened back there?

Ashlynn shook her head as she followed Garrett out

to the car. She'd taken the time to shower and change, but she still couldn't push past that scene in the kitchen. He'd almost kissed her. She was certain he'd wanted to. But the real surprise had been her reaction. She hadn't pushed him away. She hadn't even told him no. In fact, she was quite certain that she'd encouraged him. Her face warmed at the idea that she'd practically thrown herself at him…and he'd rejected her. Again. Would she never learn her lesson? They were together in this only because they shared a son. No need to relive a relationship that had left her devastated. No, she wouldn't go down that path again. Her heart couldn't stand it.

They were both quiet as Garrett drove, and she was thankful for that. Other people might have believed they had to keep her talking and upbeat, but Garrett seemed to respect that she needed quiet to regroup. She'd never been one for chitchat and she didn't find comfort in having groups of people around her. She much preferred solitude and was glad Garrett remembered to give her that space.

He took the exit from the interstate into downtown Jackson then parked in the garage attached to the police station. He walked beside her, his hand reassuringly on her back as they entered the building.

Vince looked weary as he led them into the room they'd designated as a command center for her case. There was a large whiteboard up front where they posted photos and evidence relevant to the case. She saw her own photo along with the one of Jacob they'd used for the Amber Alert.

"Have there been any hits on the Amber Alert since we left last night?" she asked Vince.

Vince nodded. "We're continuing to follow up on them all but so far nothing solid. We were able to obtain video footage from several of your neighbors' security cameras that showed a suspicious white van in the area. We ran the tag and discovered it was stolen from a dry cleaner's two days ago. Someone removed the decals but it's the same van. We added that description to the Amber Alert and several people have reported seeing it, but unfortunately that type of van is very popular with businesses."

She stared at the crime scene photos of Stephen and Mira. Their deaths seemed so brutal and so unnecessary. But, then again, was murder ever necessary? Ashlynn knew they were dealing with someone with no respect for human life, and that frightened her because this was also the person who had her son. She closed her eyes as a wave of sorrow washed over her. Had Jacob witnessed Mira's death? How scared he would have been. A motherly ache pulsed through her and her arms yearned to hold him and reassure him that everything was going to be fine.

Garrett's hand touched her back again and she found it comforting to have him so close. It was just the strength she needed to push through her maternal emotions and look at this case with a prosecutor's eye.

"Has forensics found anything from the crime scenes that might be helpful?"

Vince obviously noticed her change and he perked up, too, and went into total business mode. "According to the medical examiner's preliminary notes, the attacker slashed Mira's throat from behind. Based on the angle of the incision, he would have to be right-handed and at least six feet tall. He also found material beneath her nails, so it looks like Mira scratched the perpetrator during the struggle. He's running it for DNA. Hopefully, we'll get a hit but that will take a while. We're still waiting on fingerprints and fibers found at the scene.

"Also, we've been looking into Mira's background, but so far we haven't identified any risks in her life that could have made her a target. We haven't found any prior drug use or connections to criminal elements. According to family and friends we've interviewed, she didn't have any romantic attachments and no one knew of anyone who might want her dead. As of right now, unless we receive any new information, we're going to operate under the assumption that her death was collateral damage in the attack on you and your family. I've got detectives following up on recently released prisoners with either a connection to you or a history of crimes against children."

She nodded, thinking the police were doing all they could to put a good case together for prosecution. But it didn't help get them any closer to finding her son. She stared at the board. Mira's leads had fallen through and the Amber Alert tips hadn't yet produced any viable leads.

"What about the bomb in my car?"

Vince grimaced. "So far, not much. No witnesses saw anyone suspicious around your car yesterday. However the fire marshal does believe military-type explosives were used to detonate the bomb. It wasn't the make-it-in-your-basement type."

"So we're dealing with someone who has access to automatic weapons and explosives," Garrett stated wryly. "Terrific."

"What can I do?" Ashlynn asked Vince. "I need to do something."

"Going through your case files is the best thing you can do right now. You know those cases better than anyone else. You'll be more likely to notice something that stands out. And hopefully this press conference will elicit some other leads for us to follow up on."

She felt her insides begin to quiver. Jacob was out there somewhere, possibly hurt and definitely frightened, and they were no closer to bringing him home than they had been the moment he'd been taken. She folded her arms across her chest to try to maintain her composure and scanned the room. These men were doing all they could to find Jacob, but even she knew their abilities were limited. They could follow leads but once those leads went cold, the chances of finding Jacob diminished. She knew the statistics. Kids who weren't recovered in the first forty-eight hours were unlikely to be found alive…and time was ticking down for finding Jacob. But without God on her side, she wasn't sure that was going to happen.

Ashlynn braced herself as she and Garrett crossed the street and entered the building that housed the offices of the district attorney. Her coworkers, with their pitying glances and sorrowful expressions, were the worst. She didn't want to be here where all this emotion might make her totter over the edge, but she needed to do something to occupy her mind or else she wouldn't have to worry about other people's sympathies pushing her over the edge of reason. She would slide there all on her own.

Again, Garrett's hand on her back was a comforting support. Her gratitude at having him beside her outweighed her desire to flee from him and wallow in her anger and bitterness at how he'd rejected her again this morning. Each time the thought popped into her head, she pushed it back, reminding herself that she'd been emotional and she had a history of making bad choices out of emotion instead of reason. She couldn't be that person any longer. Jacob was depending on her to be logical. She needed Garrett to bring Jacob home and that angered her. She shouldn't need his help. He didn't deserve to be able to abandon them and then swoop in and be needed. It wasn't right. But then nothing about this situation was fair.

She headed for her office and Garrett closed the door behind them. Walking to her desk, she slid into her chair, basking in the familiar comfort of it. Being a prosecutor had been her dream for a long time, ever since she'd found herself testifying against her foster mother and becoming friends with Judge Warren. Then only an ADA, he had walked her through the process, then taken her under his wing, mentoring her throughout college and law school. He admired her tenacity and determination, he'd told her. He'd been a wonderful support for her and she wasn't sure she would have made it to the position she was in without him. Now this was her office and she was good at her job. But she would gladly give it all up to have her son back.

Garrett's phone buzzed at his side. He glanced at the screen. "They need me across the street. I'd rather you not leave the office. I'll come get you when they're ready for the press conference."

She nodded. "I always keep a spare makeup bag in my desk. I'll try to look my best."

Bridgette Myers, her assistant, rushed into the office. She stared after Garrett as he left, her eyes wide and her mouth open in surprise, and Ashlynn saw her mouth the word *wow* as she approached Ashlynn and enveloped her in a hug.

"How are you holding up?" Bridgette asked. "I cannot believe this is happening to you. A car bomb? Being shot at? Your son kidnapped and your ex-husband murdered?" She listed the previous day's events as if Ashlynn hadn't lived through them. "I just cannot believe someone I know has this happening to her." She handed over a cup of coffee and Ashlynn thanked her once she stopped talking long enough to take a breath.

"I won't be here long," Ashlynn said. "I'm going to be part of a press conference about Jacob's abduction—"

"I heard about that," Bridgette interrupted. "I can't believe it's come to that."

"I just stopped by for my extra jacket and makeup bag that I keep in my desk."

"Sure, the one you use before court."

"That's right. The police also want me to look through my case files for the last several months. Could you gather those together and have them ready for me to take with me after the press conference?"

"Sure. No problem. Can I do anything else for you, Ashlynn?"

"No, not really, although I don't believe I'll be very productive on my current cases. I wonder if I can get Roger to reassign them until Jacob is found." Roger was the ADA in charge of case assignments.

"I don't see why he wouldn't. I've heard people talking already this morning and everyone is willing to help out however they can. I'll take care of it."

Her door swung open and Ken stepped inside. "Ashlynn!" He pulled her into a hug and he was like a big papa bear. She and Ken had become close over the past six months since he'd joined their staff. Although he worked for the entire office, Ashlynn noticed he volunteered to take on a lot of her cases.

"I know you have other cases to work on," she told Ken, "so I appreciate you taking the time to help with finding Jacob."

He waved away her thanks. "Whatever I can do to help, I will. I want to be involved with this, Ashlynn. He's a cute little fella and I don't want to see anything happen to him. Whatever you need, I want you to call me."

She nodded. "I will." She glanced from Ken to Bridgette and felt a rush of tears burn her eyes. It meant so much to her to have friends like these during this difficult time. "I want to thank both of you for being here for me. It means a lot." She gulped back emotion. She didn't have many friends, and that was by choice. She'd learned at a young age that letting people into your life generally meant letting them hurt you, and that instinct to keep people at arm's length had only been confirmed by Garrett's desertion. But these were two people she worked closely with and she considered them both much more than mere coworkers. Bridgette's eagerness to help in any way and Ken's experience-filled encouragement had garnered her trust in them both.

Bridgette's eyes filled with tears and she dabbed them away. "I'll go start gathering those files for you," she said, then hurried out.

"Files?" Ken asked. "What files?"

"My case files. Garrett and Vince are convinced Jacob's abduction might have something to do with one of my cases, so I said I would go through them and see if anything stood out."

"Ashlynn, I'm taking care of that. I've already started searching through them. I haven't come across anything suspicious so far, but I'm making progress."

"I know, but a second pair of eyes never hurt. Besides, I need something to do besides sitting around making myself crazy wondering if Jacob is safe."

He nodded as if that notion hadn't occurred to him. "Of course. I'll help Bridgette gather those files and bring them over to the police station so you'll have them after the press conference."

She thanked him and watched him walk out. She went back to her desk and pulled out her makeup bag, knowing she would need a ton of concealer to hide the bags under her eyes this morning. She pushed it away. It didn't matter what she looked like. Today, she wasn't a professional prosecutor. She was just a mother whose child had been snatched from her. No one would care how she looked.

She picked up a stack of mail on her desk and sorted through it, instead. She tore one envelope open and pulled out a sheet of paper. A photo fell to the desk. She picked it up and saw it was a snapshot of Mira with Jacob at the playground. She turned it over and her heart stopped as she read the scrawled words across the back.

What kind of mother leaves raising her child to someone else? You don't deserve to be a mother.

Ken walked Ashlynn across the street to the police station. Garrett met them at the door and once she was safely inside, he loaded the box of files Ken carried into his truck. The police had retrieved it from Stephen's house during their investigation into his murder, and he'd been glad to trade in the BMW for his own vehicle. "Thank you for doing this for Ashlynn," Garrett said.

"Absolutely," Ken said. "I never had kids of my own so I consider Ashlynn to be like a daughter—or maybe a kid sister since we're not that far apart in age. That little lady holds a special place in my heart even though I've only known her a few months." He glanced at Garrett. "Do you have any kids?"

Garrett's heart skipped a beat. If Ken had asked him that question yesterday, the answer would have been different. But he was in no mood to explain all that to anyone. Ashlynn could share that story if she chose to. His mind was still trying to wrap itself around the fact that he was a dad. It still seemed unreal.

"I'm glad she's got someone else watching her back," Garrett told him instead then shook the man's hand.

"Take care of her," Ken said, then he marched across the street to the DA's offices.

Garrett headed back into the police station. He poured two cups of coffee and handed Ashlynn one of them. Her hands were shaking, and he knew it wasn't because she was chilly. She tightened her fingers around the cup and breathed in the coffee vapor.

Dressed in smart slacks and a blouse, she looked beautiful but sad. She was wearing that expression he knew so well, the one that was full of utter despair and hopelessness. He'd seen it before and he hated it even more now. She couldn't lose hope. He would find her son…his son…their son. He sighed. His brain was still trying to comprehend what he'd learned last night and he was more determined than ever to find Jacob and bring him home. He'd made a promise to Ashlynn and he meant to keep it.

The press conference was a good idea, although he still wasn't sure Ashlynn was up for it. But she had to be, and he wasn't leaving her side until it was over. He sat beside her and tried to find words that would reassure her. "We'll find him, Ashlynn. We'll bring him home."

Her chin quivered and tears pooled in her eyes. "This is my fault."

He sighed wearily. They'd already been through this. "No, it absolutely is not. I had no right to suggest it was. I was wrong and I'm sorry."

"I wish everyone believed that." She reached into her pocket and pulled out a slip of paper.

He opened it and saw the words scribbled on it. "Where did you get this?"

"It was on my desk with my mail."

He fought he urge to crumple the paper. It was evidence and he had to preserve it, but it was truly nothing but garbage. "No one believes this."

"Someone does."

"Ashlynn, you and I have both seen our share of terrible mothers. You are not like her. You would never intentionally hurt your child."

She shuddered. Few people besides Ashlynn would know he was referring to Kathryn Rollins, the foster mother who had nearly killed her. After suffering her abuse for years, Ashlynn had stood up to her and nearly been beaten to death for it. Had she again stood up to the wrong person and now her son was paying the price? He saw guilt written across her face and grabbed her arm turning her to him. "This is not your fault," he told her again, his tone pressing her to listen and believe him. "Jacob's abduction is not your fault. Someone is targeting you and I will find out who."

She stared up at him, her countenance full of hopelessness and despair. He was more determined than ever to wipe that expression from her face for good. But he knew he would need all of God's help to do so.

Please help me find Jacob and bring him home safely.

He couldn't concern himself with the logistics of what home meant yet. First he would find his son, then they would unravel everything else.

In preparation for the press conference, Ashlynn went to the ladies room and splashed her face with cold water. She was glad now that she hadn't bothered with the makeup because it would have just been washed away. She pulled on the jacket from her office, smoothed down her hair and stared at herself in the mirror in the ladies room.

Someone knocked on the door then opened it. Garrett stood protectively just outside. "They're ready for you, Ash."

She closed her eyes and tried to gather her confidence. She didn't know how she was going to get through this without breaking down. Vince had told her she didn't have to speak, but she knew she did.

Although she was still miffed at him for his words last night, she was glad Garrett was with her. His strength was a comfort to her in this trying time. She didn't know why God was allowing this to happen. Why Stephen had to die. Why Jacob had been kidnapped. She'd only thought her world was falling apart before when her marriage had ended, but now she knew she'd been so wrong.

The press was already set up outside the police station. And even though it was December, the day was mild and the bright lights were hot. As Vince stood to address the press, Ashlynn noticed he was sweating.

She listened to his official statement. "Yesterday evening, the body of twenty-one-year-old Mira Randolph was found murdered. Miss Randolph was working as a nanny for the family of Assistant District Attorney Ashlynn Morris. The child in her care, four-year-old Jacob Morris, was reported missing and is considered an endangered child. An Amber Alert has been issued. ADA Morris has been the target of multiple attempts on her life and the child's father was found murdered in his home late last night. We are coordinating with other law enforcement agencies in the state and surrounding states, as well as the FBI. Anyone with any information about these murders or the whereabouts of four-year-old Jacob Morris are instructed to phone the JPD. A tip line has been set up for any information the public has. All tips will be investigated."

Ashlynn didn't know how she was even still standing. The press was a blur surrounding her. Her only strength was Garrett behind her. She felt his presence holding her solid as Vince took questions from the reporters.

"Do you believe this has anything to do with ADA Morris's job as a prosecutor?" one of the reporters called out.

"We're investigating that possibility along with others."

After several more questions, which basically led to Vince's reassurance that they were investigating every possibility, he turned to Ashlynn. "ADA Morris has prepared a written statement. She will not be taking questions."

Vince moved aside and Ashlynn stepped to the podium. This wasn't the first time she had addressed the press. She knew most of their names. She'd met them before and discussed other cases. But this was different. Now, she had to face them not as a member of law enforcement, but as the victim of a crime. She didn't much like being on this side of the story.

She stared past the reporters and looked into the cameras, addressing the kidnapper. She took a deep breath to steady her nerves. She wanted to scream and rant and demand that Jacob be returned and even thought about threatening the kidnapper with full prosecution and every legal means she possessed, but she didn't. It was a given that the person responsible would be prosecuted, but she knew threats and rants would do no good right now. Whoever had taken Jacob from her wanted to see her emotionally fall apart. Was the kidnapper out there now, watching and waiting to see her lose it? She thought he was and decided he wouldn't get the satisfaction of seeing how his actions had affected her.

She held up the photograph that had been distributed to the press and spoke as calmly as she could. "My son, Jacob, is four years old. He's funny and he's smart and he loves playing with his blocks and watching cartoons. I know he's frightened and doesn't understand what is happening right now. He's only a little boy and I ask the person or persons who took him to please drop him off safely at a hospital or fire station. Whatever your problem with me, he is not a part of it. I don't know why you are targeting my family, but I'm begging you to please return Jacob. He misses his family and we miss him."

She stepped down as reporters shouted questions to her and snapped her picture. Vince returned and reminded them that Ashlynn would not be answering questions. She stepped off the podium and hurried into the safety of the courthouse before she broke down in front of the cameras. She wouldn't let them see her lose control, but she also knew she couldn't hold it back much longer.

She leaned against a wall, stopping to catch her breath and compose herself. It wasn't fair this was happening to her. Her little boy didn't deserve this. A wave of fury rushed through her and all the anger and bitterness she'd felt moments ago for the kidnappers now focused on God. He was the one who had allowed this to happen to them. He was the one who could have prevented it. Tears streamed down her face and she pounded her hands against the concrete walls.

As her emotion was spent, she realized she wasn't alone. She felt someone behind her watching her. She turned to see Garrett standing there, his face set and determined.

Suddenly, he grabbed her hand. "Come with me," he said, pulling her down the hall. "I have an idea I want to check out."

"What? Where are we going?" she demanded, wiping at her wet face.

He stopped and turned to her. "I may know a way to find your son."

Chapter Five

The idea had occurred to him during the press conference when he'd glanced at all the news vans parked near the courthouse steps. The white van the neighbors had seen might be the key to finding Jacob and he knew a way to possibly locate that van.

"Do you remember a guy named Mike Webb?"

"How can I forget him? I see his name on my roster every few months, but he always manages to avoid conviction."

He nodded. That was the guy. "He's a major player in the car theft business. At least, he used to be. I'm glad to know that hasn't changed."

They'd each shared their tales of difficult childhoods and bad choices they'd both made, so Garrett knew Ashlynn was aware he used to steal cars for Webb back in his younger days before the army cleaned him up.

"Well, I thought I might be able to track him down. Maybe he can tell us who might be into stealing white vans in town."

"They probably all wind up in his chop shop," she said. "The police have put together a task force to track down the car-theft ring operating in town. They haven't been able to locate him. Why do you think you can?"

"Because he knows me. I used to work for him. He wasn't a bad guy. And I'm sure he would never be party to ripping a child from his mother."

"Garrett, he's a criminal."

"So was I," he reminded her. "Everyone deserves a second chance to do the right thing, don't they, Ash?"

She hesitated, perhaps wondering if he was talking about the car thieves or himself. Did she think he was hinting around that he wanted a second chance with her and Jacob? He hadn't really meant it that way and didn't want her to get the wrong impression.

He pressed the point. "You're searching through your recent convictions, you've got Ken looking into any recent prisoners released, and Vince and the police are following Amber Alert leads and investigating the deaths of your nanny and Stephen. I don't know if this will amount to anything, but if it might, shouldn't we follow it? I have to try."

"You didn't mention this to Vince?"

"No, because I don't know if it's going to go anywhere. I'd rather not get the police involved if it's just a dead end."

He wondered briefly if her duty as a prosecutor would hamper her ability to get on board with his idea. He didn't have to wait long to find out.

She nodded. "It's a good idea if you think he'll talk to you."

"I believe he will, only..." This was the part of the

plan she wasn't going to like. "I don't think you should come with me. These guys may not want to talk if they know you're a prosecutor."

"Garrett, you were standing next to me during the press conference. Won't they have seen you on TV?"

"If anyone questions me about it, I'll just say you've hired me to find your son."

He knew she would prefer to go in with a full police task force and so would he, but they didn't even know yet where to search. Plus, this was a connection the police were unlikely to be able to provide.

He reached out and stroked her arm. "I don't want to leave you behind. I would prefer to have you with me. But in this case, I think it's necessary."

"No, I understand. You can't exactly get your former friends to open up to you with a prosecutor standing by your side. I'll stay at my office and use the time to look through my case files."

He nodded. "You should be safe there. No one is going to attack you in an office full of people."

He escorted her back to her office before he left.

He hadn't been lying when he'd said he would feel better having her with him, but her status as a prosecutor would only hinder him. He was better off working this lead alone.

Garrett chuckled, realizing there was a time not too long ago when working on his own would have been his preference, but not now. Not since Ashlynn had stepped back into his life.

Ashlynn had a difficult time concentrating on her case files. The words and information seemed to merge together. She couldn't focus because all she could think about was Jacob and wondering if he was safe, and Garrett and wondering if he was making any progress. It seemed the police weren't getting any closer to finding Jacob. She hoped Garrett was having more success.

A knock on her door made her look up. She smiled, happy to see Judge Warren step inside. "Come in," she exclaimed, welcoming him into the office. She reached up and hugged his neck. He was one of the few people who'd been there for her throughout the years and she cherished his friendship and advice.

"I saw the press conference. I'm sorry this is happening to you. Do the police have any leads about your son?"

"They're following several, but nothing concrete so far."

"I'm so sorry to hear that." He handed her a plate with plastic wrap on it. "My wife made these brownies. I remember how you used to like them so I thought I would bring them by. It's not much, but it's the least I can do."

She smiled at the gesture. She'd been a twelve-year-old battered girl the first time he'd offered her some of his wife's brownies and, yes, she had liked them. He'd never forgotten that, and every now and then he brought her some. And it was always too many. Generally, she took a couple for her and Jacob then placed the rest in the break room for the office to share. But his gesture meant the world to her because it proved that someone did care about her. She took the plate and gave him a big hug and a sincere thank-you.

"If I can do anything to help, please call."

"I will, Judge. Thank you."

He turned and sauntered out, and Ashlynn spotted

Bridgette standing by her door. She walked in holding a steaming cup of coffee.

"Oh, brownies," she exclaimed, used to indulging in the treats from Judge Warren's wife.

Ashlynn laughed at the familiarity of the situation. It made her feel just a bit better. "Help yourself," she told Bridgette.

Bridgette set down the coffee, unwrapped the plastic and bit into one of the brownies. A satisfied look crossed her face. "So good," she said. "Mrs. Warren sure knows her stuff when it comes to baking."

"She always has." Ashlynn took a few of the brownies from the plate then replaced the cover and handed it to Bridgette. "Would you place these in the break room for everyone to share?"

"Sure. Oh, I brought this for you." She pushed the coffee toward Ashlynn. "I thought you could use it."

"Thank you. I could." She bit into one of the brownies and washed it down with the coffee.

"How's it coming?" Bridgette asked. "Are you finding anything?"

"Not yet, but I won't give up. If there's something in these files that can help tell me who took my son, I will find it."

"I'll let you get back to work, then." Bridgette walked out, carrying the plate of brownies with her while Ashlynn turned back to the files.

She meant what she'd said about not giving up. Judge Warren had always encouraged her to fight for what she wanted and this was one fight she wouldn't lose. She would find a way to bring Jacob home.

But she realized she wasn't fighting alone and that gave her comfort. Garrett was out there now, tracking down leads. She was thankful he'd come back into her life just when she needed him and his skills as a ranger. She thought about her earlier railing at God. She didn't know if Garrett's return to town was divine intervention or just plain good timing, but she was thankful nonetheless.

She spent the next half hour poring over her records but then her eyes began to blur. She was having trouble concentrating and realized she'd read the same passage three times and still didn't know what it said.

She rubbed the bridge of her nose. Her eyes were tired and she supposed the strain was finally catching up with her. She glanced at her coffee cup, now empty again. She needed a refill, but instead of bothering Bridgette she got up to fetch it herself. She needed to walk, to stretch her legs and get her blood pumping or else she was going to fall asleep at her desk. She forced her legs to move. They felt like dead weight as she left her office and headed down the hall. Maybe she should have buzzed Bridgette instead, she thought, but it was too late for that.

She entered the break room and saw no one was there. That was a relief because she wasn't up to making awkward chitchat with her coworkers or rehashing all that had happened. There was a full pot of coffee, though, and it was still warm so someone had made it recently. For that, she was thankful.

She poured some into her mug and doctored it the way she liked. Her brain still seemed to be in a fog and she felt groggy. And the coffee didn't seem to help. She gripped the counter as the room began to spin. Something was wrong. She shouldn't be this tired. She felt more like…more like she'd been drugged. She saw the plate of brownies on the table. That was the only thing she'd eaten recently. But it couldn't be…they couldn't be. She stumbled to a chair and fell into it.

Suddenly, someone grabbed her from behind. Something tight and hard dug into her neck. She was being choked!

She pulled at her neck, trying to dislodge whatever was cutting off her air supply, then flailed her arms behind her. They felt like stone pillars and moving them was difficult, but she kicked and clawed and fought, knowing she had to do whatever she could to survive.

Her attacker pulled her to her feet and Ashlynn's head started spinning. She fought the urge to lose consciousness, knowing it would be the end of her. Fear pulsed through her and she wished Garrett was there. She reached up and jabbed at her attacker's face, hoping to connect with his eyes. Her fingernails dug into something like fabric. A mask. Just like the man who'd been shooting at her at her house had been wearing.

One of her kicks hit the cabinet and sent her coffee mug falling. It hit the floor, shattered and coffee splattered. It was hot when it hit her and Ashlynn groaned but her attacker did, too, obviously splashed with the scalding liquid. He loosened his grip just enough that Ashlynn managed to get her hands between her neck and the offending wire he was using to choke her.

She heard footsteps and voices, and her attacker

swore and shoved her. Her head hit the cabinet hard as she went down to the floor. When she looked back up, the break room door was swinging shut and he was gone.

She glanced at her hand, which was cut and bleeding either by a shard from her coffee mug or the wire her attacker had choked her with. Her fingernails had also snagged pieces of the mask he'd used to cover his face.

The door opened and Ashlynn tensed. Had he returned to finish her off? Bridgette stepped inside and Ashlynn breathed a sigh of relief. Hers must have been the footsteps that had frightened her attacker off.

"Ashlynn!" Bridgette rushed to her side, crunching on the shards and kneeling beside her. "Are you okay? What happened?" She hurried back to the door and opened it, shouting out. "Someone get help. Ashlynn's been attacked."

Pain was radiating from her neck, but the dull throb from her head overshadowed it. She'd hit the cabinet hard and the room was spinning, but that could also have been from being drugged.

"You're bleeding," Bridgette said grabbing for a towel and pressing it to Ashlynn's forehead, where she hadn't even known she'd been hit. She must have fallen on one of the shards or cut herself when she hit the cabinet.

"Who did this to you?" Bridgette asked, her face full of concern.

A wave of nausea rolled over Ashlynn before she could respond. She leaned over and the next thing she knew she was flat on her back. Bridgette's worried face hovered over hers then faded away as Ashlynn slipped into darkness.

* * *

Garrett hurried to the ER when he got the call from Vince about Ashlynn being attacked at her office. He kicked himself for being so foolish. He never should have left her, but at the time it had seemed like the only way. He'd never dreamed she would be in danger in her own office.

He hurried inside and found the room where she was being observed. His gut clenched when he saw her lying on the bed. She looked small beneath the hospital blanket and had an IV hooked up to her and a bandage across her forehead and around her hand. But she managed to give him a weak smile when she saw him. "Hi."

He reached for her non-bandaged hand and squeezed it, as much to comfort himself as to comfort her. "What happened?"

"Someone attacked me in the break room. But that's not all, Garrett. I think I was drugged. If Bridgette hadn't come along, he might have killed me."

"How could someone drug you?"

Tears pooled in her eyes. "Judge Warren brought me a plate of brownies. I had one before this whole incident happened."

"Judge Warren? Why would he want to drug you?"

"I don't know, but I don't see how else it could have happened."

Guilt rushed through him. He should have been there to protect her.

Vince knocked on the door and entered. "I'm glad you're here, Garrett." He glanced at Ashlynn. "How are you feeling?"

"I'm okay," she said, but her voice was small and weak.

"Did you find out who did this?" Garrett demanded.

Vince shook his head. "I've spoken with several of the people in the office at the time. No one saw anything."

Garrett sighed wearily. "How could they not see anyone?"

"It's a busy office and people are always coming and going. They don't have security cameras in the offices but they have them on the front doors. We'll search through the footage, but honestly we don't have a clue who we're looking for."

Ashlynn shook her head. "I didn't get a good look at him. He had that same mask covering his face as before. I grabbed it."

"No one saw a man in a mask, but that's easy to pull off and stuff into your pocket. We were able to get fiber samples from under your nails. They might provide some information. I also spoke with your assistant. She claims she also ate one of the brownies the judge brought you and nothing happened to her."

Ashlynn nodded, obviously thinking back. "Yes, she did have one. I watched her eat it."

"She also said she brought you coffee. The drugs could have been in that."

"Do you think Bridgette is the one who tried to drug me?" Ashlynn asked.

Garrett shook his head. "That's not likely. If Bridgette was the one drugging you, she could have easily told the police that the brownies made her sleepy, too. That would have focused suspicion away from her."

"True, and it was definitely a man who attacked me

in the break room and Bridgette is the one who spooked him. And I can't think of one reason why Bridgette—or Judge Warren, either, for that matter—would want to kill me."

Vince glanced at Ashlynn. "Well, we'll follow up with Judge Warren and we're also having the remaining brownies and your coffee mug, what's left of it anyway, analyzed, but those will both take some time. Meanwhile, I'll have an officer posted at your door."

"That won't be necessary," she said. "They're releasing me soon. My injuries aren't that serious."

"And I'll be here until she's released," Garrett said. He wasn't leaving her unprotected again.

Vince nodded. "I'll let you know if we have any further questions," he told Ashlynn, then he walked out.

Garrett looked at her. "I shouldn't have left you."

"No, you had to focus on Jacob. Did you find out anything?"

"Not yet, but I'm not giving up. I don't want to leave you unprotected again, though. I'll phone Josh and see if I can drop you off at his place. You'll be safe there for the rest of the afternoon and it'll give you time to rest up. Don't worry. I trust him. He won't let anything happen to you."

"Are you sure he won't mind?"

"I'll call him but I know he won't. He does private security for an international company so if he's not off on an assignment he generally works from home."

"Fine, but I'd like to stop by my office first. I was going through my case files. I can pick them up and continue while I'm at Josh's."

"Ashlynn, you're supposed to be resting. You were nearly killed."

"Maybe you're right, but Jacob is still missing and I won't get any rest until he's home."

He had no choice but to agree, knowing she wasn't going to sit back and do nothing while her son...while their son...was missing. Wow, he still couldn't wrap his brain around the notion that he had a son.

He made the call to Josh and confirmed that, yes, he would be home and, no, he didn't mind one bit keeping an eye on Ashlynn for a while. Garrett stayed with her while the nurse finished the discharge paperwork and removed the IV.

Finally they left the hospital and drove downtown, back to the DA's offices. Ashlynn was pale as he parked and cut off the engine.

He gently touched her arm. "Are you sure you want to go back in there?" He hadn't considered how going back into the office where she'd been attacked would affect her, and by the ashen tone of her skin he doubted she had, either.

"I can run upstairs and get the files. Or, better yet, have someone bring them down."

"No," she said doggedly, unbuckling the seatbelt and jutting out that determined chin. "I'm going. I won't be terrorized this way."

He grinned at her stubbornness. When it didn't infuriate him, it made him proud.

Garrett walked with her to her office where she loaded the stack of files she'd requested into a box.

She was stuffing a few more, along with her notepad and pens, into the box when she turned and saw him staring at the photo of Jacob on her desk. He picked it up and outlined Jacob's image with his finger.

"He has my eyes," Garrett noted, his voice cracking with unguarded emotion.

"I know. You can't imagine how confusing it is to love someone so much who reminds you of someone—" She stopped herself. She'd been about to say "someone who'd let you down so much," but she realized how that would hurt him.

But she hadn't caught herself in time. "Someone you hate?"

"I don't hate you, Garrett. I never did. Even when I thought you'd rejected us, I couldn't hate you." She placed a comforting hand on his arm.

He covered her hand with his own, then replaced the photo on the desk and moved his hands to her face, softly caressing her cheeks. "I know I've let you and Jacob down before, Ashlynn, but I promise you, I won't rest until I bring Jacob home."

She stared up into his eyes. She saw a man where she used to see a boy and she saw determination and grit and…something else. A vulnerability she recognized. His finger stroked her lips and she saw him glance at her mouth as he drew nearer to her. Her heart jumped a beat. Was he going to kiss her? And what would she do if he tried?

She couldn't deny there was still such an attraction between them and she couldn't stop herself from remembering the safety of his arms embracing her. He'd always been her rock of strength and faith.

But then the cold reality hit her.

He hadn't always been her rock.

He felt the change in her too and backed away.

She shook her head. "I'm sorry, but I can't. How can I allow myself to fall for you when I can't trust you to stick around? I loved you so much, Garrett, and you shattered me. I can't go through that again. Besides, I need you to put Jacob front and center now."

He nodded and stepped away from her, but she saw the pain in his eyes at her rejection. She didn't really want to hurt him, especially now that she knew he hadn't meant to hurt her, but she had to keep her focus. She couldn't lose herself in Garrett again. She had Jacob now and she had to protect him. He'd already lost so much.

Garrett walked over to the box of files. "Is this everything?"

"Yes, for now."

He picked it up. She noticed how his muscles contracted beneath his shirt and felt a sigh of regret for what might have been.

They were back at Garrett's truck when Ken approached them with a file. "I'm glad I caught you," he said. "I didn't want to talk inside. Judge Warren checks out. He has no outstanding debts, no family connections with legal troubles. In fact, he's set to retire from the bench in a few months. He and his wife are planning to travel once he's retired. He seemed shook up when he learned what had happened to you and he was adamant that the brownies were not drugged. I think he was kind of hurt that anyone would even suggest it."

Ashlynn shook her head. "I have a hard time believing Judge Warren would try to harm me. He's my mentor. He's been like a second father to me all these years. I should talk to him and apologize."

Garrett nodded, but she could see he was more anxious to question the judge than apologize.

"What about Bridgette?" Garrett asked. "She brought you the coffee."

"Yes, and she's brought me coffee many times before. She's never drugged it previously. Besides, she wasn't the one who attacked me. In fact, she probably saved my life. And why would she want to hurt me?"

Ken ventured a guess. "Could be jealousy."

"Over what?"

"Everyone in the office knows Bridgette and her husband have been trying to have a baby and can't. Maybe she snapped and decided she would just take yours. It's possible she's obsessed. She snatches Jacob and then tries to kill you to get you out of the way. Jealousy has a way of making normally rational people do things you would never believe."

"That's ludicrous. Lots of people can't have children. That doesn't mean they're willing to resort to murder and abduction in order to become parents. There are other ways to have a child. Adoption, for instance."

Ken shook his head. "Maybe but not for former drug addicts. This is the reason I didn't want to talk inside the office. I ran a background on Bridgette's husband, Bruce. He spent six years in prison on drug charges and burglary. No agency is going to give someone with his background a child."

Garrett seemed excited about this new bit of information, but Ashlynn shook her head, dismayed. "I never knew that about her husband, but that still doesn't mean she's behind this. I find that very hard to believe. She's been a loyal friend to me."

Ken put away the files. "Well, I turned over what I discovered to the police so they can follow up on it."

"Ashlynn, we can't discount these incidents," Garrett said. "Whoever drugged you was nearby. No one saw anyone suspicious in your office or around your car when the bomb was set. Don't you see? Whoever is behind this is someone who can get close without raising suspicion. This person, or people, are targeting you. They have Jacob and now they want you out of the way. We can't just discount people because of an emotional connection. We have to follow up on every angle."

"Wouldn't I know if someone close to me was trying to kill me? Or wanted to take my son?"

"Not necessarily. Betrayal hurts so much because it is someone you trusted not to betray you."

She saw something in his face and got the idea he knew a thing or two about betrayal. Well, so did she because she'd been betrayed by him. She bit back that comment. He didn't need that reminder and it would only be cruel to bring it up again. She had to focus on the fact that he hadn't intentionally abandoned his family. He hadn't known about Jacob when he'd ended things with her. She needed to believe that because it helped to ease the sting of rejection.

* * *

Josh greeted them both then ushered Ashlynn into the den where she would have privacy while she sorted through her files but where he could also keep an eye on her.

Garrett shook his hand. "Thanks for doing this. I shouldn't have left her alone in her office, but I thought she would be safe there." He grimaced. "I was wrong."

"Not a problem," Josh assured him.

"If I text you a few names, can you do some background work on them?" He was starting with those in Ashlynn's inner circle—her ex-husband and her co-workers, including the DA and several of the police officers she worked closely with. "Her nanny was also killed. I would be inclined to think this was about her if Ashlynn's ex-husband hadn't been killed, as well. Someone is targeting her. I need to find out who."

Josh nodded, understanding. He knew about betrayal, having discovered his friend was behind his niece's abduction and a human trafficking ring operating out of their hometown. "Consider it done. Levi is coming into town tomorrow for an appointment at the neurologist. Want me to pull him in, too?"

Garrett nodded. "I'm hoping this will all be over and done with quickly, but I wouldn't mind having you both on alert in case I need backup."

"I'm here if you need me," Josh told him.

Garrett thanked him, said his goodbyes to Ashlynn and turned to leave.

I'm here if you need me. Garrett had known he could count on Josh to be there for him. It was one of the great things about having a band of brothers he trusted completely. He would always be there for them if they needed him and he could count on them to be there for him. Having that kind of backup was one of the reasons he'd decided to end his solitary lifestyle and return to life among people. He'd been in too many situations where he'd gotten in too deep and no one had had his back. He'd had to fight and claw and too many times shoot his way out of trouble.

He'd been shot, stabbed, beaten and even poisoned once, and each time he'd struggled with knowing he was alone in the world with only his determination and skill to protect him. They had protected him and they'd brought him home each time he'd rushed headlong into peril, but more and more the times between assignments had begun to feel more like loneliness than solitude. It was a feeling he doubted any of his ranger brothers understood. He knew they worried about him and his willingness and determination to find danger.

The doctors he'd seen had called it survivor's guilt and assured him it would eventually eat him alive or get him killed if he didn't deal with it. They'd surely been right and even though he was still plagued by the feeling that he shouldn't have walked out of that ambush alive, he didn't want to nurse it alone any longer.

Now, with Ashlynn in trouble and his son—*his son*—missing, he was more pleased than ever before that he had the backup of the rangers on his side.

Chapter Six

Years ago when Garrett had been a dumb kid working the streets, Mike Webb's chop shop had been housed on Raymond Street. He started there but was unsurprised to find the building had been torn down. The very nature of Mike's business meant he had to relocate often. But there had been a few meeting points, places where people would go to be found. Usually it was to buy drugs, a pastime he'd never ventured into, thankfully, but they were also places where someone could find information.

Garrett drove to several of those places and posed questions to people he encountered, but he saw no one he recognized. The players were all young kids and they either didn't know the names he dropped or were playing dumb. He figured it was probably the latter. They didn't know him from Adam and they weren't giving out details to strangers.

He sighed as he got back into his car. This was another dead end, just as Ashlynn had predicted. He hated most that he'd let her down again. She'd acted as if she hadn't been too optimistic about this panning out but he'd seen a glimmer of hope in her eyes and he disliked dashing that.

There had to be some way to reconnect with his old crew, aside from just parking his truck with the doors open and yelling at the top of his lungs that he was leaving the keys inside, then waiting to see who showed up. Although he would be willing to do that if he thought it would help him find Jacob.

He was definitely feeling the pressure as the hours passed with no ransom demand and no leads. He would do whatever it took to bring Jacob home. He wanted to get to know his son and have the opportunity to be a dad. He'd grown up without a father and now that Stephen was dead, Jacob could be looking at the same kind of future. Garrett didn't want that for him. He'd never thought about being a father, but now that he knew he was, he wanted to be a part of his child's life. But first he had to find Jacob and bring him home safely.

He tried three more spots where his old crew used to hang out but still made no headway. Things had changed too much in town in the years since he'd been gone. And more than just the town was different. He was, too. He'd once been at home here, but he wasn't that same dumb kid who used to steal cars for Mike Webb for a hundred bucks a pop. He'd made it out of this neighborhood. The army had cleaned him up and given him a skill and a purpose.

He glanced around and spotted mostly young kids on the streets. This was why he'd accepted when his friend from church had asked him to volunteer to men-

tor inner city kids. He had something to offer them—
hope that if he could make it out, they could, as well.
And speaking of his mentoring…

He spotted a familiar face walking along Harris
Street—Adam Greer, the boy he'd been at the courthouse to support yesterday when he'd run into Ashlynn.
He didn't even know what had happened in Adam's
mother's case. Adam stopped at the corner and Garrett saw him push a bill into another boy's hand and accept something that he quickly shoved into his pocket.

He sighed, disappointed. Adam's mother was a drug
addict. Was he buying for her or following in her footsteps? Either way, Garrett couldn't sit back and allow it
to happen. He threw his truck into gear and roared up
the road, stopping in front of Adam and jumping out.

"Mr. G., what are you doing here?" the boy asked,
using the nickname they'd given him, forgetting that
Garrett was his first, not his last name. He'd gotten that
sort of confusion his entire life.

"I saw that drug buy, Adam." He pulled open the passenger door. "Get in. Let's have a talk."

Ashlynn set down the file she was reviewing and
sighed. Nothing had turned up that might be related to her
son's disappearance and she was becoming more and more
certain it had nothing to do with one of her past cases.

She took a break and stood from her spot curled up
on the sofa in Josh and Elise's living room. Placing
her file on the coffee table, she stretched her arms and
legs. There were photographs on the fireplace mantel,
including one of Josh and a teenage girl who must be

the niece Garrett had mentioned before. She also spotted a picture of a group of men in uniform and picked it up, thinking this must be Josh and Garrett's ranger team. Searching the group she found Garrett kneeling on the front row.

Someone cleared his throat behind her, and she realized she'd been caught snooping. She turned and saw Josh standing at the doorway.

"I'm sorry," she said, replacing the photograph.

"It's okay," he told her. He walked in and motioned toward the image. "That was our team before the ambush." He glanced at her curiously. "Did Garrett tell you about that?"

"He did mention it." Actually, he'd done his best to skim over the details of the event that had ripped their relationship apart.

"Only six of us made it out that night." He pointed to each man as he said their names. "Matt, Levi, Colton, Blake, Garrett and me." He pointed to a tall, lanky redhead. "That was Marcus, Garrett's best friend. Has he mentioned him?"

She shook her head but wasn't surprised since Josh had already told her the rest of these men hadn't survived the ambush. She looked at the wedding photo of Josh and Elise next to the photo of the rangers and felt a pang of jealousy. They'd gotten their happy ending. "Did you know about my engagement to Garrett?"

He nodded. "Yes, we knew. When he rejoined the group after that leave, you were all he talked about. He was crazy in love with you, Ashlynn." Josh stuffed his hands into his pockets and looked weary. "We all lost so much that night. We each dealt with it in our own ways. Garrett ran from it. He took off and I didn't even see or hear from him for months. He just lost himself. But one thing he never lost was his devotion to the rangers. Whenever any one of us has needed him, he's been there."

She sighed. That statement did not make her feel any better. He could be devoted to his friends but not to his family. "He wasn't there for me when I needed him."

"I know he let you down, but you have to know that's not who he is. That was a bad time in his life and he messed up. You're having a hard time trusting him and I get that. When I first met Elise, I didn't trust anyone. I didn't want to depend on another person because I was afraid of being disappointed."

"How did she change your mind?"

His lips twitched into a smile. "She didn't. God changed me and because He did I was able to let Elise inside. All I'm saying is that I know what it's like to step out on a limb without knowing if you're going to fall or not. But I also know Garrett cares for you. I think he probably never stopped caring about you."

She was suddenly uncomfortable with the direction this conversation was going. Of course he would stand up for his friend, but he didn't understand how badly she'd been hurt or how frightened she was that Garrett would leave her again. She just couldn't take that chance on him. "I'm trusting Garrett to find Jacob because I really have no other choice. But I can't trust him with anything else, not now, maybe not ever."

His phone buzzed and he pulled it out and glanced at the screen. "It's Garrett. He's pulling into the driveway."

She hurried to the door to wait for him, anxious to

know if he'd found anything that might help lead them to Jacob. She watched his truck pull into the garage and he got out a moment later.

"Well?" she asked before he even made it inside. "Were your old contacts able to offer any information?"

He shook his head. "No, my old contacts were a bust. However—" he opened the passenger door and grabbed the arm of a young boy, pulling him from the car "—my new contact might just be able to offer us some information. Ashlynn, meet Adam Greer, my mentee."

Adam was just a young kid who appeared nervous as Garrett stood over him. He plopped down in a chair and spent five minutes staring at the floor.

"I caught him buying drugs for his mom downtown. Despite the fact that she was just convicted yesterday and given a year's probation, she talked her sixteen-year-old son into scoring some junk for her."

Adam flushed with embarrassment as Garrett continued.

"We started doing some talking and it turns out Adam has an idea where Mike Webb's shop might be."

"How would he know that?" Ashlynn asked.

The boy glanced up at her. "My mom and her boyfriend used to steal cars for Mike in order to get money for drugs. She called me to pick her up there once even though I didn't have a license at the time or a car. I had a friend drive me over there. That was only about six months ago."

Garrett nodded. "We drove by the place, and I'm sure I saw a white van parked out back. It could be our van. It's worth checking out, don't you think?"

"Absolutely. We should take a look." She glanced at Adam. "Thank you for helping us."

He shrugged. "Mr. G. told me about your son. My mom has been in and out of jail my whole life so I know what it's like to grow up without a mama. Your boy should be happy to have one that cares about him."

She saw pain on his young face and remembered Garrett telling her yesterday—was it really only yesterday this all began?—that Adam had been at the courthouse to see his mother who was addicted to drugs. She didn't have to wonder what kind of turmoil he'd lived in. She knew it firsthand, and she felt bad for him. He was fortunate that Garrett arrived in his life to help guide him.

"I'm not anxious to take down old friends," Garrett said, "but if Mike's at all connected to Jacob's kidnapping, I won't hesitate. Our son is more important to me than old loyalties."

It warmed her heart to hear his proclamation. She saw him glance at Josh, whose eyebrows were raised in surprise. He obviously hadn't heard the news about Jacob and Garrett's connection.

He grinned at Josh and nodded. "You heard right. Jacob is my son."

"What are you going to do with him?" she asked, motioning toward Adam.

"I'll phone my friend Dave, the one who suggested I be a mentor, and ask him to come get him."

"So, what do we do now?" she asked. "I doubt we can obtain a search warrant based on just a generic white van."

He shook his head. "It'll be dark soon. I say we wait

a few hours then go by his place and do some recon-
naissance work of our own. If we see the van and can
determine it's the one involved in Jacob's abduction,
then we'll call in Vince and the police."

She nodded but she couldn't hide the expression of
worry on her face. Could she stand one more lead not
panning out? What if nothing came of it? Then they'd
have wasted precious time in finding Jacob.

Another thought occurred to her. "Won't there be
security?"

"I'll bring my tools, just in case, but Mike never
trusted security systems. He knows too many hackers
to believe in secure. He had some guard dogs six years
ago, but mostly he just relied on his own reputation to
deter thieves. No one wanted to cross him. I'm hoping
that's still the way he operates."

"Yet we're going to cross him."

"Not unless he's involved in this someway. Don't
worry, we'll be careful." Garrett squeezed her shoulder reassuringly. "We will find him, Ash. We'll bring
him home."

He pulled her into his embrace and she went willingly, finding comfort in his strong arms and solid
chest. He made her feel safe and reassured, and she
longed to lose herself here and not have to face the cold
realities of life.

She closed her eyes, breathed in the musky scent
of Garrett's aftershave and found herself lifting a silent prayer that God would be on their side. She didn't
know if it would help, but at this point, she was willing to try anything.

* * *

The street was nearly deserted when Garrett parked his car across from Mike's shop. It was a simple large warehouse with a fence surrounding the perimeter. Inside the fence were car parts and pieces of vehicles. It looked like a mini junkyard. Garrett was trained to infiltrate compounds and he'd used his ranger training many times to rescue hostages. Breaking in wouldn't be a problem. The real problem would be convincing Ashlynn to stay in the car. One glance at her and he knew that wasn't going to happen. He hadn't been able to convince her to stay back at Josh's house and he instinctively knew she wasn't going to stay in the car, either. All he could do was make the best of it and watch her back. Still, he couldn't resist one more try.

"Are you sure you want to do this?" he asked her. "I can see the headline now. ADA Arrested for Breaking and Entering."

She flashed him a determined look and that chin jutted out again. "I'm going."

"Fine. But I'm going to walk the perimeter alone first. I'll see if I can locate the van. It was parked out back earlier. Let's just hope it's not inside the shop being stripped of its parts. I'll also look for vulnerable points in the fence." He opened the door but she grabbed his arm, stopping him, her face full of doubt and mistrust.

"Don't you go in without me, Garrett."

"I'll be right back," he assured her.

He got out and hurried across the street while she scrunched down in her seat so as not to be seen. He suspected she wouldn't stay down long before she peeked out to see what was happening.

Walking along the east and west sides, he found two decent entry points. He was about to head back to the car when he noticed something in the lot. He reached for his compact binoculars and zoomed in, spotting the white van parked behind the shop near the back door. Its parts were still intact. He doubted that would be the case in a few hours.

He reached into another pocket for his pliers and knelt down, quickly cutting into the fence and feeling only slightly guilty at not keeping his word to Ashlynn. He tried to tell himself that she wasn't trained for this, and it was true, but mostly he wanted to keep her out of danger. If anyone walked out of that shop and spotted him, it would be game over. He knew from firsthand experience that Mike Webb was a dangerous man. He didn't want Ashlynn anywhere near him.

Garrett slipped through the fence and moved silently to the back of the building. Noises from inside indicated they were working, probably chopping cars. He imagined Ashlynn angrily fussing at him in the car for continuing on without her, but then he doubted she could see him from her vantage point.

Moving toward the back of the van, he opened the door softly. He didn't know exactly what he was looking for to indicate this was the same van from the security feed, but he didn't have to wonder long. His gut clenched when on the back floorboard he spotted a small stuffed bunny. Business vans didn't have children's stuffed toys in the back of them.

He grabbed the bunny, his heart breaking at the thought that not only had Jacob likely been inside this van, he'd been taken out without his stuffed animal for security. Had he cried for his lost friend and was he crying now for his mother? Garrett's blood boiled at the thought that whoever had him had been so careless with Jacob's needs. He was determined they would pay.

God, please comfort Jacob and keep him safe until we bring him home.

He tucked the bunny into his jacket and softly closed the door. All he had to do now was make it back to the fence and to the car; then they could alert Vince that they'd located the van and let the police swoop in and recover it.

But he froze when he spotted Ashlynn slipping through the hole he'd cut into the fence. His heart dropped and fear rushed through him. What did she think she was doing?

He motioned for her to get back, but she obviously couldn't see him.

His heart raced at the notion that any one of those men inside could step out and spot her and then she would be in danger. He pulled his gun and headed her way, praying he could get her out of here in time.

She'd obviously spotted him crouched against the side of the building and changed her direction, moving toward him despite his signaling for her to get back. But Ashlynn froze mid-step when the door to the shop opened and someone stepped outside.

"Who are you?" a male voice asked.

Garrett didn't recognize the voice. He had to stop this guy before he called out for his friends.

Garrett leaped up, grabbed the guy's shoulder and rammed the gun into his back. "Don't say a word," he commanded in a hard, hushed voice. Ashlynn re-laxed as the man lifted his hands and followed Gar-rett's prompting.

She hurried past the door and joined Garrett. "What are you going to do with him?" she asked, her voice also low.

"The only thing I can." He reached into his pocket and slipped her the keys. "Go back to the car and start the engine and be ready to get out of here. I'll be right behind you."

She nodded and turned, quietly heading back. He watched her climb through the fence.

The man shook his head and chuckled. "Fella, you don't know who you're messing with. Do you have any idea whose place this is you're robbing?"

"I'm not robbing anyone. I was just checking some-thing out."

"This isn't a library. These cars belong to Mike Webb. Heard of him? He'll kill you and your girl for breaking in here."

"I think Mike is about to have his hands full with something else," Garrett said, pressing the man hard against the outside wall. "Like kidnapping a little kid."

"What? Mike ain't into kidnapping kids. He's no pervert."

Garrett pulled the bunny from his jacket. "Oh, yeah? Then why did I find this inside the white van parked behind the shop? Who does this belong to?"

The man looked at the stuffed figure then swore

under his breath. "We just got that van in today. We didn't have nothing to do with a kidnapping."

"Who brought the van in?"

"A guy named Meeks. Randy Meeks. He's not a regular, but Mike buys cars off him from time to time. Look fella, I don't want any part of a kidnapping."

Garrett stuffed the bunny back into his coat. He spotted Ashlynn back at the car and knew he couldn't wait much longer. Soon this guy's friends would come looking for him. "I appreciate your help," he said before slamming his gun into the back of his head. The guy uttered an *oof* then slipped down the side of the building. He would have a headache when he awoke, and he would certainly spill what he knew about Garrett and Ashlynn's visit to Mike. They needed to get back to the precinct so Vince could arrange for the task force to raid this shop before these guys cleaned it out.

He hurried back to the car and slipped into the driver's seat. Ashlynn had the engine running and he quickly took off. Ideally, he would stick around and watch the place, making sure they didn't start hauling things away, but he couldn't risk that, not with Ashlynn beside him.

He dialed Vince as he drove and updated him on what they'd found. Vince assured him he would have a team ready to raid the warehouse within the hour. When he was certain they weren't being followed, Garrett pulled over the car and got out, slamming the door hard. "What were you thinking?" he demanded, turning to Ashlynn, who got out from the other side and walked around the car. "Why did you follow me? You could have been killed."

She shrank back at his angry tone then jutted out her

chin in defiance. "You promised you'd be right back but you went in by yourself anyway. What were you doing?"

"I did what I had to do."

"I knew I shouldn't have trusted you."

He hated the way she hissed out those words, but he didn't back down. What she'd done hadn't been smart. "I didn't want you to get hurt, Ash."

"You don't get to decide that for me, Garrett. I'm a grown woman and a prosecutor. I can make my own decisions." She huffed away and folded her arms angrily over her chest, but after a moment turned back to him. "What did you find?"

He sighed. He wanted to be angry with her because she had been reckless but also because it put off having to show her. He pulled the bunny from his jacket. When she saw it, her eyes widened and her chin quivered. He hated that look. It cut him to his core and he vowed he wouldn't rest until he could wipe it away.

"Wh-where did you get that? That's Jacob's bunny."

"It was inside the van."

She took it from his outstretched hand and hugged it to her chest. When she looked at him, her eyes were knowing and determined.

"He was inside that van."

Garrett nodded, then pulled her into his arms as tears slipped down her face. His own emotions were threatening to burst through him. "We'll find him," he told her, doing his best to reassure them both.

They turned around and drove back to watch the warehouse to make certain the men inside didn't move the van before Vince and his team showed up. She shouldn't have been so hard on him. Ashlynn knew that, but she was still angry that he'd left her behind. He'd promised to come right back, but he'd broken that promise and gone into the compound alone. Yes, she knew it had been reckless to follow him, but she'd just been so mad. But when she remembered the man's surprised expression when he'd stepped outside and the fear that had gushed through her, she knew she'd truly messed up. If Garrett hadn't been there, this man could have hurt her and she would never find out what had happened to Jacob. She was thankful for Garrett's intervention, but it still burned her that he'd broken his word to her...again.

The police finally arrived and stormed inside. The group had obviously been alerted by the man who'd discovered her that they were in trouble, because they looked as if they were preparing to clear out. They were boxing up car parts for shipping and stripping the remaining cars inside. Several of the men tried to run but were quickly caught and returned.

Once the shop was secured, Ashlynn walked with Vince and Garrett to the van outside. Vince pulled open the door and peered inside before shutting it and turning back to them. "I've got a team waiting to tow this van back to the station for processing." His eyes blazed with excitement. His team had just taken a chunk out of the car theft ring plaguing the city and he was one step closer to finding a kidnapped child. It was a good night for him in a professional sense.

As the police secured the scene, Ashlynn noticed Garrett looking around. He appeared agitated and angry. Finally she walked to him and placed her hand on his arm.

"You okay?"

He nodded but sighed wearily. "I was just thinking about that guy who walked out of the shop. That was me once upon a time. I look around at all of this and I realize how amazing it is that I made it. I found a way out of here, but most of those kids I grew up in foster care with never did. What kind of future does Adam have with a drug-addicted mother who has him already buying her drugs for him?"

"He has you," she said admiringly. "He could use a good role model."

He looked at her, his green eyes blazing through her. "You have to know this wasn't the future I planned, Ashlynn. I would never have abandoned you and Jacob. I made a vow to myself that I wouldn't be that kind of dad. I never wanted my son to live without his father."

She nodded. "I understand that, but it happened and I can't forget that. Judge Warren used to tell me that you can tell a person by his actions, not by his words. That's how I try to live my life now. I've opened up my heart too many times and had it broken. I won't take that risk again, especially not with Jacob's heart."

He pushed back a strand of hair from her face and pressed it behind her ear. "I've thought about you every day since that night I left you. You never left my thoughts no matter how hard I tried to push you out of them." He shrugged. "I was dumb and I made a mistake that I can't undo. But I want you to know how sorry I am, Ash. I let you down and I hate that I'm one of those people you place in that category."

She struggled to hold back the tears as they walked

to his truck and got inside. She hated it, too, and wished more than anything she could learn to trust him again.

While the van was being processed, Garrett and Ashlynn returned to the police station so Garrett could use the police database to look up the name the guy they'd encountered had given him—Randy Meeks.

It didn't take him long to find a file under that name. "Looks like Meeks is no stranger to the criminal justice system. He's been arrested for business burglary, assault and robbery."

"And soon to be added—kidnapping," Ashlynn said as she looked over Garrett's shoulder at the extensive list. His mug shot revealed a small-statured man with beady, dark eyes.

"Do you recognize him?" Garrett asked.

She shook her head. She'd never seen him before.

"Well, he can't be the man who attacked you. He's only five foot six. But he could be working with him."

"I've been through my files. I've never prosecuted this man."

Garrett scrolled through the file onscreen to the last known address then frowned. "The only address on file for him is listed as invalid." He slammed his hand on the desk in frustration. "This guy is the key. I know he is."

"I'll phone Ken," Ashlynn said. "He has a knack for locating people who don't want to be found."

When he answered, she passed along the information they had and asked him to do what he could.

"Where did you say you got this guy's name?"

"A chop shop in the west part of town where we

found the van that might have been used in Jacob's kidnapping. One of the men working there told Garrett a guy named Randy Meeks had brought it in. We have to track him down. He could be the key to finding Jacob."

"Ashlynn, he could have been lying about the guy who brought in the van."

"Maybe, but he gave us a name and that name belongs to a real person. Just do what you can, Ken."

"All right. Let me do some research on this guy," Ken said. "I'll get back to you when I know something."

She clicked off the call and looked at Garrett. "He doesn't seem very hopeful about finding him."

"He will," Garrett assured her. "And if he doesn't then we'll find another lead to the kidnappers. We're not giving up, Ashlynn. We will find Jacob and bring him home."

She was grateful once again for his strength and assuredness. It was the only thing getting her through this nightmare. And no matter how she tried to fight it, she found herself believing in him, trusting him. She was still a long way away from allowing him to become a permanent part of their lives, but it was nice start.

Early the next morning, Garrett received a call from Vince with the preliminary lab results on the brownies. He listened, then hung up and turned to her.

Ashlynn held her breath, waiting to hear. These results could mean she'd been betrayed by her own mentor and someone she considered a dear friend.

Garrett looked at her. "Preliminary results found no drugs in the brownies."

She breathed a sigh of relief and only then realized how nervous she'd been, believing the judge could have been involved. Then she remembered Ken's words about how hurt Judge Warren had been at the accusation.

"I should go apologize to him," she said. "I shouldn't have doubted him."

Garrett nodded. "We'll go, but this doesn't completely exonerate him, Ashlynn. These are only preliminary results. We still need to be careful who we trust."

Garrett drove, and as they approached the house of Judge Warren, Ashlynn tensed. This man was her mentor and her long-time friend. But the closer she came to facing him, the more she remembered Garrett's warning that the killer had to be someone close to her. She was glad Garrett was beside her as they walked up the front steps and rang the bell, even though she knew he had different reasons for wanting to come. As he had with Stephen, he wanted to look the man in the eye to ascertain for himself whether or not he was involved.

Judge Warren opened the door. His usual cheerful smile vanished when he saw her and she hated to see that change.

"Ashlynn, I see you brought your bodyguard with you," he said, glancing behind her to Garrett. "What can I do for you?" She cringed at his icy tone.

"I was hoping we could talk," she said.

He opened the door wider and motioned them inside, then led them into a den and offered them both a seat. "I would offer you something to eat or drink, but…" He trailed off, his point made.

Ashlynn felt her face warm at his hurt tone. She'd

known him too long to believe him capable of any kind of deceit, much less kidnapping and murder. However, her son's life was at stake and she couldn't rely on her feelings to guide her even in this matter.

"A wise man once told me that a good prosecutor couldn't allow emotion to guide her thinking. It was good advice. And even though my regard for you tells me absolutely that you weren't involved in this, I still had to consider the possibility." She hoped he could see the pleading look in her eye and hear the apologetic tone of her voice. She didn't want to accuse him.

He sighed knowingly and nodded. "You're right. I'm just a silly old man wearing my feelings on my sleeve. Of course, I had nothing to do with drugging you, Ashlynn. I brought those brownies to your office for the same reason I've brought them many times before, just to be friendly." He glanced toward the kitchen where she assumed his wife was. "Also, because ever since my wife retired from teaching, she bakes all day long and if I ate everything she made, I'd be as big as the side of a house. That's why I started sharing her goodies with friends."

Ashlynn nodded, relieved by the honesty she saw in him. "My assistant ate one of your brownies, too, and nothing happened to her so we had pretty much discounted the fact that the drugs were in the brownies. This morning we learned lab results appear to corroborate that."

"But you still had to investigate the possibility. I confess, I wasn't thrilled to be interrogated by the police. I'm too used to being on the other side of the table."

He reached out and took her hands in his. "But I do understand."

Mrs. Warren appeared at the doorway wiping her hands on her apron. "Charles, I wasn't aware we had company. You should have come and told me. Hello, Ashlynn."

"Hello, Mrs. Warren. How are you?"

"I'm doing well." She approached Garrett and held out her hand. "Alicia Warren."

He shook her outstretched hand. "Garrett Lewis."

"Ashlynn is here asking about an incident that happened at her office and Mr. Lewis accompanied her."

Mrs. Warren gave a sympathetic look. "Yes, I heard about your son, Ashlynn. I'm so sorry. Have there been any leads?"

"We're following up on several," Garrett commented, "but nothing concrete yet."

"That's terrible. Can I get either of you something to drink or eat?"

Ashlynn saw Judge Warren's eyes widen. He obviously hadn't told his wife about the police's accusations about her brownies. Ashlynn figured he'd wanted to spare her feelings. But there was no way she would ever eat another brownie again.

"Thank you for the offer," Garrett said, "but we've got to be going."

She was grateful for his tactful response.

They said their goodbyes and Judge Warren walked them to the front door.

"I do hope the police find your son, Ashlynn."

She smiled at his sincerity and thanked him.

As they walked to the car, Garrett glanced her way. "What did you think?"

"I hate hurting him. He was always so good to me. He was my mentor, Garrett. I find it difficult to believe he had a hand in this."

Garrett shrugged. "Vince's interview with him didn't raise any flags and given the lab results, I think it's safe to say he wasn't involved."

"I hope you're right. I would hate to think someone so close to me would do something so terrible."

But if Judge Warren wasn't responsible for Jacob's kidnapping, then who had her son?

By that afternoon, Ken managed to track down an address for Randy Meeks and Ashlynn was thankful he was on their side. Even Garrett confessed that he was impressed with Ken's abilities. He drove to the address Ken had given them. It was a run-down apartment building on the west side of town. Ashlynn was glad Garrett was by her side. They took the steps to the second floor and Garrett pulled his gun. He pounded on the door and called for Meeks to open up.

When no one answered, he kicked in the door and burst inside. This was no time for niceties, not while a child was missing. The place was a mess, with clothes and food and garbage littering the floor. Ashlynn glanced around, part of her hoping Jacob wasn't being kept in such dirty conditions but also hoping he was here and she could take him home.

Garrett checked the rooms then holstered his gun. "No one is here."

Ashlynn pulled out her cell phone. "I'll have Ken run his financials to see if there's been any hits on credit cards. I also want to get a warrant for his cell phone records."

Garrett nodded his agreement. "I saw a group of kids in the parking lot. I think I'll go talk to them and see what they know about their neighbor Meeks. Maybe they have an idea where he might be."

She nodded and watched him walk out. As she waited for Ken to answer or his voicemail to pick up, she scanned the apartment, disgusted by the way in which Meeks lived. It took her back to her childhood days when she'd still lived with her father. His drinking binges had often left their home looking like this, although even then Ashlynn had done her best to try to tidy up. But she'd quickly learned to steer clear of him when he was drinking or face the brunt of his alcohol-fueled abuse. Cleanliness had taken a backseat to safety.

Ken's voicemail finally picked up and she left him a brief message explaining what she needed. She put away her phone and picked up a framed photograph from its spot on an end table. There was something familiar about the faces in the group photo.

Suddenly, the door slammed behind her. She turned and gasped as a man she recognized from his photo as Meeks lurched at her, clamping a sweaty hand over her mouth and a knife's blade to her throat.

Chapter Seven

The photo fell from her hand as Meeks pressed the knife deeper into her neck.

"Stop struggling," he commanded, pulling his arm tighter around her. His breath on her face was hot and menacing as he spoke. "You're looking for your little boy?" he hissed. "Well he's gone."

Panic gripped her. No, he couldn't be gone. This man was only trying to frighten and upset her. Couldn't he see the pleading in her eyes? Could he see how much she needed her baby back in her arms? He had to have some notion of a conscience, didn't he?

Garrett opened the door. Surprise when he saw them quickly turned to steely determination. He drew his gun as Meeks spotted him and pulled her closer, using Ashlynn as a shield.

"Drop it or I snap her neck," he hollered.

Ashlynn saw the result of all Garrett's years of training. He didn't flinch. He braced his arm, aiming his gun and moving inside the apartment. His jaw was set and his hands steady. "Let her go."

"I said drop it," Meeks demanded again, his snarl high pitched and uncertain compared to Garrett's calm, cool response.

"That's not going to happen."

Meeks tightened his grip, causing Ashlynn to cry out in pain as the knife dug into her neck.

"Okay, okay," Garrett said. He carefully placed his gun on the floor, his eyes never leaving Meeks. "There. I'm unarmed. Now, let her go."

"Why are you in my house?"

"We're looking for a child that was kidnapped yesterday afternoon. He was in the van you returned to Mike Webb's place."

"I didn't take no kid," Meeks insisted. "I just returned the van for a friend."

"That's a lie," Ashlynn cried. "You just told me he was gone."

"Shut up!" Meeks hollered, digging the knife in again and causing Ashlynn to cry out in pain.

But Garrett didn't react to her cry. He stood calmly, nodding, his hand on his hip. "I believe you. What's the name of the friend?"

"I'm not a snitch like those guys Webb has working for him. I don't inform on my friends."

"I admire your loyalty. But you see we have a problem because that's my friend you're threatening with a knife, and I'm also extremely loyal to my friends. We need to work something out here before anyone gets hurt."

He took another step into the room, but his voice never wavered. Ashlynn noticed the hand on his hip slowly moving toward his belt, then she spotted a flash of metal as Garrett slung something at Meeks.

He groaned and released her, grabbing his thigh and screaming out in pain. Ashlynn slipped through his grasp and out of the way as Garrett retrieved his gun from the floor and had Meeks in custody in what seemed like one fast movement.

Her heart was pounding and a lump of gratitude rose in her throat. Garrett hadn't allowed her to be hurt. He'd protected her, just as she'd instinctively known he would. A wave of thankfulness and grief overwhelmed her and she buried her face in her hands, unable to hold back the rush of emotion that enveloped her.

Garrett placed a hand on her shoulder and his voice was full of worry as he knelt beside her. "Are you okay?" She thought she heard a slight quiver in his voice but she dismissed it. Surely she'd imagined it. Based on what she'd just witnessed, nothing could frighten this man.

"I'm fine," she assured him, then took a deep breath and allowed him to pull her to her feet. She looked and saw Meeks tied up with what appeared to be the cords from the window blinds.

Garrett's hand was heavy on her shoulder. "Are you sure you're all right? He didn't hurt you?"

She heard that quiver again and looked up into his face. His brows were furrowed and worry pierced his eyes.

"Really I'm fine," she said again, this time resting her

head on his shoulder. His arms tightened around her and she felt the rapid beat of his heart just beginning to slow. It was unbelievable to her that his heart could have been racing when he'd appeared so calm.

The thought hit her that, had Garrett not come back into the apartment, Meeks might have killed her and she would never see her son again. The realization that he'd played a part in kidnapping her son came blazing back to her, pushing away any residual fear she'd experienced from Meeks's attack.

She pulled from Garrett's arms and lunged at Meeks. "Where is my son?"

Garrett's arms tightened around her waist, preventing her from getting too close. The man sneered at her with his eyes but he didn't respond to her demand for answers.

Garrett pulled her aside and knelt in front of Meeks. "We're looking for the little boy you helped kidnap yesterday. Tell me where he is and it'll go easier on you."

"I don't know anything about kidnapping a boy."

"The van you sold to Mike Webb yesterday was used in an abduction and murder. Now, we know you're involved, and I'm certain you know the charges for kidnapping and murder can be steep. Help us out and help yourself out by telling us what you did with the boy."

He looked at Garrett then at Ashlynn and sneered again. "She doesn't deserve to be a mother."

His words dug into her soul deeper than any knife could stab her. The photo she'd received with the note came back to her. The similar words confirmed he'd sent it.

Garrett too seemed surprised by his words. "Why doesn't she deserve to be a mother? What's she done?"

He turned his glare from Ashlynn to Garrett. "I'm not saying another word. If you're arresting me, I want my lawyer. If not, untie me and get out of my house. This is unlawful imprisonment."

Garrett stood and faced her, then blew out a frustrated breath. "I'll call Vince." He touched her arm ever so slightly, almost a caress against her skin. She shivered but told herself it was less from his touch and more about the worry of the situation. Meeks knew where her son was and he wasn't talking. It was now nearing forty-eight hours since Jacob had been abducted. Were they running out of time to find him?

Garrett called for backup and soon had Meeks in a patrol car on his way to booking. Meeks still hadn't uttered a word about where Jacob was, but Garrett could tell he knew. What really shook him was Meeks's statement that Ashlynn didn't deserve to be a mother. His words mirrored the note that had been left on her desk. He had to be the one who sent it. Did he know her personally? Or was he some psycho who'd seen her on TV and decided women with high-powered careers didn't make good mothers?

She'd denied knowing him so that left psycho stalker. That meant Jacob could be anywhere.

When Vince arrived with his team, Garrett updated him on the situation. "We should start by uncovering any known associates of Meeks's. I also want a full detailed financial analysis to look for any anomalies."

"I'll call one of my officers back at the precinct and get them on that," Vince assured him.

He glanced over at Ashlynn on the phone, no doubt with Ken, giving him the same instructions, probably. She slipped her phone into her pocket then curled her arms across her chest. He knew she was trying to keep it together, but her breaking point was near. Meeks was the only lead they had right now and he was a good one. He hoped and prayed if they couldn't get Meeks talking that something would show up on his financials.

Garrett walked over and put his arms around her. She was shaking, fighting to hold herself together. She was trying to remain strong and she was one tough lady. Who else could have been through the past hours with the grace and strength she'd exhibited?

He didn't give any credence to what Meeks said, either. He couldn't imagine she wouldn't be an amazing mother. She'd always had a nurturing way about her. He wondered how many people had seen beneath that tough exterior to the generous and loving woman inside. Had Stephen seen that side of her? Few others would have, he decided. She wasn't one to let people get too close to her because she'd been brokenhearted too many times. With shame, he realized he'd caused her that same pain even though he'd been trying to do just the opposite and protect her.

Even though she was an ADA, she was also a victim, so Vince asked her not to touch anything. It could corrupt the chain of evidence that might be used against Meeks during a trial of kidnapping her child. Garrett was certain Vince would have preferred she wait outside or go back to the precinct, but Garrett was determined not to let her out of his sight again. He'd taken his eyes off her for only a few minutes and look what had nearly happened. He wasn't taking any more risks with her safety.

He took over the job of entering the evidence the team collected into a logbook, examining each item carefully first, while Ashlynn watched.

He picked up a framed photograph that looked old and worn. He turned it over and saw a group of kids together for a shot. It didn't look like a sports team or class photo, and nothing about it captured his attention. He wrote it in the log and turned to place it in a bin.

But Ashlynn grabbed his arm to stop him and stared at it, jogging his memory that it had been at her feet when Meeks was holding the knife to her. Had she been looking at it before the attack against her?

"What is it?" Garrett asked. "Do you recognize this photo?"

She nodded, but she'd turned a shade whiter. "I do." She stroked her hand over the image of the woman with the dark hair and wide smile. "I saw this before but I couldn't place where. Now, I remember. This woman in the back is Kathryn Rollins, my foster mother."

This time Garrett gaped. He took back the photo and stared at it. "Are you sure?"

"I could never forget her face. She tried to present a happy front to the world, but her eyes were cold and hard and so was she. Her hair is shorter in this picture, which is why I guess I didn't immediately recognize her." She pointed to another adult. "That's her husband.

He was a wisp of a man who did whatever she commanded."

Now Garrett understood. Ashlynn had been in an abusive foster home before she'd come to the group facility where they'd first met. She'd been beaten severely by her foster mother and had later testified against her about the atrocities she'd suffered at the woman's hands. He looked down at the photo and the image. This was the woman who had caused Ashlynn so much pain and suffering. "This was your foster mother?"

This didn't make any sense. Why would Meeks steal an old photograph of Ashlynn from when she was a little girl? What would he possibly want with it? "When did you last see this photograph? Had you noticed it missing from your house?"

She shook her head. "No, this isn't my photograph. I had one similar to this but I tore it up and threw it into the fireplace years ago. I couldn't stand looking at the smug smile on her face and the happy image she tried so hard to portray to the world."

He stared at the photo again, trying to process this new information. If this wasn't Ashlynn's picture then it must belong to Meeks. Had one of these freckled-faced boys grown up to be Meeks? And if so, why had he targeted Ashlynn?

Somehow, they had to convince Meeks to talk. He was the key to figuring this all out.

Ashlynn watched through the two-way mirror as Vince questioned Meeks. She'd been in this spot many times in a professional capacity and each time she'd wanted the detectives to find that hot button that would get the suspect talking, but she had never wanted it more than she did now. She needed Meeks to talk. He was the crucial link to finding out where Jacob was being held and who was involved.

But Meeks remained tight-lipped. He claimed he knew nothing about the van in question and nothing about a kidnapping. Ashlynn tried to remain calm but inside she was screaming. The mother in her wanted to claw his eyes out until he told her where Jacob was. The prosecutor in her wanted to toss the book at him and send him away for years. Neither reaction would garner them the information they needed.

Vince exited the interview room, his expression full of disappointment. "He's not talking," Vince said.

She'd seen that for herself through the two-way mirror, but to hear Vince sound so defeated still bothered her. He didn't believe they would get Meeks to tell what he knew, meaning this lead was quickly drying up.

"He's definitely not the right build to be the man who was in your house," Garrett noted.

She shook her head. "Nor the man who attacked me in the break room. He's too skinny. Yet it seems too coincidental that we were in the same foster home." She still couldn't believe this all could have some connection to Kathryn Rollins. As far as she knew, the woman had died in prison so she surely couldn't be acting out a revenge scenario. Ashlynn took the file from Vince. "Let me speak to him."

"That's not a good idea," Vince cautioned.

"It's better than doing nothing." She opened the door

and walked into the interview room before he could protest.

Meeks stared at her then shifted nervously in his seat. "I don't have anything to say to you," he told her, his voice full of bitterness and bite.

She pulled the photograph from the files and slid it across the table toward him. "We found this in your apartment. Apparently, you and I were in the same foster home together. Which one is you?"

He stared at the photo then cautiously, as if he wasn't sure about acknowledging it, pointed to a redheaded boy on the end.

She glanced at the picture. "I remember you, Randy. You liked to pick flowers from the yard and give them to Kathryn. She liked them, didn't she?"

He nodded. "She always put them in a glass of water on the windowsill."

Ashlynn nodded. "The house smelled like honeysuckle because of it. That was nice. She was good to you. She wasn't so kind to me."

He lowered his head, obviously aware that her statement was fact.

"How long were you with the Rollinses?"

"Four years. Until she went to jail because of you."

She jumped to defend herself. "She went to jail because of her own actions." Ashlynn bristled and knew she'd misspoken. He'd obviously been happy there and he blamed her for breaking up his family. She had to try another tactic. She pulled the photo of Jacob from the file. "This is my son. He's only four years old. He has nothing to do with any of what happened all those years ago. Please, Randy. Please, if you know anything about him, I just want to bring him home."

He stared at the picture then shook his head. "I don't know anything about your kid and I wasn't involved with any kidnapping. That's all I have to say without my lawyer."

Her heart fell. He'd just shut her down and she knew from experience he was unlikely to offer any information once his lawyer arrived.

She gathered the photos and walked out, aware that she was likely wearing the same expression of disappointment she'd seen on Vince earlier.

Vince sighed then nodded to her. "Don't worry. I'm sure we'll find something inside that van that will get him talking. I'll go put a rush on the lab."

As he walked off, Garrett took her hand. Ashlynn felt a shiver when his fingers closed over hers. His hand was large and strong and she felt so small and comforted by his touch.

"Try not to worry," he said softly. "We found Meeks and we'll find others that will lead us to Jacob."

"I just want him home," she said. She swiped at a tear that slipped from her eye but another followed it and then another so she gave up and let them fall. What did it matter if Garrett saw her crying?

He reached up and wiped away a tear, his finger stroking her cheek tenderly. Once again, she was glad he was here. She needed him by her side. This was one time she didn't have to do it all herself. She had another person she could depend on who understood her need to find Jacob.

She hoped, even dared to pray, she could trust him to stick around this time.

* * *

After the disappointment of being unable to get Meeks to talk, Ashlynn needed to get away from the police station for a while. She asked Garrett to drive her and he agreed. But she hadn't realized how entering her own neighborhood would affect her. They passed her street and Ashlynn felt a pang of sorrow. So much had happened here. Mira had been murdered, Jacob had been stolen from her and she'd been shot at.

Garrett pulled into Olivia's driveway and they got out. Olivia threw her arms around Ashlynn the moment she opened the door, and Ashlynn knew she'd made the right decision in coming here. She needed the encouragement her friend offered. She greeted Garrett, then pulled Ashlynn into the house. She poured them both a cup of coffee, then placed one in front of Ashlynn. "How are you holding up?"

"I can't believe this is really happening. And now this all may have a connection to my past. I feel like my entire life is falling apart." Tears filled her eyes, but she didn't push them back. This was one place she felt comfortable showing her emotions. "I just want him back. I want to hold him and rock him and tell him I love him. I'm so frightened I may never get that chance again."

Olivia glanced at Garrett, who was outside on the patio, standing guard while also giving them some privacy. "I can't believe I finally got to meet the ranger. He's just as hunky as you described. No wonder Stephen didn't measure up."

Ashlynn gasped. "What? That's not true. I did love Stephen. He was a wonderful husband. He's the one who left. The divorce was his idea, not mine."

"Yes, he was a wonderful husband and a good father. You should have appreciated him more."

Ashlynn frowned. Why was Olivia attacking her?

Olivia set down her coffee cup then sighed. "I'm sorry. I shouldn't have said that. You're already going through so much. You don't need me piling on."

"Do you really believe that about me?"

"Ashlynn, I love you, but nothing is ever good enough for you. You had a great husband, a sweet little boy, a nice home. I don't understand why that was never enough for you." Her voice faltered and Ashlynn realized Olivia was going through something herself. Her friend had lost her husband and her son in a car wreck three years prior, and Ashlynn was certain Jacob's abduction was only bringing up painful memories for her. She'd bonded with Jacob, often offering to babysit or take him for an afternoon at the park.

Ashlynn couldn't help the way her eyes kept being drawn to the photos on the mantel. Olivia's son had been four when he'd died, the same age as Jacob was now, and Ashlynn noticed the two boys shared similar coloring and stature.

Was it possible…?

She pushed that thought away immediately. Olivia was her friend. She would never betray Ashlynn in such a manner. But Ken's words kept floating to her mind. He'd been talking about Bridgette, not Olivia, but she felt they were still applicable. Jealousy was a powerful emotion that often led rational people to do the unthinkable.

Could grief have turned to obsession for her friend?

Ashlynn set her coffee mug on the table. "May I use your bathroom?"

Olivia smiled. "Of course. Go right ahead. I believe I'll go see if your ranger friend would like a cup of coffee."

Ashlynn walked down the hall but glanced back, making sure Olivia was out of sight before she rushed through the house checking each room, throwing open closet doors and even looking behind the shower curtain. She found no sign of Jacob and for that she was relieved, but that didn't mean her friend wasn't involved.

She saw herself in the bathroom mirror and realized she was the one who'd become obsessed. Look what her anxiety had led her to. She was accusing her friend and searching her house. She buried her face in her hands and let the tears come. She wanted this to be over and she wanted Jacob home.

Olivia had been right when she'd said those things. Ashlynn should have been more appreciative of what she'd had. It was a revelation, a wake-up call. She'd been so focused on what she didn't have and how life kept pushing her down that she hadn't stopped to appreciate all she did have. Stephen had tried to tell her as much and she hadn't wanted to listen, but now, too late, she realized the truth.

God had been trying to bless her all along but she hadn't been paying attention.

As they left Olivia's, Garrett watched Ashlynn gently touch the raw mark around her neck from Meeks's attack. Anger still burned in him over that and he knew

Meeks should be thankful Garrett wasn't the kind of man to exact revenge. His heart hammered just remembering the look of terror on Ashlynn's face when he'd entered and seen the knife to her throat.

As it was, Meeks wasn't talking. And a text from Vince delivered more bad news. They hadn't uncovered any evidence in Meeks's apartment that could link him to Jacob's abduction. As of now, only the van and the unknown witness Garrett had spoken to pointed to his involvement. And they hadn't been able to track down the guy Garrett had cornered outside the shop. Garrett suspected he had headed home the moment they'd left and was long gone once the police arrived.

He and Ashlynn had reluctantly returned to the cabin, each hyperaware that forty-eight hours had passed and they were no closer to bringing Jacob home.

He walked over and tossed another log onto the fire in the fireplace as Ashlynn remained curled up on the couch.

"How do you do it?" Ashlynn asked him as he poked the fire.

He glanced up at her. "Do what?"

"How do you have such faith? I confess I've never been much of a religious person, but I envy those that have faith. Everything seems to work out for them."

He looked back at the fire. "God never promised we wouldn't have trouble. He only promised to be with us through it. Even the most faithful have times of trouble." He was thinking of Marcus, who had been one of the most faithful men of God he'd known. It hadn't prevented something bad from happening to him.

Her tone hardened. "Well, He hasn't ever been here for me."

He turned back to look at her and was devastated by the sadness on her face. "He's always been there, Ashlynn. We don't always see Him or feel Him, but He's there."

She folded her arms tighter against her chest and seemed to sink farther into the couch. "I wish I could believe that, but it feels like He doesn't care about me at all. My life has been one terrible thing happening after another. He could have intervened. He could have kept Kathryn Rollins from beating me nearly to death. He could have prevented my mother's death. He didn't do any of that and I would be okay with it if He had only intervened when Jacob was taken." Tears slipped from her eyes. "He's just a little boy. He doesn't deserve to be punished for my faults."

Garrett moved to sit beside her on the couch. "What are you talking about? What faults?"

"I don't know, but it must be something about me or something I've done to make God hate me."

He was horrified that she could actually believe that, but he could see she did.

"God does not hate you, Ashlynn."

"Then why does He keep punishing me?" she asked, her voice choked with emotion.

He quickly pulled her into his arms and hugged her tightly. She didn't protest, and after a moment she leaned into the crook of his shoulder. He held her while she wept for her son and for all she'd been through.

When her tears were spent, he watched the fire and

listened to the steady sound of her breathing as she slipped into sleep. He wished he could do more, say more, to help ease her pain, but he had no answer to why God hadn't intervened. Evil existed in this world. Garrett knew that firsthand. He'd witnessed the evil of men during his time with the rangers. God had not intervened to stop the ambush that had taken the lives of his friends. He'd struggled with that, too, and had never come up with an answer.

But what he did know, what he'd come to count on, was that God had been right there with him during that terrible time and every day since. They surely needed some of that divine intervention right now to find out who was behind the attacks on Ashlynn and where they'd taken Jacob. Once again, his mind drifted to the idea that he was a father and he could imagine a life with Jacob and Ashlynn, as part of a family, but a nagging doubt reminded him that he wasn't cut out to be a father.

He tensed when he heard movement outside.

He slid carefully away from Ashlynn, letting her remain asleep against the arm of the couch as he got up and walked to the back door. He reached for his gun and stepped outside, his ears alert and listening for the rustle. Logic told him it was only a raccoon or a possum, and it probably was, but he needed to be certain.

He heard movement again from the side of the house and raised his gun. He shone the flashlight into the area and walked in that direction. More rustling sent his senses reeling. Someone was out there in the woods.

Just then, someone jumped from the shadows and

tackled him, forcing Garrett to the ground. The man slammed his fist into Garrett's face sending blinding pain soaring through him. But his only thought was of Ashlynn asleep inside. He had to get to her.

He blocked the man's next punch and shoved him hard away, crawling over and smashing his own fists into the intruder's face, then grabbing his gun and hitting him again. The man groaned and immediately collapsed. Garrett knew he'd lost consciousness.

The lack of direct light meant he couldn't get a good look at the man's face, but he could see enough to know he didn't recognize him. He was, however, the right build to be the man who had attacked them at Ashlynn's house, and the automatic rifle he carried further cemented that reasoning. He pulled out his phone and was about to call Vince for backup when another rustle of movement grabbed his attention.

The guy on the ground wasn't alone.

There was someone else in the woods.

Garrett grabbed the automatic rifle, hopped up and hurried back into the house. The cabin was compromised and they had to get out now.

Chapter Eight

He pulled Ashlynn awake. "They found us," he said, and although her eyes were blurry when she first roused, they immediately cleared. She quickly slipped on her shoes.

Her eyes widened when she saw the rifle he carried. "Where did you get that?"

"I knocked one of them out, but there's at least one other person out there. Possibly more."

He grabbed her hand to leave just as something crashed through the front window, hit the floor and rolled across the floor. Garrett immediately recognized it as a flash bomb. He'd seen his share of them in combat and had used them often in his search-and-rescue missions.

"Get down," he hollered, pulling her behind the couch with him and covering her with his body as the bomb exploded, basking the room in white light and emitting an awful squeal and smoke. The blast sent his senses reeling, as it was meant to do, but he had enough of his wits to pull off his overshirt, rip it in half and hand one piece to Ashlynn. "Cover your mouth and nose." He pressed the fabric to his face and reached for the rifle. They had to get out of here, and fast, before they both passed out from smoke inhalation or the assailant busted into the house and shot them.

The flash bomb had come through the front window, which wasn't good. The car was parked out front and they needed to get to it if they hoped to escape. They would be sitting ducks if they tried to make it out on foot.

He slid the keys into her hand. "I'm going to cover you. I need you to get to the car and start it."

She nodded and started to move toward the door, doing her best to stay low. He followed her, and once they reached it, he dropped the mask and threw open the door.

"Run!" he shouted at her, firing indiscriminately into the woods as Ashlynn ran for the car. He followed her, keeping a steady stream of gunfire going. She started the car and he slid into the passenger seat.

"Go!" he said, once he was inside.

The moment they pulled away, the gunfire started again, coming from the trees to the north. Garrett leaned out the window and shot back, but bullets hit the car and Ashlynn screamed as one shattered the back window. But she didn't let up on the accelerator.

Good girl, he thought. He emptied what remained of the rifle's ammunition into the woods then tossed it and reached for his pistol.

Garrett looked back and saw a man emerge from the brush. He lifted his gun and fired several shots, one of which obviously hit a tire because Garrett heard a loud pop. Ashlynn screamed as the car spun out of control and slid off the road into a ditch.

Garrett took only a moment to recover from the adrenaline pumping through him before kicking open his door and climbing out. He reached inside, hurrying Ashlynn along before the shooter came after them.

"We have to take cover," he said pulling her into the woods, glad she didn't bother pointing out to him that he'd told her they would never make it out alive on foot. The woods were their only choice for safety now.

He glanced back at the cabin. He couldn't see the man anymore, but he would be following them soon. Garrett wanted nothing more than to wait for him, confront him and demand to know why he was targeting Ashlynn and where Jacob was being kept, but right now he had to keep her alive. That had to be his priority. What he wouldn't give for some ranger backup now. He stopped only long enough to slip out his phone and dial Josh's number.

"The cabin was compromised," he said when Josh answered, and his friend responded without hesitation.

"I'm on my way to get you. There's a dirt road about a mile north of the cabin. Stay on that road as long as you can. I'll find you."

Garrett clicked off and slipped the phone into his pocket. Now they only had to stay alive until Josh could get to them.

They ran for what seemed like an hour before they stumbled upon the road Josh mentioned. Garrett was convinced they'd given their attacker the slip. The darkness had been on their side and for that he was thankful.

He heard a car approach and pushed Ashlynn off the road, down behind a clump of bushes. He clutched his gun, ready to use it if needed. He tensed, his whole body on alert at the thought of going into a firefight with only the half-full clip of his pistol. But he wouldn't let them take her. He would do whatever he had to do to protect her.

God, please help me keep her safe.

The vehicle that approached slowed as it neared them. He saw a rapid flash of the headlights in a steady beat and breathed a sigh of relief. That had been their code in the rangers, so he knew it was Josh behind the wheel. He stepped out and flagged down the vehicle. It pulled up beside them and Garrett hurried Ashlynn into the back while he slid into the front seat.

"You made it," Garrett said, so glad to see his friend.

"Are you both okay?"

He nodded then looked at Ashlynn.

"I'm not hurt," she said, but he noticed her body was rigid and tired after another close call.

Garrett turned back to Josh. "How did they find us? I can't figure that out. I've disabled the tracking on the car and our cell phones. Only a few people knew where we were." A terrible thought stung him. "There's only one answer. Someone close to us is either passing information to the shooter…or he *is* the shooter."

Ashlynn glanced at him and saw where his line of thinking was headed. "Vince."

He nodded. "Vince."

"You don't really believe Vince is crooked, do you? I've known him for years."

"Did you tell anyone where we were?"

She shook her head. "No, I didn't tell anyone."

"So only Vince knew. That kind of narrows down the pool of suspects, doesn't it?"

She shook her head. "I find it difficult to believe that Vince is in on a plot to murder me and take my son."

"It doesn't necessarily have to be him," Josh said. "He has officers under him that might have access to that information."

Garrett sighed. "Look, I haven't known Vince for that long, but we have to face the facts. Someone is tracking us and we can't trust anyone, not even the police. We'll stay in contact with them for any new leads on Jacob's whereabouts. We'll gather their information, but from this point forward everyone is suspect. We trust no one."

He locked eyes on her to drive home his point. "We're on our own."

Josh pulled into his garage and pushed the button to close the door.

"I should have brought you here in the first place," he said. "I just thought the cabin would be safe."

"I thought so, too," Garrett said. "It should have been."

Josh led them inside. "Ashlynn, you can take the guest bedroom upstairs. Garrett, you can bunk down here on the couch."

Ashlynn went upstairs but her mind wouldn't stop running. Garrett suspected someone close to them was behind the attacks on her and she was beginning to believe him. But now she was on edge. She didn't know who to trust. The only person she was certain she could rely upon was Garrett, which was a strange and new sensation.

She still had a difficult time believing Vince was behind the attacks on her, but Garrett was right. They had to be careful. However, she realized there was another person besides Vince who had known they were at the cabin.

She got up and quietly opened the bedroom door and peeked out. The house was dark and quiet, and she was glad. She needed to speak with Garrett without Josh around. She padded downstairs and found him stretched out on the couch. He wasn't asleep and jumped up when he saw her. "Hey, what's up?" he asked, his face taking on a worried expression. "Is everything okay?"

She sat beside him on the couch, uncertain how to voice her suspicion. "I know you said we couldn't trust anyone. What about Josh? Is it possible—?"

"Don't even go there," he said, stopping her before she finished her question. "I trust him. In fact, there's no one I trust more than Josh and the rangers. He's on our side."

"I can appreciate you have a connection with him, but that doesn't mean—"

"Ash, I trust Josh. Period. You have no idea what we've been through together. He would never betray me."

"I'm sure you believe that, but it's just that this is Jacob we're talking about. This is our son, Garrett. We have to think about his safety. How can we truly trust anyone?"

"If I can't trust the rangers, then who can I trust? I can't continue to live my life on the defensive, constantly wondering who is on my side and who is going to let me down. That's an exhausting way to exist."

She clenched her jaw, taking his comment as a direct hit at her. "Sometimes it's a necessity, especially when everyone around you continually lets you down."

He nodded then stood. "Okay, I deserved that."

"No, I'm not only talking about you, Garrett. Stephen, too. My foster mother. My friends. I couldn't even trust my own father to be there for me. Why does everyone I know let me down? Am I that terrible a person?"

He pulled her into his arms as her chin quivered. "No, baby. You're not a terrible person. You're an incredibly amazing, determined, powerful woman."

"Then why does everyone leave me?" Even she could hear the pitiful desperation in her voice but she couldn't stop it. It was a question she'd pondered for years. What was so bad about her that no one wanted her?

He must have seen her desperation because he grabbed her arms, sending a spark of electricity between them. "It's not because of you, Ashlynn. I didn't leave because of you. It was me. I was afraid of letting you down. I knew I could never live up to the memories of the men who died the night our team was ambushed."

She was surprised by the intensity of the pain she saw on his face when he spoke about the ambush. She'd held back pressing him about the events of that night mostly because she hadn't wanted him to use it as an excuse for his actions. But now...well, she wanted to know.

"What happened on that mountain?" she asked him, her voice soft and encouraging. "And why did it have to take you away from me?"

He gulped and pulled back from her. She saw the flash of horror and pain that spread across his face and knew he was reluctant to relive that night. She wondered again if maybe she shouldn't press him, but pushed that concern away. She'd loved him so much. She deserved to know what terrible thing had taken him from her.

His folded his arms across his chest. His stance was stiff and his jaw set. She saw how painful it was for him to relive that night and felt guilty for even asking. She had no right to demand this of him. She jumped up and stood behind him, wrapping her arms around him and resting her head against his shoulder. She could feel him shaking and knew at that moment that she wouldn't press him for details. "Never mind. You don't have to tell me."

He blew out a deep, fortifying breath. "It's time you know the truth and I suppose it's time I talked about it. I've never spoken to anyone about what happened, not even to Josh or the other rangers. There was never any reason. They were there. They knew what occurred."

He stepped away from her, unable or unwilling to look at her as he told the story. She didn't press that. Instead, she gave him the space he needed. She sat on the couch, holding her breath in anticipation of what he was about to share and lifting a silent prayer for his pain. It seemed so great.

"I was the first one in," he said, his voice cracking. He stopped to clear his throat and started again. "I was on point. My friend Marcus was following behind me and the rest of the squad was scattered out, taking different positions. Our target was a high-profile Taliban leader who'd been hiding out in the mountains and we'd finally gotten some good intel on his whereabouts. Command brought in some Delta operators along with some SEALs to lead the mission. Our part was to go in with them. They would go after the target while we cleared the compound.

"I saw Levi approach a tent. Three women emerged, all strapped with explosives. I screamed for him to watch out, but they went off right before my eyes. Levi went flying."

He shook his head in amazement. "I still don't know how he ever survived that explosion. Then shots rang out. They seemed to come from everywhere. Marcus was standing beside me and the next thing I knew he just convulsed and hit the ground. Blood was everywhere. I leaned down to help him and then it was all over me, too. I knew I had to get him out of there but everyone was shooting and shouting and screaming."

His voice cracked again, but he continued. "Smoke was thick as the night and the air stank of gunpowder and fuel. I grabbed Marcus and tried to drag him toward a building, trying to find some pocket of peace so I could check his wounds, but the shots just kept coming. The whole time Marcus was begging me to take care of his family."

She gasped at the horror of what he'd been through. But he wasn't done.

"I knew I had to get him back to where he could get some medical help. And I just panicked. I picked up my weapon and started shooting. When my gun was empty, I picked up his." He leaned his head into his hands. "I killed a lot of people that night, all in the name of war."

She shook her head and instinctively moved to him, placing her hand reassuringly on his back. "No, you were trying to survive and you were trying to help your friend."

"I pulled him up over my shoulder and carried him out. I tried to get him back to the truck." Garrett's shoulders shook. "I knew it was a lost cause. I knew he was gone, but I couldn't leave him. But then I saw Levi. I heard his moan and I saw his leg move. He was alive. I could hardly believe it. At first I thought my eyes were playing tricks on me, but he was moving. He was alive and Marcus was dead. There was no way I could carry them both out of there so I left Marcus and went after Levi. The search-and-rescue teams tried to go in after the firefight and retrieve the bodies of those who'd died…fourteen men in all…but they didn't find his body. They never did recover it. His family had nothing to bury. And when I think about all the terrible things that probably happened to his body, I shudder because I've seen the evil that lives over there and because I left him to suffer it."

"You did the right thing," she told him. "You saved Levi. You said yourself that Marcus was gone. You couldn't have saved him. What about Levi? Did he survive?"

He nodded. "He was hurt badly, probably worse than any of the rest of us that lived. And he doesn't remember a lot of what happened. Sometimes I think he's the fortunate one, not to have a memory of that terrible night."

Her heart broke at Garrett's story. He had indeed been through an ordeal and she understood how such an event could have affected him. She only wished he'd been able to talk to her about it then. Things would have been so different if she'd only known.

"I never knew anything about the ambush," she said. "No one contacted me about it and I didn't hear it on the news."

"They wouldn't have contacted you," he told her. "I hadn't had the opportunity to update my emergency information. And I didn't have a next of kin so the army didn't call anyone on my behalf. As for the news, I'm sure the government buried that story along with all the soldiers that died on that mountain. It was a failed attempt to take down a powerful enemy." The bite in his tone was real and bitter. "They wouldn't want such details broadcast."

But something he'd said touched a nerve with her. The army had had no one to contact on Garrett's behalf. It saddened her that he'd been so alone. And he'd remained alone. She had to remind herself that it was by choice. He'd had a family. He just hadn't known it.

"I stayed with the rangers for a while after that, but then I just couldn't continue. Every time I went into a firefight, I found myself reliving that night and hating myself for leaving Marcus behind. The doctors called it survivor's guilt and it nearly killed me. I was alone for a long while. I spent my time after the rangers doing things—risky things—that more than once should have killed me. I truly don't know how I'm still alive except by the grace of God. Anyway, after a while, I realized that I didn't want to be alone anymore so Josh found me this job and I came back to Jackson. I still don't know why God kept me alive that night, but I'm glad He did, Ashlynn, because now I get to be the one here for you and Jacob."

At the same time she was realizing how sad she felt for Garrett, she also realized she was in a similar situation. She'd spent her life alone, protecting her heart from getting hurt again. But it hadn't worked because she was hurting now and it wasn't because her son had rejected her. It was because opening her heart to Jacob had also meant opening it up to pain.

But she wouldn't have changed it. She couldn't stop loving Jacob any more than she could stop breathing. Having him had made her life so much richer. Nothing, not even losing him now, could take away the joy and happiness he'd brought to her life.

But that was also true for her time with Garrett. She'd held back for years, trying to protect herself from the pain he'd caused when he'd broken their engagement. But she wouldn't give up the memories of their time together, would she? Aside from giving her Jacob, Garrett had shown her what real love looked like and for the first time in her life had given her some reason to keep going after all the terrible things that had happened to her.

She hugged him tightly and he clung to her. She finally understood the circumstances that had separated them. It still hurt, but now her heart broke for him more than just for herself. She only wished he'd been able to turn to her during that awful time, that she'd been able to be there for him as a wife would have been, but she'd never been given that opportunity.

Her heart cried out for all the pain and sadness they'd both endured. *Oh, God, please help mend our shattered lives.*

The next morning, Garrett stood in Josh's kitchen and watched the morning news on TV as they replayed Ashlynn's emotional plea for Jacob's return. His mind ran over the evidence they had, which wasn't much, and knew they had to be missing something. They were still no closer to finding his son and that distressed him. He'd made a promise that he would bring Jacob home and he meant more than ever to keep it.

Speaking to her last night, sharing the details of the ambush, had been like having a weight lifted from his shoulders. Although he didn't like the way he'd lost control of his emotions and hadn't wanted her to see how weak he really was, hearing her assurances that he hadn't done anything wrong had been like a balm soothing his rugged heart and smoothing out some of the rough patches inside of him. He was thankful for that opportunity and knew he'd been right to come back to Jackson. Josh had been correct in his assertion that

Garrett needed to reconnect to life and people. He'd been alone for far too long.

Ashlynn came downstairs and joined him at the kitchen table. She looked beautiful. Her eyes were still blurry from sleep, but he could tell she'd gotten some rest. He used the remote to click off the TV then poured her a cup of coffee and handed it to her as he placed a gentle kiss on her forehead. "How did you sleep?"

She gave him a small but weary smile and sipped her coffee. "As well as I could." She motioned towards the television. "Any update?"

"No. I called Vince earlier, too, and none of the tips that have come in have led anywhere. But if he's involved, he'll want to bury any that might lead back to him."

She nodded but her heart seemed so heavy. She set her phone on the counter. "I've been trying to keep up, too, but the news apps don't have any more information, either."

"Don't you give up, Ashlynn. We're going to find him and bring him home. This isn't over."

She nodded but her agreement didn't reach her eyes. "I know the statistics, Garrett. Children that aren't recovered in the first forty-eight hours are unlikely to be found." Her voice caught as she continued. "It's already been over sixty hours since he was abducted."

He knelt beside her and rubbed her face. "I don't listen to statistics. I'm not giving up on our son…or on you." He leaned forward to place another kiss on her forehead, but she stopped him, placing a gentle one on his lips, instead. His heart hammered at the softness of her mouth and the taste of salt still lingering, most likely from a tear-filled night. He waited for her to make excuses for her action or pull away, but when she didn't, he pulled her to him for a long, deep kiss that was new and familiar all at once.

It ended when her phone rang, interrupting the moment.

She glanced at the screen. "That's Ken. I should answer it."

He nodded and stepped away from her. She picked up the phone and spoke a few words before turning to Garrett. "Hang on, Ken. I'm going to put you on speaker so Garrett can hear this, too." She placed the phone back on the counter and hit the speaker button. "Go ahead."

"I was telling Ashlynn that I did some more digging into Randy Meeks's background. After he was removed from the Rollins home, he bounced around from foster home to foster home before aging out of the program. He's been in and out of trouble with the law for most of his juvenile and adult life."

Garrett nodded. "We already know all of this from his police record."

"Oh, well, did you know Kathryn Rollins, your foster mother, Ashlynn, was being investigated as part of a baby-selling ring? Some have even speculated that someone connected to the ring murdered her to shut her up because she had agreed to speak with the FBI in exchange for a reduced sentence on the abuse charges."

Ashlynn gasped. "Baby selling? I had no idea."

"You wouldn't have. You were just a child then, and

the FBI took notice of her only after she was imprisoned."

Garrett looked at her. "It's possible someone from the ring took Jacob."

She shook her head. "That was so long ago. Why would they wait until now to target me? If they wanted to hurt me, they could have snatched Jacob when he was a baby. Why wait until now?"

Ken had the answer. "The perpetrator could have been in jail all this time and only recently got out. Or he could have inadvertently reconnected with you recently and it re-sparked his anger towards you. Kathryn made them a lot of money and someone could be harboring anger at you for costing them that money."

"It's seems so implausible."

"It's a lead, Ashlynn, and unless you have some other news I'm not aware of, it's the best one we have."

Garrett thought the other man's tone sounded harsh, but Ashlynn didn't seem to react to it. He supposed Ken was just as weary and worried as the rest of them. "You should go through your case files again, this time looking for any name that might spark recognition. Anyone from your past could be suspect."

She nodded. "I don't remember running into anyone from my past recently. I think I would know them."

"You didn't recognize Meeks," Ken reminded her and she blushed at his assertion. She couldn't deny it.

Reluctantly, she agreed to give her case files another look.

Ken continued. "I've contacted the FBI agent in charge of the investigation back then. He's agreed to meet with us and discuss the possibility that Jacob's kidnapping is related to someone involved in the baby-selling ring. I told him to meet us at your office in an hour."

Ashlynn looked at Garrett as if for confirmation. "I'm not sure how I feel about going back to that office after what happened there."

"It's a good lead, Ashlynn, and we need to talk with this guy. He may be the key to locating your son."

Garrett understood her concern, but also knew she would go. She would do whatever it took to get her son back.

"Don't worry," he said. "I'll be right there with you."

"Fine," she told Ken. "We'll meet you there."

He'd been trying so hard not to let Ashlynn get to him, but she had. He hadn't been able to stop her from sneaking back into his heart. Had she ever truly left? He'd been searching for years since the ambush, look-ing for something to bring meaning to his life but the truth was he'd had it all along. He'd just been too stub-born to realize it.

He steeled his determination and took a deep breath. He wouldn't let them down again. And once they brought Jacob home safely, maybe they could talk about becoming the family they always should have been.

Chapter Nine

The downtown streets looked eerily different from their weekday hustle and bustle as Garrett drove them to the DA's offices, but it gave Ashlynn the opportunity to really notice the Christmas decorations on the storefronts for the first time. Her heart saddened thinking about Jacob and wondering if he would be home in time for Christmas.

Bring him home, Lord, she prayed silently not even finding it odd that she'd started seeking God's assistance. If finding her son meant believing in a God that would continually let her down, she would do it. Garrett had told her that God rarely intervened in sin, but that He was always there providing comfort and guidance. She wanted His intervention so much, but she would also gladly take His direction. Other than the kidnappers, no one else knew the location of her son but God so she would place her faith in Him to lead their way. Garrett had assured her that God didn't hate her and all she could do was to hope and pray he was right and her very presence wouldn't cause Him to work against her. Jacob deserved better than that.

All the street parking spaces in front of the office were empty, so Garrett parked in one close to the building. He pulled out the box of files and carried them upstairs. She felt fortunate they hadn't been ruined after their getaway from the cabin, but Garrett had returned with Josh to retrieve his truck and their belongings, and had seen no further signs of the shooters.

She used her key to unlock the suite doors, then pushed them open to allow him inside. Just like with the rest of the building, she heard nothing coming from any of the offices, but Garrett checked them all just to be certain they were alone. They couldn't be too careful after what happened the last time she was here. Many of the associates often worked on Saturdays, but it was well past lunchtime and they had likely headed home by now. As she'd expected, Garrett returned with news that the suite was empty except for them.

She led the way into the conference room, deciding the table there would be more beneficial for the interview with the FBI agent.

Garrett placed the box with her files on the table and Ashlynn pulled out a handful of folders. She wanted to look through them again while they waited for Ken and the agent to arrive. He followed suit, grabbing one and opening it as he sat beside her. "I'm not sure what I'm even looking for," he admitted.

She sighed. "Aside from finding Randy Meeks's name in here, neither do I. But Ken thought it was a good idea."

"Where is he?" Garrett asked. "He was the one who

was so adamant about being here." He glanced at his phone. "They should be here by now."

She shrugged. "I suppose he got caught up with something. He'll be here soon." She pulled open a file and started to read through it, but the sheer volume of names she was now wading through overwhelmed her. "It feels like we're searching for a needle in a haystack and we don't even know which haystack to search in."

"We're following up all the leads. We have to consider this could be connected to one of your cases. This guy knows you, Ashlynn. He's fixated on you. He has a personal connection to you. We have to think you've come across him at some point."

She sighed. "I know. I just don't understand why someone would be targeting me or why they would take Jacob. That's beyond cruel."

And she hadn't been too thrilled with Ken's attitude on the phone, either. She'd glanced at Garrett to see if he'd noticed, but he hadn't seemed fazed by it. Was she being overly emotional? Had the strain of Jacob's abduction and some maniac trying to kill her finally gotten to her? She knew Ken cared about finding Jacob. He'd been working countless hours in addition to his duties at the DA's office to help them.

And she did have to concede his point. She hadn't recognized Meeks. That had been such a long time ago and she had worked so hard to put that life behind her. Judge Warren had told her again and again to stay laser focused on her future and never let her past define her. It was possible she'd run into someone she'd once known and just didn't realize it. Her life was incredibly hectic these days between being a mother, fighting for custody of her child and pursuing a high-pressure career as a prosecutor. But had she been so busy building a future for them that she'd allowed a snake from her past to slither back into their lives?

But digging through her past had brought up some painful memories that had nothing to do with finding Jacob and everything to do with her history with Garrett. Her face warmed as she remembered how she'd kissed him that morning and the incredible kiss he'd returned. Was it possible they could finally have a future together and be that family she'd always dreamed of? She glanced at him and her heart quickened at the idea. Had he grown into a man she and her son could finally rely upon?

She opened another file and skimmed through it, a car hijacking case. She remembered it well. The defendant had carjacked a college-aged girl, and robbed and terrorized her before she'd finally managed to escape. She'd been extremely traumatized and Ashlynn had hoped to give her some relief by putting the repeat offender in prison for a long time.

The case was especially memorable to her because it had come at the same time that Jacob had leaped from the couch and broken his collarbone. She'd been prepping for the trial when she'd gotten the call and had to leave work. She'd also missed a number of days of work caring for him and been forced to push the trial back several weeks.

It hadn't bothered her much back then. That was before they'd hired Mira, and Stephen had been out of town on business and unable to help her, but now it seemed to bring to light every reason she'd had for being angry that Garrett hadn't been around. He'd missed the broken collarbone. He'd missed Jacob's first steps and his first words. He'd missed doctors' appointments and tantrums and even a minor surgery to place tubes in Jacob's ears.

Those darker memories began to flow back to her, every moment when she and Jacob had needed him and he hadn't been there for them. She couldn't forget that. And how could she ever trust that he wouldn't do it again?

She pushed away the files and stood up, trying to stretch the knots out of her stiff muscles.

"You okay?" he asked, coming to stand behind her and wrapping his arms around her.

But she wasn't. The turmoil of not knowing if she could depend on him was just too much for her to keep continually turning over in her mind. It boiled down to one, undeniable truth—she didn't trust him.

"I've tried so hard to put my past behind me and now it seems the key to finding Jacob might lie in my past."

"I know it's hard, but it's necessary."

"It's not just hard, Garrett. It's unbearable. Why do I have to keep reliving it? Why can't these people just leave me alone? Everything in my past keeps coming back to haunt me. Even you, showing up here, dredging up painful memories."

He grimaced at her words and she sighed. She hadn't really meant to be so cruel. "I'm sorry. I shouldn't have said that."

"It wasn't my intention to hurt you, Ashlynn."

"No, it wasn't your intention, but intentions don't matter, Garrett. You did hurt me. I don't ever want to feel that way again. I realize this isn't really your fault, but I can't get past the feeling that if you'd been here, if you hadn't left us all those years ago, this wouldn't be happening. Jacob would be here with me and he wouldn't have been abducted. I know I shouldn't blame you, but I do. I've tried to get past it. I can't forget how you left us."

She pushed away from Garrett, but he tightened his arms around her. "Don't, Ash. Please, don't push me away."

"I can't do this, Garrett. I just can't."

He touched her face, stroking her cheek with his finger. "I can't pretend I don't care for you. I want you and Jacob to be a part of my life, Ashlynn. I love you. I love you both. I want us to be a family."

Her heart was divided. On one hand, she longed to fall into his embrace and lose herself. He was offering her everything she'd ever dreamed of, a life she'd yearned for all those years ago. But the other side of her heart, the side that had been battered and broken too many times, cried foul. He'd shattered those dreams of happily-ever-after and she'd worked too hard to build a life for herself and Jacob to put it at risk again, especially for someone who had already proven himself unreliable in sticking around when things got tough.

She shook her head, tears springing to her eyes. She couldn't risk Jacob's future that way. "I can't," she said, her voice choked. She turned away from him. "I can't.

This will never work, Garrett. I don't trust you anymore. I don't know how I can ever trust you. How do I know you'll be there for us?"

"I will be."

"I wish I could believe that but I... I just don't."

He sighed and dug his hands into his pockets then put some distance between them. The pain on his face was evident and sharp. She knew she'd hurt him and wanted to insist that that wasn't her intention, but then she smiled, realizing those were the same words he'd expressed to her. Neither of them meant to hurt the other, yet somehow they'd both been hurt.

"I appreciate your help in finding Jacob. I don't know what I would have done if you weren't here, Garrett, but I can't do anything else. Whatever it was we had all those years ago, it ended the day I received your call."

He nodded but didn't speak for several moments. Ashlynn turned away. There was nothing else to say. She'd made her decision and nothing could change that.

His voice was low and gruff with emotion when he spoke. "I think I'll step out and call Josh. See if he's heard anything on those background checks I asked him to do."

She nodded then turned in time to see him walk out of the conference room. She knew she was doing the right thing for herself and her son. She just wished it didn't hurt so badly.

Once he was clear of the suite, Garrett leaned against the closed door and took a long, steadying breath. Her words had stabbed him, not because they were mean but because they were true. She didn't trust him enough to allow him to be part of her life and her family. He'd lost his opportunity for a family when he'd let them down. It only cemented what he already knew. He wasn't cut out to be a father. He'd tried so hard to pretend he could do it, that he could re-create what they'd lost, but Ashlynn was right. He was a failure.

And he couldn't ask her and Jacob to take on that kind of risk. He should never have returned to town, and some part of him admitted that he had always hoped to run into Ashlynn. He hadn't sought her out, but he couldn't deny he was glad he'd seen her again.

He rubbed his face and looked up at the midday sky. It was a bright blue with little cloud cover and he stared up at it feeling better in such close proximity to his Lord. He didn't understand why God had left him here and he hoped his son and Ashlynn wouldn't suffer because He had.

Please, Father, help me to find Jacob. Don't let my son pay the price for my selfishness. And no matter how Ashlynn feels about me, keep her safe. Father, give me guidance. Light my path.

Even if he couldn't be a part of his family, he would still do everything he could for them before he let them go.

Ashlynn pulled the papers back toward her and tried to concentrate on examining them instead of the wounded look she'd seen on Garrett's face. She couldn't think about that now. She felt terrible about laying this all on him, but after that kiss this morning, she hadn't wanted to lead him on, allow him to believe there was a future for them when there really wasn't. Finding Jacob still had to be her first priority.

She glanced at the clock on the wall, noting he'd been gone for over ten minutes. That made her uncomfortable. The last time he'd let her out of his sight, Meeks had attacked her. She reminded herself that she was in no danger. The suite was empty and Garrett hadn't gone far. He was just giving her space to work. She closed one file and placed it on the read-through stack before getting another and opening it. She needed something else to concentrate on and hopefully he would return soon enough.

As she flipped through her papers, she landed on a case of domestic abuse from back in the spring. It didn't seem to have any bearing on anything and she nearly added it to the not-relevant pile until she spotted a name she did recognize—Paul Rollins. His name was listed on the defense's list of character witnesses.

She hadn't seen it previously because the case had never gone to trial. The defendant had accepted a plea for a lesser sentence. But she knew the name instantly— Paul Rollins, Kathryn Rollins's biological son. She and Meeks had been fostered in the same home where this man had also lived. He'd been a teenager in the photo they'd recovered from Meeks's apartment. She had no idea what had happened to him after his mother went to prison, but it seemed too coincidental to dismiss that his name had been in her case files. Had he come to court to support his friend during the preliminary phase and seen her there, re-sparking some anger against her, just as Garrett had suggested?

She decided to check him out, just in case. Using her laptop, she typed his name into the police database the DA's office had access to. He had an extensive criminal record. He wouldn't have made much of a character witness in her opinion. She would have torn him apart in court. But when the mug shot of Paul Rollins materialized, she gasped, recognizing the sharp eyes and features she knew so well.

Paul Rollins had been right here in her office many times, getting close to her and probably planning his revenge against her for months.

Fear pulsed through her. She reached for her phone and quickly dialed Garrett's number. He needed to know what she'd found. His phone rang once then went straight to voice mail. Now he wasn't even taking her calls? She waited impatiently for the beep. "Garrett, call me. It's important. I know who's behind the attempts on my life and Jacob's kidnapping. It's Ken."

She hung up the phone, then stood. If Garrett wouldn't accept her calls she would just have to track him down and make him listen to her. She was certain he wouldn't have gone far. He had to still be in the building somewhere or possibly outside. She walked to the window and gazed out, hoping to spot him on the front lawn. She didn't see him, but she instinctively knew he was close.

Suddenly, she heard the main suite door open and close. Was it Garrett returning? She prayed it was. She headed toward the door but stopped, frozen when she saw it wasn't him.

Ken was approaching the conference room.

Her heart raced and anger bit through her, but she wasn't sure what to do. She wanted to confront him, to demand to know why he'd deceived her and to ask if he took Jacob. But if Ken was truly behind this, she had to be smart. Jacob's life depended on it. Would he attack her once he saw Garrett wasn't around? Or would he continue to play the role of the concerned friend? That thought sickened her.

Oh, God, what do I do?

She grabbed her phone and tried Garrett's number again. It again went straight to voicemail so she shot off a text to him instead.

God, tell him to come back. I need him!

Still uncertain how to react, she turned to face Ken. But his gaze was focused on something behind her. She turned to look and saw her computer screen displaying the image of his mug shot along with his real name. His deception was now out in the open.

His eyes moved to her and his mouth twitched into a self-satisfied grin. "So, you've uncovered my true identity, have you?"

Anger pulsed through her. This man had pretended to be her friend when all along he'd been playing her for a fool. And since they were no longer pretending, she decided confronting him was her only option. "I know who you really are, *Paul*. Where is my son? Where is Jacob?"

"You'll soon find out everything." He took a step

in her direction and she instinctively backed away. He grinned, obviously satisfied at the fear his movement had caused in her. She had to get away from him, to find Garrett and end this once and for all. This man was responsible for all the heartache and pain in her life recently. He'd killed Stephen and Mira, and tried to kill her, too. And she'd led him right to herself each time, believing him a friend and confidant. He'd always known their location and had used that to his advantage in planning his revenge.

"You were the one who drugged me," she said. "It wasn't Judge Warren's brownies at all."

"No, it wasn't. I took an opportunity to distract Bridgette and slipped it into your coffee." He removed a syringe from his pocket. "In fact, I was able to get my hands on another dose. My girlfriend, Barbara, is an LPN over at the medical center. At least, she was until she agreed to run away with me and my son."

Ashlynn gasped. "*Your* son? Jacob is not your son."

"That doesn't matter to her. I've got her convinced we're protecting Jacob from you. She's a pushover for a nice smile and a sad story."

He moved again and Ashlynn did, too. She couldn't allow him to drug her again. She took off, running around the table, but the room wasn't large and he was able to reach out and grab her, taking hold of her arm and pulling her toward him. She kicked and struggled but was no match for his strength. He wrapped his arm around her neck, blocking her airway, then injected the syringe into her neck. She kicked and flailed, sending papers from the table flying, but she couldn't land a shot that loosened his tight hold on her and she couldn't breathe in enough air to even moan much less scream for help.

Finally, she went limp in his arms and felt herself fading, unable to stop it. She only had two hopes now—Garrett and God. She silently prayed for God's intervention. *Don't let me die without knowing Jacob's safe,* her heart cried.

He lowered her to the floor and stood over her. As she finally faded into unconsciousness, he whispered something in her ear that haunted her soul.

"I warned you there were a lot of crazies out there."

"Don't give up hope," Josh said when Garrett phoned him and finally spilled everything—his nervousness about being a father, his rekindled feelings for Ashlynn and even her insistence that she could never trust him. "Trust is earned. You'll just have to prove it to her. I know you have it in you to be a great husband and father," Josh insisted. "Just remember, God is the Great Restorer."

Garrett took a deep, cleansing breath. "Thanks, Josh. I needed to hear that." He could always count on his friends be to there to lift him up when he was down. One more reason reconnecting with people had been the right decision for him.

"I know you're still struggling, but don't give up believing that God is on your side, Garrett. He left you here—He left us all here—for a reason. Right now your family needs you. That's your reason."

He realized Josh was right. His family needed him

and he would be here for them. He would find Jacob and he would bring him home to his mother. He owed them both that and he needed to concentrate on that instead of on his own aching shell of a heart.

He was a ranger and it was time he started acting like it.

"Have you found anything in those background checks I asked you to do?" Garrett directed the focus of the conversation back to the finding of Jacob.

Josh didn't flinch at his abrupt change of gear. "No red flags on any of the names you gave me."

He sighed, unsure if he was glad Ashlynn had no friends who were betraying her or upset that they still had no leads.

"Thanks. I'll call you later." He hung up with Josh and walked back upstairs to the suite. He pushed open the door and immediately saw the conference room was empty. Case files were scattered on the floor, which made his heart quicken with apprehension.

"Ashlynn," he called, hoping against hope that she'd taken a bathroom break or gone to the supply closet. But he knew better. A thousand scenarios rushed through his mind. Maybe she'd thought he wasn't coming back. Would she have left without him? And where would she have gone?

He pulled out his phone and saw two missed calls from her. He kicked himself. She must have phoned while he was on the call with Josh. Why hadn't he noticed? He saw she'd left him a voicemail.

"Garrett, call me. It's important. I know who's behind the attempts on my life and Jacob's kidnapping. It's Ken."

He held his breath. She'd figured out Ken was behind this? And now she was gone. Had she gone after Ken when Garrett didn't answer? Or had he shown up and grabbed her? How had he not seen Ken enter the building? He tried her phone and heard it ring. He followed the sound and found it on the floor beneath the table.

Not good.

He dialed Ken's phone and it went straight to voicemail. That didn't really answer his question. He was the one who'd convinced them to come to the office then hadn't shown up. Had he lured them there? Or had Ashlynn gotten out before he'd arrived?

He pulled his gun and hurried out, searching the hall, the stairwell and the outer offices. If Ken had grabbed her, he couldn't have gotten far pulling someone with him. He worked his way down through the building but found no sign of Ashlynn or Ken. As he pulled open the double glass doors that led outside, fear and regret soared through him.

And that old nagging guilt returned to him. He'd let her down again.

Garrett kicked open the door of Ken's apartment and burst inside, gun drawn and ready for a fight. Josh, Vince and several officers followed him. The apartment was empty. He hadn't really expected to find them here, but it was the only place he knew to start looking. The others fanned out and checked the rest of the apartment.

"It's clear," Vince said, after checking the back rooms. "They're not here."

Garrett felt frustration wash over him. Security cameras at the DA's offices had confirmed that Ken had, indeed, abducted Ashlynn. It had shown him carrying her to his car. Garrett had taken her case files from the office, hoping to find something in them that would lead him to answers, but so far they'd found nothing. They needed to learn everything they could about Ken Barrett and quick. Why had he taken Ashlynn? Why had he kidnapped Jacob? And was he behind the deaths of Stephen and Mira? Everything seemed to point to the fact that Ken had a grudge against Ashlynn, only they still didn't know why.

He scanned the apartment. It was sparsely furnished and held no visible personal effects. In the kitchen he found a photo taped to the refrigerator. It looked like the same photo Meeks had had in his apartment. Only in this picture, a red circle had been drawn around Ashlynn's face and a big red X marked through it.

Had Ken gotten a copy of the image from Meeks? Or did he have some connection to the foster home where Ashlynn had grown up? He was frustrated by all the questions that still remained unanswered.

Vince approached him. "I've got a BOLO out for Ken's car and a trace on his phone. He must have turned it off because it's not pinging anywhere."

Garrett nodded. "He's smart and he knows police procedures." He shook his head. "There must be something we're missing." He turned to Josh. "You did those background checks on Ken. Did you find anything that seemed suspicious?"

Josh took out his phone and pulled up a file. "Nothing that raised any red flags. He's worked as an investigator with the DA's office for six months. Before that, he worked as a parole officer in Pennsylvania for twenty-six years until he moved to be closer to his daughter and her family. Exemplary performance records."

"Wait, you said he moved here to be closer to his daughter?"

"That's what his supervisors at Philly PD told me on the phone. Why?"

His gut started screaming that something wasn't adding up. "Because Ken told me he didn't have any children."

Josh pulled up the file on Ken again and Garrett watched over his shoulder as an official photograph appeared. His heart sank. "Is this from the file Philly PD sent over?"

Josh nodded. "What's wrong?"

Garrett felt a rush of dread pulse through him. The man in the photograph was gray haired and round, not sharp featured and thin. It wasn't that he just looked different. He was someone else completely. "That isn't Ken Barrett. I've never seen that man before."

Their Ken was an imposter and now they had no idea who the man they were searching for really was.

Garrett paced in front of Vince's desk as Vince spoke with the commander of the precinct in Philadelphia where Ken had supposedly worked for twenty-six years.

His face was pale when he hung up and Garrett knew his worst suspicions were confirmed.

Vince checked the computer. "The prints the DA's office has on file for Ken are faked, but we lifted prints from the conference room. We recovered a set that wasn't on file so we ran them through other databases including the military database and got a hit." He pulled up Ken's photo on the big screen. "His real name is Paul Rollins, a former army sniper."

Garrett's heart sank. He glanced at Josh and knew his friend was thinking the same thing he was. A former army sniper would be well versed in weaponry and extremely dangerous. He scanned through Rollins's file. "His mother's name was Kathryn Rollins." He looked at them. "That was Ashlynn's foster mother, the woman that nearly killed her when she was young. Her testimony helped send Kathryn to prison where she was murdered."

"So this is all about revenge," Josh said. "He's getting back at her because she had his mother sent to prison."

Garrett's blood boiled at the realization. His family was in danger all because someone wanted revenge on a girl who'd been beaten and tortured. But he had to keep his calm if he hoped to bring her and Jacob home safely.

"I'm going to call him," Garrett said, pulling out his phone. "He wiped the computer clean and made sure I didn't see him at the office, so he may assume we don't know he's the one behind all this. I'll call him to see if he's heard anything and we'll try to get a trace on his phone."

"You tried earlier and it went straight to voicemail. He's probably got it turned off," Josh stated.

Garrett shrugged. "I have to keep trying. What do I have to lose?"

Vince nodded. "I'll set up the trace."

A few minutes later, Garrett placed the call. It sickened him to speak to Ken like nothing was wrong, but he knew he had to hold his tongue if they hoped to track him.

Ken answered on the third ring. "Garrett, I heard about Ashlynn. Any news?" he asked, his voice kind and full of concern.

"No," Garrett told him. "Have you heard anything?"

"I'm afraid all I've hit are dead ends," Ken said. "I'll keep searching, but so far I've turned up nothing that could help us find her."

Vince gave him a thumbs-up, indicating that they were able to track Ken's cell phone. Garrett noted it was downtown. "Well, keep me informed," he said. But then he couldn't stop himself from issuing a warning. "If anything happens to her, I won't stop until whoever is responsible pays." He hoped the warning rang through. He didn't want Ken to know they were on to him, but he also wanted him to be on alert that Garrett was coming for whoever had taken Ashlynn.

Ken was silent for a moment and Garrett wondered if he'd hung up. Then he said sympathetically, "You really love her, don't you?"

He couldn't stop the emotion that crept into his voice. "Very much. And I won't stop until I find her. That's a promise."

Ken clicked off and Garrett instinctively knew he'd shown his hand. But Vince was already barking orders to mobilize the task force.

"We're headed downtown to the old Royal Hotel," he said. "It's been abandoned for years but there are always squatters. He must be holed up there." Vince patted his back. "Don't worry. We'll get him."

Garrett knew it would take Vince time to organize the task force…time Ashlynn and Jacob might not have. He glanced at Josh, who nodded, obviously understanding that, too. He motioned to Garrett to follow him then went outside to his car and opened the trunk. It was loaded down with enough weapons and gear to equip a small army.

"I'll phone Levi on the way and tell him to meet us there."

Josh slammed the trunk closed and they both got into his car.

He had no doubt he was going to get Ken. His days of freedom were now limited. Garrett only hoped Ken hadn't yet harmed Ashlynn or Jacob.

A heavy weight pressed on her head as Ashlynn regained consciousness. She struggled to remember what had happened to her but her memory was a fog. She tried to move her hand only to find it bound. That realization cleared her head instantly.

She pulled at her hands, then at the binding on her feet. She was tied up. She struggled to sit up and look around. She was in a room that looked abandoned, like an old house that had been left in ruins. Junk was piled in one corner, rolls of carpet lay on the floor and garbage littered the room. She looked up and realized the ceiling was also falling down in places.

She struggled to recall what had happened and remembered her discovery about Ken and his grabbing her and drugging her. She also remembered he wasn't who he'd claimed to be. Ken Barrett was a fake identity he'd used to get close to her. He was actually the son of Kathryn Rollins.

She heard movement and realized it was birds flying through holes in the ceiling. Then she heard another faint sound that grabbed her attention—the sound of a child crying. She strained to listen closer and heard the soft sounds again. Realization pulsed through her. It was Jacob! She was certain that was his cry.

She pulled at the bonds, more determined than ever to get free. She had to reach her son. She finagled the ties around her hands. When she was finally free she saw they were red and raw. But the pain didn't matter nearly as much as reaching Jacob. She loosened the ties on her feet and tossed them aside then rushed out of the room, her gait unsteady, obviously from the drugs Ken had given her. She held onto the wall and pushed open a heavy wooden door.

They were inside an old hotel. The floors were missing in several places and the walls seemed to bow, looking like they might fall at any moment. On one side of the massive lobby was what used to be the check-in desk but there were now holes in the counter and graffiti covered everything that was still standing.

In the center of the room was a large staircase that

she could tell had once been impressive and an obvious focal point of the hotel. It was easy to imagine the giant structure in its heyday and it briefly saddened her to see it in such ruin, but she had other more pressing concerns than worrying about the sad state of some old hotel. She had to find her son.

She screamed and nearly fell when a flock of birds fluttered around her then flew up to the ceiling. She grabbed the banister to steady herself, but the old structure creaked under the pressure of her weight so she regained her balance quickly. There were no doubt many critters making this place their home and probably more than a few squatters, as well, if Ken hadn't already cleared the hotel of them. As the sounds of the birds faded away, she heard the cry again coming from upstairs.

Jacob!

It had to be him.

She rushed up the stairs, the pain in her head a second thought. She used the rickety banister only when she needed to and prayed it didn't give out on her. The sound of crying grew louder as she reached the top. It echoed through the empty halls and she realized it was coming from even farther up. She followed the stairs up several more flights, chasing the sound of the cries she knew had to belong to Jacob.

On the eleventh floor, she rushed into the hallway and checked every room. Toward the end of the long hall she noticed a door that looked new and sturdy and definitely out of place. The sound grew louder as she neared it. Her heart nearly burst from her chest when she saw her son sitting on a blanket on the floor in the middle of the room. His face was red from crying and anger burned through her. Why had they left him to cry this way? And why wasn't someone watching him?

She rushed into the room and scooped him up in her arms, her heart soaring to have him close to her again and to know that he was safe. *Thank You, Lord*, her heart cried, even as tears of relief and happiness spilled from her eyes. Jacob put his arms around her neck and snuggled his face into her. She patted his back and smoothed his hair, her hands unable to get enough of him, just to feel him in her arms again.

"My, my, what a joyous family reunion."

Ashlynn froze when she heard the voice and the ice in it. She turned and saw Ken standing in the open doorway, his gun drawn and pointed at her. Behind him stood a petite, dark-haired woman she didn't recognize. Barbara, no doubt.

Ashlynn pulled Jacob even tighter against her and backed away from them. "There was never an FBI agent you wanted us to meet with, was there? You used that to lure us to the office. What do you want with us?" she demanded. "Why are you doing this?"

"You know why, Ashlynn."

"It's because I helped send your mother to jail? I was a child, Ken, and she beat me so badly I nearly died."

"I wish you had died then," he hissed. "Because of you, my mother died in prison. Because of you, I grew up without a mother." He motioned toward Jacob. "Now your son will know the same life."

Ashlynn gripped him even tighter. "Please don't hurt him. He's just an innocent child."

"So was I," Ken bellowed, then his voice softened. "I was only a teenager, but you took everything from me. I could have just killed you when I grabbed you in your office, but I wanted you to know why this was happening. I wanted you to understand that I, Paul Rollins, was the one who tore your family apart, just as you did mine."

He motioned at the woman behind him and she approached Ashlynn, reaching for Jacob.

Ashlynn backed way. "No, leave him alone! Don't you know what's happening?" she asked the woman. "He kidnapped my son and now he's going to kill me."

Barbara didn't reply but held out her arms for the child.

Ken was quick with the gun. "Either let her have the kid or I'll shoot him right here."

Ashlynn could see the serious threat in his face and knew it wasn't idle. He would kill Jacob. "What are you going to do with him?"

"I'm going to do the same thing to him that you did to me. He'll end up in foster care. Maybe he'll be one of the fortunate ones and end up with a good family." His lips formed a sly grin. "Or maybe he won't. I guess you'll never know." He held the gun up again and pointed it at her. "Now hand him over."

God, what should I do? Handing Jacob over to Ken was like giving away a part of herself, but she knew it was better than his killing them both. Jacob might have a chance to live and have a future, even if it was in foster care. Not all foster families were like the Rollins home.

But the truth was that she had little choice. If she had

to choose between her child living or dying, she would choose life for him. She wiped tears from his big, green eyes then kissed his cheek. "Mommy loves you," she whispered just as Barbara grabbed him.

Jacob screamed as the woman pulled him from Ashlynn's arms. He started crying again and reaching for her, tears streaming down his face. Ashlynn struggled to keep back her own emotion but her heart was being ripped from her chest with every scream. She closed her eyes as the woman and Jacob disappeared out the door, but his cries for her continued to echo through the empty building.

She had no choice in this matter. This was being done without her control and she couldn't stop it. She couldn't protect Jacob from the future Ken had planned for him and she wasn't going to be able to stop Ken from murdering her right here in this hotel.

Garrett had told her that God didn't often intervene in man's sins, but he'd assured her He worked to fix the wrongs caused by evil men. She looked at Ken and knew she was looking into the face of evil. She prayed God could redeem whatever Ken did here today. He might kill her, but God would still be able to restore Jacob's life. She found herself praying for her son, praying that God would keep His eye on him and give him a better life than Ken had planned for him.

And Garrett. She hated to think what would happen to him when he discovered he'd been unable to save either her or Jacob. Would he draw back into himself as he'd done after the ambush? Would he spend his life seeking revenge or self-destruction? She hoped not.

She prayed he would find a way to grieve, then move on. And maybe God would use him to find Jacob and bring Ken and his girlfriend to justice. Hopefully, he would continue searching and save Jacob from the life Ken had planned for him.

"What are you going to do to me?" she asked. She knew he planned to kill her. He'd tried many times already. He wouldn't forfeit this chance.

"Did you know the city plans to tear this building down? Well, they're not going to get the chance. There is going to be a terrible fire. When the fire department finds a body, if they do, they'll just think you're one of the squatters that calls this place home. Even if they eventually identify you, I'll be long gone with your son." He shrugged. "I had hoped Barbara could get me another syringe but she wasn't able to, so I guess I'll have to do this the hard way."

Fear rippled through her as he lunged at her. He raised his gun and slammed it hard against her head. Pain blinded her for a moment then everything faded away.

Chapter Ten

Josh pulled up and parked at the curb across the street from the Royal Hotel. Garrett had read about this place and knew the city was planning to level the one-hundred-dred-year-old abandoned building. It had once been grand, but had now stood empty for over thirty years. With the broken windows and accumulated garbage, he could understand why city leaders considered it an eyesore.

As they got out of Josh's car and moved to the back of the vehicle, a truck pulled in behind them and Levi got out. He looked robust and healthy as he greeted them both, but Garrett still saw the wounded man he'd carried out of the line of fire and remembered the man he'd left behind.

"Are you sure you're up for this?" Garrett asked him.

Levi groaned and rolled his eyes, obviously weary of people asking him that question. "I'm fine." He batted his chest. "The neurologist gave me a clean bill of health." He reached for a protective vest from Josh's trunk and slipped it on. "Now, what are we looking at inside? Multiple shooters?"

Garrett sighed and put aside his concerns about Levi and concentrated instead on the matter at hand. Vince and the police would be arriving soon, but Garrett was glad his friends were here for backup, too, because he was going into that hotel to find his family with or without the backing of JPD.

"Probably. I know there was more than one person shooting at us that night at my house. I'm pretty sure I wounded someone. One of Ken's friends, Meeks, is still sitting in a jail cell and he didn't have a gunshot wound so I'm assuming Ken has more people helping him. He must have recruited some of his army buddies."

Levi grinned and patted his back. "And you've got your army buddies helping you. Fair is fair."

Josh handed them each a rifle. "We know he took Ashlynn, and we know he's in there. Ashlynn has to be in there, too, and probably her son, as well."

"Anything else I need to know?" Levi asked.

Garrett nodded. "I'm not coming out of there without my family."

Levi didn't flinch at his words, only checked his weapon and locked eyes with him, his gaze steady and determined. "Then let's go get them."

They walked across the street and entered the hotel one by one, Garrett leading. His gun was raised and his senses on alert as the bright light of the afternoon gave way to the shadowy illumination of the hotel. Some light filtered in from the windows and the holes in the walls and ceiling, but it was very little and what made it through left patches of darkness. He scanned the lobby, noting the garbage and graffiti and junk from outside had filtered in here. But he saw no people. His pulse was pounding as he stepped gingerly on the floors, sensing Josh and Levi behind him, mimicking his actions.

Josh moved to his right to check out the registration desk while Levi cleared the downstairs rooms. Each of them gave the all-clear signal so Garrett headed upstairs.

He was halfway up the staircase when he heard heavy footsteps approaching and the sound of people talking.

"Have the charges been set?" He recognized Ken's voice.

"Yes, we've placed them strategically around the hotel. They're ready to go."

"Good, then let's get out of here."

A group of men rounded the corner and saw him a split second before he could retreat or hide. Garrett counted five men in army fatigues. He raised his gun but the man in front was quicker. He pulled his weapon and began firing. One of his bullets grazed Garrett's shoulder and he tumbled backward, rolling down the staircase. He hit the bottom and heard the floor crack beneath him but it didn't give under his weight.

Josh and Levi took cover and fired back. Garrett scrambled to conceal himself, too, as the five men in camo descended the stairs, guns raised and ready to fight. They spread out as they reached the lobby. Garrett glanced up and spotted Ken behind them along with a dark-haired woman who was holding a child. He couldn't see the child's face but felt certain it was

Jacob. He blew out a steadying breath, readying himself for the firefight. He wasn't leaving this hotel without Jacob and they weren't leaving with him.

The guy in front moved cautiously, scanning the lobby for movement. Garrett jumped out. He rushed at the man and tackled him, knocking the rifle from his hand. He didn't stay down long, however. The others turned to help him and were confronted by Josh and Levi and the shady room was suddenly filled with the flickering light of gunfire.

Garrett punched the man with everything he had but finally used the butt of his own gun to take him down. The guy slumped back to the floor and Garrett scanned the lobby for his next target. He saw it when he spotted Ken and the woman taking shelter behind the staircase.

He swooped up his gun and lunged at Ken, prepared to do whatever it took to get his son.

The woman crouched, clutching Jacob to her while Ken squatted like a snake ready to attack. He glanced behind Garrett obviously hoping for some assistance from his friends, but Garrett knew Josh and Levi had taken care of those men.

"They can't help you," Garrett told him. "Now put your hands in the air."

He saw Ken's mind working, trying to figure out what to do. He grabbed Jacob from the woman, shoving her to the floor in the process, pulled his gun from his holster and pressed it against Jacob's temple.

Garrett's chest clenched and all the air seemed to leave him. Jacob began to cry and squirm, but Ken tightened his hold on him.

"I will shoot him," he warned, and Garrett believed him. He was like a trapped animal that wasn't going to give up without a fight.

Now Garrett's mind played through the scenarios and he couldn't come up with one that could remove his son safely from Ken's arms.

God, please don't let him hurt Jacob.

He wet his lips, which had suddenly become very dry, and then pushed away a trickle of sweat on his brow. He couldn't comprehend that this man might snatch his son from him before he'd even had an opportunity to get to know him. The thought sent ripples of panic through him.

And Ken must have seen that fear in his eyes because he sneered and pressed the gun to Jacob's temple again. "That's right. Now I have the upper hand. Put your weapon down. All of you, put your weapons down or I'll shoot the kid."

Garrett lowered his rifle and nodded at Josh and Levi to do the same. He knelt, his eyes never leaving Ken's, and set his rifle on the floor.

"Good, good."

"It's going to be okay, Jacob. Everything is going to be fine." Garrett kept his voice calm and smooth, hoping to reassure the boy whose cheeks and lips were red from crying and whose face was wet with tears.

But Garrett's words seem to anger Ken. "Don't tell him that," he insisted. "Don't lie to the boy. It won't be okay. After my mamma was arrested, everyone told me not to worry because everything would be okay. Only it wasn't. She was murdered in prison, and it's all Ashlynn's fault for sending her there."

He wondered briefly if Ken held any ill will toward the others involved in sending his mother to prison, like Judge Warren who'd prosecuted her, but quickly realized he'd heaped all his bitterness and anger on Ashlynn's shoulders. He was set on his revenge and nothing was going to stop him. Garrett quickly surmised there would be no reasoning with him and no peaceful negotiations for the return of his son.

If Ken got out of the hotel with Jacob, the boy would be gone from them forever.

He reacted on instinct, sliding toward Ken like he was sliding into home plate. He kicked his legs out from under him and Ken fell. He heard the crack of the wood beneath Ken's feet and knew Josh and Levi were also on the move. But all his concentration was on Jacob, who rolled from Ken's arms as he fell and hit the floor. Garrett swooped him up and quickly put some distance between him and Ken.

But Ken wasn't giving up so easily. Garrett heard the click of a safety and knew Ken had retrieved the gun he'd dropped. He froze and turned back. Ken indeed had the gun pointed at them.

Garrett swallowed hard. His rifle was on the other side of the room and he had no way to protect them except by reaching the door. Ashlynn broke into his thoughts and he wondered if he would see her again. Ken fired and the bullet flew past him, but he quickly raised the gun to fire again.

A second shot, this one fired from Levi's rifle, went

right into the back of Ken's head. The man slumped, then hit the floor, the gun tumbling from his hand.

The woman screamed when he fell. She raised her hands above her head in surrender. Levi quickly bound her hands as he had the rest of Ken's men.

Garrett looked at Levi, gratitude rushing through him, and nodded as a way of thanks. He would have much more to say later when he was able to speak again, but for now it would have to do. Levi returned his nod then began helping Josh round up the men who'd helped Ken.

Garrett heard sirens outside and knew Vince and the police task force had finally arrived.

He carried his son outside as the police squad hurried past him into the building. He leaned against the building, taking a moment to relish the feel of Jacob's small frame in his arms. The boy was still crying, but was now clinging to Garrett, his face pressed into his shoulder.

Thank You, Lord, for this moment.

He carried Jacob to a police cruiser and opened the back door, placing the boy on the seat. He found a blanket and wrapped it around his shoulders then knelt before him and rubbed a hand over his fine sandy hair. "Are you okay, Jacob? Did that man hurt you?"

Jacob choked back sobs but shook his head *no* instead of answering. He looked small and frail, his big eyes wide with fear and his lashes wet. His chin quivered as he asked, "Where's my mommy?"

"She's going to be fine," Garrett assured him, rubbing his hand over the boy's hair again. He knew in an instant he could spend hours looking into this child's face and being mesmerized by his chubby cheeks and big, round eyes. This was his son, his child, and it would take months, maybe even years for him to wrap his head around that.

But he couldn't take that time right at the moment. He had to hand Jacob off to an officer to watch over him because five little words kept pulsating through his brain, words that could mean devastation for his and Jacob's future.

Have the charges been set?

Ken Barrett had planted bombs inside the Royal Hotel.

He ran back inside, fear igniting his steps. He had to get to Ashlynn. He had to find her. She hadn't come when she'd heard the gunfight which meant she was either tied up, unconscious, or…

He grimaced. He couldn't even go there.

He pushed back through the revolving doors and saw officers hovering over Ken's body. Josh and Levi were speaking with Vince and the other detectives, obviously unaware of the bombs. They must have been too far away to have heard Ken ask about the charges.

"There's a bomb in the building!" Garrett hollered and everyone's head popped up. "Ken asked his men if they'd set charges. That must mean there's a bomb in the building, or possibly several."

Josh motioned outside, toward the group of men who'd been Ken's accomplices. "That's why those guys were so eager to be taken out of here."

"Everyone out!" Vince shouted, waving his hands. "I'm calling the bomb squad."

Garrett headed for the stairs but Levi gripped his arm. "Where are you going?"

"Ashlynn is still missing and probably somewhere in this building. I can't leave her."

He nodded. "Then I'm coming with you."

"Me, too," Josh said.

Garrett didn't bother trying to talk them out of it. In truth, he was glad for their decision.

"I'm going to question those guys," Vince called to them. "Maybe they'll tell me exactly where they hid those bombs."

Garrett nodded then headed up the steps, wondering how much time they had. Had the bombs been on a timer? He hadn't seen one. If they'd been on a timer, there was no telling how many precious minutes they had before they detonated.

As he reached the stop of the stairs, he heard the boom of an explosion then the crack of wood as the ceiling above him collapsed.

Time was up.

Ashlynn coughed, smoke choking her as she regained consciousness. It was billowing in beneath the door. Dread filled her and she felt physically ill. Ken had started a fire…and he had Jacob. She crawled to her feet and stumbled toward the door but felt the heat of the fire outside through the wood. She grabbed a piece of cloth and tried to turn the doorknob.

Locked.

He'd locked her inside to die in the fire. She hadn't seen a room with a door anywhere in this hotel when she was searching for Jacob, but one look at the shiny new hinges and she knew Ken had hung it just for this purpose.

Without her cell phone, she had no way to call for help and her only way out was blocked. She hurried to the window and looked out. She was on a high floor, too high to jump, but she had no choice. Her only chance of surviving and getting Jacob back was getting out of this room. She would take everything else step by step.

Oh, Lord, please guide my steps. Keep my son safe. And please bring me through this safely.

She pulled at the window but it wouldn't open. In her fear, she wanted to break down and cry but that wouldn't do any good and it would only use up valuable time and energy. Ken had planned well. This was probably the only room in the entire hotel with a working door and glass in the window.

She coughed as the smoke started getting to her. How she wished Garrett was here. She should never have been so hard on him. She shouldn't have said those terrible things to him because she knew they weren't true. It had only been her own insecurities surfacing. She could trust him. Ironically, she knew that now when she couldn't even tell him. Was she going to die with him believing she never loved him?

Despite what she'd told him, she knew Garrett would come for her. Yes, he had let her down once before, but she realized she'd allowed that anger and bitterness to color her judgment. She'd wasted her life worrying about being hurt so much that she'd closed herself off to truly loving someone…and from allowing God to work in her life. In her heart, she knew Garrett wouldn't stop searching until he found her and that gave her comfort.

The question was would he make it in time to save her? Or to save Jacob?

Anger ripped through her at the thought of all that Ken had taken from her. She thought of her son and of Ken carrying him out. Jacob had been crying for her and that riled her up even more. She needed that adrenaline kick. She picked up a piece of wood and rammed against the window this time calling on that extra boost of energy. The glass shattered.

She brushed away pieces of broken glass from the sill and stuck her head outside, taking in a big gulp of fresh air. She could see police cars with their flashing lights on the street below and hope filled her. They'd found her. They were coming for her. But when she looked down she realized the fire truck's ladder was extended but wasn't long enough to reach the floor she was on. She was on her own unless she could make it down a few flights of stairs.

Suddenly the door exploded behind her sending fragments of wood and metal into the room. She screamed and hit the floor, but a piece of something sharp sliced into her back. She cried out in pain and very nearly curled up to die.

But she didn't. The police cars were outside which meant they had found her. Garrett had to be down there and he would not let her die here in this hotel. He would come for her just as she'd known in her heart he would. She had to stay alive for him, for a second chance to tell him she loved him and to introduce him to his son. More than anything, she wanted to be a family with him.

She thought of how he'd told her that terrible things

happened to people but that God was always with them. She believed him now. She felt God's presence here in the room with her, providing her comfort and reassurance that she wasn't alone.

That had been the worst part of her life, she realized. Not that unspeakable things had happened to her, but that she'd been forced to endure them alone. She'd never been surrounded by people who loved her enough to stand beside her during times of distress. She realized now she hadn't needed anyone besides Jesus. He'd always been there for her and with her, whispering His love to her and asking for her trust. He didn't hate her. He'd loved her so much that He'd died for her on the cross.

And suddenly she knew He was someone she could absolutely trust with all her heart. She was going to get through this because of Him.

She edged nearer the window again, wincing against the heat of the fire that was now pressing into the room. She climbed through the window, shards of hot glass digging into her hands and knees. She dangled her foot until she felt something solid beneath her then carefully stood and moved along the ledge, pressing herself against the building for support. She was afraid to look down, afraid of losing her balance and falling or just being paralyzed with fear. But she wasn't giving up. She needed to reach another room where the fire wasn't raging so badly. If she could get there and make it down to a lower floor then the fire department could reach her. It was her only chance of surviving this.

Guide my steps, oh Lord. Guide my steps.

She inched along the ledge until she came to the next window. This one had no glass, but one peek inside told her she had to keep going. The flames were already inside this room and swiping at the walls. She moved back the other way but the same thing was happening in the window of the room she'd just left. She was trapped. She couldn't go back inside and she couldn't move past either window. She was stuck on this ledge on the eleventh floor of the Royal Hotel.

She only thought things couldn't get any worse until she heard a loud noise and looked down at her feet.

The ledge beneath her was cracking.

Levi grabbed Garrett's collar and pulled him backward as a chunk of ceiling nearly fell on top of him.

He started digging through the wreckage, trying to clear a path, but Josh grabbed his arm. "We can't make it up that way."

"I have to get to her," Garrett insisted, fear and adrenaline propelling him.

"It's too heavy," Levi insisted. "The staircase is about to collapse."

As if in response, the wood of the staircase creaked and gave way, sending all three of them falling. A thick coat of debris landed on top of them, threatening to bury them again. Garrett gathered his senses as quickly as he could and crawled out of the rubble. The staircase was no longer connected to the floor above them. The head of it lay in a heap on the lobby floor. It was gone along with his best chance of reaching Ashlynn.

Coughing brought him back to the situation. Levi

pushed aside several pieces of rubble and climbed to his feet. Josh did the same. They both appeared to be unhurt.

"We have to find a way up there," Garrett told them. "I can shimmy up a rope to reach the next floor."

"This whole building is about to collapse," Josh said. "If you try to anchor a rope up there, you'll bring the whole second floor down on top of you." He coughed and looked around at the garbage surrounding them. "What's left of it, anyway."

He shook his head, waving off their concerns. "I have to try."

"It's too dangerous," Josh hollered, then both he and Levi took one of Garrett's arms and pulled him towards the exit.

"I can't leave her," Garrett insisted, struggling to break their holds.

"We'll find another way," Levi said. "This isn't over."

But all Garret could see was the image of Marcus's body as Garrett left him. He wouldn't leave Ashlynn behind as he had Marcus. He wouldn't!

They dragged him outside and Garrett saw the men who'd been working with Ken. He hurried over and confronted one, pulling on his shirt. "Where's Ashlynn? What did Ken do with her?"

The man shook his head. "I don't know," he said, but his tone implied that he did know but didn't care to share it.

"Where is she?" Garrett screamed, seriously on the verge of losing control of himself. He was glad Josh and Levi were there to pull him back.

"Mama!" Jacob cried, his scream carrying over the sound of the sirens and the fire hoses.

Garrett had heard the boy's shrieks ever since leaving the hotel, but this one, this cry for his mother, sounded different. He glanced at Jacob, who was squirming in an officer's arms and reaching out, pointing back up at the hotel.

Garrett turned to look and felt his blood go cold when he saw a figure move on one of the top floors where the fire was raging. But she wasn't inside the hotel. She was outside on the ledge and fire was bursting through the open windows around her.

"Ashlynn!"

He was about to bolt back into the building when several hands stopped him.

"You can't go in there," Josh told him. His face was covered in dirt, but his expression was firm.

"I have to. Ashlynn is up there."

"We'll find another way," Levi said. He, too, was covered in dust, but his eyes were locked on Garrett's determinedly. "We're not giving up on her, but you can't get up to that floor that way. We've already tried, remember?"

Garrett nodded his understanding. He heard them. He knew what they were saying was right, but he had to get to her. He couldn't stand here doing nothing and watch her die. Their hands didn't move from his arms until he relented and turned back. He raked his hands over his face. There had to be a way to reach her. *Oh, God, please help me save her.*

He lifted his eyes upward. He wasn't alone, but he

knew he needed more help than the rangers or even the police could give him on this one. He needed God's guidance. He lifted his eyes upward and noticed a cross atop the building beside the Royal. It was lit up bright with Christmas lights. That's what he needed to see—something to help his mind focus. He wouldn't hear God's wisdom if he allowed panic and fear to guide him. He closed his eyes and tried to clear his mind, concentrating only on the image of the cross. But when he opened his eyes again, he saw something else.

The building with the cross matched the Royal in height and the side facing the old hotel had windows. If he could get inside that building, up to that floor, he could crawl across to where Ashlynn was trapped on that ledge.

"I need rope," he said, causing both Josh and Levi to look up. He knew Josh was going to remind him that roping up wouldn't be possible, but before he spoke, he followed Garrett's gaze and instantly seemed to reach the same conclusion.

"I have a grappling rope in my truck," Levi said and took off running to retrieve it.

Garrett ran to the building with the cross and up the front stairs, only to find the doors locked tight.

"I'll have the police call the building manager," Josh said, but Garrett shook his head.

"No time." He pulled his gun and fired several shots at the locks, then kicked the door open, causing an alarm to sound. The gunfire also caused a roar among the street full of police behind him. He ignored it all and headed for the stairs. The alarm could barely be heard over the police and sirens and roar of the fire next door. He would gladly pay for the door he'd busted and any other damage he did, but he had to reach that top floor.

He heard Josh's footsteps on the stairs with him as he climbed and finally burst through the stairwell door and into one of the offices with windows facing the Royal. He pushed open the window and leaned out. "I'm coming to get you, Ashlynn," he called out to her.

She must have heard his voice over the roar because she looked his way. Relief flowed over her when she spotted him, momentarily drowning out the fear in her expression.

"Hang on. I'm coming."

She nodded her understanding but remained pressed against the building. She was breathing heavily and he knew she was frightened, but he saw something else in her face now. Hope.

Levi appeared moments later carrying his grappling ropes and launcher. Garrett was glad he had those. He'd thought he might have to improvise something that wouldn't be as safe.

"Try to get it close to her," Garrett instructed as Levi loaded up the grappling gun. He half expected Levi to give him that *duh* look because it was so obvious a direction, but he didn't. Garrett pointed to a window only a few feet from where Ashlynn stood on the ledge. "See if you can hit that window right there."

He took aim then stopped and looked at Garrett. "This won't be very stable. The building is compromised, so don't take your time."

"Understood," Garrett said.

Levi took aim again and shot. The grappling hook hit the empty window sill then bounced off, not connecting. Levi unlatched the rope and it wound back up. He reinserted the hook and fired again. This time, it connected with the open window about a foot from Ashlynn.

"Got it!" he shouted. He pulled on the rope to make sure it was secure and nodded at Garrett.

Garrett felt his fear turn to steady determination. He couldn't think about the consequences. All he knew was that he had to reach her. He allowed Josh and Levi to secure the ropes around him.

"They're fine," he barked, as they double-checked them, knowing it was only his agitation at work.

Josh tightened them. "They're not fine. This rope could be the only thing that keeps you both from plummeting to the street below."

Garrett stared at Ashlynn out on that ledge and the fear in her face was nearly more than he could stand. "I have to get to her."

"The rope isn't stable," Levi told him. "I can't guarantee it will hold with the building crumbling around it." He wasn't saying it in a way to try to talk Garrett out of going because he was sure Levi knew nothing was going to change his mind, but rather just for clarification.

Josh touched his shoulder. "We'll be praying for you," he said before tapping Garrett's shoulder in a way that meant he was good to go.

Garrett whispered a prayer of his own then released the lever and zipped across the expanse separating the two buildings. He grazed the crumbling ledge of the Royal then kicked his feet until he felt the landing. He spotted Ashlynn, still frozen in fear, and shouted to her over the roar of the fire and the noise.

"Ashlynn, come toward me!" She was still a good distance away from him and the fire that raged inside was still blocking her path, but she nodded and took a deep steadying breath before she started moving his way, inching along at a snail's pace. He watched her, the horrible feeling of being unable to do anything to help soaring through him. He didn't dare try to hurry her. If she fell, that would be the end. He reached out his arm for her, coaxing her along like a child learning to walk.

"Come on, baby. You can do it."

Fear shone in her eyes but she locked her gaze with his, nodded and kept moving, her hands pressed against the building and her feet sliding along the ledge. The heat of the stone she was clinging to had to be unbearably hot against her skin, but she didn't show it.

He held his breath. She was only a few inches from him now, nearly close enough that he could reach out and grab her. He stretched his arms, pulling the expanse of his gear to the edge of functionality. She reached out her hand for his and he coaxed her along.

"You've got this, baby. You're nearly there."

He saw her face change a second before the ledge cracked beneath her feet. "Garrett!" she screamed as it gave way and crumbled, sending her falling.

Something hard grabbed her, stopping her in midair. She looked up and saw Garrett's hand firmly around her arm. Her other arm was dangling along with her feet, and she was certain she heard a collective gasp from the crowd below.

Every muscle in his shoulder and arm seemed to tense and his face grimaced in pain, but he pulled her up slowly.

"Hang on, Ashlynn. I've got you. I'm not letting you go." His voice was clipped, but the determination on his face was very real.

His jaw tensed as his hand slipped on her skin. She felt his grip giving way and saw a spot of what looked like blood on his sleeve brighten and get bigger. His shoulder had been injured yet he was still holding on to her with all his might.

That was love.

He tightened his grip and took a deep breath then hauled her quickly toward him.

She used her other hand to grab hold of his vest.

"Pull yourself up, baby," he said and she did.

Finally she clutched his shoulders and wrapped both arms around his neck. His body relaxed, but his non-injured arm tightened around her.

"I've got you," he whispered, breathing hard. "I'm not letting you go again."

Fear rippled through her, along with relief and gratitude, but they weren't out of danger yet. They were still hanging on a rope in the air far from the street below and she wasn't yet convinced they were out of danger.

But she wasn't alone. Garrett had come for her just as she'd known he would.

He tied the rope around her and secured it to the pulley. But it was useless a moment later when fire burst through the windows and the structure began to creak. Ashlynn noticed his friends motioning for them to hurry. She could bask in her thankfulness once they were safely away from the Royal Hotel.

He pushed off the building, but the rope above them went slack as the top of the hotel began to crumble.

"Hold on!" he shouted to Ashlynn as their lifeline gave way and sent them falling. She burrowed her head into his shoulder and held on tight as they swung toward the other building.

They hit the side of the building hard. Garrett took the brunt of the force with his back and she doubted that was by accident. He'd steered them so he would be the one to sustain the hit, and she could see from the way his face paled that it hurt. It hurt her, too, causing her breath to leave her for a moment as pain riddled her body. She lost her grip on him and nearly slipped away, but Garrett pulled her tighter against him.

He used the building as leverage, swinging outward then back to the building, this time aiming for a window near where they'd landed before. He had to hit it twice before it shattered and he could grab hold of the ledge. She saw blood and knew he'd cut his hands on the glass. But he steadied them and carefully unhooked her from the rope.

She climbed through the window and was nearly bent over with relief to be back on solid ground. Garrett followed and she glanced up at him. He looked bloody and tired, but his eyes shone with happiness.

She threw herself into his arms and he swept her up in them, claiming her lips with his, as relief and elation flowed through her with so much joy she thought it would overwhelm her. She'd never been so grateful in her life and so thankful that God had brought them to safety.

But she realized it wasn't over. She suddenly pushed away from him as thoughts of her son rushed through her. "Jacob!"

He pressed a finger to her lips to quiet her. "He's safe," Garrett quickly reassured her. "We caught Ken leaving the hotel. He's dead and all those working with him are in custody. Jacob is fine."

She relaxed and leaned into him, realizing she'd been wrong before. Now, she'd never been so grateful. Her child was safe, her tormentor dead and the danger to them gone. She looked up into Garrett's wide, green eyes and felt herself finally, blissfully relax. Tears pooled in her eyes and she didn't bother trying to stop them. "I knew you would come for me," she whispered to him. "I knew you wouldn't let me down."

He pressed his forehead to hers. "I'm never leaving you again," he said, his voice low and gruff with emotion. "Never."

She gave a small sigh of relief as she settled into his embrace and he closed his arms around her. "I believe you."

She heard heavy footsteps approaching and shouts. Garrett glanced towards them. "That's just Josh and Levi coming to make sure we're okay." He shrugged. "Let them wait." He took her face in his hands and kissed her long and hard.

Epilogue

Ashlynn parked her car in the garage and entered her house, noting how quiet it seemed. Fear darted through her for a moment, reminding her of the day she'd returned home to find Mira dead and Jacob gone, but that fear quickly dissipated when she walked toward the back door and heard Jacob's squeal of delight coming from the backyard.

She pushed open the sliding doors and smiled when she saw what was happening. Garrett had Jacob across his arms and was spinning around, flying him like an airplane. Jacob was loving every minute of it.

"Faster, Daddy," Jacob hollered, causing Ashlynn's heart to fill again at her son's use of the name.

She smiled at their antics. It had taken a while for Jacob to warm up to Garrett, but Ashlynn's encouragement had helped the boy along. Jacob had been through a lot in the past few months. He missed Stephen, who he called his first daddy, and missed the way Mira made him PB and J sandwiches. And he still occasionally awoke screaming in fear that the bad men were going to come get him again. But the therapist she'd taken him to had assured her that the nightmare would eventually fade for him now that he once again had a stable home environment.

It pained her to think of all the time Garrett had spent alone when he'd had a family here. He should have been with them from the start and while she still didn't understand why God had allowed them to be separated for all those years, she was thankful He'd brought Garrett back to them.

"Mommy's home," Jacob cried, and Garrett set him down, whispering something into his ear and sliding something into his hand.

Jacob ran to her. "Mama, Mama, I got this for you," he said in his sweet little voice.

"What is it, baby?" She held out her hand and he placed something in it. She expected another flower picked from the grass or a slimy frog he'd found hopping around, but the object he placed in her hand was small and round and shiny. It was a ring…an engagement ring.

She glanced up at Garrett, who was grinning big and broad.

"What is this?" she asked, her breath on hold as her heart skipped a beat.

He pulled her to her feet, grasping her hands in his. "I love you, Ashlynn, and when I was away from you and Jacob my life didn't have any meaning. I was an empty shell of a man. You brought me back to life. You and Jacob gave me back the one thing I thought I'd lost, a reason for living. I don't ever want to be without you again. Will you be my wife?"

She couldn't have stopped the waves of giddy laughter that erupted in her even if she'd wanted to. Her heart swelled and tears pooled in her eyes. "Nothing on this Earth would make me happier than becoming your wife, Garrett."

"Mama, why you crying?" Jacob asked.

She scooped him up and hugged him. "Because I'm happy, baby. I'm so very happy."

Garrett slid the ring onto her finger, then leaned in and kissed her.

She had her son back and the man she loved with her. Most of all, she had the family she'd always dreamed of having.

God had truly blessed her with everything she'd ever wanted.

* * * * *

CHRISTMAS CAPTIVE

Liz Johnson

For Amy, the best kind of friend.
I'm so thankful for you!

And for all of the second chance sweethearts,
whose love is richer because of forgiveness.

We love Him, because He first loved us.
—*1 John* 4:19

Chapter One

When Petty Officer Jordan Somerton stepped onto the lido deck of the cruise ship *Summer Seas*, he'd have gladly given a month's salary to be on land.

That wasn't something he usually thought. Not after almost ten years in the navy, eight of those as a SEAL. Sea. Air. Land. It didn't matter to him on any given mission. He was comfortable in any and all.

Only this wasn't a mission. And he wasn't aboard a naval ship.

"Jordan!" his aunt Phyllis called from the starboard side of the hardwood deck. As she waved her hand, enough bracelets to sink a liner half this size jangled around her wrist. He wasn't usually called Jordan by anyone but his family. His team called him River. As in the Jordan River.

But he didn't think he could avoid Aunt Phyllis by pretending he didn't recognize his own name. Not with her eyes on him like a laser. So he smiled at her and circled around the outskirts of the crowd, his back always to the wall, facing the collection of Somertons and Sutcliffs mingling around the pool.

A ship with a pool. What a waste of space.

But Aunt Phyllis didn't seem to agree. She shuffled over, dragging his youngest cousin, Stephanie, in her wake.

"Hi, Steph," he said, leaning down to hug her shoulders and kiss the top of her head. Even though she had just graduated from high school, their standard greeting seemed fitting since he'd spent most of his growing-up years living with them. "How's college?"

She shrugged, but it did nothing to dim the smile on her lips and her flashing white teeth. "Okay."

Phyllis pouted. "She met a young man and wants to go to his house for Christmas."

Stephanie's eyes bugged out. "Mo-om!"

Jordan tried not to laugh, but Stephanie's face was just too good to hold it back. "Sorry, kiddo. Welcome to being an adult single in this family. I wish I could tell you it gets better." He shook his head. "It doesn't."

She glanced toward the corner of the pool, where Stephanie's sister and her fiancé stood, hand in hand, staring into each other's eyes. A little too in love for his taste.

"But they never teased Kaneesha."

"It's because she's been dating Rodney since they were thirteen. Everyone's known this week was coming forever." He just hadn't been planning on their wedding taking place on a cruise ship somewhere in the middle of the Caribbean a week before Christmas. "Just wait until you bring a guy home." He rolled his eyes. "I can't wait to see that!"

Phyllis was already frowning, clearly picturing her baby walking down the aisle. Suddenly her eyes shifted in Kaneesha's direction. "Speaking of bringing a date to family dinner…"

Her voice trailed off and his stomach hit the deck. Rodney, in his sharp gray suit, took a step to the side as a third person joined them.

Amy Delgado. Long brown hair flowing behind her. Full skirt dancing around her knees in the ship's breeze. Bright pink lips curved in an overflowing smile.

Words failed him.

She was stunning. And he would have noticed that, with or without the elbow to his ribs from Phyllis. He grunted. She pouted.

"I can't believe you let that one get away."

Yeah, yeah, yeah. He knew. He'd botched that. Badly. And he didn't blame Amy for hating him.

The broken date hadn't been entirely his fault. He'd blame that on the Lybanian terrorist who had suddenly popped out of hiding and tried to take over an otherwise peaceful village where a slew of American aid workers had set up shop. When the US government called on him to do his job, he'd done it. Even if it meant breaking a date he'd kind of been looking forward to.

But the lead-up to it—the *before*-the-date misunderstanding in front of his entire family that had required an apology date—that was all on him.

He was lost somewhere in the memory when Neesha waved at him. "Come over here."

No. That was a bad idea. Because Amy was staring at him now, too. And putting the two of them together never ended well. But when the bride called, he'd go running.

"Neesha, you look beautiful." He greeted her with a kiss on the cheek before shaking his soon-to-be cousin-in-law's hand. Then he shoved his own into the pocket of his black slacks.

But his cousin wasn't about to be so easily mollified. She stared at him like a sniper's spotter, her gaze intense and lips in a stern line. He made a silly face, hoping to distract her from that frown before Aunt Phyllis saw it.

The bride should always be smiling, she'd scolded him before they left the port in Miami. *So I don't want to hear a word about how much you hate cruise ships. Understood?*

Yes, ma'am, he'd said, because any good South Carolina boy knew better than to argue with the woman who had raised him without complaint since he was six.

But his faces didn't do a thing to change Kaneesha's grumpy expression or alter her reproachful tone. "Amy said you haven't practiced your dance yet. You know all of the bridesmaids and groomsmen are joining us for the second dance, and I don't want it to be your first time dancing together."

He met Amy's dark brown gaze over Neesha's shoulder. Though her eyes said she wasn't particularly pleased to see him, she still mouthed an apology for landing him in hot water. It was quite possibly the first time she'd ever apologized to him. He was the one with all the practice in that department. But he wasn't fooled into believing that this meant they were on the same team. In fact, he was pretty sure they were playing different sports. And whatever this was, he was perpetually three steps behind.

Between Amy's cold shoulder and his family's nagging, he knew there was no chance he was getting away from this trip without making everyone mad at him, one way or another. That's why he'd prefer being in the field. At least then he had a clear objective—and a team to back him up if he ever got in over his head.

"Are you even listening to me?"

He jerked his mind back to his cousin. "Of course I am."

Kaneesha narrowed her eyes and put her hands on her hips. "Uh-huh." Jordan's attention shifted back to Amy. The gold highlights in the navy blue dress made her deep brown skin glow, and the highlights in her wavy hair shone in the late-afternoon sun.

"It's good to see you, Amy."

She nodded, the briefest acknowledgment. Then asked, "How's Will?"

Of course she'd ask about his SEAL teammate. She'd been friends with Will Gumble for years. The fact that she'd barely acknowledged Jordan's status as anything more than a barnacle on the hull of a ship meant they hadn't progressed past prolonged apologies.

"He's fine. Jess is about to pop. Will's pretty excited about being a dad."

She offered a flicker of a smile. He knew she still took credit for getting Will and Jess back together after ten years apart. And he had to give Amy credit. As a

DEA agent, she'd been able to get Will set up with a false identity and thrown into a drug cartel's compound where Jess had been held captive. Working together under the noses of their captors, they'd managed to save the day—and Will had won Jess over.

Suddenly their foursome became five, as a young girl bounded up to them from the dance floor.

"There you are!"

All four adults turned to the girl, whose pink cheeks couldn't hide her delight or the effects of the brisk wind. And Amy's eyes, always so expressive, grew round. "Elaina, what are you doing here?" She gracefully dipped to look the girl Jordan recognized as her eight-year-old niece in the eye. "I thought your dad took you back to your suite after dinner."

Elaina shrugged. "I came to find you. I didn't want to stay in my room." A shadow of doubt crossed her face, and she reached for Amy's hand. "My dad had to make a secure call from the captain's office again. I was lonely."

Neesha's smile blossomed, and she bent to give Elaina a hug. "We can't have our flower girl spending the evening all alone. Come on." With a tug, she led Elaina and Rodney toward the dance floor and began to spin.

Amy crossed her arms as her gaze narrowed on her niece, and Jordan could do nothing but shove his hands deeper into his pockets, unsure what to say.

After a long pause, she spoke, barely loud enough to be heard over the thumping music coming from the DJ in the corner. "I worry about her. Ever since her mom died, it just seems like Michael is working more and more."

Jordan nodded. Not that she deigned to glance in his direction.

"It's hard for a little girl when her dad isn't around."

He knew she had some personal experience on that front. Her parents had split when she was young, and her dad hadn't really been a part of her life. But despite a nearly twenty-year history between them—she was Neesha's best friend after all—she'd never talked about it with him. Their conversations had rarely dipped below the surface.

Fair was fair, though—it wasn't as if he'd ever chosen to confide in her. She knew about the circumstances of his childhood—messed up as it had been—because Neesha couldn't keep from spilling every single bean she had. But it didn't mean they talked about it. Ever.

Amy's soft voice pulled him from his thoughts again.

"I tried really hard...but when Michael was sent to Lybania and I was transferred..."

Yeah, he knew that Michael Torres was now the US ambassador to Lybania. Jordan had actually met him after the mission that forced Jordan to cancel his sort-of date with Amy. But he couldn't admit that he'd met Amy's brother-in-law before this cruise. Not when the mission was still classified.

"Mmm-hmm." It was more grunt than acknowledgment, but it was enough for her to jerk her head up, her gaze sharp and surprised, like she'd forgotten who she was talking to.

"You don't have to pretend like you want to listen

to me." Her tone wasn't bitter, but there was a distinct crispness in her words.

"I'm not pretending." If they could smooth over so many months of awkwardness between them just by talking about other people, he'd be happy to listen to her for hours. But he knew it wasn't that simple. Even if neither of them wanted to talk about it, they still needed to address the elephant on the lido deck. Rubbing the top of his head, he stared at his shoes for a long moment. "Listen, Amy, I'm—"

With a swift wave of her hand, she cut him off. "Please don't. We've been through this enough times. You've apologized. Your teammates have apologized on your behalf. I'm just surprised that you haven't sent your pastor to apologize."

He tried for a laugh, but it came out dry and throaty and wholly unlike his normal chuckle.

When she looked into his eyes, hers were sure and unflinching. "I accept your apology." Only her tone suggested the exact opposite.

"But we can't be friends?"

"I think it's better if we aren't. Don't you?"

She didn't give him time to answer. She just stalked in Neesha's direction, flashing a smile at Elaina as she danced across the hardwood floor, leaving him to wonder if he'd ever get a second chance.

He wasn't used to accepting defeat. Especially not after battling through the rigors of the BUD/S—Basic Underwater Demolition/SEAL—training. He'd been pushed to his limits both mentally and physically, and ever since then, giving up hadn't been part of his MO.

Throwing in the towel on whatever he and Amy could have been didn't sit well with him.

They were stuck in a floating party together for five more days, so he might as well spend the time figuring out how to get her to really forgive him.

"Rodney can dance!"

"Not as well as you." Amy laughed, spinning Elaina around the dance floor as a DJ played her favorite Cyndi Lauper song from the 80s.

Elaina threw her head back and smiled up at the sky as it faded to ink, her stick-straight hair swinging wide around her shoulders. "Can we do this all night?"

"No." Amy gave Elaina her best fake-stern look. She had a real stern one, too. But she saved that for drug runners and cokeheads with big guns.

"Oh, please. I don't want to go back to my room." There was a slight tremor in the girl's voice that put Amy on her guard. Elaina wasn't the type to whine. If she said something was wrong, she meant it.

"Why not?" Amy knew for a fact that Elaina and her father—and their bodyguard—were staying in one of the very best suites on the ship.

The girl looked up, then down at her feet. "My dad's not there and it...it feels like someone's watching me."

The hairs on the back of Amy's neck jumped to a salute. Helping Elaina make a more controlled turn so she didn't bump into the other dancers peppered across the floor, Amy picked out her next question carefully. "Has your dad been leaving you alone? Has he had to make a lot of calls?"

Elaina shrugged but turned it into a shimmy as the music hit a faster beat. "This is the fourth time since we left. Probably something for work."

Amy mimicked her niece's movements, but with her mind engaged elsewhere, she was always a half a beat behind the music.

She couldn't picture anything but her brother-in-law's face. His dark hair had turned gray at the temples, and she couldn't be sure if it was from Alexandra's battle with cancer or his new role for the State Department. His smile, which had captivated Alex from the start, had turned haggard.

Amy stared at her niece, her features so much like Alex's had been. But Elaina's eyes were shadowed, haunted.

Amy knew Michael's focus on work had Elaina feeling lonely and neglected, but this didn't seem like mere sadness. Elaina actually seemed afraid. Could she be right about someone watching her? But who? And why?

The girl yawned loudly.

Maybe she was just tired.

But there was something about the way her voice shook when she said she felt like she was being watched. As far as cruise ships went, this was a fairly small specimen. But there were still enough people aboard that no one was really alone. At least, not for long. Maybe Elaina was just tuned in to the constant buzz of human activity.

Or maybe someone *was* watching her.

An elbow bumped into her stationary shoulder, and

Amy jerked back, her fist automatically cocked beneath her chin.

But when she met her would-be attacker's eyes, she realized it was only Jordan and let out a quick sigh.

"Sorry about that," he muttered. "You okay?"

"I'm fine."

He opened his mouth as if he wanted to continue their endless apology dance, but she was done. Done with him. Done for the night. Done forever. So she took her excuse and ran with it. "I have to get Elaina back to her suite. I'll see you tomorrow."

He nodded, and if he tried to say anything else, it was lost as the DJ turned the bass up.

Grabbing Elaina's hand, she spun the girl toward the edge of the dance floor and the nearest exit. "It's off to bed for us," she singsonged despite Elaina's frown. But the yawn that cracked her jaw once again proved that the girl was ready for some peace and a full night of sleep, whether she'd admit it or not.

As they climbed the steps to the next level, Elaina asked, "Do you think my dad'll be there?"

"We danced for almost an hour, so I'm sure he's back from his phone call by now. And he's probably worried about you."

Elaina shook her head. "He'll know I'm with you." Suddenly the smooth skin of her face wrinkled with concern. "Will you stay with me if he's not there?"

Amy's heart tripped at the fear that laced the girl's words. Something was clearly off. Something that she couldn't quite pinpoint. But after five years with the DEA and three with the Marines before that, Amy had learned to listen to fear. She refused to let it control her, but a little healthy fear had kept her alive more than once.

"Of course. You know I'll always stay with you."

With a squeeze of her hand, Elaina rested her head against Amy's arm. "Promise?"

The plea was familiar. Probably because Amy had asked it herself a hundred times when she was about her niece's age.

But before she could respond, a wave of goose bumps rushed down her arms. Along the interior hallway there wasn't a breeze off the ocean to chill her. But something had set off her internal alarms.

"You okay, Aunt Amy?"

She whipped her head around to look behind them. The hallway was empty. "Sure." She tried to sound more certain than she felt.

There was a weight on her skin, like someone was watching them. Except they were all alone...weren't they?

And yet the sensation of being watched was as tangible as Elaina's hand in hers.

Maybe it was habit or so many years of training, but Amy grabbed the girl and pushed her into a shallow doorway, using her own body as cover. Amy measured her breaths to keep them silent, but Elaina knew no such trick. Her gasps were ragged, and they echoed in the corridor.

She couldn't identify the source of her concern, and this was the first time she'd felt this way on this cruise. But there was no doubt. Something was going on.

It had scared Elaina.

And now it was turning up every single one of Amy's protective instincts.

She peeked out from the little notch, looking both ways, but saw no one. Not even a shadow. The hallway lights had been dimmed, but there was still plenty to illuminate a moving figure.

And there was no one there.

She backed up, pulling Elaina with her and pressing the girl against her side. "Stay close."

Elaina nodded against her.

Heart thumping faster than usual, Amy took another look behind them. Maybe it would be better to backtrack. To find someone else from the wedding party.

Or she could keep going to the nearest protected place. Elaina's suite.

With slow, methodical steps she worked her way to the end of the hall, where it intersected with another. There she peeked around the corner. Two large forms were approaching and Amy jerked back, pressing Elaina against the wall behind them. Stretching a finger across her lips, she made the universal sign for quiet as heavy footsteps drew nearer.

"Where's the girl? She was supposed to be back by now."

"I don't know. I was with you. Remember?"

It sounded like the sarcastic guy got punched, and his groan echoed.

"Shut up. Don't try to be funny. I'll call the boss. He'll know where the ambassador's daughter is."

Elaina flinched, a gasp escaping. She flung a hand

over her mouth and stared at Amy with wild eyes that asked the only important question. *Are they talking about me?*

Of course they were. What were the odds there was another ambassador's daughter aboard this ship?

Amy felt suddenly sick, bile rising in the back of her throat. This had gone from an instinctual concern to a serious threat in seconds. They had to get out of there, away from these men, who had clearly been watching Elaina.

"We don't know where she is. She's not back at her room yet," said the guy who'd announced he was going to call the boss.

The undeniable crackle of a walkie-talkie bounced down the hallway, but Amy couldn't understand what had been said.

"Sure. We'll get her before they arrive." Shoving his friend, he said, "Start looking."

Who was *they*? And what exactly did they want with Elaina Torres?

Whatever it was wasn't good. And Amy couldn't wait around to find out.

The deep voices dropped low, and then their footsteps stopped for a long moment before one took off in the other direction. Her heart kicked into overdrive. This was their chance to make a break for it.

Leaning down, she whispered to Elaina, "Hold my hand and don't let go."

"Are we going to find my dad?"

They were going to find safety and get help. No matter what.

Chapter Two

$\backsim$

Amy held Elaina's hand so tightly that their fingers shook. Or maybe that was the rest of them. Still, she pulled the girl in her wake, keeping her steps as silent and swift as possible. The halls were nearly deserted, most guests enjoying the entertainment on deck.

Her rough breathing echoed so loudly in her own head that she couldn't hear if either of the men had spotted them. And if they did, would they recognize Elaina as their mark?

"Hey!" The booming voice behind them seemed to rattle the cabin doors. "Stop!"

They'd been spotted. And apparently recognized.

Elaina slowed down, trying to look over her shoulder, pulling on Amy's arm.

"Keep running," Amy ordered. "Stay with me. Don't look back."

The little girl nodded, but her shorter legs stumbled as she tried to keep up.

There wasn't time to stop and boost Elaina onto her

back, but neither could the girl's smaller feet keep up on her own. Amy pulled her close and swung her into her arms, the additional weight making every step twice as hard.

Another hallway crossed in front of them. One that would lead to the stairwell that would take them back to the deck. Then they'd be in the open. And maybe near security.

Please, God, let there be a security guard on the deck.

Feet slapping the carpet, she held every muscle in check as they approached the turn, leaning to counter-balance the weight in her arms.

"Stop right there!"

She hunched her shoulders against the anticipated gunshot, then remembered she was on a cruise ship, not in the field. She expected the possibility of being shot at on a DEA assignment. She wanted to believe that she wouldn't have to deal with that here, on the ship where no one was legally permitted to carry weapons, but she couldn't be sure.

The problem was that she didn't know what to expect here. She hadn't gotten a good look at the men talking about Elaina. There was no intel to identify their motive, their usual methods of attack or a list of their weapons.

If she'd been in the field, alone or with her partner, she'd have looked for a strategic place to make a stand. She'd have turned and fought. She'd have disarmed first and asked questions later.

But right now there was no place to stash Elaina where she would be safe. And the girl's protection was all that mattered for the moment. Making a stand would put the girl at risk, so it wasn't an option.

As they rounded the corner, Amy caught sight of the man chasing them. She couldn't make out his features at this speed, but his wide shoulders stretched out the same black suit she'd only glimpsed before. And he charged after them, his big feet eating up the passageway as if he were an angry bull. There was something in his hand, something big and deadly stretched out in their direction.

He did have a gun.

Speed was still crucial, but she also concentrated on remembering to dodge and weave. She swooped to the left then returned to hugging the wall.

Anything to keep him off center and ensure that if he shot, his bullet would miss.

Dodge and weave.

Her mantra matched the speed of her footsteps as she flew down the hall.

They just had to keep running faster than the man behind them until they lost him. Or found someone who could help.

But the corridor seemed to be deserted, every cabin door shut tight.

Suddenly Elaina's whole body jerked, her grip around Amy's shoulders nearly breaking as she cried loudly. Amy swallowed the scream that rose in her throat as the shift in balance nearly tripped her, forcing her to come to a momentary stop. Tears filled Elaina's eyes, and between trembling gasps she said, "My hand slipped. Sorry."

Amy dismissed the apology with a wave, hoisting the girl higher on her hip and holding on tighter. But in the moments it took to get moving again, Amy glanced back at their pursuer. He'd stopped, planting his feet shoulder-width apart and raising his gun at arm's length.

Her heart leaped to her throat, and she stumbled as she flew toward the end of the hall and a glowing red exit sign, always keeping herself between Elaina and the gun.

Please. Please. If they could just make it through that door, they might find help.

Amy crashed against the metal handle, shoving it open and tumbling against Elaina as the telltale whistle of a bullet fired through a silencer zipped toward her back.

"Go. Go. Go." She cheered herself on, forcing herself to watch her feet and cling to the banister with her free hand.

Her shoes clanged loudly down the metal stairs. But there was no time to worry about silencing them.

That man was willing to take a shot when one of the cabin doors might have opened up at any moment. He either knew something she didn't that made him believe he wouldn't get caught, or he had nothing to lose.

Or both.

Probably both.

Her head spun as they sailed around a turn and another set of clanging footsteps joined hers.

He was gaining on them. He'd reach them long before she could get Elaina to safety.

Dear God, help us. It was the only prayer she could manage as her heart kept up a steady tattoo. *Go. Go. Go.*

And then another whistle, so high-pitched that she felt rather than heard it, sailed past. The shot splintered the corner of the door frame as they barreled through it. Elaina screamed.

Good. She could scream all she wanted now. Anything to gain some attention.

But the deck was empty, and the sound was lost on the wind as they rushed into the open.

Where was everyone? Had the entire ship migrated to the lido deck for more fun with Neesha and Rodney?

She whipped around to see how close their pursuer was. The clanging of his feet against the metal steps gave him away. He wasn't visible yet, but he was closing in. And she couldn't risk leading him to the party. There were too many innocent lives there. People she loved. But she and Elaina were sitting ducks out here.

Where to go? Where would they be safe?

Out of the corner of her eye, she saw the closed door of what looked like a small storage closet. But as she turned toward it, she ran directly into an unmoving chest.

Large hands clamped on both of her shoulders, surrounding Elaina and stopping her midstep. "Amy? Are you all right? I thought I heard someone screaming."

She had to peer all the way up into his face to get a good look at Jordan, but even then her eyes wouldn't quite focus on him. Her shoulders twitched as she tried to check behind her.

"Amy." His tone was clipped, his eyes darting from her to Elaina and back. "What's wrong?"

Everything in her melted. She hadn't even known

she'd wanted his help, but now that he was here, she recognized him as exactly what they needed. "Someone's chasing us. Shot at us." Her words came out on a pant, but she flung her finger out behind her and met his gaze for a brief second.

If he needed to think through his actions, it took him only a fragment of a second. He grabbed them both, shifting them out of the line of view of the stairwell. "Stay right here. Don't move."

And then he ran toward the doorway. But instead of going into the stairwell, he slipped to the side, his back against the white outer wall, his ear pressed in.

She took a step to follow him, but stopped as Elaina let out a small sob. "It's okay, honey," she said, cuddling her niece close. Everything inside her cried out to help Jordan take care of this guy, but she couldn't possibly carry Elaina into that kind of situation, and leaving her behind was equally impossible, so she held her position with watchful eyes.

Their pursuer had reached the bottom of the stairs, and the pace of his clanging steps had slowed.

But it didn't calm the tantrum of her heart. Or loosen the way Elaina's skinny arms squeezed around her neck. Pressing Elaina's face against her shoulder, Amy tried to hold her tight enough to keep both of them from falling apart.

But she couldn't look away from Jordan, whose shoulders rose and fell in a steady rhythm. His face was a mask of calm, and he closed his eyes for a long second.

She wanted to scream at him, to tell him to pay attention. He was going to miss it all, and she and Elaina would be easy pickings for their pursuer. But she bit her lips until they stung and she tasted the coppery tang of blood.

And suddenly the entire world seemed to explode. Everything happened at once. A wicked Glock 23—silencer attached—came through the entrance, their pursuer holding it straight out and ready to fire. But before the rest of him could make it through the doorway, Jordan squeezed his hands together, raised them over his head and brought both of his arms down on top of the other man's. There was a sickening crack, and the gun flew across the deck as the man groaned and swore. But before he could do anything more, Jordan landed an elbow to his sternum.

The man in black crumpled to the floor.

Years of training told Amy to secure the weapon, but when she tried to put Elaina down so she could grab the gun, Elaina whimpered and refused to let go. So she took her with, racing for the gun, scooping it up and pointing it at the still man on the ground.

"Are you all right?" Jordan asked, his hands swiftly moving up and down the beefy arms and legs of their pursuer, searching for additional weapons. Suddenly he stopped and stared hard at her. The gentleness he'd displayed with his cousin earlier in the evening was gone. Replaced by something that could only be called his mission face. It was all hard angles and firm planes. The teasing smile that he so often used had disappeared. Even the little cleft in his chin seemed especially dark.

And she was so busy studying his face that she nearly

missed his repeated question. "Amy, are you all right? Were you hurt?"

"What? No. We're fine. You're fine, right Elaina?" The girl nodded despite the persistent trembling of her chin.

Amy's own adrenaline was dropping fast and making her hands shake, but she held on to her niece and kept going. "A little shaken up, but we're all right. Who is this guy?" Her words came out on a rush, but they seemed to be all Jordan needed before going back to work, confirming she had scooped up the only weapon.

When he was satisfied, Jordan pulled the man's arms behind his back, which launched a loud groan.

"Might have cracked a bone there," Jordan said. As apologies went, it wasn't much. But somehow she didn't think he spent much time telling bad guys he was sorry.

And that was just fine with her.

"Go find an officer or security guard and bring them back here."

"But there was another man, too. He went the other way, but they were talking. What if he comes to see what's keeping his friend?"

He looked into the silent stairwell, but shook his head. "If he shows up, I'll handle it. The two of you go now."

His blunt orders made her hackles stand on end, but she fought the urge to tell him she could take care of it. She could. Usually. In any other circumstance.

But she was responsible for Elaina. And she'd rather die than leave the girl open and vulnerable to another attack.

Jordan was skilled and experienced. And no matter how much she hated admitting it—especially to herself—there were few people she trusted to handle an unexpected threat more.

When she found a security officer, it took a bit of convincing to get him to follow her back to the scene. But the gun in her hand, which she'd emptied of bullets, piqued his curiosity.

"Guns aren't allowed on the ship." He looked equal parts confused and angry, his pasty cheeks going red and splotchy.

"I know." She'd left hers at home, locked in her gun safe. And it was a fair guess that Jordan had done the same. Amy felt a little bare without her weapon, and she wondered if Jordan felt the same way. Either he felt as unprotected as the day he was born or he didn't even notice because he was fully equipped to use his hands to neutralize any threat.

Downed man in a black suit was exhibit A.

For the moment, they had no idea how the man had gotten a gun on board. But that would have to wait. "We need to see the captain."

The guard agreed, and followed her and Elaina back to Jordan, who stood over their pursuer like a hunter showing off his haul.

As the trio approached, the guard let out an audible gasp, and she tried to look at Jordan through his eyes, to consider what it would be like to see him for the first time. He'd been a part of her life for almost as long as she'd been friends with Neesha—more than twenty years. So the big shoulders and towering height didn't frighten her. The size of his biceps and strength in his grip didn't intimidate her. No, they made her feel...

Well, it was better not to think about how they made her feel.

After more than sixteen years of daydreaming about how he made her feel, she'd realized just how wrong she'd been.

It was better for her—better for everyone—if she just moved on.

Only she couldn't deny that, in this moment, he made her feel safe. And she'd never been more grateful.

The big guy in the black suit groaned again, his head lolling to the side as the officer cuffed him. It took both Jordan and the comparatively puny guard to drag the man upright. And it seemed to take hours to make it across the ship and down three levels to the security office. They'd gotten a few strange looks, but most of the ship's guests were too wrapped up in their own vacation to give more than a passing glance to a man leaning on a security guard and another man, who could have been his friend.

When they finally arrived, Amy sank into a chair, Elaina by her side. As she wrapped an arm around her niece, she whispered to a nearby security guard, "Can you get her father down here? He was in the captain's office not too long ago."

The guard nodded, and Amy squeezed her hands together in her lap to keep them from trembling.

His hands were still shaking.

Jordan tried to hold them still, but there wasn't much

he could do to stop the adrenaline charging through him. What kept him on his feet during a confrontation always left him feeling a little out of sorts when the conflict was resolved.

But as he stared through the window into the make-shift cell at the unconscious man, and then looked back at Amy, he could do little more than thank God that he'd heard Elaina's screams and gone to investigate. There was no telling what the man would have done when he'd caught them. But while Jordan was glad he'd been able to protect Amy and Elaina, he needed more information if he was going to be able to continue keeping them safe. Question number one: Why had the man been chasing them?

And as much as he wanted to beg for answers, Elaina's stricken face left him mute. She'd have to rehash the whole ordeal when the captain arrived, so he'd patiently wait for that.

Well, *patiently* was a subjective word.

He paced the confines of the little room. The security guard manning the office, who had identified himself as Paul Cortero, had called Michael Torres and then leaned back in his big black chair, his hands resting over his stomach. He didn't look terribly disturbed or concerned that a man carrying a heavy-duty hand-gun with a silencer had just attacked a woman and an eight-year-old girl. In fact, his eyes were closed as he rocked in his seat.

Incompetent fool.

Those were the kindest words Jordan had for a man

like Cortero, who showed so little concern for the people whose safety was in his care.

But calling him every name in the book wasn't going to locate the other man Amy had mentioned or resolve this issue.

So he kept on marching because movement helped him think.

Suddenly the metal door flew open, and a short, thin man barreled into the room, followed by a much larger shadow of a guard. Michael Torres usually had a big, commanding presence, despite being several inches shy of six feet. But right now his eyes were filled with panic as he surveyed the room.

Elaina jumped from her chair and flung herself into her father's arms. "I was so scared, Daddy. He was chasing us, and he said he had to find me." The words were muffled, but the terror in them was real.

"It's okay, honey. It's going to be okay."

Except a gnawing feeling in his stomach told Jordan that they couldn't be so sure of that. This situation wasn't something they could control. At least not yet. Not with at least one more man out there.

When Elaina pulled back with tearstained cheeks, she grasped for Amy's arm. "Aunt Amy was so great. She saved me."

Torres hugged his sister-in-law and mouthed a thank-you.

She nodded, but there was no accompanying smile. And a tick at the corner of her eye suggested that she had news. News that no one was going to want to hear.

And Jordan was entirely sure it had to do with what

Elaina had just said. The man chasing them had been after the little girl.

His stomach took a nosedive, but before he could analyze the situation further, Torres turned toward him.

"Somerton." He gave a curt nod, his eyebrows pulled together. "How did you get involved in this?"

Jordan cringed, wishing he'd had a second to remind Torres that, as far as the rest of the world was concerned, they'd had no reason to ever meet.

Amy cut in, "Wait. How do you know each other?"

Torres turned back to Amy but was spared finding an explanation when the door to the office opened again and the captain marched in. His white jacket shone under the sterile lights as he reached to shake the ambassador's hand.

"I wasn't expecting to see you again tonight."

"I wasn't, either." Torres's face was pinched as he looked down at Elaina, her arms still wrapped around his waist. "It seems my daughter and her aunt ran into some trouble outside our cabin tonight."

The captain motioned toward the chairs to indicate they should sit down while Cortero scrambled to give his seat to the ship's senior officer.

As the captain introduced himself, Jordan forced himself to stop pacing and slid into the chair beside Amy, who shot him a look that said she wasn't going to let her question drop.

"I'm Captain Robertson." He directed his introduction to Elaina, who was perched on her father's leg. He barely looked at Jordan and Amy and ignored Torres's bodyguard standing in the corner. "I heard you had quite an evening. Can you tell me about it?"

Elaina nodded, her dark hair slipping over her shoulders. "I was with Aunt Amy. We were at the party for Neesha."

"And then what happened?"

She looked at Amy, who gave her a gentle smile, before continuing. "We were almost to my room, and then we heard some men. They were talking. About me. Said they had to find me. Aunt Amy and I tried to get away but one of them followed us. He yelled for us to stop, but we didn't. Then there was a high-pitched whistling sound. It was weird, but we got to the stairs."

Even though he'd seen the gun, Jordan cringed as Elaina gave her trembling account of being shot at. It didn't sound like she even knew what that whistle had been, but he did. And it was enough to make him sick.

Two thugs looking for a little girl when her father and his bodyguard were away from the room. Armed and dangerous and willing to use violence to get their way.

That wasn't coincidence.

"How do you know they were looking for you specifically?" Robertson asked.

Amy filled in the gaps Elaina had left. "The two men were talking loud enough that we could hear them from around the corner." She met Jordan's gaze and held it, the anxiety there present and accounted for. "One asked the other where 'the girl' was. They called her the ambassador's daughter." Amy nodded toward Torres. "When they didn't find her, they radioed someone they called 'the boss.' Then they split up and one headed right for us, so we made a run for it."

Leaning forward, Jordan tried to put the scene together in his mind's eye. "Did they say anything else? Or indicate who was in charge?"

Amy chewed on her lower lip, turning it pink and plump. But it was Elaina who added, "The man said they had to have me before *they* arrive."

Jordan sucked in a sharp breath but held it because he couldn't risk cutting her off if there was more to the story.

Torres didn't hesitate. "They? Who's they?"

"He never said." Amy wrapped her arms around her stomach, as though she could ward off the chill from this conversation.

But Jordan was lost somewhere in the simple words Elaina had repeated. Everyone else had focused on the *who*. But he was stumped on the *how*. His forehead puckering as he tried to work it out, he wondered if maybe the girl had simply gotten the words wrong. "Arrive? They said *arrive*?"

Amy's deep brown doe eyes grew even larger, and he could tell the emphasis hadn't been lost on her. "Yes. That's exactly what he said."

"How exactly does someone *arrive* on a cruise ship in the middle of the ocean?"

Chapter Three

No matter how many ways Jordan flipped the questions over in his mind, there was no answer for them and no rhyme or reason to what the men had said—or what they'd tried to do.

Someone had attempted to kidnap the daughter of the ambassador to Lybania. On a cruise ship. In the middle of the Caribbean. But why try to abduct the girl on a ship where there were a finite number of places to hide her once they captured her? Why choose a ship with equally limited ways for them to escape from the people who would be searching for Elaina until they pulled into port? They weren't even scheduled to arrive in St. Thomas for two more days.

Even more puzzling was the imminent arrival of the illusive *they*. He had no idea who that could be. And even less where or when their arrival might take place. The arrival that had been mentioned would have to come by helicopter or boat. But either would draw significant attention. Is that what they wanted?

His only clue was *soon*. Because the men Amy had overheard had been in a rush to get their hands on Elaina.

But that left a whole lot of holes in his intel.

What he needed was information from the man in the black suit, who had finally begun to wake up and was holding his arm like he'd received a lethal blow. Bah. It had barely been a tap. Just enough to bring him down. If he didn't like it, well, then he shouldn't shoot at women and children.

Which brought Jordan right back to another question. How'd he get a gun on board the ship? Had he snuck it through security? Had it been stashed in his suite waiting for him? And why would he shoot at Elaina if his goal was to kidnap her?

The questions pounded like a woodpecker against steel. He was getting exactly nowhere.

No matter how long he paced, the walls of the security office were as confining as the unanswered questions in his mind.

Amy, too, had stood when the captain excused himself for an urgent call. But Elaina slumped in her father's lap. "Can we go back to our room now?" she mumbled against his chest.

"No!"

Torres jumped as Jordan, Amy and the bodyguard all yelled the same word at the same time. But the ambassador's eyes were knowing, even as Amy slipped into the seat she'd just vacated to rub Elaina's back. "We'll get you a new room." *A safe one.*

The last line was unspoken but louder than her other words.

Suddenly the door swung open and the captain and another man in a starched white jacket—the second in command—entered.

"My apologies," the captain said. "This is Julio Xavier, my staff captain."

Jordan shook Xavier's hand but skipped the pleasantries. "The ambassador, his daughter and their bodyguard need to be moved to a new suite right away."

Captain Robertson nodded and motioned to Torres, who stood, still holding Elaina. "I'll take care of it personally. Follow me." Just before he slipped out of the office with Torres and Elaina, and their bodyguard following closely, he turned back to Jordan. "Xavier oversees security and is in charge of our prisoner."

Jordan nodded but addressed Amy instead of the staff captain. "It's been a long night. You should get some rest."

Her lips pinched at his words, and she pressed flat hands together in front of her so hard that her arms shook. He could almost see the steam coming from her ears.

She was clearly exhausted, and he'd assumed that she'd be grateful for the chance to get some downtime, knowing he'd handle things here. Apparently not.

He scratched at the back of his neck and frowned at Amy, who gave him one shake of her head before turning toward Xavier and pointing toward the glass window into the single cell.

"With your permission, sir, I'd like to interview this man."

Jordan stepped forward to interrupt. After all, he wanted to do the interrogating.

But Xavier was focused on Amy, shaking his head at her. "It's my jurisdiction. I'll take care of it."

"Sir, I'm a DEA agent and that little girl's aunt. And that man shot at me today. I'd like to know why."

The staff captain ran his hand along his jaw, pinching his features as though in deep thought before letting his gaze land on Jordan. "Suppose you're DEA, too."

"No, sir."

Xavier visibly relaxed.

"SEAL teams."

The older man's pinched expression immediately returned. "SEALs, huh? So you've worked with terrorists before."

Jordan wasn't quite sure where this line of questioning was going, but he'd answer nearly any question to get a chance at asking a few of his own. "No, sir. I don't work *with* terrorists."

"Ha." Xavier's chuckle was as dry as dust.

"What do you say you let us stick around?" Jordan said. "We'll stay out of your way."

Amy cleared her throat as if she wasn't willing to make that concession, but Jordan kept going.

"Maybe ask a follow-up question or two."

Xavier rubbed at his chin for a long moment before glancing at Cortero, who had remained silent in the background. "I guess that's fine."

As jails went, this one looked more like a hospital,

all sterile white walls and a bench that looked like it belonged in an accessible shower. It wasn't exactly homey, but neither did it suggest that the man in the black suit would face serious consequences for his actions. Which left Jordan with a distinct feeling of unbalance.

Xavier began his interview in a calm voice. "I'm Julio Xavier. What's your name?"

The thug shook his head. He attempted to cross his arms but winced when he bumped his forearm. "I need to see a doctor. That guy broke my arm."

Amy shot Jordan a look, and he shrugged. He'd take the man—or any other—down again in a minute if he threatened Amy or Elaina.

Xavier sucked on his long tooth. "First, you have to tell me your name."

The big man squinted hard, his eyes nearly disappearing in his round face. His bald head didn't do anything except make his face look fatter.

After a long staring contest, where the staff captain didn't back down, the man said, "Dean."

"Is that a first name or a last?"

Again, he stared like he was trying to figure out what Xavier wanted to hear. Jordan couldn't stop his hands from rubbing together or force his feet to stand still. Not when there was another man out there, probably still looking for Elaina, and this man in front of him was answering none of the questions burning a hole in Jordan's gut.

Maybe it was a good thing he wasn't doing the questioning because Jordan suddenly had patience for no one and nothing.

Come on, man. Get it going.

But the staff captain kept his pace slow and easy. "Is your first name Dean?"

The man shook his head.

"Your last?"

Finally a nod. Now they were getting somewhere. Mr. Dean had half a name, and Xavier nodded to Cortero. "Look it up."

The security guard did as he was told, turning to the computer on the desk before him, his fingers making the keyboard clack. "First name?"

The man in black responded with silence, long enough to make Jordan's blood begin to boil. He shot a scowl into the cell, but it was Amy who spoke up.

"Now."

One word. One syllable. It was all she needed.

"Eric. Eric Dean."

Jordan couldn't contain the smile that bubbled into place, and he shot Amy an approving nod as Cortero typed in the first name.

"There's no one by that name on the passenger manifest."

Amy drew in a quick breath. He could feel it more than hear it. And he was pretty sure they were thinking the same thing.

This man had either lied about his name or found a back door onto the ship. With a gun.

And he wasn't alone. There was at least one other dangerous person working with him, and they were both working for someone else. But if there *was* a back entrance, there could be a whole lot more than that.

"We're going to need your fingerprints to confirm your identity," Xavier said.

But Eric shook his head. Hard. He looked like a five-year-old refusing to go to bed. "I'll wait to see the doctor first. And then I'll wait for the local authorities in St. Thomas."

His words were straightforward and clear, but something about his expression made Jordan's skin crawl. He wasn't scared or upset, or even resigned to his fate. He seemed to be suppressing a smile at the thought that he'd ever have to face the consequences of his actions. Either he was a sociopath or he knew something that Jordan didn't.

Jordan guessed that when it came to this situation, there were a lot of things he didn't know.

And that didn't sit well with him.

Turning to Amy, he frowned, trying to figure out how to convince her that pressing Dean for answers was a dead end. But she beat him to it.

"We're not going to get anything out of him tonight," she said. Then she looked right at Xavier. "Will you call me if he gets talkative?"

He nodded, and she strode toward the exit. As she walked out into the hallway, Jordan waved at Xavier and chased her down. "Hey, where do you think you're going?"

Amy didn't have the energy left to fight with Jordan about where she was going or why. In fact, all she really wanted to do was crash in her bed and sleep until this night was nothing but a bad dream.

But that wasn't an option.

So she stopped and put her hands on her hips, looking way up into his face. "I'm going to talk with Michael. Because whoever this Dean guy is, he was serious about finding Elaina. If someone's after her, it's got to be because of Michael. And anyone with the audacity to try to kidnap an ambassador's daughter isn't going to stop after one failed attempt."

Her stomach clenched as she spoke the words aloud.

It was one thing to know they were true. Another entirely to speak them.

Jordan didn't look surprised in the least, and his brown eyes only turned darker. "Then I guess we better find their new room."

He said it casually, as though they were stuck together, and she couldn't help but blurt out the truth. "You can go, you know. Get some rest. It's late. It's been a long night, and this isn't your problem. I'll be fine."

He shrugged, not bothering to reply to her dismissal. "Let's swing by the captain's office to get their new suite number."

She frowned but didn't have any choice except to follow him, racing to keep up with his long strides.

"I'll handle it. She's my responsibility."

His eyebrows bunched together as he stared at her. "What about her dad? Isn't she *his* responsibility?"

Amy's chest tightened, her hands drawing into fists. How could she possibly explain that while she loved her brother-in-law and understood that he had an important job, lately he'd been breaking promises to his daughter and missing family dinners. She knew he cared deeply for Elaina, but he was neglecting her, all the same. Maybe Amy saw it because she knew the signs. Because she'd lived through it. But she wasn't eager to parade the pain of her own childhood, so she squared her shoulders and clarified, "She's my niece. And I won't let anything happen to her."

Jordan stopped short, and she nearly bumped into him. He faced her and bent until they were practically nose-to-nose. "Neither will I."

And as though that closed the door on any argument, he began walking again. She had to run to catch up. But there was a piece of her—infinitely small—that smiled at his announcement. She'd rather have a partner in this than not. Jordan wasn't the partner she'd have chosen— but when it came to her niece's safety, she'd take any help she could get.

In no time at all they reached the captain's office, received Michael's new suite number and arrived at the cabin. Jordan lifted his hand to thump the side of his fist against the white wood, but Amy grabbed his forearm before he could connect.

"What are you doing?"

The lines around his mouth deepened, his eyebrows angling down. "What do you mean? I'm knocking." He spoke like she was a child, and she glared back at him, wishing he wasn't quite so much taller than she was.

"Elaina might have fallen asleep. So maybe don't wake her up and scare her socks off by pounding on the door in the middle of the night."

With a frown and a shake of his head, he stepped

back and waved his hand in front of the door. "By all means. Show me how it's done."

Oh, she could show him a thing or two.

And she would...if Elaina wasn't in jeopardy and there wasn't at least one thug still free on this ship.

Rolling her eyes at him, she gently rapped on the door with the edge of her knuckles. *Bump-bump-buh-buh-bump. Bump. Bump.*

The door quickly opened, and Jordan whispered in her ear as Michael led them into the suite, "No fair. You didn't tell me there was a secret knock."

"You didn't ask."

"Hmm?" Michael looked up, his eyes wild and dark hair thoroughly disheveled as though he'd been running his fingers through it all night. He probably had. "Did you say something?"

"No." Amy gave the room a quick visual sweep, taking in Pete standing beside the closed door on the far side of the room. That had to be Elaina's room, and it was clear that Michael's bodyguard wasn't going to let a soul past. That, at least, unwound one string from around her lungs.

Michael's restless marching threatened to tie it right back up.

"Can I get you something to drink?" she asked, shooting a quick glance toward the kitchenette to her left. It had a not-quite-full-size refrigerator tucked between two lengths of Formica countertop. Each slab was bare save for a coffeemaker that could make only one cup at a time. "Water? Tea? Decaf?"

Michael's eyes were trained on the floor, and when he looked up again, they narrowed in confusion. "What?"

She glanced at Jordan, whose eyes mirrored the concern she felt. With a gentle sweep of his hands, he encouraged her to keep going.

She lowered herself to the edge of the chocolate-brown sofa. "Michael, why don't you sit down with me for a minute? Talk to me. Tell me what you're thinking." Keeping her voice low and even, she managed a half smile, which didn't garner any reaction from her brother-in-law.

"Michael, what happened tonight?"

He stopped pacing, slammed one hand on his hip and stabbed the other through his hair. "You were there. You're the one who told me."

Taking a deep breath through her nose, she let it out through tight lips, trying to formulate a line of questioning that would lead to answers.

She needed to know what he knew. And she needed that info now.

But she was going to have to guide him there.

Jordan cleared his throat from across the room. He'd taken up a chunk of space outside the kitchen area, leaning a shoulder against the wall. His arms were crossed over his chest but the relaxed angle of his neck made him seem...what? She couldn't quite put her finger on it.

At ease, maybe.

And somehow it helped her breathe just a little easier.

Maybe Michael picked up on that, too. He took a step, then paused. Then he sank into an overstuffed armchair.

"The man in the cell tonight," Jordan began slowly, thoughtfully, "have you ever seen him before?"

Shoulders slumping until his arms rested on his knees, Michael shook his head. "No."

Jordan kept his voice low and easy. "Had Elaina ever seen him before?"

"I don't think so. No. I'm pretty sure she hadn't."

Jordan scratched at his chin, his gaze going to the ceiling like he was formulating his next question. "Do you usually go on vacation with a bodyguard?"

The question made both Amy and Michael snap to attention, and she stared at Jordan.

"I'm just saying," Jordan continued, "Lybania's a high-risk area, so I'm sure you're provided with a protection detail when you're at the embassy or traveling in Lybania. But I don't know very many ambassadors who vacation on US soil with a bodyguard."

"We're not on US soil," Michael said.

Jordan uncrossed and recrossed his arms, his gaze never wavering. Silence lingered too long and too heavy to last.

Even the silent bodyguard in question shifted from one foot to the other.

Finally Michael put his hands over his face and sighed.

"I think someone is trying to kill me. And now they're coming after Elaina."

Chapter Four

Now they're coming after Elaina.

The words rolled around Amy's head and filled her with dread.

She shifted on the couch, stretching all five feet and nine inches of herself across the cushions to try to relieve the pressure at the back of her throat. It didn't help. Neither did closing her eyes.

The truth remained.

And, with it, the fear.

She knew about fighting and facing down the ugliest that the world had to offer. Her experience in the DEA had shown her the worst of what people were capable of doing to one another.

But in those scenarios, the ones needing to be rescued were faceless and often nameless. Their rescue was a mission, an order. She went in because it was her job. She cared about doing it well and gave her all to making the world a safer place, but at the end of the day, it was still just a job. It had nothing to do with her family.

But Elaina as the target of a kidnapping and maybe attempted murder? This was personal. Amy would protect her niece at all costs.

No matter what Jordan said.

And he'd had plenty to say while Michael had explained what he'd meant about the danger he and his daughter were in.

There had been death threats at his office in Washington. Letters mostly. But then there was a bomb scare. The DC police department hadn't found any sign of an explosive, but it was obvious that Michael had been spooked even as he tried to brush them off as extremists. Of course, the threats in Lybania didn't come in the form of letters or phone calls. There were no warnings, just attacks. He expected that in the field. But in the States? Not so much.

"The Department of Foreign Services officers said it might be good for me to get out of town for a while so they could investigate." Michael had looked up at her with pleading eyes like a basset hound, begging her to understand. "I probably should have told you, but I'd hoped it wouldn't be necessary. I thought we'd be safe on a cruise. I mean, we're in the middle of the ocean, right? And that's why I only brought Pete. I figured one guy wouldn't stand out too much in a crowd, and he'd get the job done."

The bodyguard had stood silently as Michael laid out everything he knew. And when it was his turn, Pete corroborated the story. "We didn't see any indication that there would be trouble here on the cruise."

The room fell into silence until Jordan eventually spoke. "Any idea who's behind the threats?"

Michael hunched his shoulders, leaned on his knees and shook his head. "The DFS is running through a list of possibilities, but given the tensions in Lybania, it's a challenge to narrow things down, especially since we aren't sure of their agenda. There haven't been any demands made." He rubbed his hands together, keeping his head low. "It's not unheard of for threats to be made against ambassadors, but since the assassination…" Then he looked up, staring pointedly at Jordan.

Amy stared at Jordan, too, waiting for a reaction. But there was no movement of his features, least of all the furrowed brow of confusion.

Her chest clenched.

A little over a year ago, a high-profile Lybanian terrorist had been killed. Shot by a sniper at five hundred yards.

And, as far as she knew, no one had ever taken credit for it. Right along with the rest of the world, she'd assumed that the Lybanian government had taken him out to destabilize the terrorist group.

But that look in Michael's eyes, directed at Jordan… it was knowing. Concerning.

"Have things in Lybania been unsettled since then?" she asked.

Michael shrugged. "It's hard to say. How do you compare mayhem to mayhem? The terrorists are fearless, and they have been for years. You know about those aid workers who were kidnapped a few years back—taken in broad daylight."

Jordan and Amy nodded. One of their mutual friends had been a relief worker rescued from the Lybanian terrorists by Jordan's SEAL team.

"The factions are growing—it feels like there are new terrorist cells every day." Michael sighed. "I thought the assassination might bring some peace to the region. And it did. For about a week. Now everyone is clamoring for power. Some seem to want American aid. Others just want us out of the Middle East altogether."

Jordan caught her eye with a tick of his head. His look spoke volumes, spelling out all the same concerns that she had and adding a gut punch to go with them.

They were most likely dealing with Lybanian terrorists who had tracked the ambassador to the cruise ship and sought to strike against him while he was relatively unprotected. But exactly what faction they represented and what they wanted—beyond Elaina—wasn't clear.

Which made the terrorists even more dangerous.

If she knew what they wanted, she could try to get it for them. Or at least *act* like she was getting it for them until backup arrived.

But first they had to get backup on its way.

Jordan beat her to the question. "Have you been in touch with Washington tonight? Do they know what's happening?"

Michael's eyes grew to twice their normal size. "No." His hands fluttered and his voice rose as he pointed toward the door beyond Pete. "I was too busy taking care of Elaina."

Jordan's hand gesture was low, nonconfrontational. "It's okay. But we need to let them know right away.

They can send the Coast Guard or get some help from the port at St. Thomas." It was less suggestion and more order. And Amy was glad it had come from the SEAL. Even though she'd been thinking the same thing, her brother-in-law could more easily ignore her, thinking she was overreacting. She was practically a little sister to him.

But there was something unyielding about Jordan that demanded a response.

Michael jumped to his feet, his gaze traveling to Pete and then back to Jordan. "I should. Yes. That's right. I'll make the call right now." He picked up the corded phone sitting on the end table beside the couch and punched in a quick code. "This is Ambassador Torres. Tell the captain I'm on my way to see him. I need to use his secure phone line." There was a long pause. "When did they call? They're still on the line?" He hung up without any warning and marched toward the door.

"My office just called for me. The captain's assistant was just dialing me right now. They're waiting on the line. I've got to go take this." With a hand on the doorknob, Michael said, "I'll be back soon."

But Pete marched toward him, then stopped short. "You're not going alone, sir." His gaze darted toward the bedroom door, the war with him clearly visible. He couldn't be in two places at once.

Michael held up his hand. "Stay with Elaina. I'll be fine."

Pete's eyebrows formed a deep V, and he crossed his arms. "I don't think—"

Amy stood. "I'll stay with Elaina. You and Pete go.

Just make sure that someone in Washington knows what's going on. Even if they can't get here right away, they can still do some digging for us, and maybe figure out who we're dealing with. Any new information could help."

Pete's stance relaxed, and he nodded. But Michael wasn't quite so sure. His grip on the door handle tightened until his knuckles turned white.

"I'll stay, too." Again, Jordan's tone implied a decided course of action rather than a suggestion. And while she'd appreciated it earlier, this time it made her hackles stand up.

"We'll be fine." The words came out sounding just as confident as she felt. Which wasn't quite as confident as she'd like. Especially when Jordan's eyes narrowed another fraction of an inch. He seemed to be questioning her abilities without saying a word.

And that wasn't fair. She was trained and fully capable. And, yes, a little tired. But that wasn't going to keep her from protecting Elaina.

She squared her shoulders and spoke to Michael, but her gaze remained on Jordan. "Go now. You'll be there and back before anyone has any idea that you were even gone."

Jordan gave a quick nod, and Michael and Pete disappeared with the quiet snick of the closing door. But Jordan remained. And even though he was silent, just knowing he was so close by scraped at her nerves.

Maybe it was her God-given independence. Perhaps it was her competitive nature wanting to prove her own abilities. It could be the way his very presence reminded her of her most embarrassing moment.

Her insides did a full flip. This was neither the time nor the place to think about how he'd made her a laughingstock in front of his whole family. Taking a deep breath, she pressed her hands together and tried to form an argument that would give her a moment's reprieve from his presence.

Suddenly it was there.

"What about Neesha? Do you think someone should check on her? If Dean and his partner know about Elaina, they might know she's part of a bridal party."

His posture whipped to attention, and she couldn't hold back a smug smile. She'd thought of something he hadn't.

"Right. Yeah, someone should make sure the rest of the family hasn't been targeted to get to Elaina." He pulled his cell phone from his pocket and waved it at her. "Call me if there's even a hint of trouble."

"I can't call your cell."

He looked at his phone like it had betrayed him, rather than being hobbled through a lack of cell towers on the ship. "Fine. Text me, then."

They'd all paid for the Wi-Fi service while on board—and it would cover their texting, too. "All right."

He stepped toward the door, but turned back toward her. "Be careful, okay? Stay alert."

She wasn't a rookie. And she almost told him so, but he interrupted her.

"There are a lot of people on this ship who care about

you." He turned away but spun back before adding almost as an afterthought. "And Elaina."

After she locked the door that he shut behind him, Amy let out a soft sigh and looked around the suite. It was furnished in the same muted colors as her own cabin. Only this one had three times as much space—and that was just in the living area. Two couches faced each other, and she checked behind each. Then she opened every interior door. The closets were empty save for the standard ironing board and hotel hangers. The kitchen pantry contained a small basket of pre-stocked food items.

Everything was in its place.

Which didn't account for the nagging sense of unease that was tingling at the top of her spine. But since she saw nothing out of place, she had to believe she was just being paranoid.

So she had laid down on the sofa and stared at the ceiling, waiting for Michael's return. Fifteen. Twenty. Thirty minutes passed.

But the low buzz of anticipation still hummed through her, and she pushed herself to her feet, wandering the room and checking the locks again.

She moved to Elaina's door and pressed her ear to the center. All was silent on the other side, so she turned the handle and opened it a crack. Elaina lay in the center of a queen bed, her arms stretched out to each side and her dark hair wild across her white pillow.

Suddenly a bump against the exterior door made her jump. It was soft, almost like someone had tried to muffle the sound.

She held her breath and waited.

Lord, let that be the creaking of the ship.

Something bumped again.

And the door handle gave a gentle jiggle.

Heart suddenly hammering in her throat, Amy ran for the door, peeked through the peephole and nearly swallowed her tongue. A giant black shoulder hunched in her view, the man's face turned away. She wanted to scream, but discipline held the noise in. He was clearly working on the electronic keypad as another shadow fell across the hallway behind him.

The dull thrumming of the ship dissolved until all she could hear was the rushing of blood through her ears.

They were back. They were coming for Elaina.

And Amy was the only person standing between them and the little girl.

Racing across the living room, she reached the far side of a sofa and shoved at its end. It didn't even budge. She leaned against the armrest with her shoulder and gave another hard push. Nothing.

The furniture was probably bolted down in case of severe waves.

She huffed and spun around, searching for anything that might not be screwed to the floor that she could use to barricade the door. The four chairs around the dining room table looked too flimsy to hold the door in place, and the wooden credenza along the far wall didn't even tried to hide the bolts holding it in place.

She gave another frantic spin. Made another desperate search.

Finally her gaze landed on the mahogany coffee table between the couches. Its legs were ornately curved, but the rectangular top was solid and nearly two inches thick.

Dragging it across the carpet, she stumbled, lost her grip and fell hard on her rear end. But she wasn't getting points for style.

All that mattered was Elaina and her safety.

After several attempts, she got the table into place and shoved it beneath the door handle. It sat at a good angle, but it wouldn't keep the men out indefinitely.

And then what? Then she'd have to face them. At least two of them. Maybe more.

She'd fight for that little girl until she died.

But then what would happen to Elaina?

She couldn't even consider it, so she gave the table another shove, smacking the wood against the metal handle of the door. The crack must have alerted the men on the other side, as they dropped any pretense of subtlety. A shoulder or foot slammed into the door without preamble.

She needed help. Fast.

She ran across the room and snatched up the receiver for the suite's phone. It was dead. No dial tone. Nothing. It had been working thirty minutes ago, so they must have cut the phone lines. Maybe the ones between all of the rooms. Maybe just this room. It didn't matter.

These men knew that Elaina had been moved to a new suite. And they'd cut her new room off from the rest of the ship.

Except for maybe Wi-Fi.

She yanked her cell out of her pocket. There was only one person she could think to text, so she whipped a message out to him.

They're back.

At the crack of the splintering door frame, she nearly dropped her phone. But the metal security lock was still in place and its rattle filled the room right along with the grumbles of one of the men on the other side. He cursed long and low in a language that was both foreign and somehow familiar.

As she sprinted toward the bedroom door, her phone buzzed in her hand.

Hide. Now. On my way.

She could almost hear the growl of Jordan's voice.

With each step she took, the lock rattled. The table shook. She flinched.

And getting to Elaina wasn't going to save her. Not if these men were armed.

"Break it down." The heavy accent couldn't disguise the man's sinister intent.

"I'm trying," his comrade said.

Just as her hand reached the cool knob of Elaina's room, wood fractured and Amy dove into the bedroom.

"Aunt Amy?" Elaina sat up in bed, rubbing her eyes. "What's happening?"

"Shh." Pressing one finger to her lips, she scooped the little girl up with her other arm and whisked her toward the closet. "We have to be very, very quiet."

"But—"

Amy pressed her hand over Elaina's mouth briefly and shook her head hard. She mouthed the word *quiet* and prayed that her niece would understand, even in the darkness that covered the room.

Elaina squirmed in her lap as Amy squatted inside the confines of the closet, peering through the wooden slats into the blackness of the room. For a moment the only sounds were Elaina's strangled breaths and fidgets and rustling.

Then came a grunt and something that sounded like a copper pot being ripped in half. The security lock had been breached.

Where are you?

Her phone lit up, bright enough to illuminate Elaina's wide eyes and quivering lips, and Amy hated the fact that she'd been forced to leave her service weapon at home. She hated that she'd sent Jordan away.

In the closet. Elaina's room.

Are they inside yet?

Almost.

Suddenly something crashed to the floor. It had to be the table she'd put in place. It was followed by more swearing and some stomping.

They'd given up even pretending to be subtle or quiet, either because they didn't fear the ship's security or because they didn't believe security would come.

Stay put.

She flipped her phone over, pressing the screen against Elaina's back to keep the light from reaching into the room beyond, revealing their location. But the men weren't in the bedroom yet. Their footfalls circled the living room as she pulled Elaina closer, tucking baby-soft hair under her chin. She pulled the phone away from Elaina's back to pass along one more message.

They're here.

Tell me everything you know.

A weight settled on her chest, and she had to fight for her breath. She knew what that meant. Jordan wasn't going to arrive in time. And he needed every bit of information she could give him.

Lifting Elaina into the farthest recesses of the closet, Amy whispered, "Stay put and stay silent. No matter what."

Elaina nodded, and Amy settled a plush terry-cloth robe over the girl with a quick prayer. "Lord, protect my sweet girl."

"Aunt Amy, too."

The hushed prayer made her eyes burn, and she looked heavenward with only one prayer on her heart. *God, save us. Please. Please. Please.*

And then she made her thumbs move as fast as they could across her phone, forgetting punctuation and spelling.

Two men at least
Wearing blck
Thick accent probably MidEast
Dark hair

Suddenly the bedroom door slammed open, and a dark form yanked the blankets off the bed, growling when he found it empty. "Where is she?" he yelled to his friend in the other room.

Not afraid loud

The man's form turned around the room then marched toward the bathroom. It was empty. Next he'd check the closet. She knew that without a doubt.

Amy had only one option. Abandon her spot and try to distract them to keep them from finding Elaina.

Leaving her phone at her feet, Amy stood slowly, taking several deep breaths through her nose and releasing them slowly, silently.

The rings on the shower curtain hissed as they were wrenched across the metal bar.

It was now or never. Her only chance.

But no matter how much training and experience she'd acquired over the years, her hand shook as she twisted the handle and pushed the door open. Stepping out of the closet, she closed the door silently behind her, pressing her back against the smooth wallpaper.

The heavy step beside her interrupted her prayer.

Time to go.

She launched herself at the man, hitting him well

below his center of gravity and knocking him back against the wall. His head cracked against the door frame, and he screamed.

But it didn't stop his meaty paw from slamming into the side of her face, setting off fireworks in her line of sight.

Suddenly there were two of him in front of her, and she swung at one, only to realize he was the result of double vision.

Then her arm was snapped behind her back, her shoulder blade wrenched as the man's companion joined the fray, wrapping an arm around her throat and tightening it. She sucked at the air, clawing against him, but even when her nails dug into his flesh, he didn't let up.

A kick to his companion as he pulled himself up from the floor didn't help. It only earned her another fist to the head.

The room spun and her already limited vision blurred even more.

No. No. This wasn't...

God, save Elaina.

Right before the entire world went black, she heard the wild cry of her niece.

Chapter Five

Jordan had never run so fast in his life. The muscles in his legs cried out for a break like they hadn't since his last week of BUD/S. And the wooden deck might as well have been beach sand for all the progress he was making.

He just couldn't move fast enough. He couldn't get from his sister's room to Michael's suite in time.

Risking a glance at his phone, he checked for another text from Amy.

She'd sent a string of texts, giving information on the men that had been only a few feet away from her. Armed and dangerous. And inside the suite.

And there had been nothing since then.

His mind immediately filled with images of Amy facing those thugs. She'd fight. She'd fight like a bobcat to protect Elaina. But as strong and well-trained as she was, the odds were sharply against her.

Had he given her a bad direction? Would she have had a better chance catching them off guard by attacking from the start? Or should he have sent her to hide elsewhere—would there have been better weapons available in the kitchen?

His heart skipped a beat.

He jumped out of the way of a couple meandering along the deck and hurdled a deck chair that had been left in the open lane.

God, let me get there.

Why had he agreed to check on Neesha and Rodney on the very opposite side of the ship? They were fine. Oblivious—which was just what he wanted for them.

So he'd taken himself out of the fight. For nothing.

Don't think about it. Don't dwell on it.

He had to keep reminding himself of that or he'd go crazy. He'd learned early in his training that if he got too far inside his own head, his body would falter. And right now, Amy and Elaina were counting on him to stay strong.

Snatching one more breath of sea air, he spun into a stairwell and bolted up the steps.

Around every corner and at every crossing, he expected to see Amy and Elaina. Perhaps it was only wishful thinking.

But surely they were being toted away from the scene.

And if they were, he was ready to fight for their freedom. His muscles tensed, and he made a stiff fist as his arms pumped to keep him moving. He was ready.

Unless she'd been...

Could she have been killed? Dean had been willing enough to shoot at her earlier. And while the men had mentioned capturing Elaina, that didn't mean they would leave her aunt alive.

Bile rose in the back of his throat as he raced down the hallway, mere steps from the ambassador's new suite. The one the captain had promised was secure. He was thirty yards away. Twenty. Ten.

So close. But everything was silent, save the droning of the ship.

There wasn't a nosy neighbor poking his head out of his cabin. No steward cleaning up. No security patrolling. And there certainly wasn't a peep coming from inside the suite. Which meant that Amy was gone... or dead.

If she'd been able to contact him, she would have.

His stomach heaved again as he crashed through the doorway, past the cracked frame and into the ransacked living room. He nearly tripped over a destroyed coffee table, two of its legs ripped clean off.

And then he realized what he was seeing. The table had been wedged against the door to keep the intruders out for as long as possible. She'd done just what he would have.

Good girl, Amy.

He took careful, silent steps around the carnage on the carpet toward Elaina's room. It, too, was silent. Only the signs of a struggle had been left behind. The ripped shower curtain in the bathroom. The overturned lamp. Amy's phone smashed as if it had been stepped on.

He knelt to pick up the pieces at the door of the closet, giving it one more cursory glance before letting out a loud sigh through tight lips.

"Elaina!"

Jordan jumped up and raced toward the cry, knowing what he'd find.

Michael Torres's eyes were wild as he surveyed the wrecked room from the doorway. When Jordan caught the ambassador's gaze, Michael flinched. "Where is my daughter? I... I didn't mean to be gone so long."

The pleading in his voice was too much, and Jordan could only shake his head.

"And Amy? Where's she?"

Jordan took a quick breath and blinked against a strange burning at the back of his eyes. "She's gone, too."

Amy woke, clawing at her neck, but the arm that had been there was gone. And her breathing, while rapid, wasn't painful, though a swallow nearly set her throat on fire.

She blinked against the light from above in an attempt to calm the throbbing behind her eyes and rose onto her knees. Grabbing at the lip of the metal panel on the wall, she pulled herself to her feet, swaying with the motion of the room. But whether the ship was truly rolling or it was all in her head, she couldn't tell.

Squeezing her eyes closed, she leaned into the unmoving wall.

And then it all slammed back into her. The attack. The men. Elaina's screams.

"Elaina!" Her cry was hoarse as she launched herself at the metal door. It didn't budge, even when her shoulder slammed into it. She crumpled to her knees again, hanging on to the handle that refused to turn.

Elaina. She had to find her niece. Now.

There was no telling how long Amy had been out or when they'd been separated. She didn't even know where she was.

With her eyesight still slightly blurry, she took quick inventory of the room where she'd been left. It was actually more storage closet than room. Two of its walls were lined with metal shelves at least six feet high. Big plastic jugs of pink and blue cleaners filled every inch of wall space, leaving about four square feet for her to maneuver. Just enough to spin around and find exactly nothing helpful. There were no tools, no exits and no phone on the wall.

Nothing.

She heaved a sigh and turned one more time, just for good measure.

The room smelled of disinfectant and seawater, and she immediately tried to figure out where she could be in the ship that would make the saltwater smell strong enough to push the odor of cleaning products to the background. But she couldn't picture it.

Suddenly someone on the far side of the door bumped against it.

Scrambling for a place to hide, she pressed herself into the corner closest to the door, nearly tripping on a metal doorstop. The door swung out to open, but at least she could be in the last corner they'd see.

And then what?

She needed a plan, but her mind was still cloudy,

still rolling with every wave. And the throbbing on the left side of her face was an ever-present reminder of the fist that had hit its mark at least twice. All the same, she concentrated on holding herself together, dealing with the moment.

Maybe there's only one.

Watch the door.

When he opens it, slam it into his head.

Great idea. *If* she knew for sure there was only one or had any clue what was waiting for her on the other side.

Before she could take another breath, she had her answer.

"What are you doing?"

The words were said by a nasally voice with a heavy accent.

"Checking on her."

And he had an American buddy, which meant there were at least two out there.

She gasped for a breath and held it, waiting for the door to open, trying to prepare her trembling muscles to fight back. But her arms felt heavier than an anchor, and when she brought her knee up in a practice kick, she barely managed to lift it to her waist. Everything inside her felt limp and weakened.

"The boss wants to see you," the first man said.

His friend grunted. "It can wait."

"They're on their way. He wants to make sure we're ready."

"We're ready," the American grumbled, but his retreating footsteps said that he'd agreed to follow his friend.

Which gave her exactly she-had-no-idea-how-long to find a way out.

She sank back against the wall, tipping her head up and whispering a quick prayer. "Lord, what am I supposed to do? I'm stuck. I'm sca-ared." She hated the way her voice caught on the word. Hated more how her chest tightened on the truth. "I'm... I need your help. I don't know..."

Her voice disappeared on a wheeze as her gaze landed on a square vent about two feet off the floor, its metal slats thin and dark. The shelves on either side of it had blocked her view before now, but it was there nonetheless. The whole cover was maybe a foot and a half wide, but she twisted her shoulders, already imagining wiggling her way into the ductwork beyond. It didn't matter where it led as long as it was far away from this cramped closet and the men who had put her here.

Pressing her ear to the door, she listened for any sign of their return. But all was silent except for a low clanging of metal against metal.

This was her chance. Maybe her only shot.

And she wasn't about to throw it away.

Diving for the grate, she jammed her fingers into the slim margin between the metal and the wall to try to pry the cover away, but the space was too narrow. Her fingernails barely fit into the gap, and they weren't strong enough to pry the metal free.

Running her fingers around the edges, she double-checked that she hadn't missed a screw holding it in place. But she didn't find even one.

She just needed something strong and slender to wedge the grate out.

She surveyed her options. The bottles of cleaning products were useless. She needed a screwdriver or a file or some pliers.

But her captors hadn't bothered to leave her a tool set.

Letting out an impatient breath through tight lips, she closed her eyes and tried to picture everything in the room. The only empty wall was the one beside the door. Where she'd stepped on the doorstop.

Perfect.

She lunged for it, swiping it from the floor and racing the two steps back across the closet. She prayed the narrow end of the wedge was sharp enough to work as she jammed it against the metal. *Please. Please. Please.*

Only the tip slipped into the crevice, and she wanted to throw it against the wall.

"Why won't you work?"

She slammed her fist down against the doorstop. It groaned further into place.

"Yes," she whispered, giving it another hit with the heel of her hand, which ached at the treatment. Then she grabbed one of the jugs of cleaning fluid and banged it against the doorstop, forcing it to make more space between the wall and the metal. And again. And again. With each strike the doorstop sank a millimeter. Just a few more and she could leverage it to open the grate.

Suddenly the voices outside the door were back.

"Why even bother to open the door? She's still

locked in there." The one with the Middle Eastern accent was still arguing against checking on her.

"I told you. We need to keep an eye on her and make sure she can't get away. She can recognize me."

His words didn't make any sense. Or maybe she was mishearing them beneath the wild tattoo of her heart to the rhythm of her internal mantra. *Quiet. Hurry. Quiet. Hurry.*

Any noise that made it through the door could give them real reason to check on her. But staying put and giving up on the grate wasn't an option.

"What do you really want to do in there?"

Oh, God.

It was the only prayer she could manage as her stomach lurched. If this man really felt threatened by her, and the idea that she might be able to identify him, then maybe he was looking for an excuse to come in and kill her.

She had to get out now.

With one final blow of the jug, the doorstop dropped into place. Grabbing the end of it, she pulled as hard as she could, jarring the metal vent cover away from the wall. It only opened up half an inch of room, but it was enough to squeeze her fingers into the crevice and pull as hard as she could.

The man with the American accent seemed to have heard the noise because he said, "I told you." Then the door handle shook.

Her heart leaped to her throat, its thundering beats surely audible even on the far side of the door.

But the door didn't open.

"Let me in," he said to his friend, who apparently had the key.

Please don't. Please, no. Hold on.

As the men continued to argue, Amy gripped the cover and pulled with everything inside her. Her arms strained and fingers burned as they slipped. *God, help me. Please.*

With one final wrench, the vent cover gave way with a flurry of dust. Slamming one hand over her mouth to keep from coughing, she gently laid the grate on the floor with her other hand.

Bending, she stuck her head into the open shaft. The ventilation system wasn't remarkable, only a tunnel framed in metal. But eventually it would open somewhere else. By definition, it had to.

And anywhere would be better than here.

Pulling back, she glanced down at her gear. She was still in the navy-blue sundress she'd danced in at Neesha's party. Although she wasn't quite sure how much time had passed since they'd enjoyed such a carefree moment, the fabric looked like she'd slept in it for a week. It was wrinkled and crumpled and the hem had been torn. And somewhere along the way she'd lost a shoe. It wasn't the ideal outfit for this type of escape, but she'd make it work.

It wouldn't have mattered if she had been in a mascot costume. She was getting into that vent and out of Dodge.

Suddenly the argument on the other side of the door ended with a resigned, "Fine."

It was followed immediately by the sound of a key sliding into the lock.

No time to lose. She dove into the metal tunnel, pushing herself forward and wiggling against the cold flooring. The metal bowed and groaned a bit, but she didn't stop, reaching forward and clawing her way deeper into the dimness. Her body blocked some of the light from the room behind her and there wasn't much ahead.

She couldn't tell where the vent was headed, whether it dropped off or took a sharp turn.

It didn't matter.

She scrabbled her way deeper inside, pushing with her feet and squirming. Just as her feet cleared the edge of the vent, the door behind her crashed open, slamming into the wall behind it.

"What the…" The man's voice faded away before returning with a full-blast string of curses. "Where is she?"

Amy couldn't gain much traction against the slippery metal without causing a ruckus, so her movements were slow—always, always with an ear to the men in the room. When they saw the open vent, they'd know where she was.

And she prayed they'd be too big to follow her.

Also that they wouldn't have a clue where to find the exit to the vent shaft.

"She was in here. I'm telling you, I put her here myself."

The sickening thud of fist to flesh reached her, and she cringed.

"Well, then, where is she now?"

"I don't kn—" Even with his thick accent, it was clear the instant he realized the truth. "There."

Amy gave up stealth for swiftness, scrambling as fast as she could.

Hurry. Hurry. Hurry.

The staccato tattoo of her heart seemed to beat in time with the words.

Suddenly a hand latched on to the ankle of her bare foot and jerked her backward, forcing her to give up all the ground she'd gained.

"Get back here." His growl was low and lethal, and nothing could have convinced her to stay where she was.

With her remaining high heel, she gave a sharp kick in the direction she hoped was his head. His piercing scream proved that she'd hit her target as he released her.

Feet still kicking, she crawled like she had through the obstacle course all those years ago, like there was a Marine drill sergeant screaming her name and her entire future rode on it. She'd done it then so that now—with her life really on the line—she'd know she had the ability to dig deep to find whatever she needed to escape.

Her captor's string of curses died off as she reached the point where the metal made a sharp ninety degree turn to the left, putting her out of his reach. Thankfully, she'd been right in her guess that neither of the two men could fit into the vent.

"Find her. Get her back. She can't escape!"

Fingers hooked around the corner, Amy pulled herself to the end, thudding against the metal wall, and scrambled down another dim corridor.

The voices of the men faded behind her, clearly angry that they couldn't follow.

Wherever she was going, she had to get there fast.

Elaina was still out there. Somewhere.

And that man—the one who thought she could recognize him—wasn't going to stop until he made sure she'd never recognize anyone again.

Chapter Six

The ventilation shaft took a steep dive, and Amy could do nothing to keep from picking up speed as she slid down. Curling her shoulder against her ear, she braced for impact a moment before she crashed into the wall at the bottom of the chute.

Readjusting her position, she flexed her right hand to ward off any numbness from the harsh impact and took in her surroundings. The wall she'd slid into was the top of a T, each side reaching out until it was lost to darkness. But to her left, the darkness was interrupted by small pockets of light, representing glimmers of hope.

She scrambled in that direction, slipping against the cold metal. After several long minutes, she reached an illuminated patch and discovered the source of the light. A wall vent was tucked into a small alcove, and there was just enough room to lie on her back and wedge her feet against the slats of the vent's cover. With a careful kick, she sent the grate crashing into the room.

A woman shrieked, but Amy wasn't deterred. She

slipped through the opening feetfirst and dropped to the floor of a small cabin.

The majority of the room was taken up with a queen-size bed; a pile of towels sat in the center of the duvet. A woman in a gray uniform cowered on the far side of the room, her hands covering her mouth and eyes wide.

"I'm sorry," Amy said. The words were scratchy at best, so she reached out her hand as though she could calm the maid's fears. "It's okay. I'm just…"

There wasn't any *just* about it. And there certainly wasn't an easy way to explain why she'd popped out of a wall. So she pointed at the door. "I'll go." But then she looked down at the grate still on the floor and scooped it up to shove it back into place.

"I think I should call my supervisor." The maid pushed herself out of the corner and squared her shoulders. Her voice was shaky, but she seemed determined.

Amy glanced over her shoulder and stared hard at the young woman. "Yes. You probably should." She wrinkled her forehead, playing out possible scenarios for a split second before adding, "But don't expect me to wait around to meet her. I'll be talking to the captain soon enough."

The maid only blinked in response as Amy made a dash for the door. But before she shut it behind her, she turned back for a little clarification. "Can you tell me where we are?"

"The bottom deck."

Basically steerage. Perfect. She glanced down at the gray dust that now covered her skin and most of her dress and tried not to think about how many people she'd run into between here and...

Well, here and finding help. And then finding Elaina.

She set off down the hallway, but in only a few steps she grew annoyed with the uneven gait from wearing one shoe. After ripping off her heel, she held it and ran.

The hallway wasn't crowded, but neither was it empty. Many people stared at her as she raced along the carpet. A mom pulled her children out of the way, and Amy tried to smile in response.

But she couldn't make herself feel anything but urgency. The pounding of her feet echoed a terrible cadence playing in her head. *Get there. Get there.*

But where was *there*? Where was her precious niece being held?

When she reached the elevator bank, she paused for breath and tried to wrap her mind around where she needed to go.

She had no idea where Elaina had been taken. She didn't even know where *she'd* been kept.

Glancing back down the hallway, she quickly mapped out where she'd ended up. And if she'd gone down at least one—but maybe two—decks within the air shaft, she couldn't have been held anywhere on the lowest level. She'd gone left and left again to end up on the starboard side of the ship.

The elevator dinged, and she paused her mental mapping.

Maybe she could find her way back to the storage room. Maybe not. But she couldn't risk it alone. Not when there were definitely men looking for her. She had to talk to the captain. And then she had to find backup.

And there was only one man on this ship she trusted to watch her six.

Jordan was ready to punch a hole through the wall.

So far, he'd been able to find no sign of Amy or Elaina. It was like they'd vanished. In the middle of the sea.

He jogged back toward the ambassador's second suite—the one where the abduction had taken place—hoping the security guards who had arrived after Torres was whisked away to his third cabin had found something Jordan had overlooked in the room.

Unlikely.

But he'd never wanted to be wrong more in his life.

As he rounded a corner into the final stretch of hallway, a bit of navy blue fabric fluttered and then disappeared. An image of Amy in her blue sundress—that same color—flashed across his mind's eye. Then it was gone.

Whoever was wearing that shade of blue seemed to have gone into Torres's suite, but there were too many doors—and a handful of guests coming and going—between his position and his destination to be entirely sure.

Perhaps his eyes were playing tricks on him.

No. That couldn't be.

He trusted his vision. He had to. His entire career was based on being certain that what he saw through his scope was true. His eyes didn't play tricks on him.

And if his memory wasn't faulty either, then Amy could be back.

His heart skipped a beat, and his feet kicked into a higher gear.

After weaving through pockets of other passengers, he finally arrived at the damaged door and stopped in his tracks.

There she was. Her long, slender arms were crossed at the wrist over her chest—one hand, strangely, held her shoe—as she made a slow circle, surveying the destruction for the first time in the light of day. Her bare feet turned in quarter steps. Everything about her, except for her eyes, seemed cloudy, subdued. Her bronze skin was almost gray.

He'd never seen anything quite so wonderful.

She looked up in his direction just as she completed her turn. Her eyes flashed open even wider. And somehow he was across the room and pulling her into a hug before he even realized he was moving.

"Amy." It came out as barely a breath as he pressed his cheek to the top of her head.

Her arms wound around his waist, holding him tight, as she pressed her face into his chest. "I'm okay. I'm fine." Suddenly she tried to pull away, but he couldn't let her go just yet. "I'm gross."

She wiggled free, but not all the way. He kept his hands on her arms, holding her near, sweeping his gaze over her to confirm she was there. Safe.

"I'm so gross," she repeated. "I'm covered in dirt."

"Do I look like I care?"

Her forehead wrinkled and then released with her sweet laugh.

But her humor wasn't enough to erase the memories of the night before. "I thought you were gone." His heart picked up and his voice nearly failed him as he relived the moment when he'd seen her smashed phone and thought for a brief moment he'd never see her alive again. "You *were* gone."

"I was." Her lip trembled for just a moment, but she bit into it hard as her eyes seemed to look right through him. "I knew there were two of them, and that I wouldn't be able to take them both down, but we couldn't hide forever. When he came into the room—" she swung her head toward Elaina's door and winced at the action "—I couldn't wait. Inside the closet, we were trapped. I ducked out when he checked the bathroom, and when he came back out I went for his knees."

Her muscles tensed beneath his grip, clearly recalling the rush of adrenaline it had taken to attack a man probably twice her size. And Jordan could do nothing but listen as he ran his hands down to her elbows and back up to her shoulders, squeezing gently, praying firmly.

God, let me catch whoever is responsible for this.

Her fingers touched her throat, drawing attention to the purple mark there. "The other man got his arm around me here." There wasn't even a tremor in her voice, and he wanted to tell her that he knew lifelong sailors with less gumption. But she seemed to need to say this, and he couldn't risk having her shut down.

"He clocked me hard on my cheek." Her hand moved to the bruise there. "I thought that was it. When I felt myself start to pass out, I figured they'd get rid of me on the spot."

He'd thought the same thing. But it wouldn't do either

of them a bit of good to say as much, so he clamped his lips closed and nodded, prodding her on.

She didn't take the hint. Instead the distance in her gaze deepened.

"What happened after that?"

She shook her head slowly and pinched her eyes closed. "I heard Elaina scream. I heard her, but I couldn't fight back. I couldn't get to her."

"Did you see her again after you blacked out?"

"No." She opened her eyes slowly. "I woke up in a storage closet. It was locked, and I heard at least two guards on the other side of the door."

Something like hope sprouted inside him. If he could get to where she had been held, maybe there'd be someone still lurking around or a clue to help their search. "Where is it?"

Amy's eyes flashed with something close to regret. "I'm not sure."

How could she not be sure? Hadn't she paid attention to her surroundings when she'd escaped? *Keep track of where you've been and where you're going.* That was basic military training. And Marines were better than basic. She hadn't been with the DEA so long that she'd forgotten. "Why?"

"I escaped through an air vent, and I didn't have a ready map."

There was a touch of sarcasm in her last words, and despite everything else going on, he had to smile. "Well, if that's the excuse you want to go with."

Squaring her shoulders, she stared him down as though she could read his doubts. "I *was* paying attention, but it's not easy to count off strides when you're crawling through metal tubing in a dress with one shoe." She held up her blue strappy sandal, and he was suddenly glad she hadn't thrown it at him. He probably deserved it.

"I'm pretty sure it was on either the second or third level from the bottom. I slid down a good section and ended up in a cabin on the lowest deck."

That made sense. "What's on those levels?"

"I don't know, but I thought the captain might be able to help. There have to be blueprints for the ship, right?"

"Sure."

She looked around quickly, like she was just now realizing where she was. "I thought Michael would be here."

"The captain set him up in a new cabin, and security was supposed to be searching this room for clues."

"Oh. Right. I... I should have realized that." Her mouth dropped open, her eyes blinking slowly for several silent seconds. He had a sudden urge to pull her into his arms again. To hold her until his heart returned to a normal speed. To reassure her that it would be all right.

But all the reassurances in the world couldn't make her safe, or return her niece to her side. A promise didn't guarantee an outcome. After all, his dad had promised that he'd be back at the end of his shift. He'd promised to be at Jordan's Little League game. He'd promised to take the family to the movies that weekend.

He'd made a lot of promises he hadn't been able to keep.

Jordan refused to do the same.

Some things couldn't be controlled, but some could.

And not making promises about the uncontrollable was one he could do. It hurt too badly to be the one left with broken promises.

Amy licked her lips in a slow, thoughtful motion, and suddenly her fear fell away. She shrugged and straightened. "We need to talk to the captain. He has to know what's going on on his ship. And we need to find Michael. I want to know who called him last night, and why he was away from the room for so long. It seems like too much of a coincidence for the attackers to come when he and Pete weren't there. And I want to know everything he's mixed up in. Something isn't adding up. We have to figure out what trouble Michael's in."

"Yes, ma'am." He gave her a mock salute, and she cracked a half smile before shaking her head. Yes, he was teasing her—but he agreed with her, too. He'd been thinking the same thing. Michael had to be their next step.

"And Neesha?"

Her words hit a gut punch. "You think she's part of this?"

Eyes wide with surprise, Amy shook her head. "No. Of course not. I just want to make sure she's safe. Did you tell her what's going on?"

He laughed, breathy and bitter. "I'm not even sure *I* know what's going on." But Amy's gaze didn't shift, and the intensity there held him in place. "She was fine when I saw her last night. But I haven't told her about Elaina—or that you'd been take-en." He swallowed the catch in his throat—the one that said if he never spent another night sweating her absence, it would be too soon—and tried to force a smile into place.

Amy's eyes narrowed for a split second, and he felt like a bug under a microscope, unable to hide from her inspection. And then she gave a small shake of her head and stepped back.

"Sure. No reason to scare Neesha. This is still her wedding trip," she said. He nodded in agreement. "And we're going to get Elaina back before Neesha has to know anything."

"But first, maybe we should find you some shoes."

She glanced down, and her grin flashed for a brief moment. "That would be nice. And maybe a shower and some clean clothes."

"And some water and a bite to eat." He flipped the tip of one of her curls, which was surprisingly soft. "And even a brush for your hair."

She swatted at his hand and moved toward the door. "I just need to be in something easier to run in. Easier to fight in."

"You think they're going to be coming after you again?"

"I know it."

She sounded dead serious and absolutely certain in a way that struck him hard in the chest, and he rubbed at a spot in the center as though he could soothe the strange ache. "What makes you so sure? They're after Elaina, right? They have her, so why waste time looking for you?"

She stopped abruptly and he nearly ran into her back. "I didn't tell you." It wasn't really a question, but there was a hint of surprise in her voice. "I wasn't thinking... The men guarding the storage closet. I heard them when I was escaping."

He narrowed his gaze and leaned in close like that might help him hear her better. "What did they say?"

"One of them—he had a nondescript American accent—wanted to get rid of me. He said that I might recognize him."

Jordan released a quick breath, wishing the tension at that spot in his chest would let go as easily. "Did you see him? See his face or any distinguishing markers?"

She shook her head hard and fast. "No." Then she chewed on her lower lip for a long second. "It was so strange. Of course I didn't see him. At least not clearly. It was dark, and his face was in the shadow, and I went for his knees. I only really saw his legs. He hit me in the head, so by the time I saw his face, there were two of him. Both blurry. Then I was out cold.

"Even then, why would it matter if I could recognize him?"

His stomach took a sharp dive as he rubbed his hands together slowly. *Think, Somerton. Think.*

But there were too many questions, and intel was sparse.

He took quick inventory of what he knew. Michael had received an unexpected phone call, and kidnappers had taken advantage of that to abduct his daughter. Elaina was still missing. Someone thought Amy could recognize him. And he'd be looking to silence her.

A shiver raced down his spine, and he tried to shake it off.

It didn't work.

The tingling sensation only traveled to his arms and down to his hands, no matter how tightly he squeezed his fists. It was a reminder that he was personally involved. But how could he not be?

She was Neesha's best friend. He'd known her most of his life. And he still had to figure out a way to apologize for the debacle at his aunt's house last winter when he'd so thoroughly embarrassed her.

Their lives were entwined. Amy was in danger. A child he knew was missing. Of course he had a personal connection.

That shiver didn't mean anything more.

He wouldn't let it.

Shoving aside his wayward train of thought, he circled back to the last place he'd been. Intel. He had to get some more information, and he had to keep Amy safe.

"Just let me get cleaned up," Amy said. "I'll be five minutes, tops." She made her way toward the door, but he stopped her with a gentle hand around her arm.

"Maybe you should stay with Neesha and Rodney."

Her eyes lit with fire as if he'd just insulted her momma. "You did not just say that to me."

"Listen, Amy." He let go of her arm and scrubbed at the dome of his head. "Someone's looking for you, and we don't even know who he is."

Her narrowing eyes had him second-guessing his tactic, but he'd started down this path. It was probably too late to back out now. "I'm only saying that these guys are armed. We're not. It could be dangerous." Man, he sounded stupid.

He was stupid.

And she didn't have to say a word for him to know she agreed with that assessment wholeheartedly. The pinch of her lips and lines between her perfectly arched eyebrows told him everything he needed to know.

Finally she took a little breath. "I believe what you meant to say was that you've been sniper backup for Marines before, and you'd be honored to do so again."

A bubble of laughter caught in his throat. The situation was the furthest thing from funny, but Amy was amazing and in the running to be his favorite partner. His swim buddy and best friend since SEAL training, Zach McCloud, was great, but Zach rarely jabbed at Jordan the way Amy just had. And he didn't even know he'd been missing out on it.

Amy was his favorite combination of whip-smart woman and stunning field agent. Regardless of the nine inches and seventy-five pounds he had on her, she wasn't going to back down.

Coughing back the chuckle, he nodded slowly. "Absolutely. That's exactly what I meant. I'm glad we're on the same page."

"Good." With a curt nod she marched out of the room, her back ramrod straight. Whatever light Michael would shed on this situation and whatever they faced, she'd go after it the same way, chin high and eyes focused.

They were both going to need that same determination to get Elaina back.

Chapter Seven

A̲my was a breath away from strangling her brother-in-law. She sucked in air deeply through her nose and released it slowly through tight lips, but the breathing exercise wasn't helping to calm her down. After fifteen minutes of questioning, he was still far too hesitant to share any information about the political issues that might have led to the kidnapping of his daughter.

"Michael, you have to tell us. You understand that Elaina's life is on the line, right?"

The ambassador paused in his slow pacing of the room and shook his head. "I know. But I don't have any information. Nothing that will help."

From his place propped against the wall next to the cabin door, Jordan caught her eye. His big body looked relaxed, but there was a fire in his eyes that promised her she wasn't alone in believing that Michael was lying to them.

"Isn't it possible that someone called you so that you and Pete would leave your room so they could come for

Elaina?" She tried to keep her voice even as she worked through the scenario in her own mind. But the pieces didn't fall into place.

"It wasn't about her. The call came from the State Department in Washington, and that's all I can tell you."

Jordan sniffed, quiet but questioning. "Do you trust the person who called you?"

Michael sank to the couch and dropped his head into his hands with a sigh. "I have no reason not to."

They were getting nowhere. And they were moving at a turtle's pace on the way.

Amy pressed a hand to her chest and tried to stop the fist that seemed to clench her lungs. When that didn't work, she stalked across the room, stopped at a porthole and stared across a mile of smooth blue. It was calm outside, but her insides held a raging storm.

It was Jordan who finally ended the silence. "What about the death threats that you mentioned before?"

She spun and stared at Jordan before letting her gaze jump to Michael, who looked just as surprised about the question. They'd covered this already.

Jordan scratched at the top of his head, right where his hair was growing back after a close shave. He worked his jaw a few times, his eyes looking toward the ceiling. He appeared to be mentally sorting through the same mixed-up puzzles she was. But maybe he had better pieces to work with. She prayed it was true.

"This person, who called you last night—" Jordan's gaze dropped to spear Michael "—do they know about the threats?"

"What does it matter?" Michael stood again and resumed pacing the length of the couch. "Why are we still talking about the phone call? Why aren't you out there looking for her? Why am *I* not looking for her?" He marched toward the door, and his mostly useless shadow of a bodyguard followed, but Jordan held up his hand to stop them both.

"We have been. We will again." Jordan's voice was smooth as silk, but there was a steel bar running through it, calm, collected, sure. "But if we're going to be able to find her and keep her safe, we have to know what we're up against. Who these guys are and why they've taken her will help us guess how many there are, how they're armed and how willing they are to die."

Michael's swallow was audible as his Adam's apple bobbed. "Why would they want to die?"

Jordan's eyebrows rose, his forehead wrinkled in waves for a split second. "Are you playing naive, Mr. Ambassador? You've spent the better part of three years in a country more or less run by terrorists. You know that terrorist leaders are able to cultivate a loyalty that will lead others to commit terrible crimes and willingly lay down their own lives in the process."

"But—but those are terrorists."

Jordan pointed his finger into the hallway and nodded. "They sure aren't candy stripers. And whoever they're working for has them convinced that human life is disposable."

Michael looked visibly stunned, like he hadn't quite realized the extent of the situation, and it made Amy sick. How could he be so smart, such a savvy politician and also so extremely myopic? It wasn't like him. It wasn't normal. And it was keeping them from getting the information they needed to rescue Elaina, which infuriated her.

She stormed past him, banging her shoulder into his just for the flash of pain in the process.

Michael jerked back, slapping a hand to the point where they'd connected, and she looked back to see tears welling in his eyes. Suddenly he fell to the couch, covered his face with his hands and let out a terrible sob. "They're going to kill her!"

"Who?" Jordan left the wall and nearly hurdled the couch to drop by Michael's side.

Amy couldn't seem to get her muscles to move. She stared in silence as Jordan asked the pointed question.

"Who's going to kill her?"

"I don't know. They didn't identify themselves. They were on the phone when I got to the captain's office, and they told me not to contact the authorities or call for help. Or even tell a security guard. I'm not supposed to tell anyone—especially not you." Once the floodgates opened, he seemed unable to stop, the words tumbling out without thought or order. "He said they have eyes on me, and if I did anything like that, they're going to kill Elaina. I'll never see her again."

The panic in his voice couldn't be faked, and it tore through her even harder than her own fear.

"Did they tell you what they want?"

"No. But they said they're watching me, and they have big plans for me."

"Big plans?" Amy dropped to the opposite couch and leaned forward, trying to read anything on Michael's face through his fingers.

He looked up from his hands and nodded slowly. "That's exactly what they said. I don't know what they want from me. I tried to get them to give up Elaina and take me instead, but they just laughed."

Jordan rubbed his hands together, his forearms still resting on his knees. "They must have something on the burner. After all, they're expecting someone else to arrive."

Michael jumped, jerking his gaze to Jordan. "Do you have any idea what it is they're after?"

"I don't. But they don't want you. They want to control you. And Elaina's the best way to do that. They know you'd do anything to keep her safe. And they're going to ask for the moon."

"I can't give them the moon. I can't give them anything." Michael's voice had taken on a panicked tone, and Amy reached for his arm to give it a gentle squeeze.

"It's going to be okay."

Jordan stood and laid a big hand on Michael's shoulder. "We'll find Elaina. You don't have to fear them."

Michael jumped to his feet, too. "I'm going with you."

"No, you're not. You're going to stay here with Pete. You're not going to let anyone into this room, and you're going to let those eyes on you think that you're complying."

Michael looked at Amy and suddenly reached out to hug her. "Be safe. Find my girl."

"We will." She marched past Jordan and out the door, letting it slam behind her.

In the next instant it opened again, and Jordan followed her with one final warning to Michael. "And don't talk to Neesha. If I find out you ruined her wedding..."

The warning died off as the door slapped closed again.

And then it was just the two of them in the hallway—well, them and a raucous family leaving their suite a few doors down. Amy ignored the others and stared hard into Jordan's deep brown eyes, trying and failing to read what he was thinking.

"What's wrong with him?" she finally whispered. "Why didn't he just tell us?"

He reached for her hands, his calloused fingers wrapping around hers. "He's afraid. Maybe it was the best he could do."

She ripped her hands free of his grasp and slammed them on her hips. "That's worse."

And it was. She and Alexandra had heard that over and over growing up. *He's doing the best he can*, their mom had said.

Well, his best wasn't good enough. Not her father's. And certainly not Michael's.

And neither was Jordan's. Not when he'd embarrassed her and then—on the date that he'd planned, as a way to make it up to her for the previous debacle—he'd left her waiting, her hair done and in a new dress that had cost more than a month's worth of groceries. He'd left her waiting for what felt like hours, every minute just like her childhood. Waiting. Waiting. Forgotten.

Jordan had convinced her once that she could trust him with more than a mission. And it was almost like he was trying to again.

She wouldn't be so gullible this time.

Instead she took a deep breath. "I'm going to find her."

"I'm going with you."

She shook her head, her heart battling with her head. She could use his help, but every minute with him was another reminder that she'd sat on her couch waiting for too long. "You don't have to."

His laugh was completely devoid of humor. "You're kidding, right? I know I'm not a blood relation, but I still care about her." And there was something else he didn't say, something that lingered in the air for a long moment and almost seemed to imply that Elaina wasn't the only member of her family that he cared about. But Amy didn't ask for clarification. She didn't want it. She just wanted to get moving, to do something.

"Maybe it would be better if we split up." She'd meant it entirely in relation to finding her niece, but for a moment he looked like she'd slapped him in the face, like she'd ended a relationship they'd never had.

He recovered quickly, and a sarcastic grin settled over his lips. "I thought you said you needed sniper backup."

"I never said I needed it." Wow, she sounded hostile. But how was she supposed to tone it down now when everything he did made her want to simultaneously throw her shoe—the high-heeled one—at him and fall back into his arms. Not that she'd liked his comfort.

She had not.

At all.

Except maybe a little tiny bit.

And later she would find that bit and extinguish it.

If he had been anyone else in the world, she would have expected him to put his hands up and surrender. He wasn't. He didn't. Instead he put his hands behind his back and leaned forward, towering over her just enough to make her blood boil. Again.

"Agent Delgado, I'll be your backup or your sidekick or anything else you want to call me. But I'm not letting you out of my sight again."

His eyes flashed, and her stomach swirled, and she wanted to scream—but she refused to show him that he affected her that strongly.

"As far as I can tell, we have two options." He ticked off one finger. "We can either attempt to find the closet where you were being held and pray that Elaina is somewhere nearby." Then he ticked off another. "Or we can see if a night in the holding cell has made our friend Eric Dean more talkative. I was thinking… Well, where would you suggest we start?"

"I suggest you quit pretending you don't have an opinion."

That made him laugh, rich and real and contagious. She couldn't help her own spurt of a giggle that followed. The tension that had made her neck stiff and shoulders sore was still there. But, somehow, by his side, it was a little easier to carry.

"I think we should start with Eric. I'd still rather know what we're looking for than what we're not."

"But Elaina—"

"Is still on the ship. They'd have to bring a helicopter or a boat in to get her out of here. And as far as we know, no one else has *arrived*." He leaned heavily on the last word, a reminder that the man who chased her had had information about the someone else who was going to join them.

Suddenly the disorientation she'd felt when she woke up alone in that closet returned, making her head spin and her breath catch. And Elaina had, or was going to have, that same experience. Or worse.

She grabbed his forearm and dug her fingers into his flesh. "We have to get to her."

To his credit, he never flinched as he gently removed her grip, one finger at a time. "Let's figure out where she is first. And then I promise—I'll do everything in my power to help her."

It wasn't quite the promise she wanted. It wasn't a guarantee of Elaina's safe return.

But maybe it was enough for now.

There was an inherent problem with the idea that someone was chasing Amy because he thought she could identify him when she really couldn't. It meant that someone was watching for them, knowing exactly what they looked like, while they could walk right past Amy's attacker and not realize it was him until it was too late.

It left Jordan to trail her across the ship and pray that they weren't spotted. There were only so many back passageways and closed stairwells they could take on the way to the security office. And if she was spotted and targeted first, her pursuer could be on top of them without a shred of notice. Or worse, he could take a position and get off a handful of shots before Jordan even knew there was imminent danger.

Jordan closed the distance between himself and Amy, his chest nearly touching her back.

She didn't slow down, but she shot him a sharp glare over her shoulder. It clearly said he should take this opportunity to back off.

He responded with a look that he hoped said that wasn't going to happen on his watch.

She picked up her speed, and he stayed on her six, trying not to notice the way her curls bounced with each step or her subtle vanilla scent as it wafted off her.

Before they rounded the final corner to the security office, the sounds of an argument reached them. At first the words were muffled, though clearly agitated. But as they turned into the hallway, the reason for the disagreement became clear.

"Where is he?" The short man had his back to them, but Jordan knew that voice, even in a growl. Staff Captain Xavier.

The other man was dressed in a deep blue security uniform, his hands clasped behind his back and facial features tight. He shook his head frantically. "I told you. I don't know."

"That's not good enough. You've been on guard duty all night." Xavier got into the younger man's face, stretching to his full height and wagging a finger beneath his nose. "How did you not see anything? He couldn't have just escaped."

Amy pulled up short, and Jordan nearly ran into her, grabbing her arms to stop himself from sending both of them to the floor. She glanced at him, and he nodded as icy fingers slowly made their way into his chest.

Neither the guard nor the staff captain had uttered a name, but they both knew.

Eric Dean—their only source of information on the kidnappers aboard the ship—had disappeared.

The security guard hung his head low. "I must have fallen asleep, sir. But I don't understand it—I wasn't even tired. I've worked every night since we left port in Miami. I drank my coffee like always, and I was fine. But then all of a sudden I woke up, and he was gone."

"Did anyone else come into the security office?"

"Only you, sir."

Xavier stabbed his fingers through his salt-and-pepper hair and growled low in his throat, just loud enough to carry to Jordan and Amy. "That's not good enough. We have people in—" He turned a bit and must have caught sight of them because he suddenly whipped all the way around. Lips tight and brow furrowed, he nodded at them.

Amy stayed rooted to the garish blue carpet, so Jordan stepped around her, reaching out his hand toward Xavier. "Sounds like bad news."

"I'm afraid so." His handshake was limp, his gaze curious as it reached past Jordan's shoulder and focused on Amy. "I'm... I'm surprised to see you here. I had heard from the captain last night. He said there was an issue. Mr. Torres explained..."

That explained the confusion on Xavier's face. He knew that Amy had been taken, and apparently he thought she couldn't handle a reminder, so he tiptoed around the subject. He didn't know Amy. And he hadn't counted on her resourcefulness and ability to escape. That was classic underestimating. Amy was tougher than most gave her credit for.

She was tougher than Jordan had thought, too. He'd known she was stubborn, of course. No one easygoing would have hung on to a grudge for a year just because he'd canceled a date and said something stupid in front of his family.

But Amy had.

Tenacious. Stubborn. The kind of woman who would crawl a mile through a nasty, dirty air duct to free herself and find her niece.

The staff captain had no idea who he was dealing with.

Suddenly she was by his side, her shoulder nearly pressed against his.

"Dean is gone?" she asked. "But where? When?"

Xavier shot a scowl at his subordinate. "We're looking into that. But we don't have any solid leads at the moment."

"Can we look around?"

With a small shake of his head, Xavier said, "It would be best if you didn't distract the personnel in there. We're still running a full security operation."

Not very well, as far as Jordan could see.

He had to clench his fist and bite his tongue to keep from saying it out loud. Amy was the one who rescued him from offending the staff captain.

"Do you have any indication where my niece may be? Any tips from passengers about strange activity?"

"No." His word was clipped, but something about the stoop in Amy's shoulders must have prodded him to elaborate. "But that's not unusual. Passengers on a cruise are so focused on the fun and the food that they don't pay attention to what's going on around them. I'd say at least three-quarters of our current guests are from cold-weather climates. They're just so happy to be out of the snow and ice that they can't see past the swimming pool.

"And the ambassador said he didn't want to alert the other passengers. He thought it might trigger the kidnappers, who could hurt his daughter."

Amy nodded. Jordan sighed. It was a fair cover story, but Jordan knew that Michael had been thoroughly frightened by the call he'd received the night before.

"But my team and I will keep an eye out for anything unusual."

"We'd appreciate it."

Xavier reached into his shirt pocket and pulled out a white card. "Here's my direct line. You can call it from any phone on the ship. If I don't answer, someone from my team will. Now, if you'll excuse me, I need to deal with…" He tipped his head toward the security officer still behind him.

Jordan led Amy back the way they'd come and didn't stop until they'd reached a secluded spot. Then he stopped her short with a hand on her elbow and leaned low to tell her what he was thinking, but she beat him to it.

"Something is way off here."

"I know." He scrubbed the top of his head with his knuckles. "How do you just lose a detainee?"

"And why was there only one guy guarding him?" Amy added. "There should be two always. Everywhere. That's basic stuff."

He nodded. In BUD/S they were called swim buddies—the guy you knew had your back no matter what. But the navy wasn't the only branch of service that knew the importance of working in teams. From schoolchildren to fire fighters to military people, they all employed the buddy system.

So how had an experienced staff captain allowed one man to let another escape?

It was a ridiculous question. "He didn't escape on his own."

"I know. Someone let him out." Amy worked on her lower lip with her teeth and twirled one of her curls around a finger. "My guess is someone laced the guard's coffee."

He'd been thinking the same thing and picked right up with her. "A double dose of ground-up standard sleeping pills would do the trick."

"Probably."

"Which means—"

She cut him off with the exact words he'd been about to say. "Someone on the inside is helping Dean and probably a whole terrorist cell."

"You need to be careful." The words popped out before he even thought about them. They were true, but they wouldn't have been his usual warning to his partner. But they were the first thing to pop into his mind.

Her nose flared and eyebrows pinched together. "Me? Why just me? You're not bulletproof, you know."

"Why, Amy." He fluttered a hand in front of his face and batted his lashes in his best impression of a Southern belle. "With all that sweet talk, I might start to think you really care."

She rolled her eyes at him. "Seriously, Somerton? We're about to go into a thicket of terrorists, and you're making jokes?"

"If—" The words got stuck and he cleared his throat before trying again. "If I didn't laugh in the downtime, I'd never get to laugh. And that seems like a pretty sorry life."

Her lips dipped into a thoughtful frown, but the corners of her eyes wrinkled like she was fighting a smile.

And suddenly he wanted that smile. Not just because it was beautiful—which it was. He wanted her to smile because he'd caused it. He wanted to make her laugh and see the light shining in her eyes because she liked being around him.

He wanted her to like him.

Not for his sniper skills or the Trident pin that marked him as a SEAL. Not for his bank account, which was pretty anemic, anyway. And certainly not for his face, which he'd been told by more than one woman was fairly attractive.

He just wanted her to like him for him, for Jordan the man.

The realization made his head spin, but there was no turning off the truth.

They'd been at odds for so long that he'd forgotten he genuinely liked her.

It wasn't as though he'd ever go back on his promise

to himself, though. So long as he had a job that put him in the line of danger, he wouldn't be in a relationship.

Not that he'd think about Amy in those terms, anyway.

But that didn't stop him from enjoying an interaction with a female friend.

He grinned hard, trying to get Amy to follow his lead. But she shook her head.

"You're ridiculous."

Was that a note of humor in her voice?

"You make it sound like a bad thing," he said.

"I do not." She didn't give him time to continue the argument, waving her hand to push the conversation behind them. "Where are we going? To find that storage room?"

"Sure. Do you have what you need?"

Her hand immediately went to her waist and the holster that should have been there. "I guess so. You?"

He smiled, commiserating—he missed the weight of his rifle—and nodded. "Same."

They took off for a back stairwell, moving silently and in sync, Amy leading. She kept a hand pressed the wall, balancing as they moved downward, quickly but steady enough to keep from drawing attention. Voices above them echoed across the metal steps, but they didn't see anyone until they reached the second level.

Amy cracked the door open and poked her head out, immediately ducking back into relative cover.

"What's out there?"

Her lips pursed to the side. "Staff. Housekeepers, cooks, busboys. All in uniform."

"Makes sense, I guess. We can't be far from the kitchen, can we?"

She nodded. "And I was put in a supply closet. Maybe near the housekeeping HQ?"

"Makes sense to me." He wiggled between her and the door and peeked into a hubbub of activity. Kitchen staff in their ivory jackets pushed carts of food toward a service elevator, jockeying for position with the housekeeping units barreling down the narrow hallway. A variety of uniforms hustled to their destinations, generally with heads bowed, focused on their tasks.

"It would be easy to be overlooked here, wouldn't it?"

"I'm sure that's why they chose this spot," he said. "They probably put you in a laundry cart, covered you with a sheet and strolled right past a hundred other people."

She shivered. "Well, let's try to blend in." Shooting him a glance that said it might be harder for him, she ducked through the door, and he had no choice but to follow.

He did stick out in the crowd—and not just because he wasn't wearing a uniform. His eyes were higher than the top of every other head in the hall. But at least that gave him a clear view of the general layout and the people packed into the buzzing throng. The air smelled of soap and bleach and a sharp fish dish that cut through everything else.

He bent to whisper in her ear. "Does anything look familiar?"

"I was unconscious. Remember?"

Right. Obviously. So what exactly were they looking for?

"The door was metal, and it had a silver-colored handle. At least, on the inside."

"Sure." He bit his tongue to keep from pointing out
that all the doors were metal with silver-colored han-
dles. It wouldn't be helpful, especially when it was
pretty clear from her slowly stooping shoulders that
Amy didn't have a clue where they were going.

He hadn't really expected her to.

But he'd hoped. For Elaina's sake. For Amy's sake.

He'd wanted at least a clue.

Instead they were going to end up empty-handed.
Again.

As they neared the end of the hallway, metal pans
thundered against each other and the din of voices
picked up.

The words jumbled together to make mostly nonsense, but Amy held up her hand and stopped so suddenly that the women behind him slammed into his
back. The maid immediately stepped around him,
shooting him a scowl and mumbling something under
her breath.

Jordan shifted Amy out of the main flow of traffic
as her eyes darted in every direction.

"I remember the sound of clashing pots and pans. I
could hear it in the closet. They were muffled, but I'm
sure of it. I couldn't have been far away."

He looked around, following her lead, but nothing
struck him as unusual or out of place. It was just the
ship's bustling hub.

"Well." He shrugged, only one ridiculous plan playing in his mind. "If you were down here, then maybe Elaina is, too."

"I hope so." Her voice barely reached him over the din, but her movements were sure. Before he could even tell her his wild idea, she'd implemented it, grabbing the nearest door handle. The door swung open, and an invisible cloud of steam swept over them. Industrial washers and dryers clanked and tumbled in the relatively shallow room.

As she stepped inside, she looked over her shoulder and silently challenged him not to follow.

They'd already decided that wasn't an option, so he ducked after her, checking every nook and cranny.

They poked into every open door and knocked on the few locked ones, but there was no sign of the storage closet. And no indication that Elaina had ever been there. Everything looked exactly as it should.

But they knew the truth.

This was only a facade covering something sinister.

And the sinister knew how to hide.

As they exited another empty laundry room, Amy sighed. "I don't understand. I thought for sure that we'd find something."

"I know." He wanted to pull her into his arms. To comfort her. As a friend would.

But somehow he knew that she wouldn't appreciate that, so he pointed upward. "Let's regroup and figure out our next steps. Maybe Xavier has some new information about—"

A sudden commotion at the entrance to the kitchen

jerked his attention away from her and made his skin crawl. Every hair on his arms stood on end as voices raised.

"I'm telling you, I saw her." The voice had an American accent, and Amy's entire countenance changed when it registered with her.

She whipped around and stared toward the man, but she didn't have Jordan's height or his vantage to look over the heads of the crowd.

"There are two of them." He kept his voice low and spoke directly into her ear, even as a shiver racked her whole body. "One blond and the other definitely Middle Eastern."

"Where? Where is she?" the blond man screamed in a high-pitched voice, pushing people aside and crashing into a service cart.

With closed eyes, Amy said, "That's him."

Jordan didn't wait for her to repeat herself. He simply spread his hand across the small of her back and steered her between obstacles.

"Where did she go?" the high-pitched voice said again. "Find her!"

The clatter of a bumped cart and the hollers of an angry housekeeper behind them threatened to steal his attention, but he forced his gaze to methodically sweep the path ahead. Back and forth, checking for potential hurdles.

Amy's pace picked up with each step, and he used his free hand on her arm to keep her pace more casual. "Don't draw attention," he cautioned her. "Not until we get to the stairs."

She gave him a curt nod, and he focused on following his own instructions. It was so much easier to say than to do with a man looking for her in the bustling crowd. The same with keeping his breathing even when his lungs wanted to burst and his body ached to make a break for it.

"Get over here. Help me out!"

Jordan risked a glance over his shoulder to see three more men join the blond. All wore jackets with conspicuous bulges. Even without his training, he'd have recognized that they each carried a weapon.

His heart lodged in his throat. This was not the place to take them on. It couldn't be. So he forced a warning past the pounding at his Adam's apple. "He's got more company."

She sucked in a loud breath, and he took it as confirmation that she understood. They were outnumbered, outarmed and in the middle of a ship full of defenseless civilians.

He couldn't afford for their pursuers to catch up.

The mass of people parted, and the stairwell door appeared to their left.

"Are you ready to run?"

"Always."

He gave her a little push. "Now."

She was running before he'd even finished the word.

And the shout that followed picked up right where he left off. "After them."

Chapter Eight

Amy slammed her shin into the first step and nearly landed on her face, but a thick arm around her middle caught her in time. Fire shot up her leg and she hobbled for several strides, drawing on all of her training to ignore the pain and push through.

Jordan kept his hand on her, pushing her forward and holding her upright, somehow relieving a fraction of the pressure that released a burst of flame with every step.

Not that she needed his help. But she wasn't going to complain or pull away. Especially as they rounded the next flight and the entrance door crashed again. Booted feet slapped against the metal stairs. The din of each footstep made her heart pump a little harder until she was gasping for air.

It didn't help. There wasn't enough oxygen in the Amazon to slow her breathing to normal. Her ears rang with the rush of adrenaline zipping through her system.

But there was also a quiet voice in her ear. "You've got this. Keep going."

It was soothing and calming, but he stopped at the same time as a hole burst out of the wall in front of her. Another quickly followed, and she ducked out of instinct.

"Nope. Keep going. As fast as you can."

Keep going. Keep going.

She just had to do it. She just had to keep her feet moving.

For Elaina.

The thought of what could be happening to her niece gave her another burst of energy. It was followed by a low chuckle in her ear. "Found something more, did you? Go. Go."

Grabbing the railing, she swung up to the next flight, only then realizing how damp her palms had become. But swiping them down her pants was guaranteed to throw off her rhythm, so she pushed through.

Suddenly the tenor of Jordan's voice changed. "This deck."

Which one was it? She'd lost count of how many they'd covered.

Jordan yanked open a door, pushed her through and rushed after her. Was there a chance that the noise of the door opening had been drowned out by the sound of the men behind them? She could only hope so, because the clambering had grown louder, proving that those men were gaining ground.

How could such big men move so quickly?

But there wasn't time to analyze. There was only time to look for a hiding place. And pray that the terrorists wouldn't fire into the crowd of sunbathers and revelers who packed the deck, soaking in the December rays.

Suddenly Jordan steered her into a small alcove. Lifeboats hung overhead, and for a moment, she thought he might boost her into one.

Instead, he pressed her against a wall of unforgiving wood and hovered over her, his face so close that she could feel his breath on her skin.

Her heart slammed into her rib cage as her mouth went dry, and she tried to look away, but there was nothing but him. Up and down. On each side. He surrounded her. Big and broad and ever the protector.

He made her feel small. Petite. Secure.

It was a feat few men had ever managed. Not when she wore a uniform. Not when she was five foot nine in her boots. Not when she normally carried a weapon most men had never fired.

She wished she didn't like the way he made her feel so much.

Even as she knew her body should be returning to normal after that run, her lungs continued pumping and her heart still beat rapidly. She bit into her suddenly quivering lip. But it wasn't just that that was shaking. Her hands and legs wouldn't stop trembling, either.

It was a lethal combination, fear, adrenaline and this strange awareness of the man in front of her.

He turned his head, likely searching for their pursuers, but it served only to highlight the line of his jaw. A day's worth of beard had grown there. It looked rough but somehow still soft. And before she realized it, she was reaching to run her fingers along it. Catching herself just in time, she yanked her hand back to her side as he turned to her.

"They're coming."

"Are we running again?" She hated that she sounded out of breath and confused.

He shook his head. "You saw those couples kissing on the deck?"

"Yes." She couldn't have missed them. Limbs tangled and lips pressed together, they'd refused to take their displays of affection out of the public eye.

And then it struck her, sending her stomach to her toes.

"You want to do that?"

"It's dark in here." His voice dropped until she couldn't tell if it was his tone or the words that scrubbed her nerves over a washboard and hung them out to dry. "We'll look like every other couple out there, like we just wanted a little privacy."

"Or we could take them head-on."

She didn't know why she spit it out so quickly. The idea of kissing Jordan wasn't *so* awful. She'd known him forever, and he wasn't bad-looking.

That's a big fat lie, and you know it, Amy Delgado.

Okay, he was better than not bad-looking. More like perfectly, classically, ideally handsome. Like he should have starred on one of those TV shows about special forces operatives turned cops.

But he'd also made a complete fool of her in front of his entire family a year ago, and then stood her up for the date that was supposed to be his apology.

"I'm going to kiss you. Right—" he peeked around the corner for a split second "—now."

Suddenly his hands cupped her face, tilted it back and his lips touched hers.

The entire world vanished.

If he'd surrounded her before, now she couldn't tell where she ended and he began. His calloused hands on her cheeks were surprisingly tender. While his lips remained gentle, there was an urgency in the connection.

It pulled at her, tugging her heart until it skipped a beat, making her forget how to even stand on her own feet.

Grappling with the wall behind her, she found nothing to hold on to, so she reached forward and grabbed the front of his black T-shirt. Her hands clenched into fists as she twisted the cotton fabric just to stay standing.

His arm slipped around her waist. An enormous hand spanned the width of her back as his fingers brushed against her spine. Pulling her closer, he paused for only the briefest breath, and she took advantage of it.

She couldn't seem to draw in enough air.

Her pulse raced and her head spun.

Beneath her grip on his shirt the beat of his heart felt strong and steady. It picked up speed with every thump until it was flying as fast as hers.

Then, without warning, he pulled away.

"They're past us now."

Amy's chest rose and fell like she'd just run a mile flat out, but Jordan wasn't out of breath. He gave no indication that the kiss had meant anything at all to him.

And her hands were still knotted into his shirt.

She dropped them, twisting them together behind her back and looking anywhere but at the perfect bow of his lips as she tried to figure out how she'd so easily forgotten they were even being chased. It didn't take long for her roaming gaze to meet his, and he popped one eyebrow in question.

But what he was asking remained unclear.

Are you all right?

Probably.

Was that okay?

Better than.

Do you want to do that again when no one's chasing us?

Definitely not. No. Absolutely never. Maybe.

Why was there even a question? The answer should be a given. She didn't like him. Everyone knew it. She hadn't even tried to pretend that they were on good terms, despite Neesha's repeated pleas for her to let go of the grudge.

But that was so much easier said than done. He'd humiliated her. And then, when she'd given him a chance to make up for it, he'd skipped their dinner date and hadn't even bothered trying to cover his lie.

Her fists clenched hard, and her blood rushed through her veins.

He'd claimed he was called up on a mission. He'd asked his teammate, his best friend, Zach, to call her to cancel the date. Of course he'd called her after she'd put on her new dress, applied thirteen coats of mascara, wrestled her hair into something resembling a French twist and sat on her couch for forty-five minutes.

And the rest of SEAL Team Fifteen? They were all conveniently still in San Diego. Probably right where Jordan had been that night, too.

In town with something better to do.

And she had spent that night alone and passed over.

She clenched her teeth so hard that her jaw ached, and she had to squeeze her eyes closed as she worked it out.

Jordan had treated her just like her dad used to. He'd made big promises—Disneyland, the zoo, even a trip to the mall to buy her a new teddy bear. And each time she'd sat on the couch and waited for him to arrive.

Every promise had been a lie. All of them.

And as a little girl craving her absent father's affections, they'd crushed her spirit.

But not anymore. She was a grown woman now, and she wasn't about to let Jordan do the same.

So why on earth would she think about kissing him again? For any reason?

Except that there had definitely been a connection, a spark, and she'd be lying if she tried to deny it.

She rolled her eyes at herself and leaned her head back against the wooden slats that made up the wall as he checked the deck again.

"They're definitely gone."

"Good."

"Did you recognize his voice? Was the American the same one you heard this morning?"

Her face pinched together as she thought about it. "I

think so. But it was noisy in the service area. Still, how many Americans can be chasing me?"

His lips pursed, and he scraped his fingers along his beard, the low rasping a reminder that she hadn't taken advantage of maybe her only chance to do the same.

Don't think like that.

"Those men are looking for you. Now." Jordan pulled her from her wayward thoughts, his eyes crinkling at the corners as he frowned.

"You just figured that out, Somerton?" The question popped out before she even realized she wanted to ease his concern. She swatted at his arm, and like lightning he caught her fist in his own. Mouth suddenly dry, she croaked the rest. "I thought you were top of your class."

Without even acknowledging that he still held her hand captive, he said, "If they came for Elaina, they knew she was part of a wedding party."

A brick sank to the bottom of her stomach. Couldn't they just go back to the kissing? Even her own internal battle on that was better than trying to understand what these terrorists were after.

"Maybe they knew you were connected to Elaina."

She pinched her lips together. "They saw us together. Yesterday—was that just yesterday? When Eric Dean chased us. He saw us."

"Right. But what about before that?"

"Before the cruise?"

He nodded, and some of the mixed-up puzzle pieces in her mind began to fall into place. Or, at least, they fell into the correct piles. And sorting them might be half the battle.

"So what? They're not targeting Elaina because of me—it's Michael they're after."

Jordan released her hand and waved a finger in the air to keep her attention. "Stay with me on this. They captured Elaina because of Michael but they captured you, too. Why? Just because you were with her?"

"Right. Why else?"

"Because you could identify one of them."

Puzzle pieces scattered again, and she let out a slow breath. "I'm not following you."

"I assumed when you said you'd overheard a man say you could identify him that he thought you'd seen him when you and Elaina were taken last night."

"That's right."

He shook his head. "What if that's wrong?"

"Jordan, you're not making any sense."

"I'm sorry." He took a deep breath, and when he spoke again, his words were slow, almost methodical. "These men have shown they're not afraid to fire their weapons on this ship. They're clearly familiar with it and have hiding places. If you were just another hurdle between them and Elaina, why keep you around? Why not just kill you and get rid of your body?"

She blinked and sucked in a quick breath. "I have no idea."

"They're chasing you now. But what if they were always chasing you?"

A deep throbbing began behind her left eye and she pressed her fingers against it in a vain attempt to relieve some of the pressure, only remembering the bruise that swept across her face when she accidentally pressed too hard against the tender spot.

"What if Elaina wasn't the only target?" he said.

She held up one finger as her stomach took a spectacular nosedive. Pressing her other hand to her lips, she squinted at him and shook her head before asking a question she sure didn't want to know the answer to. "What makes you ask that?"

He answered it with another question of his own. "Was the man you heard in the storage closet one of the men that took you and Elaina last night?"

With a tight-lipped sigh, she shook her head. "How would I know? It was dark. I was hiding in a closet for most of it. And even when I came out, there weren't any lights on in the bedroom. I never got a good look at their faces."

"But did either of them have an American accent?"

Forcing herself to relive some of the worst moments of her life, she closed her eyes and let the scene play out. Big men. Loud. They crashed through the door. They spoke. One in broken English, the other was better at it. Their words played along, the soundtrack of her memory marked by Elaina's frightened breaths and the grasp of her little hands on Amy's arm as they sat on the floor of the closet.

But there was no born-and-raised American. None.

Her eyes flew open. "No. They weren't American. Not the ones last night." Her breath caught on a half sob as the truth struck home. "So how could I recognize someone who wasn't there?"

"Exactly. He thinks you'll recognize him from some-where else."

"But where?"

Jordan could tell the exact moment Amy realized that this situation wasn't what they'd thought it was. Her face went pale, turning her gorgeous bronze glow into a faded painting, and her eyebrows nearly met in the middle of her forehead.

They were in trouble. And if it was tied to someone Amy would recognize from her work, then that meant it was DEA kind of trouble. But how did that connect to Michael and Elaina?

Amy was clearly lost in thought, pressing her fin-gers to her lips. The reminder that his lips had been there only a moment before was like a kick in the shin.

Was he going to remember that kiss—the way she'd clung to him and all of his senses had shut down except touch—every time he so much as looked at her lips?

No. No he was not. He had been trained better than that.

He was disciplined and controlled. And he would not lose his mind over a simple kiss with a woman who fit in his arms like she'd been made to be there. A woman who kept up with his every step. A woman smarter than he'd given her credit for.

She was tough and strategic and fearless. And when she twisted a strand of her hair around her finger, she was immensely feminine.

He looked away from the shiny lock of hair and tried not to remember how it had felt to thread his fingers through it only moments before.

She bit her lower lip, her white teeth pressing into the fullness there, and his head spun.

This was bad. So bad.

Concentrate. He only had to concentrate on the mission. And this Christmas cruise had certainly become one.

He cleared his throat, not trusting his voice, and tried to get his mind back on track. "So maybe this has something to do with both you *and* Michael."

"But what? Elaina is basically our only connection. I rarely talk with him these days, except to check on her or plan a visit." She crossed her arms over her chest, and her forehead wrinkled in a look that he was coming to recognize. "I mean, last night it sounded like you'd spent more time with him this year than I have."

The training that had eluded him a moment before kicked in hard. He clamped his mouth closed and stared straight ahead.

She was asking why Michael, the Lybanian ambassador—not Michael, her brother-in-law—had recognized him.

And he couldn't say a word. He couldn't explain how bad he felt that he'd had to cancel their date because he'd been sent wheels up with another team in need of sniper. He wasn't free to talk about that mission or the Lybanian terrorist who had been threatening the lives of dozens of Americans and hundreds of Lybanian nationals.

"I'm sorry. I can't tell you why that is."

Her eyes narrowed, but her voice remained laid-back. "You say that a lot, don't you?"

"What?"

"That you can't talk about things."

There weren't words to explain. That mission and so many others were classified. He wasn't ever at liberty to talk outside of his team about where he'd been or where he was going.

And maybe as long as he had to keep his secrets, he'd never be able to convince her that he hadn't meant to stand her up that night.

Finally he shrugged. "It's always true."

She rolled her eyes and pushed away from the wall, cutting the distance between them in half. He held his ground and didn't back up or look away. But he forced himself not to think about how sweet she smelled this close to him.

"Listen," he said. "I get that for whatever reason you don't want to believe me, but—"

She raised her hand and slashed it in front of him. "We don't have time to hash out your lies and secrets."

Lies? He wanted to yell that he'd never lied to her. Ever.

But before he could, the phone in his pocket chirped.

Where are you? Have you seen Amy? She's supposed to be at the spa with us!!!! And she's not answering her room phone or returning my texts!!!!!!!

"It's Neesha. She seems upset. Lots of exclamation points and no emojis."

Amy's jaw dropped open, and she wrung her hands. "I forgot. It's the girls' day at the spa. She'll be worried about me."

"Yeah. Apparently she's been texting you."

Amy held up two empty, helpless hands. "My phone is gone."

"I know. I saw what was left of it."

"I… I need to see her. She has to know what's going on. It was one thing to keep her in the dark when we thought they were just after Elaina. But now that we know they're looking to capture me, too… If they go after her looking for me, she won't be safe. She needs to know to protect herself." Amy took a step toward the deck and the sunlight that had shifted to reach its fingers into their little haven. "But…"

But they needed to find Elaina before whoever was arriving arrived.

She didn't even have to speak the words aloud. He knew they needed to split up—him to continue the search and her to warn Neesha. And if he couldn't tell her every story and reveal every secret, then at least he could continue where she wasn't able. Even if he'd much rather the two of them stayed together, and everything inside him screamed that he shouldn't let her out of his sight.

But he had to trust her. Because even when she'd been taken, she'd figured out a way get back to him.

He just prayed she wouldn't have to again.

"I'll go find Michael and get to the bottom of whatever you have in common—whatever would make them go after both of you."

The very thought gave him heartburn, and he pressed a fist against his chest to stem the flow. Usually he could control his body's reactions on a mission.

But he'd been able to control exactly nothing when it came to Amy Delgado.

"Okay. But you won't go after Elaina alone, right?"

"I won't. Where do you want to meet back up? When?"

He looked toward the bow and then the stern, picturing the ship's layout and trying to choose a relatively safe place. "What about Michael's second suite, where you were taken last night? There's no real reason for the tangos to come back to that spot. Plus there's still plenty of security buzzing around."

"All right. I'll see you there." She looked at her watch. "Forty-five minutes."

He nodded, peeked out of the alcove to be certain their pursuers were long gone and ushered her into the crowd.

His hand was still at the small of her back, and he looked down into her eyes. They nearly glowed beneath the sun's rays, but he couldn't even begin to read her thoughts. The relaxed line of her jaw was either a facade or a testament to her experience and strength.

Finally, they had to part ways. Before he knew what he was doing, he bent and pressed a kiss to her cheek, which was like satin. "Be careful."

Her eyes flashed with something, but it was gone before he could read it. Then in a quiet voice she said, "You, too." She turned to go, but caught his arm before he'd fully turned away. "Forty-five minutes."

"I'll be there."

Chapter Nine

Jordan set off for the ambassador's current room, his senses on alert and a strange sensation in his chest. It felt oddly like fear, but not for himself. It wasn't about failing the mission—or really about the mission at all.

Something deep inside him wanted to give the feeling a name, but something more experienced promised that that would be a terrible mistake.

And then, before he knew it, his mother's face flashed before his eyes. He approached a row of deck chairs facing the swimming pool and nearly stumbled into them, pausing to catch his breath.

The memories were almost twenty-five years old. The knock on the door and the uniformed Charleston PD officer holding his hat in his hand. *Ma'am, I'm so sorry. There's been a shooting. Officer Somerton's been killed.*

His mom had dropped to the floor as if the words had hit as hard as any bullet ever could, tears streaming down her face.

Jordan had hidden beneath the kitchen table. He'd pressed his hands over his ears so he wouldn't have to hear about the man who had tried to shoot his girlfriend but who had killed Jordan's father instead. His dad had been on a routine domestic disturbance call, and it had cost him his life.

At the time, all it meant to Jordan was that his dad wasn't going to come to his baseball game. They weren't going to the movies together. And he wasn't coming home. Ever.

But in the following months it had become clear that it meant so much more. It had meant his mom couldn't make it out of bed to feed him before school. Still wasn't out of bed when he came home. Forgot to wash herself and gave up trying to care for him.

That's when he began to realize that death could be so much more than sadness and grief. Sometimes death stole the living, too.

Jordan thanked God for Aunt Phyllis, who had swooped in all those years ago and given him a place in her loud and wild home, free from the grip of depression and the stink of the unwashed.

And that was why Jordan didn't get serious with girls.

He refused to be the reason a woman received a visit from a navy chaplain. He wouldn't ever put his wife through that.

So as long as he was on the teams, he wasn't going to have a wife. He couldn't.

No matter what this strange pressure in his chest suggested.

He took another shaky breath, glad he'd made it down a level and to the port side of the ship without incident. Somewhere between the alcove and the cabin, he'd gotten lost in memories of his mother and in questions he'd never asked himself before. Was the trade-off worth it? Would he rather be a SEAL than be in love?

And there was no doubt in his mind that Amy was the reason he was even contemplating such thoughts.

If ever there was a woman worth giving up everything for, she would be the one.

This train of thought did him no good, and he tried to excise it by pounding on the door of room. But as soon as he realized how ominous that knock sounded, he cringed. Maybe he should have employed the secret knock Amy had used before.

As it was, the light on the other side of the peephole went dark for a moment, then a low voice asked, "What do you want?"

"It's Jordan." Not that Pete hadn't seen for himself. "I need to speak to the ambassador."

All was silent for a long minute, and Jordan passed the time by taking a moment to really survey the row of rooms that lined the hallway and covering a jaw-cracking yawn.

Scrubbing his hand down his face, he pushed fatigue to the back of his brain and tried to focus on the layout before him. A potted palm tree in the corner was decked with white twinkle lights in a nod to the holiday season. And every door had a small wreath attached to it.

A twenty-foot evergreen dressed in its finest ribbons and bows had filled the grand foyer. He rolled his eyes

just thinking about it because ships were not supposed
to have foyers. They were supposed to have flight decks
and mags for storing weapons and ammunition.

But Neesha had wanted to be married on a Christmas cruise, so she'd chosen a floating ship of frivolity.
Only it wasn't quite so frivolous now.

He stared at the dancing lights on the tree for another
second before he realized that one of the lights never
wavered. And it wasn't the same soft white as the others. It was more yellow and unblinking.

Strolling toward it, he nodded to a gray-haired couple
holding hands and whispering as they wandered down
the passageway. As he drew closer to the plant, he realized why the light wasn't flashing. It wasn't part of
the decorative strand at all. It was attached to the wall
about at his eye level.

A security camera.

Well, how many of these were hidden around the
ship? And what had the security team seen that they
hadn't shared?

"Petty Officer?"

He turned toward the ambassador, who leaned warily
out of his doorway. "Just looking at the tree," Jordan
said as he marched back to Torres. "I need to speak
with you about Amy."

"Has she been taken again?"

"No." At least, he hoped not. He told himself that
she'd be fine getting to Neesha. And if she ran into trouble, she could handle herself. "But I think that whoever
took your daughter has a connection to Amy, as well."

Torres waved him inside and pointed to the striped

sofa in the living room. "How can that be? I'm sure this is all related to those death threats I was getting in Washington. Amy had nothing to do with them. She didn't even know about them." Plopping onto the opposite couch, he ran his fingers through his hair until it stood on end. "Has there been any sign of Elaina?"

"No. We scoured the service area near the kitchen, and there was no indication she'd been there. But we did run into someone who we believe was one of the attackers. Someone with an American accent. It seems he thinks Amy can recognize him."

"But Amy's okay?"

Jordan squinted. "She's fine. She's checking on Neesha and the bridesmaids." Running his palms down the legs of his jeans, he took a breath and tried to find the right questions to ask. "Why would someone targeting your daughter be afraid that Amy could recognize them?"

Torres shrugged one shoulder. "I have no idea. Could it be a coincidence?"

"No." He didn't bother with explanations. He also didn't bother believing in coincidences. It never paid off.

"Then I have no idea. I hadn't seen Amy in months until this cruise. We talked maybe six times all year, and that was mostly because I answered the phone when she was calling for Elaina."

"Mostly?" Jordan latched on to the innocuous word. "When was it not that?"

Michael's face puckered, and he stared at the ceiling. "When...when...when I met her team to thank them for the drug bust."

"Drug bust?" Jordan's stomach clenched and twisted, and he rubbed suddenly antsy hands together. Why had no one thought to mention a drug bust?

"Amy's team was working a drug smuggling case. Big shipments were coming through crates at the San Diego harbor—almost four hundred pounds of heroin."

"So, why were you there?" Jordan asked.

"The shipments originated in Lybania, and several of the men detained with the shipment were high-level Lybanian terrorists." Michael leaned his elbows on his knees, seemingly hesitant to share more, but after a look at Jordan, he continued, "The State Department thought it would be helpful for me to be there. After they were booked, I stopped by to thank the DEA team for their hard work. Amy and I spoke for about three minutes."

Did he even hear the words he was speaking? "You just said that Amy stopped four hundred pounds of heroin from hitting US streets."

Torres nodded.

"And you don't think someone was mad that almost three hundred million dollars of funding for their terrorist activities just went down the tubes?" Jordan had to struggle to keep his voice calm. Yelling wouldn't do any good. "Do you know what kind of arms a terrorist cell in Lybania could buy with that kind of money?"

Realization washed over Torres in visible and audible ways. First his face turned white and then he groaned. Finally he stood and paced the confines of the room. "Did they take my Elaina because of Amy? To get back at her?"

"I don't think so." Jordan stood so he didn't have to

look up at the ambassador but stayed rooted in his spot between the couches. "But I wouldn't ignore the connection to that bust, either."

Through his hands covering his face, the ambassador said, "What are we going to do?"

They needed help. But this cruise ship—an older one in the fleet—wasn't equipped with cell phone service. Calling from the room phone could alert the terrorists, too. And even if they could call for help, there was no guarantee that a ship was anywhere nearby. It could take hours to scramble help.

And they might not have hours.

"We need to get help and fast."

Torres nodded, his face grim with understanding. "Maybe they're not watching you?"

Jordan didn't hold out much hope, but he pulled his phone from his pocket, swallowing the dread that came with what he saw. "I'm not connected to the internet." He had been. Just fifteen minutes ago, he'd gotten the message from Neesha. But now his internet connection had been severed. And he'd wager that was the case for everyone else on the ship. They'd been cut off.

Torres snatched up his phone and confirmed the same. "I checked my email earlier, but now nothing."

But why do it now? Why would the terrorists alert everyone on the ship to their presence? And if they were finally ready to play their hand openly, what would that mean for Elaina?

He couldn't stand still a moment longer and paced the length of the sofa. It took exactly two and a half steps to go from armrest to armrest, then he spun and repeated his motions. At least it was movement, and maybe it would be enough to get his brain going, to think through what needed to be done, what he should do next.

"How helpful has the captain been to you?" he asked.

"Very." Torres drew his dark eyebrows into a single line, and he scratched at his chin. "He's given me three different cabins."

But somehow the terrorists still knew where to find Elaina.

"He sent a security officer by here a few times to check on the ambassador, too."

Jordan nearly jumped when Pete piped up. He'd nearly forgotten the big man was standing in the corner. He wasn't the most talkative or quick thinking of bodyguards. But he did seem to care about Michael and Elaina, which was a key part of the job description.

"And he offered me free use of his office and his secure phone," Torres added.

"Which you can't use again without alerting someone to that fact—if the phone is even working."

Torres looked up from where his gaze had been trained on the floor, his eyes darting in Pete's direction and then to Jordan. "You think that's been taken out, too? Have we been cut off? Why now?"

"Good question." And there was only one answer he could come up with. "I believe something is going to happen that will absolutely draw the attention of everyone on this ship, and they can't afford for word to get out about what's happening."

"But if we're cut off, how can we get help?"

Jordan shook head and stared at the ceiling. "The cruise line will be tracking us, and if we're sent off course for any unexplained reason, they'll alert the Coast Guard."

"But what if we're not off course?" Pete asked.

"We might be. We can pray that we will be. If I can find someone to help us, I will. Until then, you need to stay safe until we reach St. Thomas."

Sure, that sounded well and good, but he was still unarmed and facing a threat he didn't fully understand. More terrorists kept popping up. Elaina was still missing, and he couldn't afford for her to wind up in the middle of some cross fire.

But he had a suspicion that the hidden security cameras might have some useful information.

Marching toward the door, he stopped only when Torres called his name. "Where are you going?"

"I need to check in with the staff captain. I have some security questions for him."

"What should I do?" The ambassador's voice wobbled just a hint, betraying the diplomatic facade he so carefully kept in place.

"Stay put." Jordan looked back just before swinging open the door. "And pray."

Chapter Ten

Amy pulled Neesha into a hug, but that didn't stop the bride from squealing in front of the crowded spa. "Where have you been? You're two hours late, and I've been texting you all morning. We've already gotten our toes done." She held up her hand and wiggled her fingers. "And we're about to get our nails done. Sit. Sit."

Neesha was at least a few rings outside of bridezilla territory, but that didn't mean she didn't know what she wanted and where she wanted her attendants at all times on this cruise.

One of the staff members, wearing a purple smock and a kind smile, put her arm around Amy's back. "We'll get you taken care of."

"No. I can't stay. I have to meet—"

Neesha's pursed lips turned into a true frown. "What do you mean you can't stay? This is my wedding cruise. I want my best friends surrounding me, getting pampered with me. The wedding is in two days. Don't you want to look your best?"

"I do but..."

The eyes of the five other bridesmaids followed her every move, and they hung on her every word. This was not the time or the place to explain about the kidnapping. But convincing Neesha to step away from the spa would be almost impossible.

"Wait, you said you have to meet up with someone." Neesha's eyes grew wide, long lashes fluttering with excitement. "Did you meet someone? I told you it could happen anywhere."

"No." And then her memory flashed every sweet sensation of Jordan's kiss, and her entire body shivered.

"Who is it?" Camille, another one of the bridesmaids, called from the chair where the last clear coat of polish was drying on her toenails.

Meredith, who was sitting next to Camille, hollered, "I think it's that French guy who's been running around the deck in his Speedo."

Moans and groans flooded the spa, with even the employees chuckling in agreement.

Amy offered a half grin but shook her head. Even if she wasn't involved in a life-or-death mission, she still would never be interested in the French guy in need of a larger bathing suit and some heavy-duty sunscreen, if his wrinkled leather skin was any indication. Jordan was about the opposite of the rotund man.

"Very funny, Mer. Ha. Ha."

All the girls giggled again. "Then tell us who it is."

She had a sudden urge to lie and say that she was meeting up with Elaina. But lies never solved anything,

so she closed her eyes, hunched her shoulders and prepared for the worst. "I have to meet Jordan."

The squeals were deafening.

"Really?"

"Oh, Amy! He's *so* handsome!"

"It's about time. The two of you have been circling
each other forever."

"Does this mean he's off the market?"

It was Neesha's voice that rose above all of the others. "You've finally forgiven him, haven't you?" She
grabbed Amy's hands and squeezed hard. "I told you
he's wonderful. He's such a good man. He really is. He
just made some dumb choices. He never wanted to hurt
you. But now that's in the past, and the two of you together would be—"

"We are not together." Amy had to cut her off. She
didn't want to hear more about Jordan's finer qualities.
She'd been seeing them firsthand for the last eighteen
hours or so, and she didn't need another voice in her
head suggesting that she might have overreacted to his
rejection.

Maybe her grudge had more to do with her dad than
with Jordan.

But that didn't mean she was ready to let it go.

She tried to plaster a consoling smile into place.
"We've been…" She needed a word. Anything to describe what was actually happening rather than the
images in their minds. The trouble was, if they were
picturing them kissing, so was she.

Focus, Delgado. This is about keeping Neesha safe.

"We've been working on an assignment together. Nothing more."

"An assignment?" Neesha recoiled in surprise that quickly turned to anger. "You said you took time off. Jordan promised that he was on leave. This is my wedding, and I hate to play the bride card, but this is all about me. For at least two more days. Understand?" Her tone never rose, and her words were unfailingly even. But there was a steel in them that must run in the family. She'd heard the same from Jordan when he'd insisted on sticking by her side.

"I know. But something's come up." Amy tugged on her arm. "Can we talk in private? For just a minute."

Neesha looked over her shoulder at a row of bewildered faces, and Amy wished she could explain it to them all. But prewedding stress was high and the chances of all of them keeping their calm very, very low.

With a curt nod, Neesha acquiesced, shuffling behind her in flimsy oversize flip-flops. They found a dark corner of the spa, a luscious purple curtain blocking the view of the rest of the amenities.

Amy didn't dance around the subject. "Elaina's been kidnapped."

Neesha's mouth went wide like she was going to scream, and Amy pushed her hand against it.

"Don't. We can't draw attention."

After a long pause, Neesha nodded her agreement. Amy removed her hand, and Neesha stood like a stone for another silent second. And then the floodgates opened. "What do you mean? I just saw her last night. She was fine."

"I know. But they came after her last night. I was with her. And they took me, too."

Neesha's mouth opened and closed, but no sound emerged. Her eyes turned liquid, and she pressed her hands to her face.

"I'm okay," Amy reassured her. "I got away. But they're still looking for me."

"Who would do that? Why would anyone come after you? Where could they possibly take her on this ship? There isn't anywhere to go."

She made a great point. But it seemed that someone knew a secret spot that she and Jordan hadn't found because Elaina had vanished practically right in front of them. Neesha asked questions that Amy couldn't answer, so she skirted them with what she did know.

"Jordan and I are working on it, but in the meantime, I think the men who are after me know I'm part of your wedding party."

Tears leaked down Neesha's cheeks, and she swiped at them with her knuckles. "Are they going to come after me or Rodney or the girls?"

Amy had to find the kindest truth. "If you stay cautious, I'm sure you'll be fine. But I wanted you to know so that you'd be on your guard."

Neesha's lower lip trembled, as she stared in the direction of the rest of the wedding party. Amy could practically see the scenarios playing out in her mind. Her wedding ruined, her friends injured—or worse.

This wasn't the way any girl dreamed of starting the rest of her life, and Amy could do nothing but ask her friend to put on her big-girl pants and face it head-on.

"I need you to be careful, okay?"

Neesha nodded.

"Have you noticed anyone hanging around? A guy who's not part of the party? Someone who's there wherever you go."

"No. Nothing like that. But I've been a little…"

"Distracted." Amy filled it in for her. "It's okay. Just please don't go anywhere alone. If you can stay close to Rodney, that would be best. You need to stay alert. Be aware of your surroundings. And please don't say anything. To anyone."

Neesha blinked rapidly, her arms circling her stomach as though she could somehow comfort herself. "Not even Rodney?"

"You can tell Rodney, but just him. Make sure he knows to keep it to himself, and don't discuss it anywhere where you might be overheard. We can't afford to tip them off that we're coming after Elaina."

Neesha nodded slowly. "Okay, what if I see something? I should text you?"

"My phone was… I lost it."

Neesha let out a quick breath. "Okay." Then suddenly she grabbed Amy by the shoulders and pulled her in for a hug that nearly stole her breath. "You be careful, all right? I have to break in a new husband, and I don't have time to break in a new best friend, too."

Amy held on tight to the woman she'd known for most of her life, savoring the comfort. "I will. I promise. I've got to go."

She slipped out of the spa without passing the rest of the wedding party and stalked down a hall toward the elevator closest to the meeting spot. She kept her chin down but eyes alert. Her pace was even and steady, but she was always ready to take off at a flat run if she needed to.

But she didn't need to be quite so wary. She hardly saw anyone in the hallways, and those she did rushed by her, their swim bags swishing and sandals clacking along the carpet. They barely gave her a second look as they rushed to soak in the vitamin D on the upper deck, the warm and abundant sunshine a rarity for half the world this time of year.

A glance at her watch told her that she would be a few minutes late if she didn't hurry, so she picked up her pace the last hundred yards, but even as she rounded the last bend, she saw that she'd beaten Jordan. Maybe he was running late, too.

Except she'd never known him to run late. He was exceedingly punctual.

A year ago, they'd been on the same flight from San Diego to Charleston to celebrate Neesha and Rodney's engagement. He'd offered to give her a lift to the airport, and she'd been happy to accept. He'd said he'd arrive at oh-seven-hundred, and the clock in her entryway was sounding the first chime of the seven o'clock hour when he knocked on her door.

She'd been ready.

That was military time. On time and ready to roll.

He was either on time…or he didn't come at all, like the night of their would-be date.

As the second hand on her watch ticked by the minutes, a band around her lungs began to pull tight. She paced in front of the repaired cabin door, attempting to entertain herself by trying to figure out how long it had taken a carpenter to put another frame into place and reset the door.

That distraction lasted about twenty seconds. But she kept pacing, kept her feet moving and her eyes ever watchful.

As minutes turned into quarter hours, her heart picked up, playing out all the evils he could have stumbled upon. Or worse, maybe he'd decided to go it alone. Without her. Didn't he understand that she was an asset rather than a liability?

Her stomach churned, anger boiling low and endless as she imagined his face, so smug about leaving her behind.

Silly Amy. Didn't she know that his plans didn't include her?

Fists clenched so tightly that they shook, she nearly kicked the new doorjamb. She'd fallen for his false promises again. She'd expected him to follow through. She'd let herself hope that the past didn't define the present.

Stupid Amy.

As she stomped down the hall, even the lights seemed to be tinged with red and she fought the urge to push the too-cheerful-for-its-own-good palm tree to the floor.

She didn't hear the other body approaching from around the corner, and she slammed into him at full force. Big hands immediately grabbed her shoulders, the only thing that kept her from falling on her rear end as she bounced off his chest.

"Amy!" Jordan kept his hands in place and ducked to look her directly in the eye. Then suddenly he pulled her into a tight hug.

"Get off me." She tried to push away his arms, but it was a little like taking a fly swatter to a mountain.

When he pulled back, his eyes burned with something she couldn't name, and immediately his head whipped around, his gaze darting into every corner. "What's wrong? What happened?"

"You—" She couldn't keep the tremor out of her voice, anger taking over even her vocal chords. "You said you'd meet me here. And then you took off without me. You left me."

He let out a quick breath and suddenly brushed a thumb across her cheek, leaving a damp trail in its wake. Even her tear ducts were rebelling. Perfect.

"I'm sorry I'm late."

"*Sorry.* It's always sorry with you. Why not just show up when you say you're going to? Then an apology wouldn't be necessary."

He rubbed his knuckles across the top of his head. "I deserve that. I know I don't have the best track record with you, but I promise, I have a good reason for being late."

"Hmph." She couldn't get any more past the lump that popped up in her throat. Relief had begun to mix with the fury, and it was producing a whole new set of emotions that she didn't have the time or patience to analyze.

"I did some exploring. And do you know what I found?"

Arms crossed over her stomach and toe tapping, she shook her head. "I have no idea. Do I care?"

"I think you're going to." One corner of his mouth tipped up as he pulled one of her hands free and took off toward a back set of elevators.

"Where are we going? What are you doing?"

He stopped suddenly and pointed. "See that light?"

"Of course." She barely gave it a glance, but the pleased look on his face couldn't be ignored. She looked again. And her heart picked up its pace.

"That's a camera."

"And they're all over. Including in the passageway outside the ambassador's original suite. I checked. And then there's this one." He pointed in a line from the camera all the way down the hall past the door she'd just been pacing in front of.

Was it possible that the cameras had captured Elaina's kidnapping? Could they track the movements of the kidnappers from here to the girl's current location? This could be the break they needed. As long as someone on the inside hadn't tampered with the footage.

After all, someone had definitely failed to mention the cameras before now. But it was the first hope of finding Elaina she'd had in hours. And she'd take it.

Anger vanished in that moment, and she flung her arms around his waist, squeezing tight, burying her nose into his chest. "Thank you."

He tipped her head back so he could meet her gaze full on. "I'm going to do everything in my power to get her back and to keep you safe. I promised. Can you trust me to do that?"

He didn't know what he was asking of her, and she pulled all the way out of the embrace.

She wasn't going to make false promises, either. "I'll try."

"Thank you." Then without preamble, he grabbed her hand and tugged. "Let's go find those videos."

She chased him as they made their way through the ship's maze, finally popping up at the security office. He banged on the door, which rattled under the pressure.

The tinny voice of a security officer came through a box beside the door. "Can I help you?"

"This is Petty Officer Jordan Somerton. I want to speak to the staff captain. Immediately."

Whether it was the unyielding tone of his voice or the intimidating width of his shoulders, she couldn't be sure. But one way or another they were ushered into the office and given chairs at a desk within minutes.

The staff captain had yet to make an appearance but one of the security guys—he'd introduced himself as Bo—kept staring at Jordan. "You're in the navy?" His voice was hushed with wonder.

He nodded slowly, but Amy knew right where this was going.

"You ever meet a SEAL?" Bo asked.

Jordan produced a slow smile as they settled in front of a computer screen. "I've met a few."

She shot him a look that she hoped communicated that this was not the time for modesty—or for teasing men who might be able to help them find and secure Elaina.

He shrugged and finally continued. "I am a SEAL."

Bo's eyes got bigger than dinner plates. "No way. Really? Do you have a tattoo?"

Only Amy heard the tiny, exasperated sigh he released. She nudged him with her knee. "Of course he does."

After Jordan rolled up his sleeve and showed off his trident tattoo, the kid was in awe and eager to please. "Where do you want to start?" he asked.

Jordan made sure that Amy was settled in with a prime view of the screen before nodding at Bo. "Last night. Around twenty-three-thirty. Can you start in the hallway outside the ambassador's room?"

Bo asked for the room number, and then punched the information into the computer until the electronic files popped up. The video was black and white and grainy, and it showed other passengers walking to and from their rooms. There was a distinct influx when the comedy show let out, couples and families returning to their beds. And then they saw the ambassador leave his room, trailed by his bodyguard. A few minutes later Jordan left, too.

The hall was clear for several long minutes.

"Can you fast-forward it?"

"Sure." Bo did as asked, and the counter clock sped forward thirty minutes before two figures suddenly appeared. They were big and brawny, and the sight of them made Amy's stomach roll.

They watched in silence as the goons took out the door, and even though Amy knew what was happening inside that room, she held her breath. It was like wishing that a novel would turn out differently upon the second read. It didn't happen. But it didn't keep her from hoping for just a moment.

And just when she realized that her hands were clenched in her lap, Jordan reached for them. "It's okay," he whispered.

If Bo heard, he said nothing, and Amy let herself accept the comforting touch for a long moment. It didn't mean anything. But she sure was glad for the weight of his hand on hers when the two men emerged, one carrying a wiggling, lashing Elaina, a white cloth pressed to her mouth. The other carried her own limp form.

It was an oddly out-of-body experience to watch something happen to her that she couldn't remember, and the bruise on the side of her face throbbed.

Elaina got a good kick into her abductor's stomach, and he grunted, nearly dropping the girl before whatever drug they'd used in the cloth began to take effect and her limbs turned listless.

"Looks like Elaina learned something from her aunt," Jordan said.

Warmth rushed up her neck, but she said, "Of course. Delgado women aren't pushovers." She focused her attention back on Bo. "Can you track them?"

Bo frowned, his skinny pale neck revealing even more veins. "I think so. They've gone into corridor 7C." He flipped to another video, and sure enough, the two men were walking straight toward the camera, their faces clearly visible, if somewhat pixelated.

Jordan shot her a careful look. "Do you recognize either of them?"

Amy shook her head. "I think the one carrying me,

the one with the limp—I think he's the one I tackled. The one who hit me." Covering her ear and the side of her face with her hand, she tried to forget how bad that bruise was going to look in a few short days. It hadn't turned dark purple yet or Neesha would have been all over it. "But I don't know him from anywhere else."

They tracked the men through several flights and multiple passages. Several times they lost sight of the men in hallways without cameras, but with some trial and error they found them again. Bo moved so quickly that she lost track of where they were looking. But the men onscreen seemed to know back ways and deserted corridors. Even in the middle of the night it was strange that they hadn't run into anyone.

Unless…

Maybe they were getting help from the same person who helped Eric Dean escape.

Suddenly the men nodded at each other and the one carrying Elaina veered down another hallway.

"Follow the girl," Amy ordered.

"Yes, ma'am."

And then suddenly the man wasn't alone. Another man, shorter, his hair lighter, stepped into the frame. He took Elaina and clamped his hand over the rag at her mouth. But just before he disappeared into the darkness, he looked right into the camera.

Her heart slammed to a stop and then started up again, painful and abrasive.

"Wait. Can you pause it? Rewind."

Bo cued it up to his face.

"That's the man who was chasing us earlier when…"

Jordan's voice tapered off, and for a second, he looked mildly uncomfortable.

In any other circumstance, Amy would have laughed at Jordan. But now all she could see were the bitter features of the man on the screen. His nose had been broken at least once, and his lips were so thin they were barely there. He scowled as though he'd forgotten—or never learned—how to smile. And his beady little eyes spoke volumes.

Her insides were tied up in a knot and those ridiculous puzzle pieces were beginning to make a picture she could understand.

"I know that man."

Jordan nearly swallowed his tongue. He shouldn't have been surprised. He wasn't, really.

But the softness and certainty in Amy's voice made the hair on his arms stand on end. He wanted—no, needed—to hear it all. But first they needed a little bit of privacy.

"Bo, where does he go after this?"

Bo shook his head when the man stepped out of range of that camera. "I can't follow him past this point. We don't have any cameras in that deep."

"Where is he right there?"

Bo pulled up a map of the ship and showed them. "It's a stairwell that leads to the back side of the kitchen."

Jordan caught Amy's eye, and he knew she was thinking the same thing. They'd been on the wrong side of the kitchen. They'd been so close to Elaina, but they'd missed her because there were two kitchen exits. Not one.

Jordan reached out his hand and shook Bo's with a quick pump. "Thank you for your help. The teams could use good men like you."

The kid's blue eyes shone like someone had lit a candle within him. "You serious, man? You think I could do it? I could be a SEAL?"

"Only you can answer that. But for what it's worth, I think you'd stand a real shot."

Jordan grabbed Amy's hand, tugged her toward the exit and left Bo to ponder that statement.

They still hadn't seen Xavier, but there was no time to wait and no one with enough authority to send help with them. They were probably better off without it. Some of these security guards were eager to offer their services but severely under-trained—like Bo. Some were downright apathetic—like Cortero the night before. And not being able to rely on the man beside you was worse than having no one there.

Good thing he had Amy.

He smiled at her, and she responded with one of her own, tense but hopeful. And his insides tripped.

He liked her. He liked spending time with her. He liked that he could trust her. He liked how strong and independent and fierce she was. And he liked how she'd spoken to her niece at the party the night before. Soft, calming, compassionate words. She could take down an entire drug ring in one breath and comfort a frightened child in the next.

And he'd be lying if he pretended he hadn't noticed how beautiful she was while doing it all. The highlights in her dark hair shone in the sun like a halo. Even on the run, out of breath and scared, her skin glowed a deep bronze, and her brown eyes sparkled. And when she smiled—well, it wasn't safe to think about those lips for too long because that just reminded him of their kiss and how much he wanted another one.

He wasn't in love with her or anything ridiculous like that. But...but she made him wish his personal rules were different.

Maybe for the first time.

They reached a semiprivate corner outside the security office and he stopped, turning to assess her current state. The stunned expression had been replaced by one of determination.

"Why are we stopping?" she asked. "Let's get going."

"In a minute. First, tell me—who is that man?"

"His name is Bruno Stein. He's an American connected to the Lybanian drug ring that my team took down this summer."

"I thought maybe he was connected to that. Michael told me that he'd seen your team after that. It's the only plausible connection. But what happened in that operation that would set off this level of an attack? What did you do to make them so angry?"

She raised an eyebrow in question. "You mean besides confiscating four hundred pounds of heroin?"

He nodded.

"We arrested their leader, General Abkar." Her lips formed a tight line for a long second. "And I think they're going to try to use Elaina as a bargaining chip to get him back."

Chapter Eleven

Jordan raced after Amy down the passageways that they'd only seen before on the security monitor. They bumped into packs of other people on the upper decks, but as they moved into the bowels of the ship, the crowds thinned, eliminating much of their cover.

So long as there were other people around, they weren't quite as conspicuous to anyone who might be watching for them. And it was unlikely that Stein and the other terrorists were just milling around in crowds.

With each level they passed, down each ladder, the chances of running into Stein grew. So did the knot in Jordan's stomach.

By the time they reached the deck above the kitchen, he could nearly hear his own heart pounding. His shoulders were tense, his neck already stiff in anticipation of what was to come.

Even though he really had no idea what to expect.

Were they entering a swarm or a hive?

Were armed men running around without order or position, or did everyone have a place and a job?

If it was the latter, their best option was to take the men out one at a time, commandeer their weapons and hide the bodies.

If the former, their best option was prayer. Men without orders were unpredictable and often careless. They shot first and rarely bothered to ask questions later. And they tended to blend into a crowd, making them harder to identify as the enemy.

But either way, he was ready for a fight.

"Jordan?" Amy's voice was barely a whisper as they reached a corner. "Do you hear that?"

He'd been so caught up in making a plan that he'd missed whatever she'd heard. He held still, listening carefully.

All was silent save for the crashing of metal pots and pans in the kitchen below. The deck between them muffled the words, but the cries of busy line cooks and demanding chefs wouldn't be denied.

He nodded toward the floor, asking Amy if that's what she'd heard.

She mouthed *no* and pointed her chin toward the corner.

His pulse kicked up a notch, sweeping adrenaline through him.

He pointed to himself and then to the corner.

Sinking to the ground, he crawled to a better vantage point and peeked around the corner. He wouldn't be easily visible this low to the ground, so he pushed himself a little farther into the opening to get a full view.

Two men stood by the entrance to the stairs, trying—and failing—to look casual. Maybe it was the Glock hanging in the hand of the one on the left or what looked like an Uzi conspicuously tucked into the jacket of the other. Either way, they were decidedly not casual.

And they had a straight shot down a short passageway with no obstacles—or opportunities for cover—in their way.

If Jordan tried to take them head-on, he'd be hit. Without question.

And he couldn't risk Amy suffering the same.

Wiggling back to Amy, he stood and shook his head. "Not good. Two armed men—but I don't recognize them. No cover. It's a straight shot, and no way to get to them except from behind. Only that's the stairwell we're trying to get to. We need a better angle."

She chewed on her lower lip for a long second, her eyes gazing overhead. "If we play a couple that's lost…"

The image of her arm wound around his and fingers threaded between his own, her eyes gazing up at him adoringly, flashed through his mind and delivered a punch to his throat.

That didn't sound bad. At all.

But what if these men were shoot-first-ask-questions-later kind of guys?

"No."

Her lips pursed, eyes narrowing in on him. "How about if we separate them?"

"And how do you suggest we do that?"

A slow smile spread across her lips. "I have an idea, so just go with me on this."

A band around his lungs cinched tight, and he grabbed at her arm. "Don't try to be a hero, Delgado. There's a lot at stake here."

She didn't back down. If anything, she took a step toward him. "Like my niece."

"And she needs you alive." His voice rose, and he had to swallow the fear that was already beginning to take root. "We all need you alive."

"And I will be. But for now, I need you to trust me."

"I do."

Oh, Lord, what is she thinking? Don't let her get herself killed.

Amy took a deep breath and tried to give Jordan a reassuring smile as she pushed him out of sight into another hallway. "Say put," she breathed.

He nodded, but then shook his head. "If you scream, I'm coming to get you. Understood?"

"Sure." She dismissed it with flippant wave of her hand, but everything inside her seized up because she *did* understand. This was not a lukewarm promise, and she didn't have any doubt that he'd follow through.

This was the first time she'd been so certain of any man since her dad stopped bothering to show up.

But this was not the time for reflection.

This was the time for action. And pretending.

Flipping her hair over, she gave it a good shake, then pinched a bit of color into her cheeks and bit her lips to turn them red.

God, help me.

And then she let the role begin. "Jason! Jason Burke,

you come out here right now." She paused and made her panic rise, using it to fuel the character she was playing. Not too difficult when she was about to turn a corner to face two armed men. But this had to be realistic, like she had lost her charge, but not like she was ready for a weapons fight.

She ran along the carpet, hugging the wall, then stopped and screamed again. "Jason, if you don't come out right now, you're not getting any dessert." Forcing out a loud sob, she prayed they'd buy the whole scenario. "Jason."

Blood pumping hard, she rounded the corner and stopped in her tracks.

Act surprised. She had to act surprised.

Her mouth dropped open, and she batted her lashes at them, wishing she'd had enough time that morning to put on at least one coat of mascara. "Have you seen a little boy? He's six, and he has a habit of running off, but if his parents find out I've lost him again, I'm going to be in so much trouble."

The two big men stood nearly paralyzed in front of a dark wood door. Neither blinked at her for what felt like an eternity, and their paralysis seeped into her, rooting her feet and her facial features for too long.

Her gaze couldn't seem to stray from the Glock that hung a little too loosely in the hand of the man on the left. He squeezed his finger against the trigger, and her heart stopped.

This wasn't working. But she was in too deep to back out now.

Play the part. She had to play the part.

Sucking in a stabilizing breath, she flipped her hair over her shoulder and smiled again. "Have you seen him?" Holding a hand at waist level, she tried again. "Brown hair, green shirt?"

Slowly the man who was clearly covering a submachine gun under his jacket shook his head. "We've seen no one."

Amy forced herself to burst into tears—not a terribly difficult task given the rush of emotion thundering through her. "He said—" She sobbed loudly and stumbled toward them. "He said that he was going to play a game, but now he's hiding and I can't find him. And we were supposed to meet his parents twenty minutes ago."

Glock guy nodded slowly, like he understood her predicament but had no idea how to help.

Good.

"I think he might have locked himself in the men's bathroom." She covered her face with one hand, leaving just enough of a view to watch their reactions. "And *I* can't go in after him." She wailed hard at the end of it.

Please, please let this work.

Lybanians weren't known for treating women well in their country. But it was a truth universally acknowledged that men didn't know how to handle a crying woman.

They remained silent, and then suddenly Glock guy reached behind him and tucked his weapon into the back of his waistband. "Fine. I will look."

"Really?" She tipped back her head and shot him her best impression of a pageant queen smile—so toothy and bright that it made her cheeks ache. "It's just around the corner. I can't thank you enough."

Thinking twice about putting a hand on him, she waved in the direction where she'd left Jordan.

Lybanian custom dictated that women walk at least a pace behind any man in their group, and she quickly fell into place. He didn't even seem to notice.

As soon as they were outside the view of machine-gun man, she slipped her hand beneath his jacket and pulled his gun free.

Oh, man, it felt good to have a weapon in her hand again.

He turned, rage on his face and mouth open ready to scream. But she held the Glock in both hands, arms straight and level with his nose.

"How dare—"

Her heart leaped to her throat as she pressed her finger against the trigger. It always did.

But before it could fully engage, an elbow flew out of nowhere, connecting to his face. The crunch of bone as his nose shattered made her cringe, and Glock guy—or rather previously Glock guy—crumpled to the ground, an unconscious form covered in crimson streams.

Her gaze shot to Jordan, who stood over him, a satisfied grin in place. His smile turned into a half frown as he stared at her. "You okay?"

Her hands trembled slightly, but she shoved them behind her. It was just the action kicking too much adrenaline through her system. Shaky limbs were pretty normal for her in the aftermath of situations like this. "Good."

"One down." He nodded to the motionless man on the floor. "You want to get the other or want me to?"

Holding out the gun, she said, "You're the sniper."

His hands dwarfed the pistol as he took it from her. "Be right back."

She held her breath, waiting for the pop of gunfire. But it didn't come. Instead a loud voice demanded, "What are you—"

"Drop it." Jordan's voice was lethal, terrifying. And there was an immediate clatter on the floor. It was muffled by the carpet, but she knew without a doubt that machine-gun man had surrendered.

For a long moment the only sounds in the hallway were the bubbled, strangled breathing of the unconscious man at her feet.

And then Jordan reappeared, his shirt slightly twisted, face grim.

"That's taken care of." So matter-of-fact.

It was a good thing they were on the same team.

She reached out to straighten his T-shirt but stopped halfway there, her arms hanging out awkwardly. Maybe that wasn't okay. Maybe she wasn't allowed to just touch him whenever the thought popped into her head.

His brows drew close together as he stared at her hands.

Oh, forget it. This side of two hours ago, he'd had her pressed against a wall, kissing her silly. This wasn't anywhere close to that level.

Grabbing the cotton by the crooked seams, she gave it a little tug until the V of his collar pointed straight down, and the sides of the shirt lined up with the sides of his body.

"Oh." He smoothed out any remaining wrinkles with one of his hands—his other still holding the weapon. "Thanks."

"You're welcome." Because suddenly this had turned into tea on the veranda at Aunt Rosemarie's.

She should say something. Anything. Nothing could be worse than this uncomfortable silence, while one of her hands still rested on the hem of his shirt at his hip. His body was warm and alive, and a rush of gratitude set her skin on fire.

One or both of them could have been killed. Suddenly the two feet between them was too much, and she flung her arms around him, holding him tight, bumping into the pistol but not caring.

"I'm glad you're okay." Stupid. Stupid girl. She should have been able to come up with something smarter than that inane pronouncement, but the words had vanished, replaced only by the momentary need for a physical connection.

"Me?" His chuckle rumbled deep in his chest beneath her hear. "You're the one who risked everything."

"I know. It was a terrible idea."

"It's never a terrible idea if it works." His hand made a lazy circle on her back, and she shivered beneath his touch. Probably still the adrenaline leaving her system.

Sure, that seemed valid.

It couldn't possibly be that she really only wanted him to hold her. Which he did as if he'd been training for it his whole life. His steely arms were somehow both gentle and strong, and when she leaned against him, she had no doubt that he could keep her standing, no matter what.

His heart beat steadily under her ear, and she closed her eyes to the steady rhythm.

"I was a little bit scared." Her confession came out more easily than she'd imagined.

She'd always felt that she had to be so strong with him. Especially after their failed date, she couldn't show him her weaknesses or risk being vulnerable. Again.

So she'd put up her walls and kept him at bay. Staying angry with him, that was the easy part. It kept her safe. Protected. It meant she'd never risk another heartbreak.

And, oh, she'd been heartbroken. She'd never told a soul, but she'd been halfway in love with Jordan for nearly half her life.

She wasn't alone, of course. All of Neesha's friends had fallen in love with him at some point. But the rest of them had moved on.

Amy had been stuck.

Hoping. Wishing. Praying that one day he might notice her. One day he might realize that she was more than little-cousin material. One day he might prove to her that everything she'd learned about men from her father was wrong.

Only he hadn't.

He'd confirmed it all.

Starting with Neesha's engagement party.

Flames shot up her cheeks at the mere memory of that disaster, and she tried to pull away from his embrace. But the steel of his arms held strong.

"What's going on in that mind of yours?"

"Nothing."

"Liar." It was half teasing, half accusation. "We're not done, you know? But before we go through that door, I need to know that your focus is in the right spot." He took a deep breath, and her head moved with his chest. "You want to tell me what you're thinking about?"

She pinched up her face to keep anything in her expression from giving her away, wishing it was enough to make her disappear. "Not really."

"Too bad." How did he get his voice to be so authoritarian? There was absolutely zero room for negotiation or argument. And somehow she knew that if she lied to him, he'd know that, too.

"I was thinking about why this is so much easier than Neesha's engagement party."

"You mean, when you threw your entire plate of spareribs and collard greens in my lap?"

"Yes."

Every muscle in her body tensed, and so did his. How would he reply? With an excuse? An apology? Another false promise to placate her?

"I deserved it," he said.

She'd have fallen to the floor in that minute if he hadn't been holding her. "What?"

"I was a jerk. I didn't mean to be, but I was… Listen, I'd been getting a lot of pressure from my family to settle down, make grandbabies, carry on the family name. You know how that is."

Yes. She'd heard the teasing. She knew Aunt Phyllis and Aunt Ruth and Uncle Bobby weren't going to let up on him until he brought a girl home. Permanently.

Was it so terrible that once upon a time she'd hoped it would be her?

"When I showed up with you at the party, it was like walking into a firefight only to discover I'd forgotten my gun and worn an orange vest." The metal in his voice began to soften, regret lacing the words. "I tried to explain to them that I hadn't brought you as my date—that it was just easier for us to come together. We were on the same flight. It made sense to only get one rental car. Why waste the money?"

"But they didn't want to hear it."

He nodded his chin into her hair. "And when they started teasing you and me and asking when our engagement party would be, I needed to shut it down."

"Why?"

Oh, dear Lord, why did I say that? I don't want to know. I don't want to know. I don't want to know.

"They all love that I'm a SEAL, that I'm serving my country. But they don't get that it means that I don't know if I'm coming home."

He was so matter-of-fact about it that she jerked away. She must have surprised him because he dropped his arms, and she stepped back.

With his hands now free, he put one on his hip and the other at the back of his neck. "When I said that I'd never date you, it wasn't about… It didn't have anything to do with…" He let out a frustrated sigh. "You're amazing, right? You know that?"

Her stupid eyes started burning the second his voice dropped like that, and she clamped them shut, praying they wouldn't leak or give away how vulnerable she felt at the moment.

She could be hard and tough and play with the boys

at work, but at the end of the day, she was still a woman. With all the unruly emotions that came with it.

"I just… I'm not in a place to be… I can't settle down right now. With anyone. I can't make promises about a life and a future together that I don't know if I can keep." And then, as if that wasn't a strong enough dismissal, he added, "But whoever you choose, he's going to be a really fortunate guy."

"Sure." Because what other insipid response could she give?

When she finally risked opening her eyes, he was staring at her, hard. "I'm sorry I hurt you."

"Sure."

"Okay." He leaned in to her side, and she shifted to return a quick hug.

Only it wasn't a hug. It was a kiss on the cheek. Except when she moved, it wasn't just on the cheek.

His lips caught the corner of her mouth, and they both froze. Because, for at least a moment, no one was chasing them. They weren't hiding from anyone. No one was going to interrupt them.

And his lips were on hers.

His eyes flashed wide-open, but he didn't pull away.

Her heart skipped a beat, maybe two, and all the air on the ship seemed to vanish.

And in a flash she was back in his arms, his lips fully pressed against hers, his arms snaking around her back.

She bumped into the submachine gun hanging from his shoulder, and he mumbled against her lips. "Safety's on."

Good, she thought. But she couldn't be bothered to

respond aloud. There were more pressing things at hand. Like getting lost in his embrace. Like realizing that she'd never felt quite so cherished before in her entire life. Like knowing that no other man in the world could live up to this.

She rested her hands on his shoulders, then the back of his neck, her thumb doing a lazy dance against his nape. He shivered, and a low groan in the back of his throat draped over them.

He wasn't distracted the way he had been the last time—watching for their pursuers. And the difference in his kiss was black-and-white versus Technicolor.

Even with her eyes closed, she knew that everything was brighter, louder, sweeter in Jordan Somerton's arms. She wiggled closer, holding him tighter, wishing this never had to end.

One of his hands slid into her hair, and he tilted her head to the side, increasing their connection.

She forgot her own name.

Her body felt like she'd been dipped in seltzer water. Everything tingled from the top of her head to the tips of her toes.

Oxygen had become a secondary need to being this close and this connected to him. Even when her lungs began to complain, she didn't pull away.

Finally, it was Jordan who broke the kiss. Gasping for air, he pressed his forehead to hers. "I'm sorry. I haven't done that in a while."

"You mean since this morning."

"No." His head rocked against hers, and his fingers curled into her waist. "I mean, kiss someone because

. I wanted to." He grasped for another breath. "Not because I had to."

"Oh." She shouldn't be surprised. Obviously he'd wanted to kiss her. She'd just assumed that handsome SEALs had their pick of the girls.

Apparently he was serious about what he'd said before. He believed he couldn't be in a relationship, couldn't be both a SEAL and a boyfriend.

Clearly he hadn't been paying attention to the five guys on his team, who had had no trouble realizing their lives were a million times richer because of the women who loved them. Matt, Tristan, Will, Luke and even Jordan's best friend, Zach. They'd figured out that life was too short to ignore love.

Not that she loved him.

She did not.

What she'd felt as a girl was infatuation. What she'd dreamed of as a young woman was a fairy tale. What she knew now was true.

If he wasn't interested—in it with his whole heart— then he'd wind up just like her dad.

And she'd had enough broken hearts to last a lifetime.

Keeping up the wall was easier. Hanging on to the memories of the times she'd been hurt didn't feel great. But it was better than fresh pain.

"It's okay. We'll just forget it happened." Or remember that it happened and have dreams about it but never speak of it again. Ever.

That was probably more realistic.

Cupping her elbows, he squeezed her carefully. "I'm

sorry, Amy. I shouldn't have let myself get so carried away."

"Didn't you hear me? I said it's okay."

"That doesn't mean you don't deserve an apology."

There were no words to follow that. She'd had a lot of experience letting guys off the hook, but this was a first. She'd given him an out, and he wasn't taking it.

"Oh, man!"

The sharp cry made her jump back, and Jordan dropped his hands as they both turned toward the person intruding on their private moment. Bo turned his head as his neck and cheeks went red. "Man, I didn't mean to—"

His words cut off as his gaze landed on the figure at their feet. A pool of blood had collected near the thug's head, and Bo's mouth dropped open. "Is he dead?"

"No. I just broke his nose."

"Like, you broke it. For real?"

Jordan looked at the kid, who was gazing up at him like he was a superhero come to life. "Only way I know how."

Amy bit back a snort, and Jordan winked at her, his lips fighting a grin.

"I saw you take out the other guy."

Her head whipped up. "What?"

"On the monitor. I was tracking you to see where you'd go." Bo ducked his head, almost in embarrassment. "Man, I've never seen anyone do a choke hold like that."

That explained why there had been no gunshots. Jordan didn't need them to subdue a terrorist.

If she hadn't been watching him, she'd have missed

Jordan's response, an easy shrug. "There a reason you came to find us?"

"I almost forgot." Bo shook his shoulders and leaned in close, like he was about to reveal state secrets. "Staff Captain Xavier came into the security office. He was whispering with Second Officer Garfield. I don't think anyone was supposed to overhear, but I did. And I thought you'd want to know."

Jordan nodded but had to prompt Bo to continue. "Know what?"

"Radar picked up another boat coming in port side. It's headed our direction, and it ain't another cruise liner, neither."

"Is there any chance it's Coast Guard?" Jordan caught her gaze.

A tiny bubble of hope sprang to life. *Please. Please.*

"No. It's not official, and it's not announcing itself or responding to our hails."

Amy's heart took a nosedive to her toes. Her head spun, and she stumbled when the ship hit an unexpected swell.

Jordan grabbed her elbow but didn't address her unsteadiness. "Sounds like someone is *arriving.*"

They were on the same page. He remembered it, too. Eric Dean had mentioned it early on. They had to have Elaina when "they arrived." Apparently *they* were almost here.

But a ship didn't only mean an arrival. It could mean a departure.

Elaina's.

Though her mouth was painfully dry, she forced herself to speak. "We've got to find her. Right now."

Jordan didn't even reply. He simply turned to Bo and said, "You want to be part of our mission?"

"Seriously?" His fair eyebrows rose high. "What do you want me to do?"

"I need a rifle. A good one, preferably with a scope."

His face fell. "But all the weapons are locked up to keep them out of the passengers' hands. So we don't end up with one of those situations where the prisoners take over the prison. You know, like in the movies?"

Jordan waved his submachine gun in the air. "You mean like this?"

"Umm…sort of."

Jordan clapped a hand on the Bo's shoulder, nearly buckling the scrawny young man. "Listen, there's a little girl in danger. And you can either be a hero or you can get out of the way. It's up to you."

Bo had clearly never been called out by a SEAL before, and he scrambled for a response. "No, sir. Yes. I mean, I can—" His head ticked to the side and his barely there whiskers shimmered in the light. "I might—"

"Good man. Meet me on the lido deck in twenty minutes."

Bo took off running, and Amy stared after him. "You think he's going to find you a rifle?"

"Would you say no to me?"

She shot him her fiercest scowl. "Right now?"

His chuckle was throaty and it wrapped around her. "Right now we're going to find Elaina."

Chapter Twelve

Hollywood always made the terrorist's lair dark and foreboding, but the stairwell, which had until recently been guarded by two burly men with minimal skill, was rather well lit.

Jordan held the Uzi at the ready as he ran down the steps, Amy close at his six.

He was missing his flack jacket, SIG Sauer and the seven-inch blade generally tucked into his boot.

But at least he had a weapon in his hand.

As they eased into the passageway, he scanned it for any activity. There was a small commotion at the mouth of the kitchen—someone had fired up the grill a little too high, and flames licked at the white dishes on the upper shelves. A short man was yelling at two others.

Other than that, there was only one man in their vicinity. He sat on the floor, his chin resting on his chest and hands folded over the white jacket covering his stomach. Definitely not a watchman.

But something was off. He could practically smell it.

"Where is everyone?" Amy whispered.

The other kitchen entrance had been hopping, house-keeping and waiters and other staff on assignment.

It almost felt as though someone had ordered this side to be kept clear.

Suddenly a scream ripped the air into shreds.

The three men at the grill looked up then quickly down, their argument forgotten. But no one moved to investigate the sound.

Amy's eyes grew round, her lips nearly disappearing into a line. "That was Elaina."

"You sure?"

"I heard her scream right before I blacked out." There wasn't an inch of give in her voice. "I'm sure."

It had come from somewhere at the far end of the hall, so he nodded that way. They crept along the bulkhead, silent and always at the ready for whatever they might face.

He checked each door as they passed it. First he pressed his ear to the frame, then he turned the handle. But each one was silent. No commotion. No more screams.

And the ones that opened showed only storage closets.

When he opened a door halfway down the hall, revealing a room with shelves full of cleaning supplies, Amy took a sharp breath. "I was in here. This is where I escaped." Her eyes darted from the tiny cubicle down the hall and back. "I was so close to Elaina."

The regret in her words nearly sliced him open, but he couldn't let it freeze them in place. They had to keep moving forward.

Suddenly another scream echoed through the walls.

And it was followed quickly by the footsteps of four very large men. They were still a good fifteen yards away, and if their raised voices were any indication, they hadn't noticed that they were being observed.

"Shut her up." That American accent and blond hair couldn't be missed. Stein was still in the picture. And he was speaking to Eric Dean, who held a writhing Elaina in his arms.

"I told you to keep it down," Dean hissed at the girl.

Amy leaped for them, but Jordan pulled her into the closet.

"What are you doing?" The words barely made it out from between her clenched teeth as she struggled against his hold. "They're moving her, and we both know if they get her off this boat, I'm never going to see her again." There was no emotion now. She'd put it away and put on her work mask. "We have to go for her now or we'll lose our chance. Don't you see that?"

"I hear you, but charging them directly right now is not what's best for her, and you know it. What would you have me do, spray this gun into that group of men—one of whom is holding Elaina? Take them out one by one, giving them time to kill her between shots if I didn't accidentally hit her myself?"

Amy's face turned ashen, and the gun in her hand shook.

And all of a sudden he realized that he wasn't only talking to a DEA agent, his partner on this mission. He was talking to a desperate aunt who had had her niece stolen right out from under her.

"I'm sor—" he tried to say, but she cut him off.

"You're right." She jerked her shoulders back, looking in the direction that Elaina had been taken. "But I'm not going to let them get away."

"Me, neither."

"All right, so what's your grand plan?"

He scrubbed at his face, buying just a fraction of a minute to put the pieces together. "She can't be transferred to the other boat unless it's moored to this ship, right? And if they're looking for any kind of fast getaway, they're not going to use chains. Probably ropes. And ropes can be cut. In order to keep her on this ship, we have to make sure they can't get to the other boat."

He could read the annoyance in her eyes. She was ready to go in, guns blazing, but he had a plan that might actually work, even if it wasn't the tactic she'd prefer.

"You going to shoot the ropes out?"

"I'm sure going to try."

"And if Bo doesn't come through with a rifle?"

He pushed a lock of her hair out of her face. "Then we go to your plan. Blazing guns and all that."

She sucked on her front tooth for a long second. "We going to split up?"

He knew she was still focused on tactics, but there was something in the words that made his heart ache, like it might be the end of what they'd shared.

It had to be, but that didn't mean he particularly wanted it to be that way.

"I think it makes sense. I need the high ground to get the right angle to take my shot."

Which was right where Bo was supposed to meet him.

"You okay following her from a distance?" Jordan

continued. "Stein is in that group. If he sees you, he's not going to let you get away again."

Oof. Those words even hit him hard.

This was a bad idea. A very bad one. They should stick together. They should wait for backup. They should do anything but split up while hoping for the best.

But hoping for the best wouldn't get the job done. There was no backup coming, no one for them to rely on but each other.

He wasn't sending a novice out to do a job. She was highly trained and fully capable. And now she was armed.

The impressive 45mm Glock looked good in her hands, a reminder that she'd been trained and certified and was entirely competent. Not to mention strong. Determined. Dedicated. Beautiful.

And she was—the most beautiful woman he'd ever seen. All that soft-as-silk hair curling around her shoulders and those deep, expressive eyes that couldn't hide anything. Not that they ever tried to.

He'd been an absolute idiot not to beg her for a second chance on their sort-of date the minute he'd returned from Lybania.

But then where would he be? Right where he was now. Able to offer her a couple of sweet kisses and friendship and not a single thing more.

She deserved better than that. And he knew it.

And none of it changed the fact that he was going to send her out after a man who wanted to see her dead.

Yep. This was a terrible idea.

"All right. I'm going to follow them. And if I get

any chance to snatch Elaina, I'm going to take it." Her eyes sparked with fire, like she'd been working toward this her entire life. "When you snap the mooring ropes, what's your next move?"

"Truthfully? I haven't figured that part out yet."

Amy took off after Elaina, a prayer on the tip of her tongue and the top of her mind.

God, please keep Elaina safe. And me. And Jordan, too.

It had probably been years since she'd prayed for him. But somehow, in less than twenty-four hours, he'd woven his way back into her life and her mind in a very real way.

And even though they'd never be more than what they had been, she needed to know that he was out there, putting his very life on the line to save the innocents.

Pushing thoughts of Jordan out of her mind, she focused on the pursuit of her niece's captors. She had to somehow keep up with them but not get close enough for them to see her.

Her footsteps stayed silent as she listened for any sign of them.

Extra voices wove in and out of the service hallway, and she held her breath, pausing for just a moment.

Suddenly a man and a woman turned the corner in front of her, walking toward her direction.

She shoved her gun behind her back and held her breath as they approached. She hadn't seen either before, and they sure didn't look like they belonged with the terrorists. But she couldn't assume anything.

The gun in her hand was solid, and she held it with a firm—but not too firm—grip.

As they approached, the couple looked at her for only a brief moment. She gave them a curt nod and a half smile, and they passed without a word.

She let out her breath in a slow sigh and hurried along in the direction she'd been going. But even that short pause might have been too long. The men were no longer in sight. Had she lost Elaina again?

Heart thumping and ears ringing, she picked up her speed.

She had to find her niece.

But the hallway ahead was empty. And the blue carpet showed only normal wear patterns—no clear indicators of recent footsteps.

She turned around and raced toward another offshoot of the main hall. Maybe they'd gone that direction?

But it was empty, too.

Oh, Lord, where did they go?

She could barely hear her own thoughts over the thunder in her mind. They had to be here. They couldn't have disappeared so quickly. But if she chased down another hallway and it was the wrong choice, she'd lose them for good.

She slammed to a stop against a wall where two passageways merged into one, resting at the base of the Y and praying for all she was worth.

"Come on, Elaina. Tell me where you are."

The scream was high and loud and sweet music to her ears. There was no denying that it came from the left fork, and she chased its echo. Her feet were moving so fast that she nearly missed an offshoot and was half-way across its opening before she realized that it led to the service elevators, where a band of men and a writhing little girl waited.

Amy flung herself back against the wall, praying that Elaina's fuss had distracted them enough that no one realized they weren't alone. She held her breath to keep from taking ragged breaths, hope filling a balloon in her chest and then popping it before it could be fully realized.

Elaina was right there. And Amy had six bullets in her gun. More than enough to take out the four men. But Jordan's words filled her, reminding her.

She might get off one or two shots, but not before someone took out Elaina. If she could just remain patient—patient and vigilant—she could get her back.

Amy closed her eyes and waited for the next movement. A fraction of a second later, the elevator doors groaned as they opened. Heavy footfalls trampled onto the metal floor, and the doors squeaked closed again.

She waited just long enough to make sure the doors were all the way closed before rushing around the corner. Just as she'd hoped, there was a set of adjacent stairs.

It was a race.

She took the steps two at a time, her running shoes landing as softly as she could upon the metal. Sometimes they clanged loudly and she cringed. But she didn't stop. Not even when she passed a group of housekeepers in their gray uniforms. They were moving much slower than she was, and one of them grumbled as she pushed past. "What's she doing here in such a hurry?"

"She's fit," said one of her coworkers. "Probably exercising."

If only her physical fitness was all that was at stake. Amy pressed on, deck after deck. At each level she pressed her ear against the wall, listening for the sound of the elevator. As long as it kept moving, so did she.

Her legs were trembling after five decks, her heart hammering so hard she was sure the sunbathers two decks below could hear it. When she flattened herself against the wall and listened, there was only the thump-thump of her own pulse and the rasp of her jagged breath.

Holding her breath and willing her heart to slow down, she waited.

Nothing.

The elevator had stopped. This was her floor.

Leaning back to tell Jordan, she stopped herself short and shook off the feeling of being all alone, abandoned.

God, why do I always jump there?

She stared up toward the heavens and waited for an answer. It wasn't too much to ask, was it? She'd had success in her career. She'd found a way to make a difference in the world. She was respected and had been honored on more than one occasion. So why did her mind insist on reminding her every chance it got of all the times that she'd been ignored, forgotten and left behind?

Jordan hadn't left her behind this time. They'd mutually agreed that by splitting up they could cover more ground. He was off doing his part of the job. And she was doing hers.

And it meant that she'd have to wait to listen for answers.

Poking her head out of the stairwell, she made a quick survey of the situation. The elevator doors were closed, and the niche was empty, save for two service carts lining the far wall.

She raced toward the metal carts, ducking between them and out of sight just as the telltale groan of the elevator doors began. She pulled a loose bedsheet over her, maintaining only a partial view.

"Hurry up." She'd recognize Stein's voice anywhere at this point, and he spat out orders to the other three men. "They're pulling the boat in now. It can't stay docked for long. And she has to be on it when it pulls away. The general won't accept any less."

General? But Abkar was awaiting trial in a US prison. Was he pulling strings from behind bars?

Where was Jordan when she needed to talk this through with him?

Don't dwell on that, Delgado.

The entourage turned left, and she slipped after them, thankful for the silence of padded carpet compared to the clanging metal stairs she'd left behind. They went halfway down the hall and then entered a cabin—one of the most expensive on board with a semi-private deck overlooking the port side of the ship.

Right where the unnamed boat was to meet up with the cruise ship.

Her stomach sank as sure as an anchor at sea.

This was all going down on the outer deck, but she was stuck inside. She had to figure out a way to get through one of these rooms. The outer decks on this part of the boat were each separated by a partial wall, and if she could just get to one, she could work her way down the row.

It was the getting through the room that would take some effort. She needed Jordan to kick the door in. But she didn't have Jordan.

She needed help. An idea. Anything.

She twisted and spun, looking for something that would help.

And then, like a gift, a squeaking wheel rolled in her direction. She looked up just as a maid pushed one of the service carts in her direction. She was busy counting towels, and Amy jumped into the notch of a door to get out of her way. Holding her breath, she waited for the cart to stop, which it finally did. At the far end of the hall, just three doors down from the one Elaina had disappeared into.

Thank You. Thank You.

It was the only prayer that she could complete as she flew toward the cart. The maid had propped the door open as she pulled out soiled towels and sheets, and Amy didn't think twice before racing through.

"Hey. Hey, what are you doing?"

Amy didn't even pause, flinging open the sliding glass door to the private balcony. The sun was bright to eyes that had spent so much time inside the bowels of the ship, and she blinked against the white spots that flashed before her, rushing toward the partial wall that separated her from the neighboring deck.

But before she could launch herself over, the thrumming sound of a second boat reached her ears, and she looked over the railing and down at what looked like a midsize fishing boat.

She couldn't imagine the fishing boat managing the open ocean for very long—it simply didn't have the fuel capacity for long journeys—but no matter how hard she looked, she couldn't see land in any direction.

Where it had come from wasn't nearly as important as who was about to be on it, and where they were going, so she grabbed the top of the first wall and pulled herself up.

The partial wall was at least six feet tall—offering relative privacy to each of the cabins. Scrambling over it wasn't quite as easy as she'd hoped.

The last time she'd scaled a wall, it had been made of wood and boasted a knotted rope. This one was mostly metal, its panels slippery against the toes of her shoes. But she worked her legs up and up until she was on top of the wall and then slid to the floor on the other side.

It was empty save a table and two chairs, and she gave a quick peek into the room on the other side of the glass door to make sure that it was empty, too. No need to have a surprised observer as she scaled the next wall.

The second wall took a little longer than the first, her fingers and arms aching with the strain.

She hadn't used these muscles in a long time, and by the time she was on the other side of the wall from Elaina, every single inch of her trembled.

Moderating her breathing, she pressed against the barrier and peeked over the edge of the ship. The fishing boat below bobbed a few dozen yards away. And even though she'd climbed five decks, it wasn't terribly far below them. Too far to jump, but with a ladder...

And then she realized that the ship was already secured to the cruise liner. Ropes thicker than her forearms swung between the two vessels, bobbing and dipping out of the water.

Plenty of time had passed since Bo had told them security was aware of the approaching boat. Where was security now? Why wasn't the captain doing something?

She looked around frantically for help but was still alone. The crew seemed to be on vacation. Or was somehow tied to this conspiracy. Because if anyone was paying attention, there was no way they'd have let this happen unless they were in on it.

She was alone.

You're not alone. You have Jordan.

The ship rocked on a large wave. The ropes pulled tight but held. And Amy thought she might be sick. She'd expected that the arrival meant someone would be boarding the ship, but now it was clear from this angle that the boat's only goal was taking someone away. Taking Elaina away.

Okay, Jordan. Where are you? We need you.

The sliding door on the other side of the wall rolled open, and angry voices started shouting.

"There it is."

Amy peeked around the edge of the barrier, and her eye almost missed a metal wire running from the balcony straight to the boat. It didn't seem to be holding the boat secure, and there was a little slack in the line. It quivered as if someone on the other side strummed it.

"Looks stable. You ready to go?"

"Yep. My harness is good."

"Okay, put her in the vest." That was Stein. "Get her attached to the line."

It wasn't just any line. This was a zip line. Forget the ladder—they were going to slide Elaina right into the hands of someone on that boat.

No. No. No. This could not be happening.

"No. Stop!" Elaina's voice was strong and demanding, and Amy had never been so proud to be her aunt.

"Shut up!" The sickening smack of a hand on flesh made Amy recoil and Elaina wailed. "You better keep your mouth shut, or you're never going to make it to that other boat. You understand?"

Whatever Elaina was being threatened with—a gun? a knife?—made her scream, and Amy had to physically hold herself back from crashing through the wall. Pistol in hand, she laid out all of her options.

Shoot into the unseen and pray she didn't hit Elaina.

Shoot over the water to distract them but alert them to her presence.

Scale the wall and try to tackle at least two, maybe four men, risking injury and the inability to fight back.

These weren't options. They were ludicrous.

She couldn't do this alone.

God, I need help!

Chapter Thirteen

Jordan burst into the sunlight, its brilliance nearly blinding him, and he held up his arm while his eyes adjusted. The vacationers who had packed onto the lido deck were oblivious to the boat off the port side, but it was nearly all he could see. The small vessel held the telltale cranes and nets of a fishing boat, but it was capturing a different type of fish today.

Zigzagging between deck chairs and towels spread across the ground, he chose a place along the rail and took stock of the ropes strung between the ships.

The new arrival wasn't close enough to the cruise liner to make for an easy transfer. But it was obvious that the plan was to get Elaina away from the ship. So why was it so far way?

Or, better yet, why not use a vessel that could pull closer to the ship?

He turned to Amy to see what she thought. Then he remembered that he was on his own. At least for now.

Amy would be back. For sure.

For now, he had to break the ties that bound the two boats together. Said ties were made of four-inch-thick rope and loose enough to lose any benefit from tension, which was a problem. The tighter the rope, the easier it would snap when broken. Loose rope could be damaged without breaking.

He needed those ties to pull taut. And he needed a rifle.

Pulling away from the rail, he made a quick survey of the area. No sign of Bo.

Had he misjudged the young man? The kid had seemed so eager for a pat on the back and the hope that someday he might become one of the elite. Surely he wouldn't let his new hero down...would he?

Jordan had never taken advantage of his place on the teams, but he knew there were those who would do anything to get in good with a SEAL. And it was generally the young ones who wanted a trident pin of their own.

So, where was he?

"Mr. Somerton." It was barely a panted breath, but Jordan turned with a smile on his face to see Bo racing toward him, a rifle held out at arm's length. Several women screamed and jumped to their feet, but Bo paid them no mind.

The kid had a lot to learn to earn the title of SEAL, but at the moment, Jordan had never seen anything better.

"Good man." He clapped Bo on the back, accepting the weapon and weighing it in his hand. It wasn't quite right. It wasn't his. But it would do in a pinch.

"That man has a gun!" a mom screamed and frantically collected her children. "Get inside, now!"

Bo looked over his shoulder, his eyes round. "I guess maybe I shouldn't have held it out like that."

"Maybe not. But we don't have any time to lose. That ship, it's here."

"I know." Bo's voice took on an urgent whisper. "Everyone in the security office is going crazy. Made it easy to take off with the rifle, but Staff Captain Xavier has been yelling at the guys—even the ones off shift— to line the lower decks and keep anyone unauthorized from boarding this ship. And no one can find the captain."

His heart gave a hard thump. "The captain's missing?"

"Yep. No one's seen him in, like, three hours."

"Who's running the ship, then?"

"Staff captain."

This didn't line up. The captain disappearing when the other boat was meeting up with them was a coincidence he couldn't ignore. Either the captain was in on this whole thing—which would explain Eric Dean's escape—or he'd been taken out of commission.

Jordan hoped it was the later—and only temporarily. No captain would willingly give up his command. An image of the incapacitated officer flashed across his mind and made his skin crawl.

Whatever had happened, if the captain had been taken out of commission then someone else had control of the ship. And Xavier might not even realize it.

Until he knew what exactly was going down on the bridge, Jordan couldn't trust anyone. Except Amy.

And maybe Bo.

"Did you bring me any rounds?"

Bo's face broke into a broad smile. "Course I did." He reached into his pocket and pulled out a handful of ammo.

Jordan scooped the bullets up and shoved them into his pocket.

"Bo, I need you to do me a favor."

"Anything."

Jordan nearly smiled at the young man, so eager he was almost dancing on his toes. "Get this ship moving hard starboard."

"Excuse me?"

"We need to move to the right. Right now."

"But…" Bo pointed toward the bridge, his finger rolling in the air. "That's up to the senior officers. We've got to stay on course and everything."

Jordan clapped his hand on Bo's shoulder firmly, forcing him to understand. "We won't get off course. We only need to shift direction for a minute, but this has to happen. Right now. And you're the only man for the job."

"But what do I say?"

"Tell them a little girl's life is on the line. Tell them you saw her on the monitor. Tell them they're going to save her right now. Just steer starboard."

Bo's face went slack, but he quickly recovered. "Okay. I'll do it." He bolted away, and Jordan prayed the boy would find a way to get the job done.

In the meantime, he had his own job to do.

As he lifted the rifle to his shoulder, a rush of rightness flowed through him. This is what he knew. This is what he did.

But a bloodcurdling scream from across the lido deck reminded him that not everyone felt that way about a weapon in his hands. He glanced over at the young woman yanking off her headphones and jumping to her feet, clearly only now realizing what the rest of the crowd had discovered minutes before. She held a towel in front of her like it might save her life. Her lips trembled, and she never blinked, her gaze always on him.

"Ma'am." He nodded in greeting, keeping his voice low. "You might want to head inside. This is going to be loud."

She jerked her chin up and down several times before dashing across the wooden slats. Halfway to the exit, she stopped, turned back to look at her bag, and then clearly made the choice to leave it behind as she kept running.

He leaned into the railing, watching the fishing boat through the scope and following the lines across the water.

Suddenly the sunlight glinted off something he hadn't seen before. It wasn't part of the boat or the rope. Maybe it was just the crest of a wave.

Nope. There it was again. He caught his breath and waited. Again.

The stock of the rifle dug into his shoulder as he leaned his elbows on the wooden rail.

Suddenly the light hit it just right, and he realized what he was looking at. It was a zip line. He couldn't see exactly where it began, but it absolutely ended on the fishing boat.

If he'd had any hair on the back of his neck, it would have stood up on end.

They were going to slide Elaina off the ship. Most likely never to be seen again.

Unacceptable. Period.

The line was tight, which worked for him. What didn't work for him was his blind spot. From this angle there was no way to tell if anyone—such as Elaina—was on the line.

But every second he waited was another that she might be attached to that line and pushed off the ship.

Oh, Lord, let her not be on it now.

He checked his rifle once more, focused through the scope and lined up his shot.

Smooth is fast.

He took a deep breath, released it and eased his trigger finger back.

Crack.

The shot echoed and everyone on board knew someone was shooting now.

But the bullet veered left, missing its mark.

How could that be? He'd had it lined up perfectly.

His stomach sank. The scope was off. But there wasn't time to worry about that. He had to recalibrate and fire again.

He found his mark, adjusted for the errant scope and let out a prayer with his breath. Then he squeezed the trigger, and it was like the whole world exploded.

The wire snapped audibly, the sound of the recoil covering this side of the ship.

But his job wasn't done. Reloading his weapon, he

took aim at the still-sluggish ropes. He got off round after round into the lines, fraying them but not succeeding in snapping them the way he wanted to. They were just too loose.

"Stop. Put your hands up now!"

Jordan paused but kept his weapon in place as two security guards approached. They both carried pistols, arms extended and elbows locked.

Oh, man. It was going to hurt when he took them out.

He almost felt bad. They weren't trained for this— for any of it. For pirates in the middle of the Caribbean Sea. For a SEAL sniper with a rifle. But feeling bad for them didn't mean Jordan would hesitate to put them down. There were lives on the line here. The safety of the ship and everyone on it—including his family—was at risk. And, most of all, Amy was counting on him. Jordan wasn't going to let anything stand in his way.

"Listen, guys. You can put your guns down. I'm not aiming at anyone."

The rounder one looked at his skinny friend and shook his head quickly. They continued their approach. "Just put it down, man."

Jordan let the rifle swing from the strap at his shoulder and held his hands up. "Take it easy." He stepped toward them slowly, evenly, maintaining eye contact the whole time. "It's okay. I don't want to hurt anyone."

Well, that was mostly true. He genuinely didn't want to hurt these guys—though he wouldn't be opposed to getting a few blows in on Stein. But with the guards, he wouldn't do any permanent damage. As long as they cooperated. If they tried to fight back—well, he just couldn't make any promises at that point.

The men responded well to his soothing tones and their weapons lowered as he drew within three feet.

That was their biggest mistake.

His arm swept down without warning, taking both of their firearms out in one motion. Guns clattered to the deck as one man fell to his knees after it, his forearm bent at an unnatural angle. He groaned, his face going white with pain as he reached for his weapon with the other hand. Jordan stepped on the guns, sliding them out of reach.

"I'm not going to hurt you guys." Well, not much more than he already had.

"Why are you doing this? What do you want?"

He narrowed his gaze onto them. "I'm trying to rescue a little girl."

"What girl?"

That was new. Shouldn't all the security personnel have been briefed? Surely Xavier had made certain that his team was looking for Elaina. He'd said he would do that, right?

Jordan tried to rack his brain, but suddenly the ship tipped starboard.

Way to go, Bo!

He raced for the railing just as the ropes pulled tight. They held for a long breath, and he pulled up his rifle again, just in case.

Snap. Pop.

The lines snapped and then broke apart.

The fishing boat rocked in the water, keeping up with the liner but now wholly disconnected.

"Gentlemen," he said, turning back to the injured guards. "You should probably get some medical attention." The guy with the broken arm looked about ready to pass out, and Jordan rotated his wrist in sympathy. His arm barely stung where he'd made contact. He should thank Lieutenant Sawyer for teaching him that move when he'd been fresh out of BUD/S.

Scooping up their pistols, he quickly checked them for other weapons. None.

Good. They couldn't do anything else to stop him from meeting up with Amy.

As long as she was where she said she'd be.

Amy nearly dropped to her knees at the first crack of a rifle, her pistol jumping into her hand.

But the shot wasn't aimed at her.

Soon after, a second echoed over the ship, and then the zip line tore in two, the sudden release of tension whipping it back and forth.

Her neighbors shouted in languages she'd never heard before, distracted and clearly blaming each other for a terrible plan.

This was it. Her chance.

It might be her only one.

Scaling the wall, she did a quick assessment from her position perched at the top. Eric Dean and another man argued with each other as Elaina stood crying before them. Two more rifle shots came in quick succession, and the men spun toward the sound, leaning over the railing. Stein had disappeared, but the sliding door to the room was open, the curtain waving in the wind.

Elaina looked up, her gaze locking on Amy, and her mouth opened.

Amy slammed a single finger in front of her lips.

With huge eyes rimmed in red, Elaina nodded.

Amy waved to the side as another rifle round shook the ship, and Elaina huddled in the corner.

Swinging over the wall, she landed in a squatting position. Before the men even realized she was there, she got off two knee shots, almost indistinguishable from the sounds of Jordan's rifle fire.

Both men screamed, dropping their weapons, which Amy scooped up and shoved into her pockets.

She wanted to hug her niece and bury her nose in Elaina's sweet hair and never let her go again, but there wasn't time for a proper reunion, so she scooped the girl into one arm and said, "Hold tight."

Elaina nodded, and Amy burst into the cabin.

Stein dropped his phone, his mouth hanging open as she flew through the door. It took him only a split second to grab for his gun, but it was too late.

She got off two rounds that hit his stomach with enough force to knock him on his back, sprawled across the bed. She didn't stop to check on him, to see if he was dead or to disarm him. There had been four men with Elaina, and she wasn't going to wait around to run into the last.

Rushing through the door, she raced for the spot where she'd promised to meet Jordan—Michael's cabin.

The whole ship seemed to be in chaos, people screaming and cabin doors slamming. No one seemed to pay her or Elaina any mind. They were just another pair of people in a sea of confusion.

Amy didn't pay attention to the others, either—all of her focus was on Elaina's tears. She sobbed a great pool on Amy's neck, her hiccups shredding Amy's heart one piece at a time. Elaina's grip was unrelenting, digging into her neck like she would never let go.

"Honey, don't cry." The words were no better than a whisper, forced past the lump in her own throat. "You're safe now." Amy wrapped her other arm around Elaina's waist. Carrying her while running was awkward. Setting her down wasn't even an option.

"I was so-o scared."

Amy wished that she could wipe those memories away, praying they would be replaced with ones of joy and security, of flying high on park swings and hugging Michael.

"I'm going to take you to someplace safe, okay? This is all over. I promise."

But as she ran, she wondered if she could really make that promise with any hope of keeping it. Elaina wasn't in terrorist hands any longer, but manipulating Michael had been the goal all along, so their family was still in danger.

Without Elaina in their hands, what depths would the terrorists sink to?

She didn't have any idea how many more of them were on the ship or how long it would take before someone on the outside noticed that their ship was in distress.

Her stomach sank as she approached Michael's cabin. The door was closed, the hallway strangely silent. She set Elaina down and pressed her ear to the wood, praying Jordan was in there. He had to have made it back.

He'd done his part. The zip line had snapped, and

it had been enough to keep the terrorists from sending her niece to the other boat. Elaina was free. But had he been caught?

"Daddy!" Elaina shrieked when Michael poked his head out of the doorway.

Michael scooped her into his arms, holding her and crying like he'd never stop. "Baby girl. I was so scared."

"Not out here." That voice brought every nerve ending in Amy's body to life. Jordan appeared like he'd always been there, and he ushered them into the suite, closing the door behind all of them. Michael sat Elaina on the edge of the couch and knelt before her, running his hands over her limbs and whispering over and over how much he loved her.

And suddenly, Amy couldn't keep from crying. A daddy who loved his daughter. A daughter who held on like he was her newest, best and only toy.

She knuckled away the tears rolling down her cheeks and refused to look anywhere remotely in Jordan's direction.

"I feel like we're intruding on a private moment. Maybe we should give them a minute."

She nodded, and they ducked outside, sharing the tiny niche removed from the hallway. She stared at the deck. He at the ceiling.

All she really wanted to do was ask him to hold her. Not in a wild kiss or strategic play. She just wanted him to put his arms around her and whisper that it was all going to be all right now. That everything was okay and they were safe. And that he wasn't going to leave her alone.

And that he loved her, too.

Oh, dear.

That was beyond inconvenient.

She didn't love him. She couldn't.

He'd made promises only to break them. This was not the man she could love.

Yet a tiny voice in her head that sounded too much like Neesha insisted that he was a good man and that she could trust him with her heart.

Except, she didn't trust *any* man with her heart.

At some point during her mental meanderings, his gaze had drifted to her, and she jumped to attention, certain he could see all of what she was feeling written across her face. So she blurted out the only thing she could think of. "Where'd you get the rifle?"

A slow smile sneaked across his lips. "Bo came through." Then he told her the whole story of Bo and the security guards and the ship with no captain. "I'm glad that Elaina's safe, but I can't help but feel like we're not done. Pirates are still hidden on this ship."

She knew the feeling. It felt like a brick was sitting in the bottom of her stomach. "And if they can't get Michael to comply through Elaina, they're going to try something else. Aren't they?"

His eyebrows dipped together, but he didn't have time to answer before a loud voice with a heavy accent came through the speaker system.

"Ambassador Michael Torres. You have twenty minutes to report to the bridge. If you—and all of your bodyguards—do not arrive, we will shoot one passenger every five minutes."

Amy's mouth went dry and her palms began to sweat.

"And we will begin with this one."

From farther away from the microphone, but no less clear, came a voice she'd recognize anywhere. "Take your hands off me."

That brick in her stomach tripled in size, pushing all the air from her lungs and every thought from her brain, save one.

Neesha.

Chapter Fourteen

Jordan grabbed Amy's arm as she dashed down the hallway.

"Let me handle this." He tried to keep his voice steady, but there were too many pictures flooding his mind. Of Neesha being pulled from her suite, kicking and screaming, a gun to her head. Of Rodney being taken with her. Of the fear on her face and terror in her eyes. Of the smack she'd inevitably have taken across the cheek when she talked back to them.

And she would have. Because she was Neesha, and she was fearless.

And above all of those was one more image—of Amy at the mercy of these madmen.

Just the thought of it hit harder than a kidney shot, even as he tried to shake it off, to pretend that he hadn't felt the fear of losing her.

Because maybe the only thing worse than leaving someone behind was having them leave you.

That kind of pain was unacceptable. He'd spent his

entire life making sure that he'd never feel that way again—the way he'd felt when his dad hadn't come home. And he wasn't about to change his mind for a pretty smile with a fierce heart.

"I can't let you go."

She laughed in his face, but there was no humor to it. "It's not your choice."

He waved a hand at the closed door. "Someone needs to stay with Michael. Keep him from leaving this room."

Jerking her arm free from his grip, she leaned in until their faces were only inches apart. "That's my best friend up there."

"And she's my family. I'm better trained. I'm fully armed. And I'm not going to let you put yourself at risk. I need for—"

He slammed on the brakes. He'd been about to admit that he needed her to be safe and to be there and to never leave him. Because he'd never met anyone so maddeningly brilliant and tough. Because he cared about her.

Because he was head-over-heels, couldn't-wait-to-kiss-her-again, please-God-let-her-feel-the-same in love with her.

His head spun like he'd been clocked with a two-by-four.

No. Nope. Not going to happen.

Amy was the most vibrant, fierce woman he'd ever met. But he could not, would not, be in love with her.

"Your family needs you to make it home. Elaina's already lost her mom. What would happen if she lost you, too?"

It was a low blow, and he saw the instant it landed.

Her mouth went slack, then closed, then opened again without a sound except the slow release of breath.

But he wasn't going to take it back. If she found it unforgiveable...then that was fine by him.

"Stay put. Keep them safe. Let me take care of this."

Eyes narrowing, she poked him in the chest with one finger. "And what about you? You don't think you have family waiting for you to come home? You don't think people care that you're safe?"

She jabbed him again in the same spot, and he backed up a step to rub at it.

Undeterred, Amy continued her rant. "You don't think that maybe some of us would want you to come home safely so we could have at least one more kiss?"

Wait. What?

"So we don't waste whatever time we might actually have together?" Her voice rose until it echoed around them. "So *some of us* can stop *daydreaming* about being in love and *actually* be in it?"

She slammed her mouth against his, grabbing his face between both hands and holding on until he couldn't breathe. It wasn't romantic or tender, but it nearly knocked his socks off. There was so much fire in her frame, and somehow he knew that one more kiss would never be enough between them. He'd always want another and another and another.

So he forced himself to pull back.

He couldn't make heads or tails out of anything she'd said, even without the kiss that jumbled it all together. All he knew was that seconds were ticking by until those madmen killed his cousin.

"No. No one wants that from me."

He had to believe that or he'd never be able to go. And he needed to.

He took off running without another word.

By Jordan's count there were eight guards surrounding the ship's bridge. None of them in uniform and all carrying Middle Eastern weapons. That was at least twice the number of Lybanians he'd counted on. And he couldn't see inside the bridge to tell how many more he'd face in there. But it didn't matter. Neesha was going to make it to her wedding day. Jordan would stand by Rodney and watch them commit to making a life together.

Someone deserved to be happy. Even if it wasn't an option for him.

But he pushed those thoughts away as he focused on what was ahead.

Each guard patrolled a small section of the bridge's perimeter alone.

Easy targets.

Jordan worked his way toward the guard nearest him. Sliding up behind him, Jordan wrapped an arm around his neck and jerked.

The man fell to the floor immediately, his eyes closed and chest rising with shallow gasps. He'd wake with a raging headache. But he wouldn't wake up anytime soon.

Jordan moved on to the next, who also went down without a fight.

But each confrontation took time, which he didn't have to spare.

Ten minutes had already slipped by and every minute that passed lowered the chance of being able to save Neesha.

It was too risky to charge the bridge without first taking out the men standing guard. But taking them out and tying them up one by one was too slow.

A knee shot would be more efficient. No one walked away from a blown out knee, and it would certainly take them down long enough for him to take their weapons. Any shot would also alert whoever was running this ship that Michael wasn't coming. And then the innocents would start dying.

His stomach rolled, an image of Neesha lying in a pool of blood flashing across his mind's eye.

That wasn't an option. But he couldn't come up with any valid alternatives.

If only he could go back in time to three days before and tell his family never to get on this ship. If only they'd never left the port and everyone he loved was safe.

If onlys didn't get the job done.

Swinging his rifle to his shoulder, he took one step before a hand latched on to his shoulder.

He swung around, shoving his weapon into the face behind him.

"Amy?" But there was no real question to it. "What are you doing here?"

She pushed his gun out of her face with a hand that also held a fluffy red pillow. "I figured you could use some backup."

"But what about Michael and Elaina?"

She waved off his concern, a second pillow flouncing

as she did so. "They're fine. They're safe. And they'll stay put with Pete. Besides, with everyone here watching for Michael, who's going to go after him?"

"Well—" She made a valid point. Rats.

"Besides, you can't take them all out moving this slow." He jerked his head in the direction he'd been moving. "How long have you been following me?"

"Long enough." She shoved one of the pillows into his chest, and he had no choice but to take it from her. "Now, we have exactly seven minutes until this lunatic said he'd start shooting."

"And you want me to take a nap?"

She popped him upside the head with the other pillow. "Don't be a jerk. Take the pillow. Use it as a silencer. You take out a few kneecaps on that side. I'll take the other. And then we'll meet at the entrance to the bridge."

She sounded so sure about her plan that he nearly agreed without thinking. But he had an argument—a really good reason why she shouldn't be part of this operation. He was sure of it. He just wasn't entirely clear what it was at the moment.

No, watching Amy put herself in danger didn't work for him. But he'd tried telling her that. And it hadn't gone over well. And did he really have the right to hold her back? She was as trained and sure as any Marine he'd ever worked with. So why shouldn't he want her as a partner?

Because love didn't always make sense.

"Stop thinking, take the pillow and go." She looked at her watch. "We don't have time for whatever argument you're trying to make against this." With that, she dashed toward the far side of the deck, staying out of the line of sight from anywhere on the bridge.

Smart girl.

Smart woman.

Amazing woman.

"Shut up and go." He mumbled to himself as he took off in the opposite direction.

Amy aimed through her pillow and pulled the trigger halfway back. Ready to take her final shot. Well, at least her last one before they stormed the bridge. Already, her heart beat faster than it should, every thump heavy with anticipation.

All she had to do was get through this and meet up with Jordan. Then they'd free Neesha.

And then they'd call for help.

She let out a quick breath, preparing to take the shot.

Suddenly an arm wrapped around her throat and jerked her of her feet. Her Glock clattered to the floor, the pillow falling right on top of it.

She gasped and clawed and tried to scream, but her windpipe was under attack, brutally constricted by a meaty forearm.

"You've done enough damage." Her attacker swore in her ear, calling her filthy names that made her skin crawl.

All the bruises from when she'd been choked to unconsciousness the night before throbbed even further under this abuse, but she refused to succumb.

Black curtains pulled across her peripheral vision, and she kicked down against his knee, pushing herself up to steal a breath. It was enough to pull back the veil for at least a moment, but it didn't dislodge his arm.

Hanging by her chin, feet kicking and fingers clawing for freedom, all the air in her lungs dwindled down to nothing. Her neck stretched, the weight of her body dragging her down.

She was going to miss Jordan. He'd be waiting for her, and she couldn't get to him. Funny how that was all that she could think about as her chest screamed for oxygen and her muscles trembled.

This time, she'd be the one standing him up. It wasn't because of another commitment or because she'd disappeared to someplace else she'd rather be. She just wasn't going to show.

Because sometimes there was no way around it.

Deep down, she'd known that all along. But she'd held on to a grudge because it was easier to be bitter than it was to admit just how raw her heart had been worn by a negligent father. And because keeping up that wall was so much easier than risking love.

Only it wasn't easier. It meant missing out on all the amazing things that God could have for her. It meant missing out on Jordan.

She cried out as loudly as her hoarse voice could manage. The sound didn't go far, but it elicited a growl in her ear.

"Shut up!" He slammed her into the wall, and she thought her body might just splinter.

This was it. She might not survive this attack.

She was never going to see that cocky grin when she finally told Jordan that she'd forgiven him. And she had. In that very moment.

She'd choose forgiveness every day of the week if it meant a chance to be with Jordan.

But she'd missed her chance. She was never going to see him or hold him. Or kiss him again.

And he'd think she hated him.

She didn't. Not even a little bit.

Her dad, either. All those years of anger and resentment were useless. Such a waste of time and energy. She'd missed out on only God knew what kind of joy because she'd held on to hurts. The walls she'd thought protected her only robbed her.

Her dad hadn't changed.

Jordan couldn't be any more sorry than he already was.

She was the only one who had been hurt by refusing to release those memories.

What a waste.

But if she was going to meet her Maker today, she'd do it with a clear conscience.

God, forgive me for hating my dad for so long. Let him know somehow that I forgave him. Maybe he was doing his best. And no matter where he was, I was never alone. You were always with me. And be with Jordan, too. Protect him. Keep him safe. I'm so sorry that I held on to my anger when I should have shown him that I loved him.

The arm at her neck jerked again, and suddenly everything went black.

Jordan's flesh tingled as he slipped along the bulkhead below the bridge. His gaze darted across to the open deck and to the ladders leading to lower levels. All clear.

Except for that small voice in his head screaming that he'd missed something.

There was supposed to be one more guard. Where had the guy gone?

And where was Amy?

His stomach rolled, and something that could only be fear washed over him.

He didn't have time for fear on a mission. There was only focus and strategy and executing the plan. But this wasn't like any other mission. It had become something entirely different from the moment Amy had been taken the night before.

An uneasy sensation gnawed on his stomach with each step he took closer to the meet-up point. Despite the warmth of the sunshine and the blue sky, a black cloud hung low over him. He held his breath, his pistol at the ready.

Only he knew what he was going to find.

Nothing.

Just then the walkie-talkie he'd stolen from one of the guards he'd taken out squawked from the spot where he'd clipped it to his belt. "We got her," a sinister voice announced. "The DEA agent. Bringing her up right now."

Then he added, "She'll never make trouble for us again."

His heart stopped in that moment. It had no reason to keep beating. The one person he'd ever been in love with was about to lose her life. And he didn't have a plan, a backup or a hope in the world.

Jordan hid in the shadows below the bridge, waiting for any sign of Amy, counting down the seconds until whoever was calling the shots on this ship gave up waiting for Michael. As for what he'd do then…he honestly had no idea.

But he had to stay close if he was going to have any chance of protecting Neesha. And anyway, he wasn't going anywhere until he knew where Amy was.

"God, could You show up? Right now, please." His whisper was nearly inaudible as he stared toward the sky. He'd always trusted that he was heard when he prayed, but he'd still always done as much as he could in his own strength.

But now his own skill, experience and power weren't going to cut it.

Not even close.

I need You.

And then, as if God had only been waiting for him to come to that understanding, everything changed.

Two broad men strolled toward the bridge, arrogant and assured and thoroughly armed. And one of them carried Amy. Her body sagged, limp and pale.

His stomach rolled. Was she even alive?

He couldn't afford to ask himself questions like that. He could only believe that God had this covered. If he let himself dwell on the might-bes, he'd go crazy.

"Michael Torres. You have three minutes," the voice over the intercom singsonged as though he was enjoying taunting Michael, and Jordan spat next to his shoe. Terrorists liked to mock their victims. They thrived on perceived power and used psychological tricks to make their opponents feel helpless to stop them.

But it wasn't going to work.

Clearing his mind of everything but the scene before him, he played it out, visualizing every tactical maneuver. Stay low. Pie the corner—turning around a corner so he only revealed himself a step at a time while maximizing his view into the rest of the room.

He double-checked the rounds in his pistols and the rifle over his shoulder. Full magazines in each. One pistol in hand, one at the ready.

Time to go.

He ran for the entrance to the bridge and stopped just outside of the view of those inside, pressing his back to the wall.

"Get her up." The low growl sounded familiar, but Jordan couldn't quite place it. "We'll prove to the ambassador that we're serious."

Neesha screamed and Rodney yelled, but the sound of a fist against flesh quieted the room.

Perfect. Neesha, Rodney and Amy were all in there, all at risk of being caught by a stray bullet.

Jordan took a single step away from the wall, turning to face inside. Each small step revealed another slice of the room, so far showing him only empty computer consoles. The rest of the staff had either been run off or met the same fate as the captain, whatever that was.

On his fourth step, he spotted two figures. The one sprawled on the floor was clearly Amy. And the thug towering over her had to be a Lybanian, his dark hair hanging past his collar as he looked down his narrow nose at her.

"Time's up, Ambassador!"

The announcement came from both inside the bridge and the intercom above.

Before the speaker finished, Jordan said a quick prayer and fired his first shot. It hit the man's shoulder, and he stumbled backward, opening himself up to a second shot, this one to the throat.

He went down hard, just as the room erupted in shouts and gunfire.

No more hiding.

Jordan roared as he raced into the ship's control room, drawing as much attention as he could, taking a quick survey. Five men standing. The tango holding the microphone for the intercom also held a gun aimed at Neesha's head.

Pop. Pop. Pop.

He put three bullets into the man's chest, and Neesha cried out as the gun dropped to the ground before her. But she wasn't stupid. She scooped it up and aimed it across the room.

There wasn't time to check on her as he fired three more shots and dropped three more men. The last clung to his weapon and got off a rapid blast, which Jordan dodged by dropping to his knee and shooting out the other man's gun hand.

Jordan let out a low growl as he spun toward the last man standing. But he wasn't where Jordan had last seen him.

Neesha was still on the ground, her eyes wide and trembling fingers holding the gun, looking over his shoulder with an expression of shock and horror. And that's when Jordan knew. He didn't even have to turn around.

Amy was going to die.

And he was going to be sick. His stomach heaved, and he physically had to force himself to turn around.

There he was—the fifth man. The inside man. The

one who had been playing them from the start. Xavier. He was decked out in a white uniform and wore a scowl on his face as he held Amy in front of him. Her head lolled to the side, but her eyelids fluttered like she was fighting hard to recover consciousness.

His heart stopped when Xavier shifted enough to reveal the gun pointed directly at her carotid artery.

"Let her go." Jordan tried to get the words around the lump in his throat, but they came out strangled. Clearing his throat, he tried again. "What kind of man are you? You'd use a defenseless woman as a shield? Let her go."

"Somerton." Xavier cinched his arm tighter around Amy, and she groaned. "You think she's defenseless? She took out three of my guys downstairs and took off with the kid who was supposed to be my leverage. Elaina Torres was the key to getting our whole operation back up and running." He swore heavily, and spit sprayed out of his mouth with every word, as his eyes narrowed. His trigger finger bent, almost ready to pull it back and end Amy's life.

"The two of you have ruined everything! We had a plan. Get the girl off the ship, force her dad to use his connections to have Abkar extradited back to Lybania and get back in business." Xavier's eyes flashed, and his nostrils flared. "Don't you get it?"

"Get what?" Jordan asked, trying to stall. "What did we ruin?"

"Ha! Like I'm going to talk to you while you're holding a gun on me? Not likely."

Attack now or keep him calm? Jordan made a split-second decision and prayed that it was the right one.

Holding up his hands, palms facing out, he squatted and set his guns on the deck. Neesha sobbed behind him, but he never took his eyes off Xavier. "Okay. Look. I'm not armed anymore. Let her go."

"Her? *Her?* You really think I'll let her go? Don't you see? It was her stupid arrest that nearly shut us down." Spittle flew, and Amy flinched. Jordan was torn between being relieved she was waking up and terrified that she'd move at the wrong moment and cause Xavier's trigger finger to squeeze.

Oh, God, please let her be okay.

"We had a good thing going. Lybanian drugs coming in on cargo ships, transferred to my cruise ship and delivered to ports across the Caribbean. I was going to retire a wealthy man. And then she went and arrested Abkar and impounded all that cargo." His eyes bugged out. "Close to three hundred million dollars. And I was due to get ten percent. Do you know what I could have done with thirty mil?"

"Is there any on the ship now?"

"What?" Xavier's mouth dropped open, confusion washing over his face as though he wasn't sure what or how much he'd just revealed. "That's just not... We're not talking about... That's not the thing—"

He jammed his gun into Amy's neck again, and that was it.

Jordan couldn't wait a moment longer.

But just as he launched himself at Xavier, Amy's fist came out of nowhere, her elbow a fulcrum, her knuckles nailing him in the nose.

Xavier's gun clattered to the deck as Jordan collided

with them both, and they ended in a messy, bloody tangle of limbs. Xavier wailed as blood gushed down his face, which had turned a terrible shade of purple. He cursed violently, calling Amy every name in the book.

That was enough of that.

Jordan wrapped his paw around Xavier's throat and squeezed. It shut the man up, all right. He dug his fingernails into Jordan's wrist, but the pain didn't even register.

It was a gentle touch on his other arm that stopped him. "Jordan. Don't." Amy's words were barely a croak, but they were everything.

Flinging Xavier to the ground in a heap, he scooped her into his arms, holding her close and whispering into her hair, "You're okay, right? Did they hurt you?"

"My throat—" She couldn't get out more without an audible swallow. "I'm sorry. I'm sorry I didn't meet you."

She was sorry? What a crazy world this had become that she would apologize for being kidnapped by drug runners and missing their meeting.

"I don't care if you're ten years late. Just always come back to me."

She nodded into his shoulder, resting there as the announcement he'd hoped for finally came.

"*Summer Seas*, this is the United States Coast Guard. Prepare to be boarded."

Chapter Fifteen

"You're such an idiot sometimes." Neesha smacked his arm, a little too hard to be playful.

Jordan rubbed at the bruise on his biceps, although he'd lost track of just when he'd sustained it on this cruise. "What's that supposed to mean?"

She rolled her eyes at him and primped her hair, pausing just briefly to admire the diamonds in the wedding band on her left hand. "Just what I said. A perfectly incredible woman is in love with you, and you're about to let her just walk away."

"I'm not *letting* her do anything. She has a mind of her own, you know?"

"Of course I know that. Which is why she's so amazing. Well, that and she has great taste in friends." She pointed at herself. "Case in point."

Jordan nodded, but couldn't manage a smile of confirmation as he stared over the ship's railing at the Miami port. They were just an hour away from exiting this cruise, which had been the opposite of the planned floating frivolity. In fact, the only thing that had gone as planned was that Neesha and Rodney had gotten hitched.

She'd been radiant as she asked the captain—after he'd been found and released from the room where Xavier had drugged and stashed him—to please do the honors. The ship had to return to Miami, and the cruise line would be paying dearly for this in lawsuits and poor press, probably for years. The least the captain could do was perform the ceremony.

Which he'd done with pride as the Coast Guard vessel escorted them home.

At least Neesha had gotten her happy ending.

But Jordan wasn't going to get his own. No matter what Neesha said.

Amy didn't want him. Now that they were safe, Elaina was with her father and Abkar's cohorts were in the custody of the Coast Guard and headed to trial, Amy didn't need him.

And even if she was remotely interested, she'd never be satisfied with what he could offer. Which was likely a broken heart.

Neesha bumped his shoulder with her own. "What's going on in your head?"

"Nothing for you to worry about."

She slammed a hand against her hip and leaned the other against the railing, turning to face his profile. "Don't treat me like I'm a child. I've been married a lot longer than you have."

He snorted. Figured. Neesha would be quick to rub

it in his face that she'd gotten married before him. "Of course. How could I be so stupid?"

Her eyes turned soft as she rested a gentle hand on his arm. "Jordan, you're practically my brother, so you can't hide much from me. I saw how you looked at Amy when you held her."

"How? How did I look?" Rats. He had a sneaking suspicion that he already knew, and he wasn't really interested in confirmation.

"Like you'd do anything for her. Like you never wanted to let her go." A flicker of a smile crossed her face. "Like you're so much in love with her that you don't even know how to deal with it."

Leaning both elbows on the rail, he hunched over and scrubbed his bent head. "So what if I am? It's not going to change anything."

She flung her head back and crowed with delight. "For a really smart man, you can be really obtuse."

"Yes, we've covered that."

She got right into his face, her deep brown eyes blazing. "You're right. It won't change just *anything*. Love changes *everything*."

"It can't."

"Why not?"

He flung a hand out to the sea. "You know about my schedule. It's unpredictable and—"

"That's the most pathetic excuse, and you know it. Why on earth wouldn't you go after what you want?" Her voice rose half an octave, her glare accusing him of being a coward.

"Because it's none of your business." Sweat beaded

on the back of his neck, and he took a deep breath, trying to calm down.

Haughty and so confident she knew what he was thinking, she began again, "That's ridiculous—"

"Because I could die. Because she could end up just like my mom."

Neesha slammed on the brakes, her jaw dropping open and eyes unblinking.

"What? Isn't that ridiculous enough for you?" He hated the sarcasm dripping from his voice, but it was too late to reel the words back in.

Thankfully she ignored his snide remark, planting her hand on top of his. "Do you really believe that?"

He didn't dare look at her. "My dad didn't come home from a day on the force, and my mom just… withered. She gave up on life. And I'm not going to be the reason that anyone else would do that. I won't risk breaking her heart."

"First of all—" she wagged a finger right in his face "—if you think for one minute that you could die and no one would be hurt, you're delusional. My mother would grieve you like her own child, and you know it."

"Tha—"

"No. You're going to hear this, you big lug. And you're going to understand. People love you. Like really, really love you. Like there would be weeping and gnashing of teeth of biblical proportions if anything ever happened to you. But that's *never* going to stop us from loving you. We're not going to miss out on caring for you and spending time with you just because you happen to have a dangerous job. We're just going to pray for you and tell you to be careful and thank God every time you come home. Got it?"

His tongue was a twisted mess, and his pulse roared in his ears so loudly that he could barely nod.

"Second—and this is important, so pay attention—I know that what happened to your mom was really hard on you, and I'm sorry that losing your dad broke her. But Amy is nothing like your mom. She's the toughest woman I've ever known."

He opened his mouth to respond—although he had no words at the ready. But Neesha cut him off with a three-fingered wave.

"And third, if you think you haven't already broken Amy's heart, you're blind and stupid."

He blinked, searching for anything to say. But there was only the hammering of his heart against his rib cage and the air that he couldn't seem to find with each labored gasp.

She couldn't be right.

Not about all of it.

But he'd never known Neesha to be wrong. She was a know-it-all in the best sense of the word, aware and empathetic. And at the moment, right in his face.

The backs of his eyes burned, and he shoved the heels of his hands against them. If what she'd said was true, then he was passing on someone who filled his spirit and brought him so much joy for absolutely no reason.

None.

He was making them both miserable. For nothing.

He *was* stupid.

* * *

Amy wadded up a T-shirt and chucked it into her suitcase, ignoring the sizzle down her spine that demanded to know where all of her meticulous organizational training had gone.

Well, it might as well be on the bottom of the ocean as far as she was concerned.

No number of wrinkle-free tops or perfectly folded maid-of-honor dresses could change the fact that she'd stood next to her best friend on Neesha's happiest day and watched the love of her own life completely ignore her.

A searing pain slashed down her chest, and she had to lean over, pressing her hands to her knees to manage even a single breath.

This. This was why she'd been so careful never to let a man deep into her heart. This ache that felt like it would last forever was reason enough to keep the wall of protection high and well preserved.

But it turned out that wanting to protect her heart and actually doing so were two different things. She could want every single brick she'd stacked in place to still be there. But Jordan had already taken them down, one by one.

And he'd been so surreptitious about it that she hadn't realized it was too late until putting the wall back together wasn't an option.

Which basically left her with perpetually leaking eyes, a running nose and a throbbing pain somewhere near where the wall had been.

Oh, and completely without Jordan because…

Well, because he didn't want her.

She crumpled another shirt and threw it into the bag as hard as she could. Stupid heartache.

"Wow, did that shirt insult your mom?"

She jerked upright and spun, a ball of shorts in her hand.

Jordan leaned in the door frame of her cabin, his shoulders stretching the cotton knit of his own shirt. He had a half smile in place, but she couldn't stand to look at it for long. It only increased the pressure in her chest.

Turning back to her packing, she said, "What are you doing here?" A thought slammed into her mind, and she swung back in his direction. "Did something happen with Xavier or Stein? Did they escape?"

His face flashed surprise, but he quickly shook his head. "No. Nothing like that. They're both still in Coast Guard custody. All of them are."

"Good." She cringed just thinking about the lot of them. Eighteen terrorists—fourteen Lybanian nationals and four Americans, including Xavier—had been part of the plot to kidnap Elaina and blackmail Michael into using his position to arrange to have Abkar extradited to Lybania. The American government didn't negotiate with terrorists, but Lybania's unstable government would happily release one back into their country.

And the terrorists had done it all so they could return to what sounded like a very lucrative drug-running business. And when Amy had rescued Elaina, they had had to come up with a plan B—threatening Neesha and Rodney in order to flush out Michael, along with Amy and Jordan.

She hadn't planned on putting a stop to a drug ring while on vacation, but maybe she could mark this as a bonus on her DEA evaluation. Perhaps at least one good thing had come of this whole ordeal.

Actually two. She'd never seen Michael so affectionate and caring toward Elaina, who was eating it up like she was starving. And maybe she had been—for love, anyway.

A warmth flowed through her chest just thinking of how much attention Elaina would enjoy from here on out. Amy prayed it would last forever.

Suddenly she remembered that Jordan was still standing there, staring at her, and shivers raced from her neck to her legs. She tried to shake them off. "Did you need something?"

"Yeah, actually, I do." He crossed his arms, and a scowl fell into place.

"What?" The word snapped out harshly—which he deserved, given his grumpy face and suddenly unpleasant attitude. "You don't have to look so sour. You're the one who came looking for me." She scooped her socks out of the dresser drawer and dumped them into the suitcase just to give herself something to do, but she couldn't turn her back on him.

He didn't bother responding to her sharp comment. "Do you actually unpack your things when you're away from home?" His eyebrows dipped low.

"Sometimes. If I think I could be called away, then I don't bother. But it wasn't like I could be called off the ship. Why? Don't you ever unpack?"

"I've lived out of a footlocker or duffel for almost

half my life. Packed is my default. But I could be flexible with that."

"What?" His words didn't make any sense. Why was he telling her this? Why should she care if he unpacked or not? She was fully planning on avoiding him for the rest of her life. And all of a sudden she just needed him to go. Every minute he stood there, being all Jordan without being *her* Jordan, a sliver of her heart shriveled.

"I need to finish getting ready," she said, as dismissively as she could, glancing at him only out of the corner of her eye. "Can this wait?"

He shook his head once, definitively. "No."

Biting her tongue to keep from snapping at him again, she took a breath before asking, "What is it, then?"

"I owe you an apology."

So they'd made it back to this again? Well, it was probably better to get it over with now. After all, she'd decided the bitterness was too heavy to carry. She'd been released from that weight, and Jordan deserved to be freed, too.

"Thank you." She looked back at her suitcase so she didn't have to watch his reaction. "I forgive you. I never should have held on to my anger from before for so long. I'm sorry for refusing your apologies. I was really angry with my dad, who used to make plans with me and then call and cancel at the last minute. When you did that, it just brought back a lot of painful memories. But I never should have taken it out on you. Let's forget that that almost date ever happened. Okay?"

He didn't say anything, and she finally peeked at

him. His arms were still folded, but his head was cocked to the side, confusion written across his features.

What now? She glanced toward the ceiling and prayed for wisdom because this man was nearly enough to drive her to insanity. What more could she do?

"I... I'm glad to hear that. I guess."

He guessed? *Guessed?* He'd been badgering her for nearly a year with apologies, and now he sounded like he wasn't sure he even wanted her forgiveness.

She threw up her hands before slamming them onto her hips and marching toward him. She stopped with just a foot between them.

"What is it that you want?"

"You."

She felt as if she'd been hit with a sledgehammer. It had to be that because she suddenly couldn't breathe or think or process. But he kept talking like it all made perfect sense.

"You're incredible, and I was so stupid to push you away all this time." He dipped his head and swiped his big hand across the back of his neck. "I was..." He stopped, seemed to think about his words and tried again. "My dad was a cop."

"I know."

"And one day, he didn't come home." He swallowed loudly, his Adam's apple bobbing, and she couldn't not reach for his hand. But before she got there, he grabbed hers and squeezed. "My mom just broke after that. It was like the woman who I'd known and loved wasn't there anymore—like we buried all the important parts of her along with my dad. All that was left was just a shell. She couldn't care for me. She tried to, but I was mostly left on my own. And that's when Aunt Phyllis stepped in. You know the rest."

She began to nod but stopped. "What happened to your mom after that?"

His eyes glistened, and she felt like she'd waded into waters too personal, but his hold on her hand never wavered. "She died about fifteen years ago. Until then she lived in a home with others who had lost touch with reality. She never returned to her old self. All because my dad died."

Suddenly puzzle pieces began falling into place. "Jordan, you don't think…"

He nodded. "I have a dangerous job, and I can't promise that I'll always make it home. I want to. I'll try as hard as I can. But…"

"You thought that you couldn't be in a relationship because you didn't ever want to hurt someone the way your mom was hurt." She didn't even pose it as a question, and confirmation washed across his face in the form of relief.

"Stupid, right?"

"No! Who told you that?"

"Neesha."

The backs of her eyes began to burn, and she blinked furiously. "She's wrong. It's not stupid. It's kind and protective and so many other things that I love about you. But you don't have to worry about it. At least not with me."

Oh, no. That had just popped out without any planning.

He hadn't said that he loved her. But he *had* said he wanted her.

She held her breath, waiting for a response, praying he wouldn't turn and run.

He didn't. Instead he smiled.

"I know. Neesha told me that, too. And she *was* right about that."

Her heart stopped altogether, and she gasped for breath under a sudden and wonderful pressure in her chest. "Jordan?" She didn't even know what she was asking him, but he seemed to understand.

Pulling her hand to his mouth, he pressed his lips to the back of it, and lightning flashed up her arm. "Amy Delgado, I am sorry about that date that I missed, but I'm more sorry that I missed seeing you—seeing us for what we could be—for so long. You're the most incredible woman I've ever known, and you saved me more times than I can count in the last few days. I want to watch your back and have you watch mine for the rest of our lives.

"And I really, really wouldn't mind another one of those kisses."

She giggled like a teenager because what else could she do when the man she loved with all the pieces of her heart had proven that he could put it back together?

Wiggling her eyebrows at him, she said, "Did you have an ETA for that kiss?"

He stepped closer and put her hand on his shoulder. When she walked her fingers over to his neck, she could feel his entire body tremble.

He pressed his forehead to hers and drew in a deep breath. "I think it's only fair to tell you that I'm a little bit in love with you."

She wrinkled her nose. "Only a little bit?"

He chuckled from somewhere deep in his chest. "More like a lot bit."

"I'm okay with that." She closed her eyes, only a breath between them, and everything inside her zinged in anticipation. Wrapping her hand into his shirt, she pulled him closer until they were almost sharing the same breath, but it wasn't quite enough.

"And will you be okay with it if I'm called away at a moment's notice? Like, if I'm called to a specific Middle Eastern country to meet your brother-in-law and take out the leader of a terrorist cell on a night when I'm supposed to be meeting you?"

"Are you serious?" She shoved at his chest, but his arm around her waist kept her in place. "Why didn't you just tell me?"

"I have no idea what you're talking about." But there was a twinkle in his eye that belied the truth. He'd missed their date because he had been called up on a mission. Not with the rest of his team, but as a sniper to stop a man bent on killing innocent Americans.

"No matter what," she promised him.

His hand snaked into her hair, cupping the back of her head and holding her close. "I love you, Amy." Her heart soared until she couldn't even see the remnants of the wall he'd taken down.

He leaned in to make that final connection, his lips soft and urgent and filled with promises to come. The pain, the heartache, the trials had all been worth it to be in his arms and know that she could trust him with her heart.

And she would.

"I love you, too. Always have."

One eyebrow popped up. "Always?"

She shrugged. "Longer than I'd like to admit."

He laughed and pulled her close again. "I thought you hated me."

"We have plenty of time to talk about that later."

And they did.

Epilogue

Seven months later

A my snatched her purse from the passenger seat of her little coupe and tumbled out the door. The San Diego street was lined with the familiar vehicles of the SEAL Team Fifteen families, but Jordan's truck wasn't among them.

Because he'd called her to tell her he wasn't going to make it to the party this afternoon. The navy had extended his deployment another two weeks.

She'd keep waiting for him to return, but she didn't have to like it. She rolled her eyes at the memory of his phone call as she ran up the front walk to Tristan and Staci Sawyer's home. They were hosting the monthly get-together for the members of the team and their wives and children, mostly because they had a backyard big enough for all the kids to run around in.

And there were so many kids.

From Will and Jess's six-month-old all the way up to

Matt and Ashley's son, Jasper, who was almost nine, the SEAL team had ended up with enough kids to form a football team. And given the size of most of their dads, these kids could take on any opponent.

She swung open the door and turned to throw her purse on the bench in the entryway, where it always went, already calling out her greeting. "Hey, guys, Jordan's not going to make it. He's not back from…"

Her voice trailed off as she slowly surveyed the empty living room. No sign of Staci or Tristan or any of the other guys and their wives. Not even a peep from the kids.

All was silent, and it made her spine tingle.

"Guys? Staci? Ashley?"

She nearly reached for her holster, but she'd left it at home. Because this was a party, and no one was after her.

She peeked up the stairs, but there was no sound there. And then she ducked into the kitchen. Trays of burgers and hot dogs and potato salad lined the counter, but no one was eating or even hovering around the food—the way the men usually did when their wives were still setting things up.

Something was really off. She'd never seen these guys pass up food.

"Hello? Is anyone here?" She poked her head into the garage, but it was empty, too, except for Tristan's truck.

Her stomach began to churn, and she wrapped her arms around her middle. All the usual sounds of laughter, chatter and children playing in the backyard were absent.

Still, she opened one of the French doors and stuck her head through.

There, on the grass in front of a semicircle of his SEAL team and their families—more quiet and still than she'd ever seen them—knelt Jordan.

"I thought you weren't…"

And then it struck her just what she was looking at. Jordan wore a tie and slacks, and there was something in his hand that sparkled as the Southern California sun caught it. "Jordan, what's…"

He didn't move much. Just a nod of his head really, but it was enough. And suddenly she ran toward him, falling to her knees before him and throwing her arms around his neck—bumping into his outstretched hand.

"I haven't even asked you yet," he teased.

"I don't care." She half laughed, half sobbed into his neck, and his arms swept around her. He'd been gone for nearly six months on deployment, and now he was back. And that was all that really mattered. Everything else was icing on the cupcake.

"Well, I do. I want to marry you, Amy Delgado. What do you think?"

"Really? You couldn't be more romantic?" She bit into her lip, trying and failing to keep her smile at bay.

He gestured to the families behind him. To the smiling fathers, beaming mothers and kids barely containing their excitement. They bounced and danced and waved at her, the little girls whispering loud enough for all to hear. "Say yes. Say yes!"

Everyone laughed, and Jordan said, "Well, I did get this all together so I could surprise you."

"I suppose, if you went to so much trouble, I can't refuse."

"I'll take it!" He slid the ring onto her finger before planting a kiss on her in front of their entire audience. And all pretense of decorum vanished. The other SEALs hooted and hollered while their wives gushed, and the kids laughed and screamed and ran off to play.

Later, while Amy stood hand in hand with her fiancé, she leaned into his shoulder, so thankful that she'd given up her grudge and learned to love.

Without Jordan, she'd have missed out on friendships with these amazing people. Ashley Waterstone, who had taken over as director of Pacific Coast House, a shelter for battered women, had become a good friend. And while her husband, Matt, had retired from the SEAL teams last month, he was busy flipping houses and caring for their three children.

Tristan Sawyer, a SEAL instructor at Coronado, and his wife, Staci, had to run to keep up with their four adopted children, but Staci always had a smile on her face as though the frantic life of a mom of four under eight was everything she'd always wanted.

Will and Jess Gumble had welcomed their first child right after the New Year, and had eagerly offered to let Amy babysit any time she liked. Will was still on active duty, but Jess didn't seem to mind. She would spend several months with her little one before returning to her work in the laboratory as a vaccination specialist.

Luke and Mandy Dunham had two of their own kids, who looked just like their dad. Luke had returned to active duty following his knee injury, and he showed no sign of retiring soon. Mandy had sold her physical therapy practice after their first baby was born and loved being a stay-at-home mom.

And Zach and Kristi McCloud were Amy and Jordan's closest friends. So far, Zach's talk of retirement because their third child was on the way hadn't gotten Jordan thinking along the same lines. But Amy wondered if it wasn't far away. It didn't matter to her. As long as he was doing work that fulfilled him, she'd be happy. She trusted the strength of their love and knew they could overcome any challenges together—especially with this support network of people to help them through it all.

It was something special, this family that Jordan had brought her into. And she'd have hated missing out on the laughter and teasing of this wild group.

But mostly she'd have hated to miss out on Jordan.

Stretching up, she kissed his cheek.

"What was that for?"

"Because I'm so glad I don't hate you anymore."

A grin spread over his face, and he leaned close. "You can't be any happier about that than I am."

* * * * *

Get 4 FREE REWARDS!

We'll send you 2 FREE Books plus 2 FREE Mystery Gifts.

FREE Value Over **$20**

Both the **Love Inspired®** and **Love Inspired® Suspense** series feature compelling novels filled with inspirational romance, faith, forgiveness, and hope.

YES! Please send me 2 FREE novels from the Love Inspired or Love Inspired Suspense series and my 2 FREE gifts (gifts are worth about $10 retail). After receiving them, if I don't wish to receive any more books, I can return the shipping statement marked "cancel." If I don't cancel, I will receive 6 brand-new Love Inspired Larger-Print books or Love Inspired Suspense Larger-Print books every month and be billed just $6.24 each in the U.S. or $6.49 each in Canada. That is a savings of at least 17% off the cover price. It's quite a bargain! Shipping and handling is just 50¢ per book in the U.S. and $1.25 per book in Canada.* I understand that accepting the 2 free books and gifts places me under no obligation to buy anything. I can always return a shipment and cancel at any time by calling the number below. The free books and gifts are mine to keep no matter what I decide.

Choose one: ☐ **Love Inspired**
Larger-Print
(122/322 IDN GRDF)

☐ **Love Inspired Suspense**
Larger-Print
(107/307 IDN GRDF)

Name (please print)

Address   Apt. #

City   State/Province   Zip/Postal Code

Email: Please check this box ☐ if you would like to receive newsletters and promotional emails from Harlequin Enterprises ULC and its affiliates. You can unsubscribe anytime.

Mail to the Harlequin Reader Service:
IN U.S.A.: P.O. Box 1341, Buffalo, NY 14240-8531
IN CANADA: P.O. Box 603, Fort Erie, Ontario L2A 5X3

Want to try 2 free books from another series? Call 1-800-873-8635 or visit www.ReaderService.com.

HARLEQUIN
PLUS

Announcing a **BRAND-NEW** multimedia subscription service for romance fans like you!

Read, Watch and Play.

Experience the easiest way to get the romance content you crave.

Start your **FREE 7 DAY TRIAL** at
<u>www.harlequinplus.com/freetrial</u>.

SPECIAL EXCERPT FROM

LOVE INSPIRED SUSPENSE
INSPIRATIONAL ROMANCE

An undercover agent must break her cover to save someone she doesn't trust.

Read on for a sneak preview of
Blown Cover *by Jodie Bailey,*
available November 2022 from Love Inspired Suspense.

Darkness lurked in the shadows of Christmas tree lights. Sinister. Deadly.

Special agent Makenzie Fuller could almost feel it.

The bride and groom twirled beneath the raw-beam ceiling of the ballroom at Hunter's Ridge Castle.

The air seemed to buzz with danger.

Makenzie had felt this kind of hum against her skin in the past, shortly before her first partner was found dead.

Shortly before her second partner, Ian Andrews, vanished in a hail of accusations.

Makenzie took in a deep breath and exhaled. If she looked as ill at ease as she felt, her nerves could unravel almost a year's worth of undercover work. It had taken months to earn Robert Butler's trust.

"We have a problem." The voice at her elbow nearly made her jump.

She dipped her chin to the side, bringing her ear closer to Robert Butler, who'd slipped up beside her. "What can I do?" She kept her voice low, playing the part of his protector.

"There's a traitor in the room." The only agency investigating Robert Butler was her military investigative unit.

She was the only undercover agent on the case. *Traitor* would certainly apply.

She managed not to tense.

Makenzie furrowed her brows and reset her thinking into character. Her life depended on it. "Point him out and I'll handle it." That was her "job," after all. She could take the person into custody and get him out of harm's way without blowing her cover. Her team might even be able to offer a deal for testimony against Butler or his *associate*. "I'll—"

"No. This one's personal. It's been a while since I got my hands dirty. You stay and make sure no one disrupts Emma's wedding."

It would mean standing by while he killed a man.

She couldn't do that.

Slipping through the crowd, Makenzie trailed Butler.

Butler put his arm around the shoulder of the man he'd approached.

As they passed the window, the man stumbled, and his blue eyes met hers through the glass.

Familiar eyes.

Ian Andrews's eyes.

Don't miss
Blown Cover *by Jodie Bailey,*
available wherever Love Inspired Suspense books
and ebooks are sold.

LoveInspired.com